THE BURNING

D0859187

"An intimate, sweeping portrait of a country and couple divided, David O. Stewart's *The Burning Land* does what all good historical fiction should do: gives us characters to root for and brings the past so vividly to life it feels like the present. I can't wait to see how the rest of the trilogy unfolds."

—**Louis Bayard, author of *Courting Mr. Lincoln* and *The Pale Blue Eye***

"*The Burning Land* is an elegantly written, heartrending evocation of a Maine family's suffering during the Civil War and its aftermath. The battle scenes are riveting, the characters convincingly and compellingly developed. As a Civil War historian, I highly recommend David O. Stewart's marvelous novel."

—**Peter Cozzens, author of *The Earth is Weeping: The Epic Story of the Indian Wars for the American West***

"David O. Stewart has written many books, but this may be his best: a gripping Civil War novel, set in coastal Maine and with the famous Twentieth Maine Regiment, followed by an exciting account of post-war Chicago. This is a book you won't want to miss."

—**Walter Stahr, author of bestselling biographies of William Seward, Edwin Stanton, and Salmon P. Chase**

"In *The Burning Land*, David O. Stewart has vividly brought alive the landscapes and human spirit of Civil War era America from the hardscrabble coast of Maine, through the battlefields of Virginia and Pennsylvania, to the chaotic postwar scramble to survive in the burgeoning city of Chicago. To the generational drama of the tenacious Overstreet family, Mr. Stewart brings a historian's feel for the ways in which ordinary lives were shaped by extraordinary times, enriched by an unerring eye for authentic detail and page-turning prose."

—**Fergus Bordewich, author of *Congress At War: How Republican Reformers Fought the Civil War, Defied Lincoln, Ended Slavery, and Remade America***

ALSO BY DAVID O. STEWART

HISTORICAL NOVELS

The New Land, Book 1 of the Overstreet Saga

The Resolute Land, Book 3 of the Overstreet Saga (forthcoming autumn 2023)

The Lincoln Deception (2013)

The Paris Deception (2015)

The Babe Ruth Deception (2016)

HISTORIES

George Washington: The Political Rise of America's Founding Father (2021)

Madison's Gift: Five Partnerships that Built America (2016)

American Emperor: Aaron Burr's Challenge to Jefferson's America (2011)

Impeached: The Trial of President Andrew Johnson and the Fight for Lincoln's Legacy (2009)

The Summer of 1787: The Men Who Invented America (2007)

The BURNING LAND

DAVID O. STEWART

A KNOX PRESS BOOK
ISBN: 979-8-88845-153-3
ISBN (eBook): 978-1-63758-083-7

The Burning Land
© 2023 by David O. Stewart

Cover Design by Elaine Byers and Carol Sullivan,
CarolSullivanDesign.com
Interior Design by Yoni Limor

Permuted Press, LLC
New York • Nashville
permutedpress.com

Published in the United States of America
1 2 3 4 5 6 7 8 9 10

To Flora, August, Lucy, Scarlett, Rex, and Kiki,
whose story this is too

Maybe times are never strange to women: it is just one continuous monotonous thing full of the repeated follies of their menfolks.

William Faulkner, *The Unvanquished*

HISTORICAL TERMS AND PERSONS

Ames, Adelbert – A native of Rockland, Maine, Ames was graduated fifth in the West Point class of 1861. After seeing action in the Union Army as an artillery officer, he took command of the 20th Maine Volunteer Infantry Regiment in August 1862. He became brigadier general in May 1863 and left the regiment. After the war, he served Mississippi as provisional governor, senator, and governor during bitter Reconstruction years. Following a career in business, he was a brigadier general again during the Spanish-American War.

Chamberlain, Joshua Lawrence – Born in Brewer, Maine, Chamberlain attended Bowdoin College and taught there before the Civil War. He was appointed lieutenant colonel of the 20th Maine Volunteer Infantry Regiment in August 1862 and assumed command in the following May. He won the Medal of Honor for his leadership at the Battle of Gettysburg and later became brigadier general. He presided over the surrender ceremony of the Army of Northern Virginia in April 1865. After the war, Chamberlain served four terms as governor of Maine.

Chinese laundries – Immigrants to America from China in the 19th Century were excluded from some occupations by racial prejudice. Because Chinese men often handled laundry work, many turned to that trade. Though it was hard work and low-paid, many used it as a stepping stone to greater success.

Contrabands – Early in the Civil War, General Benjamin Butler of the Union Army received three escaped slaves from Virginia plantations. Although other Union officers had returned runaways to their owners, Butler (a lawyer) rejected that practice, calling them "contraband of war." Congress adopted his reasoning and accepted runaways as properly confiscated enemy property. The term "contrabands" caught on.

Copperhead – A derogatory term for Northern Democrats who preferred peace to President Lincoln's refusal to recognize the secession of Southern states in 1861. The term was drawn from the venomous snake by that name.

Double eagle – A twenty-dollar gold coin issued by the United States.

Ellsworth, Captain Elmer – A native of upstate New York, Ellsworth organized an Illinois militia company, then raised a "Zouave" regiment from New York City which adopted the colorful dress of French troops in North Africa. Ellsworth's regiments gained prominence for flamboyant and martial displays. He became the first Union officer to die in the Civil War when he removed a confederate flag from the roof of a hotel in Alexandria, Virginia and the hotel owner shot him.

Grapeshot – An artillery munition designed to injure soldiers at close range, consisting of many small projectiles clustered together, often in a canvas bag, and fired from a cannon.

Grip – An antiquated term for a small suitcase or traveling bag.

Hamlin, Vice President Hannibal – A native of Paris, Maine, Hamlin was a newspaper editor before entering politics. As a Democrat, he served two terms in the United States House of Representatives and nine years in the U.S. Senate. Hamlin's opposition to slavery led him to join the Republican Party in 1856. He was Lincoln's vice president during his first term in office. After the Civil War, he served two more Senate terms and as ambassador to Spain.

Howard, General Oliver O. – Often called the "Christian general" because of his evangelical religion, Howard grew up in Leeds, Maine, and ranked fourth in the West Point Class of 1854. Howard lost his right arm during the Civil War and won the Medal of Honor and rose to major general. After the war, he was commissioner of the Freedmen's Bureau until President Andrew Johnson dismissed him as a dangerous advocate for assisting freed slaves. He commanded troops during Indian conflicts in the West, and was superintendent of the U.S. Military Academy at West Point. He participated in the founding of the school now called Howard University in Washington, D.C.

McClellan, General George – A native of Pennsylvania, McClellan was graduated second in his class at West Point in 1846 and served during the Mexican War. Upon leaving the army, he became president of the Ohio and Mississippi Railroad. Commissioned a major general at the beginning of the Civil War, he rose quickly to command the Union Army of the Potomac in the summer of 1861 and held that post for sixteen months. His greatest success was at the Battle of Antietam, though his failure to pursue the Confederates after the battle led to his dismissal. He unsuccessfully ran for president in 1864 as a "Peace Democrat," arguing for a negotiated settlement with the Southern states. He worked as an engineer after the war and served a term as governor of New Jersey.

Meade, General George – From a Pennsylvania family, Meade was graduated from West Point in 1835 and served in the army until the Civil War, when he was appointed brigadier general. Given command the Army of the Potomac only a few days before the Battle of Gettysburg, that was his signal victory. Months later, after Ulysses Grant assumed overall command of Union Army forces, Grant also took control of the Army of the Potomac.

Mortise-and-tenon joinery – A method of construction with wood that prepares a mortise hole into which the tenon tongue is inserted. The connection may be reinforced with glue. Nails are not ordinarily employed.

Secesh – A slang term for Confederate soldiers and sympathizers during the Civil War, short for "secessionists."

Sutler – A civilian who sells supplies at a military post or camp, under authority from the military commander. Sutlers sold items, such as tobacco, that the military did not provide.

Warren, General Gouverneur – A New Yorker who graduated from West Point in 1850, Warren rose during the Civil War to command the V Corps of the Army of the Potomac, which included the 20th Maine Volunteer Infantry Regiment. Days before the war's end, General Philip Sheridan, irate that Warren did not move troops quickly enough, removed him from command. Warren remained in the army after the war, focusing on railroad construction in the Midwest.

TABLE OF CONTENTS

†

PART I

✝

CHAPTER ONE

DECEMBER 1862

The word spread fast. Corporal Henry Overstreet passed it on to his platoon as soon as he heard: Two men in Company C froze to death in their tents the night before. The bodies were blue.

The platoon gathered around campfires in the thin morning light, kicking at four inches of early December snow. They shook their heads. They warmed their hands over the flames or cradled them around tin cups of coffee with more heat than flavor.

"Glory be to God," said Joe Maxwell. "That's a hell of a thing. What in God's name happened?" The flaming red of his face reflected both the cold and his temper.

Henry kept his voice level, fitting for a corporal. "They didn't seal their tent flaps."

"And they died for it? Men from Maine shouldn't freeze to death in Virginia."

Henry met Joe's gaze. The other man dropped his eyes and muttered again, "Glory be to God."

Henry couldn't show how nervous the news made him. He resolved to check the men's tent flaps at night, to make sure they stuffed their rubber blankets into every crevice and gap. He couldn't mention this to Katie in his next letter. He didn't know how he could make sense of it for her. His fingers were too cold to write, anyway.

Captain Clark came down the row of tents, stopping to talk at each knot of men around each fire. A few men saluted but he paid little heed to the formalities. As he spoke, heads nodded slowly. Then he moved on.

"Corporal Overstreet," Clark said as he neared.

"Captain, sir."

Clark scanned the faces around the fire. Joe Maxwell loomed over the others, his sandy hair poking out from the sides of his kepi cap, the brim drawn low over his eyes even though there was little morning light to shield against. "We march at ten. This is it. The whole army. Twenty extra rounds for each man."

"Fredericksburg, sir?" Henry asked. The extra cartridges definitely meant a fight. For days they'd heard rumors about an attack on the rebels dug in there. They'd also heard rumors about attacks on Richmond, or rebel assaults against Washington. But Fredericksburg was the tale they heard most.

"Nobody's saying. The newspapers say that's where General Lee has his army, so that seems like a good guess, but it's a guess." He nodded and spun on his heel, his officer's cape billowing behind him.

"Well," Maxwell said, his eyes following Clark as he moved back up the row of tents. "The secesh can't complain about us surprising them, can they?" The others grunted in agreement. They assumed their generals weren't as smart, or as tough, or as daring as the rebel generals. That's how it had been so far.

"Eat hearty," Henry said with a small smile. "Easier to carry it in your belly than in your pack."

The march took three days. On the third, bugles roused them at three in the morning, but the march didn't start for another two hours, triggering a cascade of grumbles. The regiment stayed together on this march, all the way to the Rappahannock, across from Fredericksburg.

The rebels were dug in on the far side of the river, up on the crest of a slope that rose from the town streets. They had a commanding view of the settlement, the river, and the Union Army.

The regiment joined the rest of the Fifth Corps in a muddy field, close by the house where General Burnside had his headquarters. They stood there for most of the frigid day while the engineers tried to assemble a pontoon bridge across the river. Messengers on horseback rushed to Burnside and then rushed away.

Company E stood at ordered arms near the front right of the formation, close to Colonel Ames and Colonel Chamberlain and their aides. For once, Henry could overhear at least something of what was going on. George Young, his sergeant, kept stopping by for news.

"What're they saying?" George asked in the late morning.

"Every time we get the bridge planking up on the boats near the other side, that's when the rebel sharpshooters—they're hiding in the houses over there—start picking off the engineers and the whole business falls to pieces."

"Bad day to be an engineer," George said.

At midday, with little rise in the temperature and no orders to advance, Colonel Chamberlain approached Henry.

"Corporal," he said. The officer loomed nearly a head above him, his drooping mustache ends expressing a sadness that his eyes confirmed.

"Colonel, sir." Henry snapped off the best salute he could manage.

Chamberlain nodded absently. "Have the men eat what they have. We've no idea how long we'll be here."

"Yes, sir. And, sir?" Chamberlain had started to move away but looked back. "May they stand at ease?"

Chamberlain looked around the ranks of blue-clad men who filled the cold, soggy field. "I'm afraid not, corporal. General Burnside wishes us to be ready to march on short notice." Henry thought he could hear a soldier's skepticism in Chamberlain's voice. "Tell them they may ground arms."

"Thank you, sir."

At that moment cannons bellowed. "Ours," Chamberlain said, his eyes flicking to where cannon smoke was rising. "May they do some good."

The bombardment went on for hours, cannonballs pulverizing the empty buildings of Fredericksburg, but the Union attack never launched. Captain Clark ordered the men back a mile into night camp. The bridge was built, he reported, but the assault would be in the morning.

Henry's nerves were strung up. Everyone was cold and getting colder, but there was nothing for it but to swallow some hardtack and sleep as best they could. Henry checked from man to man, reminding each to seal his tent against the night. Joe Maxwell and Teddy Meisner sat on their rubber blankets before a fire that smoldered with damp wood.

"Might as well sleep, fellows," Henry said. Both nodded but kept their eyes on the low flames. Voices murmured close by. They were tense, all of them. They were afraid. Henry was too. Tomorrow their war would change from one of misery and discomfort to one of fighting and dying. Henry said good night. They grunted in answer.

Flagg was asleep when Henry slipped into their tent. As he lay down, Henry couldn't rest. His mind kept turning to the battle to come, the fighting. Through the long day, he had focused on each task before him, and then the next one and then the next one until now, when it was time to wait for sleep that would not come. Now his stomach tightened with the idea of gunfire, cannons, raging men tearing and clawing at each other. He wished he was somewhere else. The idea slipped from his mind as he drifted off.

* * * * *

In the morning, the regiment descended through heavy river fog to the bridge. From their high ground, the rebels could watch them across an open plain on the other side of the town.

It looked like the generals were going to fling the Union soldiers through the city, then across the exposed plain and uphill against the Confederate lines. While the regiment waited, Joe Maxwell looked over at Henry with a tight grin. "Sure hope old Burnside has some trick up his sleeve," he said, "'cause otherwise this looks to be pure murder."

The attack didn't start until midday. A Union division that had crossed the bridge during the night started out across the open field. As the blue-clad soldiers neared the rebel lines, fiery streaks erupted from the hilltop. The angry roll of explosions reached Henry a second later on the safe side of the river. Smoke bloomed from the rebel cannons. The cannonade gouged gaps in the blue lines, which seemed to melt into the ground. Some patches of blue fell back down the slope, seeking shelter where they could find it.

Pure murder it was.

Henry felt weak. His skin prickled. How could those men march up that hill to die? Would he have to do that?

Another blue line advanced, then sputtered out on the green slope, adding more slashes of blue to the ground. Then another line came on. And another. Nothing, Henry thought, was up Burnside's sleeve today. Or between his ears. The men in Company E watched with horrified awe. They breathed oaths and took off their caps to scratch their heads. Johnny Baxter's eyes were wet.

It was near the end of the short December day that orders came for the Twentieth to cross the bridge. Shells screamed overhead. Some splashed the water around them. Henry felt the air press down when a shell passed close by. Anxious men and horses ducked and weaved on the bridge. The boats under the bridge planks wobbled and swayed, threatening to spill them all into the river.

When the regiment reached the town's battered buildings, the men shed their packs. "Hey, look," a man in Company G shouted. He held up a bank note. Hundreds of them fluttered in the breeze. Henry picked one up. It carried the name of a Virginia bank. The printing was splotchy, some of the words smeared. He showed it to Maxwell, who shrugged. "Worth even less than ours," he said. Henry stuffed it into his tunic.

A hungry-looking black dog ran to the men, who crouched behind what must have been the bank building. The dog nuzzled Johnny Baxter. The young soldier placed his rifle on the ground and hugged the dog, whispering to it. Colonel Ames's shout sliced through the din. Other voices picked up his cry. The soldiers began to move. Baxter shoved the dog toward the pontoon bridge and pointed, shooing him away. The animal, his tail straight down between his legs, stared back. He was shivering.

The regiment, exposed to the Confederate cannons, filtered carefully through the ruined streets. Henry heard a thud and cry behind him. Meisner swiveled to look. "Keep going," Henry shouted, shoving him forward. Fighting to keep his legs moving, not to turn and sprint for the bridge, he couldn't understand why they were climbing the same slope where so many had already died. Didn't anyone else know this was suicide?

They broke into the open land just as the sun fell behind the Confederate lines. Grateful for the spreading dark, they advanced a short way before reaching a low ridge, still a hundred yards from the enemy. The officers decided they could advance no further. A few men fired their rifles up the slope, but Henry didn't. He couldn't see anything to aim at. Word came to settle in for the night.

Without blankets, without overcoats, Henry's platoon burrowed into the ground to get out of the wind that whistled down the slope. Moans came from the wounded men who lay around them. Some begged for water. Some for their mothers. Some for death. A few for God. Two stretcher-bearers crept past the platoon and knelt next to a fallen soldier.

"Wish they'd take the loud ones," Joe murmured to Henry. They were hard up against each other, sharing their warmth against the chill that seeped into their bones. "Jesus. We're gonna freeze. Save the rebs a lot of trouble."

"I know. The South shouldn't be so damned cold."

When the stretcher carriers came back, leaning over as much as they could, Henry whispered to them, "Hey. Any of those men dead right there?"

"On the right," came the reply.

Henry crept out in that direction. He found two corpses, one sprawled over the other. He stripped the tunic off the top man. His fingers smeared the frigid blood and exploded intestines of the bottom man. He slid to his right. Another corpse yielded a blanket and another tunic. A fourth corpse wore an overcoat. Though spattered with gore, the coat was too thick to pass up.

Henry crawled back to Joe and shared his haul. When they had covered themselves, they looked out to see Colonel Chamberlain dragging one of the corpses Henry had just plundered. The officer shoved the body to the rim of the shallow swale he occupied with two other men. Then Chamberlain turned back to drag over another one.

"Jesus," Maxwell said, his voice filled with wonder and revulsion.

Henry started up over the rim again. Joe's hand grabbed him. "My turn," he said, then pushed forward.

They positioned four bodies between the enemy and the dip where they huddled. Other forms moved in the dark, working at the same grim task. Henry covered his face and head with a dead man's tunic and pushed hard against Joe in spoon position, partly for warmth and partly to affirm that each was still alive. "Sing out if you're going to roll over," Henry said, squirming to pull the extra blanket underneath them. The wet soaked through it as he sank into mud. The weakening voices of the wounded still came through the dark.

"Reckon we'll ever get out of here?" Joe said.

"How the hell do I know?" Henry gritted his teeth. He looked longingly over his shoulder, down the slope. *Why weren't they ordered to crawl back down in the darkness?* he wondered. He could make it. He squeezed his eyes shut, tried to close his mind off.

When the morning sun sneaked over the trees on the east side of the river, Henry couldn't tell if he'd been awake or asleep. He rubbed his hands together and twisted his neck. Shots began to sputter from the Confederate lines. Henry reached for his rifle but stayed down. A bullet thumped into one of their corpses. Henry bent his head against Joe's back to stifle the scream that surged into his chest. They'd had no choice, he told himself. Colonel Chamberlain started it. He showed them how to stack the bodies.

After a few minutes, Joe said, "Gotta piss."

"Downhill."

Joe twisted around and fumbled with his pants. He leaned back against Henry and began to moan. Henry turned his head and saw the yellow arc.

"Tarnation, Joe. That'll run right back on us."

Joe's response was more moaning. The odor arrived in a few seconds. Henry closed his eyes and told himself it wasn't the worst thing about the day. He had to piss too.

After an hour, the urine stink was overpowered when a Confederate ball struck one of the corpses in the abdomen. A pop and sssss signaled the escape of gas, which enveloped them.

Hour after hour, the regiment lay there. If a blue-coated soldier raised his head, the rebels shot a hole in it. After a while, the Maine boys started to fire their rifles blindly up the slope, twisting awkwardly to load, then poking the barrels between sheltering corpses. It was an act of defiance, not a military maneuver.

By noon, their water gone, their food gone, Joe and Henry no longer paid any heed when enemy bullets thudded into the dead flesh that protected them. They couldn't move, or stand. Henry stopped thinking about getting off that slope. He wondered if he could get used to anything. Had the generals forgotten they were out here?

The sun was sinking when the enemy mounted an attack to the right, dozens coming out of their lines to flank the shallow depressions where most of the Twentieth still lay. If the Union soldiers tried to rise up to meet the attack, the rebels remaining in their trench would pick them off. Some fast-thinking soldiers stacked more corpses at the right edge of their swale, creating enough shelter so they could fire back at the attackers, who quickly withdrew.

Dark brought orders to leave. The men first began scraping out graves for the dead who had protected them through that long night and day. Henry used his bayonet. Joe favored a wide, flat rock. The wet ground yielded readily. The sound of digging ran down the slope. The graves were shallow, with barely enough dirt to cover each body. For head boards, most used the butts of the dead men's guns. Not knowing the names of the dead, they carved into the wood the number of their New York regiment.

"Duck," Joe whispered harshly as they finished the fourth burial. Henry flattened against the new grave. A pinkish light washed over him. There was no explosion, no firing. He rolled up onto one shoulder. Light streaked and flashed across the sky, sometimes in wide sheets. "I'll be damned," Henry said. He had seen the northern lights before but didn't know they showed so far south.

"What's it mean?" Joe asked, his voice filled with emotion. The colors made the sky look as bloodthirsty as the men on that slope. Could one have something to do with the other?

"Don't mean a thing," Henry answered.

When the lights had finished, the men used the dark to slide down the slope. Where the ground leveled, they rose to walk. They passed smashed wagons with wheels jutting at odd angles, decapitated draft animals, and dead soldiers. Henry wore the bloodstained overcoat he had borrowed. Joe clutched another man's blanket around him. They breathed easier when they reached the town's ruined buildings. At the pontoon bridge, Henry felt the coiled spring in his stomach begin to loosen. Rain started. Dirt spread over the bridge planks muffled their steps.

The regiment had done all right. They weren't cowards. They knew that now. They stayed together. They lost only a few killed, a few more wounded. But they had lost another battle. Their minds were sour with the horrors of that slope.

Lacking rations or shelter, they stopped for the night. Rain fell. Henry and Joe found tree stumps to sit on. Neither cared to lie down in that downpour. They wore out the night on those stumps, sometimes asleep, mostly not. Henry tried to think of Katie but couldn't bring up anything about her. Not her face. Not her words. He had her letters in a pouch that hung around his neck, but he couldn't take them out in the rain. He had only her name. He thought it over and over in the dark.

From the time they left the cursed slope until the next morning, neither he nor Joe spoke a word.

CHAPTER TWO

JANUARY 1861,
ALMOST TWO YEARS EARLIER

"Whathat the hell's it mean, they're seceding from the Union? It's not like they can pick up a state and move it somewheres else, like over to Europe. Do they stop voting? Stop paying taxes? Christ, the whole business makes no sense." George Young's hectoring baritone emerged in bursts of steamy breath. "Where's young Overstreet?" Young demanded. "He reads the papers, him and that father of his. Maybe he can explain it."

Hunkered into heavy coats, four of them sat around an open fire at the Williams Shipyard. The brittle noonday sun did little to warm their dinner break, which came halfway through their bitter-cold ten-hour workday.

"What do you care?" Billy Steele asked, his mouth full. He was on his first pork sandwich, the one he usually swallowed damned near whole. Two more waited in his food sack, which he kept near the fire—but not too close—so the meat could warm up.

Henry Overstreet's sack sat next to Billy's. "Doesn't matter what you think. There's what, six states already seceded? Didn't none of them ask your permission."

"Ah, Billy," Young answered, "someone should've told you that being born stupid doesn't mean you have to stay that way." The others chuckled. They knew that Young would target each of them soon enough, so they might as well enjoy some fun at Billy's expense. A large and loud man, George Young led this crew of joiners by force of will, not because of his modest carpentry skills.

Henry, the youngest of the crew by ten years, arrived with an armload of scrap lumber for the fire.

"There's the professor," Young cried. "Straighten us out. What the hell's all this seceding stuff about. It's the niggers, right?"

Henry sat next to Billy Steele and reached for his dinner. "Pretty much, George, if you read what South Carolina said, and they were first to go. They don't make any bones about it. They want their slaves and damned if they're not going to keep 'em."

"Hell," Young said, "I don't care if they have nigger slaves. They've always had 'em. What of it?"

Henry drank cold coffee from his canteen and wiped his mouth. "It's more complicated. See, they want to spread slavery, force it into other parts of the country, like out west. And Mr. Lincoln says no to that, and he won the election saying it."

"So what happens next?" Billy Steele asked. "Is the country just going to fall apart?"

"More important than that," Young broke in, pointing a finger at Henry, "what happens to our ship orders? This sloop we're working on right now, that's for the cotton trade. If the country falls apart, are those Southerners gonna keep coming up here for ships?"

Henry grinned, his pale blue eyes alight and his sandy hair flopping onto his forehead. "What do you boys think I am? A fortune-teller? Nobody knows what's going to happen."

"Well, I don't like it, not one bit," Young said. "Those southern bastards're just trying to push us around. I also don't much care for the idea of losing our work. Half the ships we build are for the coasting trade, and that mostly means cotton."

"Don't forget," Billy Steele said, "there's a Maine man going to be vice president. He'll look after us."

"Hamlin?" Young said. "What's he ever done? Anyway, I don't trust any of those abolition scum as far as I can throw them.

Plus, who could trust a man won't take an honest drink?" The men guffawed in appreciation.

"Why don't you ask your buddy Boss Reed what's going to happen?" Henry said. "Since you always vote the way he says."

Young's big face flushed, and he held his hands out to the fire, wiggling his fingers. Boss Reed owned the Waldoborough bank on top of his political work, which gave his word extra weight when he directed the town's citizens to back Democrat Stephen Douglas in the September vote. Men who voted against Reed's wishes sometimes found their fences torn down or their gardens trampled. There was, for instance, Elias Yates, a heavy anti-slavery man who everyone thought was helping runaways, sneaking them to cross the Medomak at night and head to Canada. Just before the election, somebody beat Yates bloody in the dark. Henry worried that his father's public disdain for Reed might earn similar treatment, but so far the boss and his thugs had left the old man alone. Having backed the loser for president when most of New England went hard for Lincoln, Reed and his boys probably weren't feeling real frisky. Other New England shipyards were bound to get government work long before Waldoborough got even a whiff.

"I swear," Young said, rubbing his hands together, "the rheumatism's already getting me like it got the old man, crippled him up like an old tree limb."

Henry chewed his second sandwich thoughtfully. "So, we've got no job after this one?"

"Who said that?" Young fired back.

"I'm asking. The other jobs in this yard are workboats, not much call for joiners on 'em."

Young sighed. "We got another two weeks here, maybe three. The Catlin yard may have a job for us. Something'll come in. Don't I always find something?"

The men fell silent. They stared into the flames as Henry fed in the new scraps. There was no point starting back to work early. Quitting time would be 5:30 whether they took the full dinner break or not.

Starting for home in the early dark, Henry passed a half-dozen yards. A couple were really boatyards, not shipyards, too small for major projects. He smiled and nodded to those passing in wagons or on horseback. His high spirits had nothing to do with his working day, or Abraham Lincoln, or the seceding southern states, or Boss Reed, or even with the prospects of George Young's crew of joiners. He was smiling for the best reason he could think of—that Katie Nash shared this earth with him and lived in his town. Better yet, he was pretty sure she liked him.

He decided to cross the river so he could walk by the Nash place. He might see her, or at least someone in her family. The river was frozen solid up there so he could cross back easy enough.

He passed the shuttered shops of the granite and brick Fish Block. Lights glittered in Medomak House, where drummers gathered in the tap room, their battered sample cases filled with cheap jewelry or patent drugs or pattern books—stashed carelessly while they washed out the road grit with beer and whiskey. Alcohol was legal in Maine again after seven thirsty years of temperance. Henry turned down the steep incline of Main Street to the bridge, passing the sawmill, the gristmill, and the foundry. The carding mill sat on the far bank.

It wasn't that Katie had ever said anything to encourage Henry, not in the few weeks since he realized how wonderful she was. But since that blinding realization hit him, she had—several times—smiled at him with those dark blue eyes. A person can fake regular smiles, everyday ones like Henry directed at passersby as he walked. But smiles with your eyes: Those can't be faked. Henry was sure she wasn't faking.

He and Katie hadn't spent much time together, not yet. Back in school he hadn't paid attention to her. She was three years younger. Then just before Christmas, she came into Winslow's store when he was buying potatoes and flour. She wore a blue cape that was more stylish than was usual in Waldoborough. She stamped the snow off her boots and hurried to the stove to warm her mittened hands. He liked that. No false courtesies on a freezing day. Her cheeks glowed a bright pink. Those eyes smiled in his direction. "You'd think I'd be used to the cold, wouldn't you?" she said.

He laughed and agreed; the cold was a shock every winter. She was fully grown now, he couldn't miss that, her chestnut hair thick and flowing when she threw back the hood of her cape. For a moment, his usual ease with words failed him, but then he started talking about the potatoes in his hands. He explained how his mother always used rosemary and pepper to fry them and how he was trying to capture how she did it. Katie's eyes grew soft. She said she'd been sorry to hear about his mother; she would have said something back then but had been away. He and his father, she added, must have a hard time getting on without a woman.

He carried her packages home for her that night. Despite the cold and the raw wind, they dawdled, feeling the spell of the evening, speaking simple words—but ones meant only for each other. Henry's senses sharpened. He heard the not-yet-frozen trickle of a stream. His nose told him what meals were being prepared in houses they passed. The lights from the houses burned in his eyes like suns.

Katie hadn't asked him to come inside, which wasn't the best sign, but it had been late. He was late for his own supper. His father had accepted the explanation without complaint, then doled out his usual succotash, a dish that always tasted like wet sand.

A few days later, Henry saw Katie at a holiday concert at the German Meetinghouse. The choirs of three churches combined to sing something by Bach. As the audience filtered out, he stole a few minutes of talk with her. When he got that smile from her again, he knew it. He was going to marry her.

Asking around, he learned that Katie had been with relatives in Bangor for much of the year before, which explained why he hadn't noticed her until that day in Winslow's. If she'd been around, he would have noticed.

In truth, Henry didn't require much evidence to conclude that she liked him. He naturally assumed that she did, since most people did. It was always that way. He never had schoolyard fights because the boys wanted to be his friend. He never wondered why. They just did. Maybe it was his cheerfulness. It could have been generosity. If he had something—food or a toy—he shared it freely. Anyway, why wouldn't Katie like him?

The challenge was moving her along to falling in love with him. He'd have to give her some reasons to get there, but he was hopeful. He knew most of the young men in town—or knew about them—and figured he measured up pretty well. He looked all right, not really handsome, but evenly constructed, without any major strangeness. He had some good qualities that a woman with serious blue eyes would appreciate. Like all Overstreets, he had a feel for working with wood, so he'd always find work. As Lewis

Overstreet's son, he was known to be well-informed, a young man who read and understood. He hadn't had any choice about that. The old man never stopped reading. Henry's older brother was named Ralph for the great Emerson, while Henry was named for some novelist named Fielding. Henry knew he should read that other Henry's books, but they were awfully long.

Henry did worry about one factor that might stand between him and Katie: her parents. They were proper. Very proper. Katie's grandfather had owned a shipyard, one that got trampled in the scramble among the town's two-fisted shipbuilders. People spoke well of how old Mr. Nash paid off his debts even though it took him ten years to do it. Katie's father, chastened by that example, lived a quiet life as bookkeeper at Gay's, the dry goods store.

The Nashes were Methodist, temperance people, and abolition-minded, none of which bothered Henry. He didn't get wrought up about religion. The Overstreets had always gone to the German church. The pastors were dull, undemanding. Henry's experience of religion never extended much past wondering at the night sky's vastness, the sort of wondering that a boy couldn't avoid. The stars seemed so near but were so far. When his mother got sick and then died, Henry felt the grip of loss and despair, but the murmurings of Reverend Schlieffer did nothing to relieve them. Nor did the pastor persuade Henry with promises about worlds Henry could not see or know, not when those promises were two thousand years old and had been retold ever since. Why, Henry had asked the pastor, weren't there any miracles since Jesus died? The Catholics had recorded hundreds of miracles since then, the pastor answered, with all of their saints. But, Henry answered, you don't recognize their saints or those miracles, do you? Reverend Schlieffer never had very good answers. When the black grip of his mother's death relented, Henry gave up on talking with the man.

The Methodists, as far as Henry could tell, had no better answers but were a lot more certain. They tended to get riled up, especially about liquor and slavery. Still, Henry couldn't see any reason the Nashes should get riled up about him. He didn't go around advertising his disbelief. He'd worked steady at the yards since he was fourteen. He was a man with a skill. He wasn't a hell-raiser—not for the last year or two, anyway. And he had no affection for slavery. An infernal practice, his father insisted, one that no civilized people would tolerate.

But Henry feared that the Nashes might nevertheless be quick to judge, even a bit narrow in their views. They hadn't done or said anything outright unfriendly. They were correct toward him. But not warm. Their reserve might stem from the reputation Henry's father had for skepticism. The old man stopped attending church a short time after losing Henry's mother, saying he preferred to examine his soul in private. Some said that Lewis Overstreet was no better than a Universalist, a group generally viewed with pity, since they would never see the next world. Lewis Overstreet ignored the talk. He spent his Sunday mornings reading and smoking.

Another possibility was that the Nashes might view Henry with suspicion as part of the old German community. The Overstreets would always fall on that side of the town's divide, even though none of them could speak much of the language anymore. When Henry confided that speculation to his father, the old man exploded.

"Why that's ridiculous." He vigorously stirred that night's succotash. "That's the same feeling against the Germans that's been around here for a hundred years. Are you sure that's how they feel?"

No, Henry wasn't sure, but there was…something. He could feel it in the way Mrs. Nash drew back at the waist from him, also in the way Mr. Nash pressed his lips into a thin line when he inclined his head in greeting. What other reason could they have not to like Henry?

As he neared the Nash house, a well-maintained clapboard affair with two rooms built onto the back, Henry slowed and straightened to his full height. He tried to peer around the curtains in the two front windows, imagining the activity inside. Katie, the oldest of four and a year out of school, might be helping with dinner or sewing or knitting, chores that Henry's mother had never seemed to finish.

When he saw Mr. Nash splitting wood in the side yard, it looked wrong. Katie's brother was old enough for that chore. But Henry recognized the opportunity. He offered a carefully calibrated wave, respectful, not too eager. The man nodded. A definite opening.

"Good evening, sir," Henry called. "Not a bad night for January." The man wore old-fashioned mittens, blue ones. What with working indoors all day, he probably wasn't used to the cold.

"Good evening," he answered. "You're looking spry after a day at the yard."

Offering his best grin, Henry stopped. "Working on a coaster right now; she's a beauty. The captain's paying extra for some fine cabinets. Mr. Young, he's our foreman, he's letting me build them. I like the work." Henry knew not to talk politics. Like most of the town, Mr. Nash was known to toe Boss Reed's line, even when it ran against his abolition ideas.

"You're a lucky man." The man let the ax head rest on the ground. "Not everyone can say that about his job."

"I hope Mrs. Nash and the family are well?"

"We're all fine," he said, leaning down to pick up a length of wood, then standing it on end. "Off to Bangor next week."

That put Henry on edge. Could Katie be leaving town as soon as he had found her? "That's a journey and a half this time of year, sir. Are you risking the railroad through Augusta, or the roads?"

"We'll take the roads in a sleigh. It'll be easier with all we're taking."

"So, the whole family?"

Swinging harder than he needed to, Nash split the wood with a thwack. He buried the blade in the chopping block. He must be rusty at wood-splitting. Rocking the blade to work it free, he said, "No, just Katie and me. She'll stay with my brother's family there, look after his little ones. They've got six, and their mother is ailing."

"Well." Suddenly there was no air in Henry's lungs. His mind bounced through the possibilities. "That's fine, helping them through the winter months, when the children are indoors. My brother and I used to drive my mother crazy in the cold weather."

Using a more measured stroke, the man split another length. "Don't know how long it'll be," he said. "She's got the consumption. Isn't that what your mother had?"

Henry nodded.

"Katie may be there a while."

Henry gave a quick nod. "I should be moving on. My father'll be waiting supper." He gave another calibrated wave and strode off. His smile was gone.

CHAPTER THREE

✝

Henry dropped into the wooden seat across from George Young. He would have to ride backwards from Waterville to Bangor, looking at the countryside that they had just passed through. Confusion over boarding had already fogged the excitement of his first train ride. When the stationmaster called passengers for Bangor, George led Henry straight to the last of four cars. It was best, George announced, to get far away from the locomotive and its flaming sparks. Before they even stored their grips, the conductor ordered them out. The car was reserved for ladies and for gentlemen who were escorting ladies. The conductor didn't think they fell into either category.

So they ran through the rain up to the second car, the one behind the car for Negros. George sank into the corner formed by his seat and the window, his legs stretched out to rest on the seat next to Henry. Uncertain what the conductor would think of such liberties, Henry extended his own legs under George's seat and began to study the car's interior. Curtains framed wide windows. A potbellied stove squatted in the center, though the early fall weather didn't require heat. The paneling was cheap pine, its whitewash scarred by rough use. Two floppy-hatted farmers faced each other, their expressions severe and dubious.

Across the aisle, a man in a black coat and extravagant cravat read a newspaper while puffing on a harsh-smelling cheroot. Henry wondered if he should have worn his good collar and cravat. They were in his grip. He was saving them for Bangor. The stranger met Henry's glance with a glare that dared Henry to remark on his cigar, his attire, or anything else on Henry's mind.

The train whistle shrieked. A bell clanged. The engine yanked the cars ahead, jolting the passengers, then rocked forward and back. Slowly the behemoth moved.

"Not much smoother than the stagecoach," Henry said. When Young cupped an ear to show he couldn't hear, Henry leaned forward and shouted over the clamor.

"Maybe," Young called back, "but a hell of a lot faster."

The train built speed, settling into a steady jounce, the passengers' bobbing heads like boiling water. Bright embers flew by his window. If a spark hit the cheap paneling, the car would ignite like kerosene, but Henry decided to say nothing. No one else seemed concerned about it.

Trackside trees blurred with the speed. The engine roar and whining rails formed a barrier between Henry and the farms and woods whipping by. The scenes flashed too quickly for him to consider them, much less imagine the lives they contained. Compared to steamboats, which Henry twice had taken to Portland, the train felt violent, like it was thrashing the land it passed over. In contrast, the heaving sea had been unbothered by man's puny motorized ship. The ocean was too vast and powerful for man. The land wasn't.

Their journey grew from a contract George landed for the interiors of four sloops that were aimed at the coasting trade. As their crew had feared, Waldoborough wasn't getting any Navy contracts. It had voted wrong in the election and its yards were too small for the steam-powered ships that were now the rage. River ports like Cincinnati and Pittsburgh were building the Navy's gunboats. But all was not lost. With Navy work crowding yards in other cities, Waldoborough could build merchant ships.

George needed to place a large lumber order with a Bangor mill. He would negotiate the deal, but wanted Henry along to judge the wood. Henry had an eye for grain and strength, and he understood the wood should be good enough, no more. They weren't building Commodore Vanderbilt's flagship.

Henry had leapt at the trip to Bangor, where Katie had been for nearly nine months. He was starved for news of her. He should have written to her, but he never had written much to anyone and couldn't think what to put down on paper to someone he had spent so little time with but was intending to marry. Anyway, he didn't have her address in Bangor, and he didn't want to ask the Nashes for it. Where would he be if they refused?

When he saw her brother Theodore, he had asked after Katie, but the boy usually shrugged and said they didn't know when she was coming home. Henry had flirted with other girls at picnics and musicales, even took strolls with a couple, but his heart wasn't in it. It never would be until he knew where he stood with Katie. That was the point of this journey for him. He and George had meetings on Saturday. When Henry had said he'd stay a day or two extra to look at Bangor, George gave him a funny look, but voiced no objection.

Across the aisle, the smoker's cheroot was down to half-length, forcing him to squint against its wispy fumes. When he tossed his paper on the seat, Henry leaned over and pointed. "All right if I take a look?" he called.

The man consented with an upward palm, then announced, "We finally won something!" He pulled the cigar from his mouth between forked fingers. "Couple of forts in the Carolinas. Our ships bombed 'em to smithereens."

Henry took the paper. It had been printed the day before in Portland. He looked for war news.

"It's about damned time," George called over to the smoker. "After that mess at Bull Run, the Navy may have to win this war for us."

The cigar smoker nodded agreement. He held out two more cheroots. Henry shook his head but George took one, pulling his legs down and sliding toward the aisle. He pulled a friction match from his vest and lit up.

Henry located the account of the battle near Cape Hatteras and read it while the others puffed and agreed that Southerners didn't know the first thing about ships. "If it wasn't for us," the stranger said, "they'd've been eating all that cotton all these years. They'll never get it to market now."

"What about the British?" Henry put in. "They're pretty fair on the water, and they take a lot of cotton. They might side with the South, eh?"

The stranger looked at him through half-closed lids. "They're not looking for another war, not with us."

George pulled a flask from his jacket and offered it to their new friend, who took an enthusiastic pull, then returned it.

The conductor called for tickets as he worked down the aisle. He turned to Young and nodded at his flask. "Now you're not going to get yourself wallpapered and raise a ruckus, are you?"

"Sir," Young said quickly, grinning and patting his pockets for his ticket. "This is my mother's lemonade, the finest in the whole state." He held out the flask. "You should taste it."

"Much obliged," the conductor said, shaking his head, "but Mother always warned me against lemonade."

The men laughed.

Bangor was a revelation to Henry, a town so devoted to the lumber business that its air carried the sweet smell of sawed wood. Its waterfront on the Penobscot bristled with barges and ships carrying felled trees, telegraph poles, boards, planks, and every other wood product. But Henry wasn't so interested in the town. He set to work at finding Katie.

The hotel clerk was a marvel. When Henry asked how to find a family in town, the man produced a city directory. Unfortunately there were seven Nash listings. Henry jotted down all seven addresses and located them on the directory map that the clerk also produced. The head of one Nash household was named Theodore. Since Katie's brother carried that name, Henry decided to start there.

Then Henry had an idea. Better to encounter Katie in an open setting, away from her family. The directory listed three Methodist churches and their schedules for Sunday services. Henry noted that information as well, asking the clerk for a description of the neighborhood of each. George, overhearing the exchange, gave Henry a quizzical look. "Had no idea you were such a holy fellow," he said. "Methodist? I thought your people were German." Henry grinned and shrugged.

Early Sunday morning, business completed, Henry strode through quiet streets to each Methodist church, the town map folded in his back pocket. He couldn't tell anything by how each church looked, so he decided to start with the one closest to Theodore Nash's address. If Katie wasn't there, Henry would slip out the back during a hymn and hurry to the next one. If he came up empty at all three, he could always knock on seven front doors.

Approaching the first church, sweat seeped into his shirt as his heartbeat quickened. He paused under a tree and took off his jacket to cool off. He thought what he might say after all these months, then decided not to plan anything. If he couldn't think of anything to say to his future wife, then this truly was a fool's errand. He pulled on his jacket and strode into the church, settling in the left corner of the last pew, a good vantage point for scanning the arriving worshippers. She wasn't with the early groups.

The pianist was starting a regal tune when Katie arrived. Her steady walk matched the song's pace. Every few steps, she peered over her shoulder at the scrubbed and polished children who followed her in duckling formation, wearing proper demeanors. An older man, doubtless her uncle, brought up the rear, his attention riveted on the two boys immediately in front of him, prime candidates for mid-sermon squirms. The Nash tribe filled most of a pew. Henry shifted for a better view of the white-bonneted girl and her pale green dress. She was lovelier than he remembered.

If the Methodists worshipped prayerfully that morning, Henry didn't notice. All of his attention was on Katie. When the final processional began, he stood to catch her eye, but she was resolving a sibling altercation. Finally, when she stepped into the aisle, their eyes met. He grinned. She looked surprised, ducked her head, and herded the children before her.

Skirting the queue waiting for the preacher at the front door, Henry slipped outside and marched up to the man he presumed to be Katie's uncle. He introduced himself as a friend of Katie's from Waldoborough, in Bangor on business. The children had commenced to chasing each other around the churchyard, shouting their joy that services were over. Katie walked toward Henry, smiling with those eyes. His head swam.

She touched the older man's arm lightly. "Uncle, perhaps Henry and I might go for a walk before I make dinner? It's long since I've spoken with someone from home."

"Of course," he said, then invited Henry to join them for dinner.

"Only if I can do the washing up, sir," Henry said. "That's the deal my pa and I have."

"Hardly necessary. We have plenty of hands for that chore." Mr. Nash inclined his head. "Until dinner, then." He stepped away.

"Katie, girl," Henry said, "aren't you a sight for sore eyes." She puckered her brow to shush him, but he couldn't stop the words. "I can scarcely believe it's true. I've been looking forward to this since the last time I saw you."

"This is pretty sudden," she said. "You didn't think to write?"

"I did, I did. But I didn't have your address here in Bangor."

Katie gave him a disbelieving look. "That seems a small obstacle, at least compared to ambushing me at church in Bangor. This is not an accidental encounter? You're not here because you've seen the error of your sinful ways?"

He couldn't stop smiling. "Not at all." He fell silent, searching her face for warmth. "Well, here we are. Might as well talk a bit. If you're of a mind to."

She suggested they go along the river. He steered her with a touch to her elbow, then withdrew his hand as though scalded.

He asked after her aunt, learning that her condition was up and down, too often down. Katie talked about her young cousins, who had become dear to her. She loved to help them with their schoolwork. She was thinking she could teach school, though in Waldoborough men usually filled those jobs, and college men at that. He told her she'd make a wonderful teacher, far better than any they had while growing up.

Henry felt like he was floating past Bangor's mills. When he commented that Bangor appeared to be prospering, she suggested they see Broadway where the lumber kings lived. Large, gabled homes loomed on either side of a road divided by the greensward. He barely noticed the houses or the street.

Katie asked what people back home were saying about the war. Most, he said, were coming around to supporting the Union despite Boss Reed and Bull Run, where the Northern troops had turned tail and run all the way back to Washington. "Hosea Robbins," Henry said, "why, he even draped a banner across Main Street calling for everyone to defend the Union, and no one bothered about it. Of course, Hosea sat right there under the banner with a shotgun for most of the week."

"Will you fight? Will you join the army?"

He'd been asking himself that question without really wrestling with it. "I don't know. The Overstreets have fought before. The first one who came to America, they called him the sergeant major; he was a real soldier. Another was at Bunker Hill."

"And you?"

He shook his head. "There's a family story. Not really a story, more like a proverb. My pa told it to me and to Ralph, drummed it into us. Supposed to be from the sergeant major. That war is butchery, unworthy of civilized men. So whatever military tradition we had, well, it's died down a bit."

"But isn't this war different?"

"I don't know." He kicked at a stone. "It's men killing each other."

"But it's to keep the nation together and to free the slaves. Isn't freedom worth fighting for?" Her eyes looked fierce. Color flushed her cheeks.

"Well, take freeing the slaves." He sensed that this might not go well, but he wanted to speak his mind. Things would never work out with her if he couldn't speak his mind. "I don't even know that it's a war to free the slaves. Not even Mr. Lincoln says that. I don't even know how we in the North have the right to force the South to do that, end slavery."

"What if right now we passed a man who was whipping a slave. Would you raise a hand to stop him? Would you walk on by?"

"No, of course I'd step in. But this is our home, here in Maine. That's not what we allow people to do. But going down to Virginia or South Carolina and telling people there what to do – that's different. Do I have more right to do that than they have to come and whip their slaves here? Don't they get to decide for themselves? Isn't that what the Union is about?"

"I thought the Union was about all men being created equal, and about liberty for everyone."

"Sure, sure. But I just don't know that it's so simple."

"What's complicated about slavery? Do you want to be a slave? If I was being held as a slave, had been taken off these streets and hauled down to Virginia where you can own slaves, would you try to free me? Or would you say that my owner had the right to decide for himself what's right and wrong?"

He was quiet for a moment, then said, "I haven't thought about it that way. No one would do that to you."

"That's because I'm not a black girl." She had stopped in front of a three-story mansion with green shutters, a challenging look on her face.

This was going all wrong. Down at the shipyard Henry was used to being the smart one, the one the others didn't challenge, but she was smart—maybe smarter than he was. She'd thought about this more than he had. He struggled for words. "I, I guess I need to think some more. I see what you're saying. I can't say you're wrong, but I'm not sure you're right either."

Her face had begun to soften, but now her lips drew tight. Her eyes went cold. "Henry, perhaps you shouldn't come for dinner. Thank you for coming to see me. That was kind. But I need to start the cooking. Please remember me to the people back home."

She spun and started off. "Wait," he called, "I'll see you home."

She didn't break stride, and he didn't follow. Unless he had something smarter to say, there didn't seem any point in it.

He spent several hours on a log at the riverside, surrounded by Sunday quiet. Bird calls filled the quiet, though Henry couldn't identify most of them, except for the quarrelsome jays. Their raucous chatter sliced through the air, warning off any who meant them ill.

He'd come all this way, tracked Katie down, only to end up sitting alone by the river. All because of politics. No, it was more than politics. Underneath it all there was a question he'd worried about. It was well and good to be against slavery. Nobody was exactly for it. But was this the time for doing something about it? For him to do something?

His brother Ralph had signed up with the first wave of recruiting and marched off for the war, but then…Ralph ended up with nothing but shame, so much that he moved to Rockport with a new wife and new baby, hoping to leave behind the story of his brief army service and its inglorious conclusion. The episode made Henry wary of the army. He hoped Katie didn't know that story. Not yet. It would only complicate matters.

When the shadows grew long, Henry set off to find the Nash home. He misread the map twice, so it was near dark when he reached his destination. It wasn't a big place. He wasn't sure how they could fit all those people in—nine of them, counting Katie. It couldn't have more than a couple of bedrooms. He stopped to straighten his clothes and smooth his hair. He took off his hat and held it with both hands.

A boy of ten answered the door. When Henry explained that he wished to speak with Miss Nash, the boy called out, "It's the man from church, for Katie."

A soft woman's voice came from inside. "Bring him to me, Michael, then run and tell Katie."

Henry stopped still when he saw her, Katie's aunt. She had the wan complexion with dots of pink on her cheek, the frail arms and lethargic air, so much like his mother when she got sick. She huddled under a quilt though the evening wasn't cool. "Ma'am," he said, "I'm Henry Overstreet."

She smiled. She had the glow of a fire that burned too bright, one that consumed from within. "I know who you are. At least I found out today, though you were quite the secret until now."

He ran the brim of his hat through his fingers. "I don't get to Bangor much. My first time, actually."

"Sit down, Mr. Overstreet." She nodded to a stool near her. When he was installed, she said, "We'll have only a moment, so please overlook my forwardness. I'm glad that you came. The Nashes, you know, they can be a crusty lot. But they often regret themselves."

"Yes, ma'am," Henry said. "I mean, we haven't, Katie and I that is, we haven't known each other so long."

"Don't give up easy, Henry Overstreet. The Nashes can smell weakness. You don't want them to get that in their nostrils." She smiled. "She's a special girl. And she likes you." She spoke the last sentence very quietly, just before turning her head to Katie, who dried her hands on her apron as she entered. "Katie, look who was able to get away from his business. I'm so glad to meet him."

Katie smiled. Maybe her eyes smiled too.

"Mr. Overstreet," the older woman said, "I believe there's some leftover mince pie that Katie made. Her pie, why, the thought that I can't have it at every meal brings tears to my eyes."

Henry protested that he wasn't hungry, though the mention of food made him ravenous. He allowed himself to be coaxed into the kitchen, where he inhaled a generous wedge of pie, testifying enthusiastically to its excellence. Curious children passed through the room repeatedly while he ate, allowing nothing like a private conversation.

"Your aunt," he started to say, then left a space.

"Tessa," Katie said.

"Yes, she's very nice."

"Yes. She makes it easy to be here."

"That must make it hard, as well."

She nodded.

He wanted to ask how long Katie would be there in Bangor but suspected the question had no answer. Instead, he said it was late and he should get out from underfoot.

Picking up his hat, she saw him out onto the doorstep and closed the door behind her. She nervously fingered the brim of his hat. "So," she said, "now you know I have strong views. Mama says no man can abide that."

"You said nothing I haven't said to myself. I just don't have very good answers."

She cocked her head and looked right at him. "Henry, don't you ever lose your temper?"

The question unsettled him. "I don't suppose I've thought about that either," he admitted, running his fingers through his hair. "I'm not much good answering your questions."

She looked at him now, her brow furrowed. "I wonder what that's like, being even-tempered. Jeddy, he's the third boy here, he's like that. Not all the time, but most of it. It seems a blessing with him."

"The only blessing I seek, Katie, is you."

She handed him his hat and smiled. He leaned over and kissed her gently on the mouth. "Henry," she said and touched his face with her fingertips.

"I don't know when I can get back here," he said. "Will you answer my letters if I write? Now that I know the address and all."

"Yes. I will answer."

CHAPTER FOUR

†

October 1, 1861
Waldoborough
Dear Katie:

I hope you can read this scrawl. I know that a neat hand shows a person of good habits, but I am naturally lefthanded so the pencil sits awkwardly in my hand. I did better with chalk on a slate in school but slates would be too heavy for the mails so you must make sense of these hen scratches. We are having a fine autumn so far; it only rained two days since I returned from Bangor which is a boon to us working out of doors. I have thought much since we spoke by the river about the war and slavery and how the two combine but have not made much advance in that way. People talk like our army soon will stroll to Richmond and end the fighting especially now with General McClellan in command though there seems to be little enough fighting and even that will stop for the winter. I don't know that I would make a soldier or that I could be much help for the army but I know that I make a good joiner and help build good ships and I know that it would be hard on my father if I was to go to war. So I will stay in Waldoborough through the winter. I hope you do not think less of me for this.

Your friend,
Henry Overstreet

October 29, 1861
Bangor
Dear Henry:

Your letter arrived on October 6, so I am sorry to take so long in writing—I was able to read every word without much effort, no matter how left-handed you are. It is very busy in this household in every season, but it was especially busy with my cousins going back to school. This is the first year for all of them to be in school, even Hannah, the smallest, which leaves more time to care for my aunt and see to the house. Aunt Tessa was very proud to watch them go off, but she also seemed sad. Based on some of the conspiring conversations I have overheard between the older boys, there are pranks planned for Halloween by some Irish boys, so ours are preparing retaliation. One of our neighbors came out this morning and found that his two horses had their tails braided to each other and they were hitched backwards in his carriage. My uncle was angry about it but it did look comical if it wasn't your horses and carriage. I don't think it did any real harm except inconvenience and perhaps some confusion for the horses who hadn't ever faced the wrong way in a harness. I don't think our boys here did it but I cannot be certain.

I am glad you continue to follow the war and think about it. Just this week we read of a battle in Virginia where a United States Senator was killed along with many other men. I hope of course for a short war with a good ending but I don't know that we will see that. As a female I cannot fight in the army though I could help in other ways and do not. So I do not think ill of you for staying with your father. I hope you will continue to write.

Katherine Nash

November 15, 1861
Waldoborough
Dear Katie:

We are getting ready for the Thanksgiving celebration, which will be next Tuesday. My pa and I will go to brother Ralph's house in Rockport the first time they'll be having a holiday in their own house and it will be fine to see Ralph and his wife Lucy and their baby who's only two months old and I am even more looking forward to the food as Ralph says his wife Lucy is a fine cook and her mother an even better one. Nothing can match your mince pie but I hope they will give it a run. With the cold weather there's been some cases of measles. The Jenkins baby has died and several others are sick. Something that has shaken a lot of the men me included is an accident down at the Tucker shipyard last week. They were launching a barkentine of good size and one of the stern lines broke free with such force that it pulled Joby Forrest a Negro working at the yard straight into the river, and then two or three timbers fell off the launching frame and fell in after him. Joby Forrest is a respected man and works as hard as any white man for his $1.50 a day so several went to pull him out which they did pretty fast but that water was cold as ice and he was pretty near ice himself. No one says why it happened except someone did not tie down that rope right which could happen in any yard any day. We all see things that are unsafe and we either fix them or try to get away from them fast, but when we hurry on a contract sometimes it's more the second than the first. Joby is still sick from his dunking in the river and not able to work. I asked George who runs our crew if we could all contribute for the family while he is home and George said yes. I think other yards are doing that too. It made me think about the black men who work as slaves and whether they are looked after when they get hurt. My father says that the slave owners always claim they care better for Negros than we do in the North but he does not believe them. We are being careful at the yards now but I guess we will be back to our sloppy ways soon. Please give my good wishes to Mr. and Mrs. Nash for Thanksgiving and to you too.

Henry Overstreet

January 10, 1862
Waldoborough
Dear Katie:

The cold here this week has been fierce and will freeze your fingers stiff before you can use a tool. We try to work near the fire that goes all day long and go over to warm our hands every few minutes but we must work as long as there is light which is not that long thank heavens. My fingers may be cold but my heart remains warm from the times we had when you were here during Christmas time. It was the first I can remember when my heart felt full maybe since my mother died. Singing carols with you and skating on the river and then the sleigh rides which were the best, at least they were for me—a man can live for a long time on times like those even in the long winter we are having. I know you are doing a Christian thing with your aunt and uncle's family and I wish only good things for them but I cannot help but wish also for you to be here. Please remember me to your aunt and uncle and my father sends his regards

Henry Overstreet

January 23, 1862
Bangor
Dear Henry:

I have news that makes me happy and I hope you share my excitement too. When I returned from Waldoborough my aunt asked to speak to me in a private way. She is so good and suffers too much. I wish the doctor would arrive some day with a magic potion and make her strong and healthy again. She said that she knows that I want to be a schoolteacher and the way I teach the children here shows that I have a talent for it. At Christmas time, my uncle spoke with one of the people who hires teachers at a school not too far away. Not the one my cousins go to but not far. They will lose their teacher in February and will offer a six-week contract for another. There are twenty-eight children of all ages and I imagine that they are the same as children everywhere—bright enough when they want to be and eager to be out of the schoolhouse whenever they can. But they have agreed to take me on the six-week contract beginning on February 18. I told my aunt that I had to help her family more than go off on a new job but she shushed me in her gentle way. She said it was time for her older ones to take on more of the work of the house and to look after her more and that I must teach them how, though they know most such things. She then spoke to the children—mostly Jonathan who is thirteen and Christina who is twelve—and they could not object to anything their mother tells them, she is so good. So that's my news. In less than a month I will be standing before a room full of children and trying to teach them. I must practice my loud voice and my stern looks. I hope my experience with my own brother and sisters and here in Bangor will help.

Katherine Nash

February 14, 1862
Waldoborough
Dear Katie:

I share your joy over the prospect of teaching the young scholars of Bangor and I expect you will have begun by the time this gets to your hand. However delinquent those children may be now I am certain you will bring them to heel promptly. It is a sore temptation to me to travel to Bangor to enroll in your class as I envy those who will have the complete attention of Miss Nash for several hours of every day.

Did you have the heavy snows that we did last week? The yards were closed for a full day while the snow fell and the wind blew a gale so the snow swirled and we could not see our work. Finally even old man Brown—we're working at Brown's now—said we should go home. I walked up the river because the wind had swept the snow off the ice in places which made it easier going. I got as far as the Miller place about a half-mile below our house and then I could see part of the roof blown off. Mr. Miller and his neighbor were standing on barrels trying to get some wood in place over where the roof was gone. I had to stop and help them which about froze my hands and feet harder than the river, but we got it covered though not very well, and Mr. Miller joined his family at his neighbor's house. We are able to move about now but not very fast without a sleigh and horse and walking on the river is the fastest way to most places. Old man Brown grumbles about not much work getting done and how he was closed for three days but it seems to me he should be grateful we come to work at all.

Henry Overstreet

March 8, 1862
Bangor
Dear Henry:

The time we have feared for so long is upon us and it must be from the cold of this long winter. My aunt has taken a very bad turn and has not been outside her bed for ten days at least and has neither strength nor appetite. The doctor is not hopeful and this noisy and happy house has become the saddest place I have ever been. The children are always quiet. Jonathan has split so much wood for the fire in his mother's room that we have no place to store it. He and his sister Christina take turns missing school to be with their mother during the time I must be teaching. Then they teach each other the lessons from that day. I feel a traitor when I trudge off in the morning to face those hard-hearted children in my class but my uncle insists on it because he says that Aunt Tessa wants it and she must have her every wish met and what can I say to that? I am a poor teacher not only because I am new but because my heart is not in it. I am counting the days until my contract ends and I can stay here with my aunt and see to her properly. I am sorry I cannot write a more cheerful letter so I will stop now.

Katherine Nash

April 11, 1862
Waldoborough
Dear Katie:

I have been slow in responding because the yards have been working extra time—even by lantern light in the evenings—to make up for days lost to the winter but also because of the news in your last which I have had in my mind for many days without having any good words to write about it. I will always be grateful for your aunt's kindness to me though I was one of the smallest moments in her life. Your description of what the house is like now nearly unmanned me as it was so much like ours during my mother's last days. It is an evil disease that takes a person slowly inch by inch so you feel the loss again and again and there can be no outcome but the one the disease demands. I still see the sadness in my father at times; it left its scar on all of us maybe my brother most of all. But you have many cares other than mine or ours. I hope you are bearing up. Your aunt is fortunate to have such a faithful niece to help care for her and her family. May she know the greatest peace in this life and any other. There has been war news of the worst sort that makes me think again of our conversation on the riverside and I can feel my mind moving on this but I know you have no time for such matters. I cannot know when we will be together again but I wish I could assist you and speak with you.

Henry Overstreet

CHAPTER FIVE

JULY 1862

Henry stood near the front of the crowd, close to the steps of the custom house and post office that served as Waldoborough's civic heart. He slapped at his neck, cursing the black fly who had overstayed his welcome. Only mosquitoes should be torturing Waldoborough by this point in the summer. Billy Steele had come with him straight from Brown's shipyard. They had rinsed their hands and faces in the river, but their clothes were stiff with dried sweat and sawdust.

"He's from around here, right?" Billy asked, his dark eyes alive with the moment.

"Some little place a ways inland," Henry answered, "but he's a Mainer right enough."

A man wearing a soft hat and farming clothes joined in. "He's a goddamned brigadier general, that's what he is. Been at every big battle, every step along the way till he lost that arm."

"Just last month he lost it, right?" Billy said.

"Yes, sir," the farmer affirmed. "And here he is, already spoiling to get back into the fight with old McClellan and the rest."

Henry stood on his toes to look over the crowd. There had to be at least two hundred there, maybe more, spilling over into the road. It was the end of a warm day in summer, a fit occasion to stop and listen to someone important talk about something important.

Henry knew about half the faces around him, maybe more, but didn't see the one he wanted to. He had told Katie about General Howard coming to recruit new Union Army regiments. She had already known about it and said she'd like to go. Maybe something was keeping her away. Or she might just be late, though that wasn't like her. She wasn't the type who timed her arrival to be noticed.

The town cornet band's rendition of "Columbia, the Gem of the Ocean" would have been more stirring if the musicians had agreed on the tempo. Billy jabbed Henry in the ribs when the crowd began to cheer. "Look at that man," Billy said, nodding at the custom-house steps, "like he's been pro-Union all along. Makes a body want to spit."

It was Boss Reed, bold as brass but looking as delicate as china, a gilt-edged Copperhead traitor standing next to a one-armed man in a blue uniform who had to be General Oliver O. Howard. Henry's eyes lingered on the general's empty right sleeve, which was pinned in place. His arm ended just below the shoulder joint. His uniform, definitely wool, had to be hot for standing in the sun.

Boss Reed began, nattering on in nasal tones too thin to carry very far. Since people always wanted to hear what the boss had to say, Henry thought, he never learned how to project his voice. The man seemed nervous today. He wasn't the main attraction, nor did he agree with the meeting's purpose. In the last election, Reed— Copperhead to the bone—had again delivered Waldoborough for antiwar candidates. Henry had heard that Reed's flunkies were trying to talk men out of enlisting, even paying for them to sign on with fishing boats rather than join the army.

Henry didn't listen to Reed's words. If he wanted to, he could hear the man twenty times a year—at town meetings or at rallies. Instead, Henry studied the genuine war hero, the son of Maine who had led fighting men against the Confederate scourge. His face wore a grim look, one that reflected the suffering of a man not yet recovered from a terrible wound. The sickroom pallor of his face contrasted with thick, curly hair. His lush mustache and abundant beard proclaimed that he was an aggressor in the battles of life. His eyes glowed with fever, either the fever of sickness or the fever of belief. He looked a mix of warrior and martyr.

When his time came, Howard took a single step forward. His face grew calm. What terrors could shipwrights and farmers hold for a man who rode into the mouths of guns? Though he stood no larger than Henry, Howard's voice was deep and resonant. After greeting his fellow countrymen and thanking Boss Reed, he made a small flap with his stump of an arm, looking like a baby chick learning that his wing moved but wouldn't take him anywhere.

"I suppose you're wondering about my injury," he said. "Folks don't appreciate the advantages that come from this." He flapped the stump again. "It took General Kearny to see them. He knew right off, because he lost an arm himself, his left arm, during the war with Mexico. When he visited me, the first thing he proposed was that we shop for gloves together!" The general paused. He allowed a small smile to play across his lips, giving the spectators permission to enjoy the joke. Gradually, everyone either grinned or laughed out loud, proud of this brave man, their neighbor. A martyr and a hero who mocked his own disfigurement.

The general wasted no time reaching his central message: that the men of Lincoln County must take up arms in the holy battle to save the Union and crush its enemies. He spoke soberly of the progress of the war, the victories at Shiloh and New Orleans, the courage of the Union men in the Virginia campaign. Even though they never reached Richmond, they'd fought for seven days straight, toe to toe with the rebels, showing how Northern men fought. There were Maine men there in Virginia, he called out; there should be more. The men here in Waldoborough should be among them. Their country needed them.

Then General Howard's transformation began, from soldier to prophet, a man who challenged the hearts of those before him. The religious echoes in his words surprised Henry. "Gird on your sword," he called out, his eyes searching the crowd, commanding every eye. "Mount your horse, come forth to the help of the Lord to smite down the high and mighty who threaten our commonwealth."

He spoke with the power of one returned from battle. "I have seen the awful magnificence of hosts arrayed in deadly strife, one with another. I have heard the fearsome roar of the cannon that rings through men's souls, mingling with the shattering peal of musketry. I have seen the awful mangling of the land and of bodies, but I know also that it is a great work to which we are called—to which all of us are called—a work for noble patriots – for hardy, true sons of Maine.

"I cannot promise you comfort. The army has no soft beds. No warm and familiar sights or smells of home. The food will disappoint you. The burdens will try your souls. The dangers will be terrible. There will be raging rivers to cross, mountains to scale, and valleys of death and steel and sorrow and blood. Let no man say that Oliver Howard promised him a bed of roses in the Union Army. But I promise you this: a cause as noble as man and God can know, the cause of American liberty, a liberty promised to all, one that we—you and I, together—will deliver to all, aided by the all-powerful arm of God in heaven."

He paused and scanned the crowd. He spoke without gesture now, keeping his remaining arm fixed by his side, his passion coursing through his words and through his voice, which bore irresistibly into Henry's head.

"We will prevail." His expression dared anyone to contradict him. "We will prevail because our fight is righteous and the Bible tells us that righteousness exalteth a nation, but sin is a reproach to any people." Howard inserted a slight throb in his words, a surge that seemed to enter Henry's bloodstream, to match his breathing, to suspend the passage of time. "Join me. Join me as I return to this sacred battlefield. Lend your two good arms to mine"—he raised his remaining arm. "Join our fellows in this great cause, with righteous courage and upright passions. You and I, together we cannot fail."

The general allowed his head to fall forward and breathed deeply. The crowd took a breath itself, then erupted in lusty cheering and hooting. Men waved their hats or threw them to the sky. Howard lifted his head and again looked across the faces before him. Brown and sunburned faces like Henry's and Billy's, smeared with dirt and grease from a day's work under the open sky. Pale, well-fed faces of men who worked as bookkeepers and men of business. And bonnet-framed faces of women, some showing hardship, others reflecting ease. He challenged each face. In their shining countenances, they blessed him for that challenge.

Edwin Clark, whose family owned the largest lumber yard in town, jumped up on the steps between Boss Reed and General Howard. He pointed to a table to his left where two men in uniform sat. He was recruiting a company, he said, for the glorious cause. As they knew, the town had approved a bounty of one hundred dollars to each recruit. All they had to do was give their names, then come by his office this evening to sign the contract and accept the bounty. He hoped to see every man there.

Henry, who came to the rally intending to enlist, moved toward the line forming at the recruiting table. He knew Billy, with four children at home, couldn't sign up.

"Hey, Henry, Henry!" George Young walked across the road toward him. The big man had cleaned up after work. He wore a nearly white shirt and black vest, buttoned up despite the heat. His face was flushed. "Hell of a talker, ain't he? Like a preacher, I'm telling you. Preaching the Word!" Henry kept moving toward the recruiting table. George fell in with him.

Henry nodded his agreement, unable to take his eyes off George's beard. Only an hour before, it had been a mix of gray and brown and red, befitting a man of his years. Now it fairly gleamed with a dark sheen and gave off a heady whiff of bootblack. "They say he does some real preaching," Henry said. "Methodist, I think."

"He's got the fire of the Lord in him." George looked around. "I wouldn't be surprised if old Edwin got his whole company signed up tonight." He looked at Henry. "You're going through with it?"

"I am. Didn't hear anything to persuade me otherwise."

Young looked at him sideways as they neared the end of the line, which stretched about twenty-five men long. "Me too."

"Yeah?" Henry grinned and stroked his bare cheek.

"What do you mean, doing that?" Young's hand went to his beard. "Don't it look right?"

Henry smiled. "George, it looks exactly like what it is. You never said anything about signing up. I don't know how that's going to go down with your Copperhead friend, Boss Reed."

"Hell, I don't care a fig what Reed thinks about this, not this war business. I've been thinking on it for a while now. Our youngest one, he's eleven now. The older boys make good enough money. We've even put some by." He looked off toward the river and shrugged. "The big problem is that I'm old so I may be no damned good to the army, but I've heard of older men signing up. And I'm still pretty rugged."

"And you've got that beard."

"Damned if I don't."

Henry didn't know the man's exact age, but he had to be closing in on forty, or even past it. "What happens to your business? Who's going to do the woodwork on all these ships?" George, his thumbs hooked in his vest pockets, kicked the ground. "Plenty of joiners on the coast here. They'll be glad to see George Young go off to war, stop taking the work away from them like I always have. Like you and I always have."

Henry held out his hand. "I'd be proud to serve with you."

George took the hand, then grabbed for his hat with his other. "Hello, Miss Katie," he said, lifting the hat.

Henry pivoted. In a gray dress with a simple collar, she looked like a queen.

"Mr. Young," she said with a smile. She placed a hand lightly on Henry's arm, then took it back. "I'm sorry to have missed the great speech. Theodore gashed himself jumping off a rock at the pond near us, and my mother made me sew it up so I'd learn how. Since Theodore was my boatman to get over here, I couldn't come until he was seen to, anyway."

"Was it bad?" Henry asked.

"Didn't hurt me a bit." She smiled, then pointed across the road where Theodore stood under a tree, a white bandage on one arm. "He'll live. He says the water was shallower than he expected, which I call a pretty poor excuse for a boy who's lived near that same pond his whole life." She squinted in the sun. "How was the general?"

Henry pointed to the recruiting table. Howard stood talking with Boss Reed. "He's right over there."

"He didn't talk you out of signing up?"

"Young lady," Young broke in, "if you'd'a heard him, you'd be signing up yourself."

When Katie looked back to Henry, he nodded in agreement. "He's a man you'd be proud to follow. Didn't sugarcoat anything.

Basically said the army'll deliver hell and damnation, but made it sound like something you'd be a fool not to join."

When Katie said she had to stop at Winslow's for some things, Henry asked George to hold his place while he walked her to the store. She took his arm.

Since her return from Bangor, they had become a regular sight in Waldoborough. Henry squired her to church sometimes, or public concerts or horse races and anything else. Twice they went off on picnics by themselves. Those were the times Henry liked best. He felt like they could talk about anything, or just be quiet together, neither of them having to say something.

When they were away from George, she asked if Henry had told his father yet.

"Tonight," he said. "After I sign up with Clark over at his yard. But I think Pa's expecting it. We've talked about the war lately. Ever since Shiloh showed how long and how bloody this'll be." After a few more steps, he added, "Then tomorrow I'll ride over and talk to my brother." He looked over at her and stopped. They had reached a place with no one else near and turned to face each other. "I've not told you Ralph's story. I don't know what to say about it."

"I know. I know about Ralph."

"You know he signed up?" She nodded. "And that he left when he learned about Lucy; she was expecting and all." She nodded again. He looked off into the woods. A bird was singing the same three notes over and over.

"That was Ralph," she said. "That's not you."

"No, but he's my brother. He'll always be my brother. I've never been quiet in my mind about it all."

"He stood by Lucy. That was a manly thing to do."

"There's men who serve who leave a wife and child at home. He could've married her and then gone back to serve out his term. He took an oath, and he broke it."

"What does he say about that?"

"He said they could arrest him if he went back. But that wouldn't make much sense, would it? To arrest a man who's come to serve? They sure could arrest him for being here, for leaving the army like he did."

"No one here's going to arrest your brother, Henry."

"But they all know. One night Pa called it a life sentence—one Ralph'll never outlive. Maybe not even when he's dead."

"Well, he and Lucy are making a go of it, aren't they?"

"I guess, though it didn't do Lucy's reputation any good either."

She reached for his hand and squeezed it. "Is that why you're signing up? To save everyone's reputation?"

He shrugged. "Mostly, you know, my own. I want to do something in this world. You know, maybe leave a mark. You don't leave a mark by sitting out the biggest thing that happens in your life."

She looked serious. "You want to be famous?"

"Not likely. I just need to be part of this. I can't say it like General Howard can. He called it as noble a cause as man and God could know. I'll always regret it if I don't go."

She nodded at him. "Okay, then." She seemed wrought up about something, but Henry couldn't ask her about it in the middle of the street.

"I'll come by tonight?"

She nodded again and turned to the store.

* * * * *

Henry climbed the stairs to the Clark office, which sat over a storage area that held boards and panels and shingles. A half-dozen signs announced that no smoking was tolerated, nor open flames.

He rapped on the office door, then stuck his head around it. "Mr. Clark?" he said.

"Yes, yes, come in. Overstreet, is it?"

"Yes, sir, Henry Overstreet." They shook hands.

"Sit over there," Clark said, pointing. "Give me a moment to get organized. You're my first victim tonight." After a minute of sorting through drawers, and then papers stacked on a table behind his desk, Clark sat facing Henry, the desk between them. "I commend your patriotism in answering the call of the president," he said. "And the call of General Howard."

"Yes, sir. The general's an impressive man." Henry felt awkward being so respectful of Clark, who was not so very much older. They didn't know each other. Clark hadn't attended local schools or consorted with Waldoborough boys. That hadn't held him back any, not with the Clark money and position behind him.

"Indeed, indeed." Clark sorted papers again, then counted crisp greenbacks into a stack. Henry hadn't yet seen the new greenbacks. He'd never seen that much money in one place, even if it was just paper. "Your father's known to be an independent man, a Lincoln man. Or so Mr. Reed says."

"My father raised us to be independent."

"Yes," Clark looked up. He fixed his gaze over Henry's shoulder. "There *is* the matter of your brother. That's come up."

"What do you mean?"

Clark nodded at the stack of bills. "Now that the town's paying this bounty, there's some who worry that some might sign up for the money, then go sign up somewhere else for another bounty. You can see that would be a concern, can't you?"

"That's not what Ralph did. He got no bounty. And he had a reason for what he did."

"Yes, I heard."

The chair legs screeched as Henry stood. He felt a rush of anger. "Mr. Clark—"

"Overstreet, sit down. You've got me wrong. I'm just explaining, as I have to with every recruit, that we will recover the bounty if your enlistment is not completed."

Still standing, Henry said, "Do you plan to talk about my brother with every recruit?"

"No. Of course not." Clark cleared his throat again. "I guess we've covered the bounty. Why don't you sit down and sign? Then you'll be a member of Company E of the Twentieth Maine Volunteer Regiment. Now, that sounds pretty good, doesn't it? We're getting together a fine group of men from Waldoborough and around here."

Henry took his time looking over the paper, then formed his best signature on it.

He was excited when he crossed the bridge to see Katie. It was near dark when Mr. Nash opened the door and stepped aside. It was Henry's first time inside the house, which wasn't any nicer than where he and his father lived, though it was a good deal neater. It showed, he decided, a woman's touch.

He and Katie sat at the kitchen table. After both of Katie's sisters came through the room on errands that seemed less than urgent, Katie stopped her brother from entering. "You're all so nosy," she said. "Just go away." She closed the door and turned to Henry. He placed the greenbacks on the table. Her eyes grew big.

"Henry Overstreet, are you just sashaying around the town with that kind of money?"

"I'll give it to my father tonight, to keep safe until the war is over. Or until my war is over. Then it'll be for you and me. Our getting-started money."

"Can I look at it?"

"Sure."

She picked up a bill and turned it over. "Who's this, the picture?"

Henry shrugged. "I'm not sure. I didn't ask. It might be Alexander Hamilton."

She placed the bill back on the stack and looked up at him. "So many are getting hurt and killed."

"Yes."

"Not you. Don't you be one of those. I won't stand for it."

"I'll be sure to tell General Lee."

"You don't need me to say that it's brave and right to sign up, but the most important thing is to come back."

"And you'll be here?"

"As long as it takes."

CHAPTER SIX

†

Athin rain fell during most of Henry's ride to Rockport, dripping off his hat brim and beading on his oilskin cape. The gray light didn't flatter a landscape mostly stripped of trees. Far from the road, a few saplings survived, too slender to reward chopping down. Despite the wet, Henry didn't push the horse. He'd ridden Cricket since he was six. A gentle roan mare, she was entitled to some consideration. Anyway, Henry had the whole day to get to Rockport, say farewell to Ralph and his wife, Lucy, and their daughter, Sarah, then ride home. He was in a thoughtful mood, trying to form memories of the land that he could hold onto after traveling south to the war.

Three wild turkeys ran single file through a meadow. Few wild creatures roamed here anymore. In their place were milk cows, hogs, horses, and oxen, all broken to man's ways. The farmhouses were humble but neat. Home gardens flourished. Here and there a cottage slumped with neglect, another farmer worn out by rocky soil and short growing seasons.

Henry tried to remember how long it had been since he'd been to Ralph's. Nearly three months, he decided; not since he helped paint the house. It wasn't more than twenty miles from Waldoborough, but it was nearly three hours each way. His father had visited Ralph a few times since then, but Henry had stayed back to see Katie. If they ever built that coast railroad they kept talking about, maybe then he and Pa could make the trip more often.

Hatless in the drizzle, Ralph met Henry in the yard with a grin and a handshake. Wordlessly, he led Cricket into the barn.

Other people thought the brothers looked alike, though neither of them thought so. They shared a well-knit, compact frame, an economical way of moving. But Henry was an inch taller and his hair was darker, while Ralph took the sun better, his skin weathering to a rich butternut. The blue-gray eyes were the same, but Ralph was always the serious one.

"The trim looks good," Henry said as he dismounted. They stepped to the barn door to look over the one story home. Smoke curled from the chimney.

"Lucy wanted the green," Ralph said. "Insisted on it."

"She was right. Downright friendly looking." Henry smiled. He took off Cricket's saddle while Ralph rubbed her down.

"We've got news of our own," Ralph said over his shoulder.

"So you know mine?"

Ralph shrugged without turning. "People like to tell me about the war, you know. Wanting to get a rise out of me."

Henry shook water from his hat and cape. "Doesn't speak too well for your neighbors."

"Folks like a story. Livens up their day."

"What's your news?"

Ralph hung the rubbing cloth to dry and led Cricket to some hay, next to the mule. "Sarah's gonna have a brother. Or maybe a sister." He smiled sidelong at Henry. "January, Lucy thinks."

Henry laughed and threw his hat high, snatching it as it fell back. "You've found something you're good at."

"We already knew that." Ralph turned and beamed as they shook hands anew. "Turns out it's not difficult."

"Let's go in so I can congratulate the mama."

He passed the afternoon with the young family and its hopes. Baby Sarah was a towhead yet, though they expected her hair to darken. She had a newfound passion for crawling. Ralph complained that Henry was going off to war just when they needed help adding a new room on the side of the house. He showed Henry some rough drawings, pointing out the wall he would have to punch through. Henry dodged Lucy's demand for news about Katie, who she didn't know very well. He still wasn't sure what he thought of Lucy as his brother's wife. She came from a branch of the Schumans that hadn't prospered much, but then the Overstreets weren't exactly merchant princes. She seemed nice enough. He could see that she and Ralph were better with each other now. Some of the tension from how they started was gone, leaving something that looked like comfort, fondness, even happiness. He hoped so.

Dinner was lamb, sauerkraut, and potatoes, with some pumpernickel, washed down with honey wine Ralph had traded for. They lingered at the table, chatting about the new room and names for the new one. Sarah squeezed a piece of potato in her fist until it squirted between her knuckles, which made her squawk with pleasure. Then she did it again. Henry played napkin peekaboo with her, a game that never grew old. No one spoke of the war.

"Well," Lucy said, reaching to take the baby from Henry's lap, "I expect you boys will want to walk the property, now the rain's stopped. Sarah and I'll do the washing."

"Wait," Henry said, "that's my job back home. I'm the professional here." He stood to clear dishes.

Lucy smiled. "You go on now. Your manners are noted, but you two need to get out from underfoot. Sarah and I'll come out when we're done."

The sky had brightened. Scraps of pale blue opened to the west. Ralph held out his hand to stop Henry when they were a few steps out the front door. "Listen," he said.

Henry waited a few seconds, then said, "What?"

"You don't hear it?"

Henry shook his head, his eyebrows gathered in perplexity.

"The sea. Don't you hear it?"

The question seemed important to Ralph, so Henry decided to play along. "Guess I thought it was the wind."

"Only three miles away, where it smacks up against some rocks. Wind must be blowing up over the water."

As they walked east, over to the stone fence that earlier owners had built, Ralph explained how he hoped to do more potatoes and hogs. "Takes money, though. Have to buy a couple more brood sows, then put some of that pastureland back there"—he waved to the south side—"under the plow. Need to rent oxen for that."

They sat on the fence, ignoring the wet, and looked back over Ralph's land. "Cash money can be hard to come by," Henry said.

"Don't I know it. 'Specially when you start out with debt."

"Pa doesn't expect to be paid back for a while. You know that."

"He may not expect it, but I do. Can't stand owing." He shook his head. "I'll tell you, there's nights I can barely eat my supper I'm so tired. Lucy puts me to bed before she does Sarah."

They both smiled. Their smiles were alike.

"So," Ralph started after clearing his throat. "You're going."

"Tomorrow's the mustering in. They say there's fifty or so from Waldoborough and thereabouts, all for this new regiment. It's the Twentieth. You were the Fourth, right?"

"Yup, as long as I lasted." They sat quietly. The wind was picking up, blowing more blue holes into the cloud-sheets. "Pa's going to get lonesome."

"Since Mama died, he's lonesome in a room full of people."

"This'll be worse."

"I know. Sorry to leave that on you."

"Least I can do, since I can't go myself." He kicked at the ground with the heel of his shoe. "Did he try to talk you out of it?"

With a half-smile, Henry said, "Not exactly. Just had a lot of reasons I should think about why maybe going off to get killed wasn't a good idea. Starting with going off and getting killed."

"That's Pa. Always got his reasons, marching in tight formation. He tell you about the sergeant major?"

"More than once. War isn't worthy of civilized beings."

"Didn't matter to you?"

"I thought of what you said, Ralph, when you were arguing with him. It's the most important thing that's going to happen in our world, in our lives. We care how it turns out, about preserving the country. How could I not want to be part of it?"

"I said that?"

Henry nodded at him.

"Full of myself, wasn't I?"

Henry smiled. "But smart." After another pause, he asked, "What was camp like?"

"Some fellows you like. Some you don't so you steer 'round them. Everybody's scared, excited too. Some cover it up by getting loud, talking big. Others by getting quiet, trying not to get noticed. And that was before we knew the war'd go on so long, that it'd take so much killing. We were foolish then, thinking we'd whip the rebels quick and hustle on home as heroes. Now it seems like those rebels know something about war—maybe more than we do." He looked over at his brother and nodded. "You'll do fine, Henry. Better than me." He shook his head.

They started walking to the back end of Ralph's land, past the stink of the hog lot. A bustle of half-grown piglets circled their mother, craning already-thick necks to get to her teats. She ignored them. "Mama'd be happy to see you farming," Henry said. "She missed it. You could see it, how she'd talk about having animals, watching crops come up."

Ralph gave his sardonic smile. "She never had to figure out how to make farming pay."

"But you like it."

"Yeah, I do. I like being out of town life. The yards aren't for me. I tried 'em, working in Pa's crew. I just felt shut off there. Out here, I'm part of the world. I can feel how it goes every day, the sun and the rain and wind. Farmers watch the weather. It's what we do. There's some around here think this is sorry land, but I don't. They'll see when I get done. And when old man Northcutt is ready to sell"—he pointed to land to the east—"I hope to make him a good offer. Put these pieces together, then you've got something."

"You've got plans."

"Most of the time, I'm thinking on them. When you're done soldiering, you could come out here too."

Henry looked around. He had no idea what Ralph saw in this place. To Henry, it sure looked like a sorry piece of land, promising nothing but never-ending work. "Something to think about, brother. Something to think about. Right now, I think the army's going to do my planning for me."

CHAPTER SEVEN

†

The men clustered around the windows of the railway car, proud of their blue wool uniforms and flush with the pay they had received the day before. They shouted to those on the platform. After only a few weeks in Camp Portland, they weren't really soldiers yet. On a good day, they could march across an open field without tripping over each other, but heaven help the officer who ordered them to turn right or left. Few had weapons. None had yet had target practice.

A single emotion united them all, including Henry: a fiery hatred for the regiment's colonel, a West Pointer named Ames whose rich store of profanity had been a revelation. On the parade ground, Ames shouted himself hoarse with bitter denunciations of his men's incompetence. He waved his sword with rage. He ordered the drum corps off the field, their ragged beats only confusing the soldiers. He ordered bumbling officers away, too, so he could try to explain the simplest maneuvers to these unresponsive dolts. Most days, the Twentieth Maine drilled longer than any other regiment, especially if it was raining. After three weeks of his abuse, the regiment was better, but not much.

"What're you fellas carrying on about?" George Young yelled over to the soldiers at the windows. "You don't know a soul on that platform. Not one of you is from Portland."

"Come on over here, Grampaw," a man shouted back. "There's a couple grandmaws asking after you."

"To you, *Private* Shelton, that's *Sergeant* Grampaw," George answered. By the second week in camp, he had given up blacking his beard, so his whiskers now were dark on the ends and mottled near to his face. Henry had offered to trim the beard to a single hue, but Young claimed to like the effect. Henry admired how the older man had become the moral center of Company E. Accustomed to leading his crew of joiners, George was rough enough to intimidate the rambunctious, yet old enough to steady the homesick.

When the men of Company E voted on their noncommissioned officers, George was unopposed for sergeant. Henry thought there'd be support for two men who had served in the British army and actually knew something about soldiering, but George had disagreed. They were foreigners, he pointed out. And Irish.

The Irish were why Henry ended up with a corporal's chevrons on his sleeves. The argument started over firewood, which the men had to gather themselves. The longer they stayed in camp, the farther they had to go to find it. Two cabins away from Henry's, the cry had risen that someone filched several armloads of good wood. Suspicion fell upon some Irish because—as near as Henry could tell—suspicion always fell on the Irish. With an assist from home-brewed alcohol available throughout the camp, the investigation ripened into a confrontation, then a brawl. Though outnumbered, the Irish boys gave a solid account of themselves, mostly because they held their liquor better.

Henry had waded into the melee and hauled off one of the most truculent fighters. The man broke from Henry's grip and turned on him, then burst out in a horselaugh. "What the hell do you think you're doing, sonny?" he said. "This here's for the grown-ups."

With a flash of temper, Henry drove his fist into the man's midsection, dropping him to his knees. "Now quit it, all of you," he shouted, breathing fire as he turned to the scene. "Colonel Ames'll have our heads if he sees this."

Henry helped up the man he had just leveled. The others, with looks that ranged from wonder to bemusement, disentangled themselves and shuffled away. Next day, when Henry's platoon chose its corporal, one of the men nodded at him and said, "Well, this one here's a grown-up."

The others smiled. The vote wasn't close. That night, Henry asked George what he'd have to do as corporal.

"Not sure," George said as he used a stick to scrape crusted mud off his army-issue brogans. "Whatever I ask you to. Maybe keep the men from grumbling about the food and anything else, which means you don't get to grumble yourself."

"That's it?"

"I'll tell you as soon as I know different." He held a shoe up to inspect it and nodded with approval. "By the by, where'd that temper of yours come from? At the yard, you was always sweetness and light."

Henry leaned back on his cot. "Guess you never riled me up."

George shrugged. "Guess we'll keep it that way."

Once the train was under way, its racket forced the men to raise their voices. Henry closed his eyes and thought back on a recent escape from Camp Portland. Some of the men had figured out that they could always get permission to leave camp by forming a group with at least a corporal supposedly in charge, then claiming they were going to practice their drill. The Sunday before, Henry had played the role of supervisor for such a breakaway group, whose members quickly split up to explore the city as soon as the camp was out of sight.

Henry had walked quiet streets until he heard music from a large stone church. He slid inside and leaned against the back wall. About half the seats were filled. A female pianist played a slow song. A violinist played along. Henry let the sad tones fill his head, breathing slowly. When his hat slipped from his fingers, he left it on the floor. He hadn't realized how on edge he had been. The notes died out gently, echoing off the walls and through Henry's fatigue. The next passage was jarring in its energy, stirring Henry upright. He was glad when it was over.

The audience, which included a few blacks, applauded vigorously and stood to honor the performers. When the clapping died down, the violinist called a woman forward who announced they would close by singing the new "Battle Hymn of the Republic." She passed out sheets with the words. When the violin started,

Henry recognized the tune as "John Brown's Body," a favorite at camp. The words were complicated. Henry lagged a half-beat behind the other singers, catching up only on the verse, the Glory Hallelujahs. When they finished, he read the words again, lingering on the phrase "fateful lightning of His terrible swift sword." The words carried the power of the Bible, of moral right, like General Howard had. He tucked the sheet in the band of his fatigue cap so he could share it back at camp. Now, bouncing on the hard wooden train seat, he fingered the sheet inside his cap.

After several hours, the regiment was impatient to arrive in Boston, a metropolis most had never seen. The train stopped before reaching the center of the city. In the station, officers and sergeants roared the men into line to march through city streets. "You will NOT," Colonel Ames shouted, his face bright red in the early September warmth, "gawk at the buildings and the people as though you have never set foot off the pig farm. You will march like proper soldiers and you will not embarrass yourself, or your comrades, or your officers. Is that clear?"

Henry was in the first line of his platoon, on the righthand end. He felt silly marching off to war without a rifle on his shoulder, but lost that feeling after the first block. He yearned to gawk at the people, both the stylish and the grubby who paused to watch the regiment. He tried to take in the sights with the corners of his eyes. The park on their right, he thought, must be the Boston Common. Or it might be. Children ran alongside them, trying to talk to the soldiers. Henry caught glimpses of backyards where other children played in mud. "They're all Irish." Henry heard a voice to his left. "Damned dirty people they are."

Compared even to Bangor, the city was immense, hundreds and thousands of buildings on all sides, stretching away in the distance. An older fellow in a sailor's canvas trousers leaned against a lamppost as though he would fall down without it. He called, "Where you from, boys?"

"Down east," George answered, "where the strong winds blow and the pines grow tall."

A gentleman waved his hat and called for three cheers for the men from Maine. Following his loud "Hip, Hip," the watchers broke into a loud "Hooray." The soldiers puffed out their chests and marched more crisply. For a moment, Henry wished that Katie could see him, with his corporal's stripes, with the Twentieth Maine, cheered by the worldly people of Boston. He would rather have a rifle, but he was still proud.

They passed into a square, then stopped abruptly at a wharf. Without ceremony, the regiment climbed the gangplank of the *Merrimack*, a steamer that Henry reckoned was far too large for the Medomak River. No shipyard in town could dream of building a ship this size.

From the *Merrimack*'s rail, Henry and his fellows watched a Massachusetts regiment approach. The Bostonians cheered louder for their neighbors, who did look more impressive than the Maine soldiers. They had rifles. Their legs moved in unison. They stood smartly at attention while they were organized to board the ship. They looked like men who knew their business. Henry was proud to be with them, but envious too. The Twentieth would have to pull up its socks.

After an hour of confusion, most of the men had found a berth in the triple-stacked bunks belowdecks, then wandered back up top to enjoy the day. On the water side of the steamer, Henry gazed at the harbor's ceaseless activity. Workboats and tugs circled fine sailing ships. In the distance, fishing boats careened through the water.

George, a newspaper in hand and his pipe in the corner of his mouth, pushed up next to Henry. "Listen to this," he said, then turned to the men scattered on the deck. "All you men, news from Virginia!"

He took out his pipe and started to read. The men grew quiet. Others drew nearer. There had been a great battle, a second one near the stream they called Bull Run. Another Union loss. The rebels might attack Washington next.

When George finished, the deck was mostly silent. A man wearing the insignia of the Massachusetts regiment called, "Three cheers for Old Abe!" The men responded with shouts for the president. Another voice rang out. "Three cheers for Little Mac!" The men answered. Soon, though, it was quiet again. The ship's bell clanged, and its whistle blew as it pulled from the pier.

"Well," George said to Henry, "I guess the fun part is over."

Henry nodded. He'd been thinking about how little he knew about war. He knew one former soldier. John Sloan had fought in

Mexico, but everyone said he made up most of the stories he told. Some of the Irish in the Twentieth had served with the British Army—and maybe deserted from it—but never fought in any battles. His schoolteachers taught about the Revolutionary War, of George Washington and Benedict Arnold, but he knew little about them.

Nor did he know much about the Southerners they'd be fighting. Jefferson Davis, the Confederacy's president, had come to Waldoborough a while back. The rich men in town, led by Boss Reed, honored him at dinners. After all, Davis was a senator and had been secretary of war. He represented the cotton growers who paid for ships that Waldoborough built. But Henry didn't think he'd ever spoken to a Southern man. He knew they owned slaves and were proud. They were supposed to have high tempers. They wanted to destroy the Union, to spit on the idea of America, the idea that all men are created equal. Was that reason enough to go kill them? And to let them try to kill him?

The salty breeze stiffened as the *Merrimack* gained speed on a steady sea. Henry wished again that he had a rifle.

CHAPTER EIGHT

†

"**W**ill you look at that," Captain Atherton Clark said, pointing toward the Virginia shore of the broad Potomac River. "If I'm not mistaken, that's Mount Vernon itself." He called to the men milling on the ship's deck. "Over here, boys. There stands the home of George Washington."

Henry and George joined the crowd at the rail. Trees obscured much of the large, white mansion. They could barely see people standing on a portico that fronted the river. "And to think," the captain said loudly, "they want to take that, all that it means to us, take it clean out of the nation. It'd be like ripping our hearts right out."

George stared as the structure's columns flashed between trees. "Professor," he said to Henry, "how many darkies you figure it takes to keep a place like that going?"

"With you as foreman? Hundreds. Maybe a thousand."

"Now, now, I mean for real. They say the darkies don't like to work, not when they're slaves, though the black fellows up our way work pretty damned good." He shook his head and pulled out his pipe. "Army's turning my language foul, ain't it? I'm losing the knack of talking without cursing."

"How hard would you work for no money?" Henry said. "You get bad food and a cold bunk, might be sold to some other place whether you want to go or not, maybe have to leave your family behind."

George smiled as he chewed on the stem of his pipe. He had learned not to try to light it on deck. "Sounds like being in the army, don't it?"

"Sergeant, you're not building my morale." Henry pushed back from the rail. "I'm going to check that the platoon's packed up." He stepped around men sprawled on the deck where they'd slept through the mild weather of the voyage.

"Corporal." The voice came from behind as Henry reached the stairs down to the sleeping quarters.

Henry turned to face Captain Clark. He had grown a bushy mustache since their first camp in Bangor. It made him look older.

"Corporal, I've noticed you with the sergeant."

"Sergeant Young, sir? Yes, I worked in his crew back at the shipyards, more than four years, sir."

"Watch that, corporal, will you? Colonel Ames spoke to us about how the army's no place for playing favorites. You don't want other platoons thinking you get better treatment because you knew the sergeant before."

The steamer lurched as its pilot threw the engine into reverse to slow for its landing.

"I can't stop knowing him, sir," Henry said.

"You can stop acting like it. It undermines his authority."

"Have you spoken to Sergeant Young about this?"

"I saw you first, corporal." Clark nodded. "That's all."

Henry saluted and left.

Squeezing through the crowded sleeping quarters, Henry found his platoon. They were evenly divided between farmers and lumbermen, all used to hard work. They mostly understood that good habits led to good work, though they could find army ways strange. Like Captain Clark's instruction that Henry and George should act like they don't know each other. Unlike the other Maine regiments they had drilled with, the Twentieth drew men from all over the state, not just one part of it. Company E, Henry's outfit, was mostly Lincoln County boys, but most were new to him. Having George at hand was a comfort.

The *Merrimack* tied up at Alexandria on the Virginia side of the river, which pleased Henry. The Union had already reclaimed part of the South. The men of the Twentieth bridled when the Massachusetts regiment marched off first. But they all had rifles, which Henry knew made a better impression.

Indeed, the Twentieth's entrance into the war zone was distinctly unsoldierly. After gathering the men on a small side street, Colonel Ames set off on horseback to find their billet. Captain Clark gave Company E two hours to look over the town in the warm, soggy air of late summer.

Henry saw George and several others walk away without waiting for him. Captain Clark had probably delivered his warning to George. Henry fell in with two men from his platoon. Passing down the streets, they stared open-mouthed and goggle-eyed, losing any trace of military bearing.

"Never seen so many darkies," said Joe Maxwell, a tall lumberman from outside Bangor. "Had no idea there were so many."

"Look at this place," Teddy Meisner said, awe in his voice. "They don't care what kind of filth they live in. Makes Boston seem clean."

Henry held his tongue but shared their judgments. At an open-air market, fish heads and guts rotted in the street next to a mound of overripe peaches. Mangy dogs squabbled over choice bits. The men veered around horse dung, waving their arms to drive away flies. The people here seemed to wait for time to take the filth away. Residents emptied chamber pots out of open windows. Henry breathed through his mouth.

They had nearly passed a three-story brick building when Henry noticed the sign over the door. "Hey," he said, grabbing Maxwell by the arm, "this is Marshall House." The others stared back. "Where they killed Elmer Ellsworth. You remember?"

Both nodded. Everyone remembered Ellsworth. More than a year ago, when the rebellion was new, he died in that hotel, the Union's first martyr, after climbing to the hotel roof to tear down a rebel flag. The hotel owner killed him. Ellsworth became an instant hero. His legend reached Maine.

"Why haven't they burned it down?" Maxwell demanded.

Henry shrugged. "Don't know. Maybe they keep it to honor him." He led them into the hotel and started up the stairs. No one challenged them. It was three flights to the roof, which looked across the river to Washington. Henry pointed out what might be the White House, where the president lived, and the Capitol. The top of the Capitol, though, was dark and misshapen, incomplete.

The men paused on the stairs on the way down. "This is where it happened, ain't it," Meisner said, lifting his hand off the banister and stepping back. "Can't believe I'm here where history happened."

"We're here to make more history," Henry said. "Better history."

Maxwell pulled his knife from his waistband and began to cut a slice from the banister. "I'm taking some of this history home," he said. Meisner pulled his own knife and set to work two steps above Maxwell. Henry said he'd wait out on the street.

Lounging in the shade of the hotel's outer wall, Henry realized one of the differences here. People—not everyone, but especially the blacks—moved slow. Even the children, the little black ones whose hair stood out in masses of tight coils. He wondered why they were so listless. Because being a slave took away any reason to hurry? Because moving fast in a hot place wore you out, while moving fast in a cold place like Waldoborough kept you warm?

"Where to?" Maxwell asked when he and Meisner arrived.

Henry pointed in the direction they'd been walking. "Let's head to the edge of town, then loop back along the river."

After two more blocks, they reached a mansion of stone blocks with a yellow flag draped over its entrance. Men in stained army uniforms lounged in the front yard. Their bored eyes flitted over passersby. Some wore slings holding injured arms, or leaned on crutches. Bandages wrapped a few heads and decorated limbs. Many were thin and pale, watching the traffic with the sunken eyes and sharp cheekbones of fever and contagion. Henry saw the accusation in their faces. Why did they suffer while Henry was hale and hearty?

He nodded at the patients. Some of them probably fought at Second Bull Run. Henry could feel the disquiet of Maxwell and Meisner. He shared it. They walked faster, eager to pass this stony harbinger of ill fortune. They completed the rest of their tour at the same quick pace.

When the regiment reassembled, Colonel Ames led them through town. The men, conscious of representing their country and their home state on enemy ground, strained to keep their lines trim and their pace steady, but the poor habits of the parade ground asserted themselves. They passed over the Long Bridge into Washington, where people on the street stared at the ragged lines of blue-clad Mainers. Some smiled. A few in Union Army uniforms laughed outright. Colonel Ames, at the front with his second-in-command, a lanky college professor named Chamberlain, rode as though unaware of the muddle straggling behind him.

Washington City was fascinating and dismaying. Far from a shining metropolis, it seemed to combine the dirt and disorder of Alexandria with the tumult of a military camp. At least half the people were soldiers, dashing this way and that on missions that Henry doubted were well-planned. Who could manage such a giant mass of men and weapons?

Cavalrymen, marked by yellow straps and yellow stripes on their uniforms, rode arrogant horses who lifted their tails to shit on the roads. Artillerymen with red uniform markings leaned against their infernal cannons, their horses and mules ignoring the endless parade, moving their own bowels when so inclined. An artillery company pounded urgently past the Maine men. The wheels of their cannons and caissons raised dust clouds. Supply wagons and ambulances added more billows of grit and disorienting hubbub.

The regiment marched through the mayhem to the arsenal. Stacked cannons rose at one end of the long building. Their ink-dark barrels delivered fire and death from the depths of hell. From the arsenal, Henry could see that the crown of the Capitol was unfinished. Supports clung to one side of its main tower, with a vertical hoist rising in its center.

"They haven't even finished the damned thing yet?" It was Maxwell, just in front of Henry. "What in blazes have they been doing down here?"

"Those Congress bastards're too busy feathering their own nests," another voice said. Snickers sounded. "What do you say, corporal? Could those shipyards of yours stay in business taking eighty years to finish a ship?"

Henry grinned. "Well, I guess our country's got good and bad in it. What we're fighting against is all bad." Looking around, he saw a couple of heads nod. He hoped his words would simmer them down.

At the arsenal, each man received an Enfield rifle with bayonet, plus forty rounds of ammunition in a cartridge box with a shoulder strap and a cap pouch. Each gun came with its own ramrod for the slow process of loading powder and ball down its muzzle. The men tried on new knapsacks, lashing their blankets on top of them, and shouldered haversacks to carry rations.

When some Irishmen complained that the British had made the Enfields, Henry spoke up. "I've used this gun. It's reliable and accurate for a pretty far piece. It'll do." The rifle raised Henry's spirits. He was no longer impersonating a soldier. He felt like one.

They marched to a stretch of empty ground nearby, then waited while officers paced off the site, stumbling at times. Each company would settle on one section. During the process, Colonel Ames dismounted and stalked the regiment, glaring at each man. He stepped back with his hands behind his back, commanding every soldier's eye. "If you can't perform any better than you have today," he erupted, "you'd better all desert and go home!"

As Ames stomped off, most of the men stared at their shoes, embarrassed and remembering how much they hated that man.

When they broke ranks to set up their camp, the soldiers learned why the officers had floundered unsteadily across the lot. It bristled with bricks, old bottles, broken furniture, and anything else the local residents no longer wished to retain.

"My stars," said a Company E man who had not yet lapsed into the army's profane ways. He stood over a pile of dead cats. "People here are lower than these poor animals."

Henry directed some men to scavenge for barrels and other containers they could fill with the trash. The others picked up anything that would burn. Soon a half-dozen open fires sent thick black smoke into the darkening sky, the plumes shifting with the breeze. Meisner had dug a metal pot from his knapsack and was heating water for coffee.

"I'm afraid it's a hardtack night," Henry said to the men huddled around the fire. "Too late to cook anything."

"No tents?" a man asked. Away from the fire, a cool damp was rising.

Henry made a show of looking around. "Don't see any." At that moment, Henry noticed George walking toward them. "Sergeant," Henry called out, "all the comforts of home, eh?"

"Every blasted one, corporal," George answered. He clapped Henry on the shoulder, then kept walking.

CHAPTER NINE

†

"**H**ear the latest about Bobby Lee?" Joe Maxwell set a load of green-looking wood next to the firepit. For the last week, he and Henry had shared a tent with four other soldiers. The sun was down to the horizon, ending another day of drilling and waiting.

Henry looked up from the letter he was trying to write. A board on his lap was his desk. "Don't tell me—he and the whole secesh army have grown wings and flown right up to New York City, captured it, then burned it to the ground."

Maxwell ignored the remark. "He's crossed the Potomac, upriver a ways. He's invading. We're going after him."

"I heard that two days ago. Also he was about to seize the Long Bridge into Washington by attacking through us here in Arlington, then take the White House and capture old Abe."

Henry turned back to his letter. He was struggling with what to tell Katie. He didn't want to worry her, so he couldn't mention the fellow in Company G who'd been fiddling with his rifle the day before and shot it off by mistake, plugging some poor clerk from Portland in the belly. They didn't know if that man would make it.

And Henry didn't want to tell her about how much Colonel Ames hated the regiment and how much they hated him. That would seem unpatriotic. And he didn't want to complain about the last four days of brutal drilling. The more the colonel berated the men, the worse they performed. Henry felt shy about saying too much about how much he missed her. He'd mention it, of course, but he didn't want to overdo it.

The problem was that his words on that page would stay there forever. If she thought they were shallow and silly, or bloodthirsty and uncaring, or weak and contemptible, he could never take them back or explain them. They would always be there, always his. She could read and reread them as many times as she wanted, thinking less of him each time. Tortured by this danger, he'd produced only two sentences so far.

"Suit yourself," Maxwell said. "But I saw a lot of messengers and officers riding hither and yon over at the colonel's tent. I believe something's truly up."

Henry pointed down the row of tents to the left. George Young was striding along, shouting to the men. "Maybe," Henry said, "you're right this time."

"Listen up," George called as he neared Henry's tent. "We're marching out at first light, so be ready, lined up in front of your tents one minute before daybreak."

"Where we going, George?" Henry asked.

George gave a head wag. "Not even sergeants know that, but I've got the same hunch you've got."

Through the evening, word spread that they were joining the pursuit of the unaccountably fleet rebel army. Henry gave up on his letter and stashed it inside his tunic. He worked with the men to get them organized. They needed full canteens, rations, and weapons cleaned and ready. It bothered Henry that he still hadn't fired his rifle. He didn't want to march into battle without knowing if it pulled in one direction or another, or if it worked at all. It made little sense to assemble an army that never tried its weapons.

The march stepped off on schedule, the men burdened for the first time with full packs—rifle, bayonet, ammunition, blanket, spare socks, canteens, rubber blanket, tent pieces, and maybe a few cherished photos and letters. Tunes from regimental bands clashed in the moist morning air. Drums provided a floor of sound for bugle calls to slice through. The Twentieth joined a long blue line crossing the Potomac. They were one hundred thousand strong. No matter how ill-prepared they might be, what force could withstand such an immense host?

After only two hours, soldiers started dropping away from the march. Unaccustomed to full packs, even fit men struggled to keep up. Some collapsed by the roadside, chests heaving and mouths agape. A few removed their shoes and rubbed blistered feet, moaning softly. Others walked slower and slower, limping, staggering, losing track of their regiments, then falling away entirely.

Henry envied the ones who fell away. He strained to haul a full load at this punishing pace, but he was a corporal so he couldn't quit. When he felt most exhausted, when he could swear his legs would give out with the next step, a nervy energy swept over him. Stopping in some shade, stretching out his aching legs, looked so good. It would *feel* so good. But it would bring shame. So he kept on, encouraging the men. If one dropped out, Henry went to him, urged that he catch up when he could. Then Henry hurried up to those who trudged on. He didn't notice the countryside, only whether it tilted up or sloped down or was rocky. By the time they stopped for evening bivouac, his platoon of twenty was only nine. Through the night, three more tramped in and collapsed in heaps. In the morning, they had to do it again.

Near the end of the third day, they paused outside Frederick City in a stretch of pretty green hills, then passed through the town. Although this was supposed to be the North, the people lining Frederick's streets looked surly, resentful.

Evidence of battle was everywhere. The town overflowed with wounded soldiers, Union and Confederate. Houses and yards served as surgeries where doctors labored in the open air, stained with blood, wielding evil-looking instruments over men who groaned and screamed. Behind one house, Henry thought he saw bodies lying unattended, stretched out like a corduroy road. He looked away.

The regiment passed a dour-looking group of captured rebels. Henry stared at them intently. They were lean, their limbs barely covered with soiled gray uniforms. They didn't meet his gaze. They looked like tough fighters.

The regiment entered scarred and tortured lands. Shell holes pockmarked the ground. Trees lay twisted in odd shapes or blasted to pieces. Sunlight peeked through bullet holes in ruined buildings.

E Company left the road to climb a low hill where they were to camp. Rumbling sounds had to be fighting, a scene of blazing cannons and whistling bullets, but they were far away. Henry was too tired to worry about them.

Dropping his pack was a heavenly release. Holding his rifle by the barrel and using it as a walking stick, he moved to a stone wall. The meadow on the other side had seen a bloody fight. Dead rebels lay where they fell, some in clusters of four or five. Some were alone, solitary in their final agonies. Or perhaps they hadn't felt a thing. Henry couldn't look away.

He climbed over the wall. The corpse smell was vile, but he ignored it. He studied the bodies, trying to guess ages, to know something about each. Young or old, tall or short, that was what he could tell. Would he soon lie on a field like this, in this way? Who would know he had fallen? Who knew these men had? A chill passed through him. The distant havoc came more clearly through the air. Each cannon roar made him flinch. The high-pitched, rattling sound—that must be rifles. Making more sprawling bodies like these. Halfway across the field, Henry turned back. He should see to his platoon.

"Where you been?" Joe Maxwell asked. Dark was closing in.

"Reconnoitering. They've been fighting close by. Still are, by the sound of it."

"Tomorrow, they say. The big battle's tomorrow. Seems like we found Bobby Lee and his friends."

Henry forced himself to eat the dry and mealy hardtack, alternating with bites of salt pork to keep some flavor in his mouth. He would need food in him.

Judging by the snores, the men fell asleep readily enough, but Henry—rubber blanket underneath and woolen blanket on top—watched the stars. He felt jangled, unsettled. He sat up when steps approached. "Corporal Overstreet? That you?" The question came in a weary whisper. Henry stood and walked to the sound. He helped the man shed his pack. It was Johnny Baxter from Bath, another shipyard man, though his specialty was planking. They had been wary of each other. Bath and Waldoborough were rivals.

"Sorry, corporal, my legs just seized up."

Henry shushed him. "Let the men sleep," he whispered. "There's space behind me." He carried Johnny's pack over to open ground. "Did you eat?"

In the shadowed moonlight, Henry could see him shake his head. "Too tired. Had a hell of a time finding you."

"Eat. Tomorrow may be hard." He clapped Johnny on the shoulder and lowered himself to his blanket.

Henry felt the mist begin to moisten his cheeks. It blurred the stars overhead.

PART II

✝

CHAPTER ONE

†

September 28, 1862
Near Sharpsburg, Maryland
Dear Katie—

I sit here on a camp stool with a board across my knees to write on and a pencil in my hand hoping you can read this scrawl which every teacher I ever had spoke ill of. I hope you and your family are well. I have tried to write this letter a number of times before but gave it up as a bad job because I want to write you a perfect letter that will make you proud to have such a one as me writing to you which is why this has taken so long to write. I have decided I cannot write a perfect letter so instead I will try to write to you as though you were sitting here on another stool and we are talking together with me telling you what went on. Because that would be a great happiness to sit with you and hear your voice and talk about the day. My days often are dull and routine but some are not.

A great battle was fought not far from where I sit and we have not lost though we may not have won either but our regiment did no fighting. We were in reserve through the battle and never called upon though there was a false alarm at day's end and we thought we would be in it then. We heard the cannons as they made a powerful thundering on a day of bright sunlight. We smelled the powder and squinted from the smoke and heard the shouts of brave men. When it was over and no thanks to our regiment, the rebel army had been drove off. The price has been high and the fighting was terrible. Now we see and hear the dead and dying and wounded and all of that presses on our souls. We had a chaplain join the regiment a few weeks ago and I thought that didn't make sense since fighting men need bullets and powder not praying and ministers but I was wrong. If it helps the men be more easy in their minds and their hearts then I am for it.

I know now I am not ready to be a soldier and how few of us are. I think how I spent my whole childhood seeing my father and others working with wood and tools around shipyards and building things. As I got older my father and my brother showed me how to do the things they knew how to do. They showed me shortcuts they learned and tricks of how to do the job faster and better so when I went to work I was ready though I had to learn much more. Soldiering is no different. Real soldiers know things about being a soldier that I don't and neither do these others certainly not our sergeant good old George Young. He is a fine fellow but a joiner and not a soldier and not a good joiner. I think now that must be why Colonel Ames hates us so much. He's a real soldier who trained to be one for years but when he teaches us simple things and we can't learn them we try his patience very much and he has precious little of that though when I get this close to war I understand why. A battlefield is no place to be confused or undecided and that's what we are much of the time. The last few days I have thought how I wish I could ask the colonel to teach me about being a soldier but I don't think a corporal can ask a colonel that.

We see balloons here that drift up into the sky with men dangling in baskets underneath and looking out over the land so they can see where the enemy soldiers and cannons and cavalry are. I wonder what the world looks like up there. It must be like having your own little mountain that you take around with you and climb up for a look when you need to. Is the view from those balloons the way God sees us?

Our army has lingered here, resting and burying the dead and letting the rebels go back to Virginia. The other day they had us all in our regiments in formation so we could be reviewed by Father Abraham who came up from Washington to see the field and the army. He rode around with Little Mac—General McClellan—and they make a humorous pair. The one so long and solemn and plain and the other so short and puffed up and sparkly with gold braid. The men cheered for both of them long and loud because the men are proud of driving off the rebels after losing to them before.

I should see to my duties and close with assurance that I carry thoughts of you very dear to me.

> Yours always,
> H. Overstreet

September 28, 1862
Waldoborough
Dear Henry—

I have no letter yet from you but we have news of the battle fought in Maryland and that your regiment was there. People here say that the mail to and from the army is not reliable, so I will write first, hoping it gets through so you know I am waiting for word that you are well.

It is dark and all is quiet even in this noisy house. Quiet except for the cricket, who keeps me company. Because crickets are good luck, Mother won't let us disturb this noisy fellow. I agree that it's better to have him around. This is a time I can concentrate on thinking about you. That is a sweet sadness and I hope you may remember me when you can. The sky is beautiful to-night. The moon is new so the stars shine undisturbed. They gather in bright groups, ready to light the way for weary travelers, offering familiar signposts and mark-ings. I think of how the stars are the same stars in the same places that people saw in the time of Jesus, and in the time of Shakespeare, and all the other times.

There is little enough to report about Waldob-orough. Our sow is fattening so we should see piglets soon, which makes my brother unhappy, since there will be more work for him. Father bought the sow to teach Theodore responsibility, so of course Theodore hates it. And he will hate it more with squealing piglets, though I suppose the sow does most of the looking after them. I don't know why Theodore is so moody about it, since Father said he can keep half the price the pigs fetch at market. I get no pay for the housework I do. The Spring-ers have had twin girls and both are doing well though they say the babies are small. The harvest is a good one and the apples have been very good. Father brought home cider tonight that a customer had brought to the store and it was tasty.

I saw your father the other day. He looks well but seems concerned for you. I am selfish enough to want a letter from you first, but then you should write to him. I have heard of a new teaching contract coming open for a school in North Waldoborough. I am thinking about try-ing for it. They may consider me young for the position and I have not been to any college, but I know as much or more than any teacher we ever had. Have you read the new Emancipation Proclamation from Mr. Lincoln? There is much excitement about it at our church. What do the men think of it, and what do you?

Yours,
Katherine Nash

October 10, 1862
Near Sharpsburg, Maryland
Dear Katie—

I have yours of September 28 and am very glad of it. We have been marching around the countryside sometimes getting close enough to the rebs for both of us to blaze away but not to much effect. Our generals do not seem to be in any powerful hurry to fight the enemy for real which makes the men impatient as we are here to fight and would rather do that however it may turn out than hang about. Our soldiers have become skilled at complaining; they complain that we are at war and that the war is being fought so stupidly and they complain that we fight too often and we fight too little and that we drill too much but that we are not as prepared as the enemy is. When we get a look at the rebels—either as prisoners or as wounded or when they are dead—we see that they are no better fed or clothed or armed than we are so we should not complain about those things but we do. I am not supposed to complain because a corporal should support good fighting spirit so I mostly don't complain or at least complain only to sergeants and other corporals. I had to place a man on report for sleeping on guard which is a dangerous thing for him to do but not much should happen to him or so I hope. We need soldiers too much to discipline one who might fight. There was one fellow who stole molasses from an officer's tent who was caught and made to stand in camp for six hours with a sheet written with "Thief" pinned to his tunic which I don't know it taught him much of a lesson.

It's the next day Saturday. I had to stop writing yesterday when I was called away to settle an argument over rations. In your letter you ask about Mr. Lincoln's proclamation about the slaves that they are free. The men talk about it some but many say they don't know what to make of it. The Irish boys say it makes them angry since they didn't sign up to fight a nigger war and they don't intend to if that's what it is. I know slavery is wrong. When I was small and asked my father about it, he said it was wrong and it still is. Seeing the darkies in Alexandria was a surprise to me; they weren't like Joby back home—do you remember him? He worked in the yards until he got hurt and lived down below the yards towards Bremen on the west side of the river. I hope he's back working now. The darkies around here have a look that seems to come from slow wits and when they speak it's like another language like their mouths are full of cotton or marbles. I wonder if they would be suited to labor like Joby where they had to figure out what had to be done and how to do it and then do it. Would they be worth paying which many of the boys say they are not. There's some black ones who come by the camp at nights to sing and dance for the soldiers hoping to get money for their small shows. Even those ones don't seem the same as Joby though sometimes when I look at them—really look at them—I can see they are watching us and trying to figure us out so they know what we like and don't like so we will give them more money. So I know they have brains and they use them. I know they have families same as us though mostly we see only men and boys here in camp. We all read the papers when there is nothing else to do and we read about how if we free the slaves then Southerners will be poorer and they can't fight us as hard. Or even how rebel soldiers will have to go home and do work themselves if they own no slaves to do the work which sounds good and fair to men in this army. I still am puzzling on it. Keep writing to me.

Yours always,
H. Overstreet

October 17, 1862
Waldoborough
My dear Henry—

I am sorry to share ill tidings with you but my mother has fallen sick again. She insists that we never speak of it so I have not told you, but she has had problems with her lungs that seem like my Aunt Tessa's but different. My aunt had the consumption and all the elements of it with the cough and blood and weakness which finally took her. With Mother it's a shortness of breath—sometimes truly fighting for the very breath of life that she seems unable to find anywhere—which she tries to conceal. She insists that it comes and goes and that it will never be the end of her but it's come now and is not going. It is bad enough that she cannot conceal it but is in bed much of the day. After being with Tessa all those months I find this hard. The doctor comes and prescribes different medicines. We give her endless cups of tea with the medicines but nothing seems to help. She sleeps sitting up when she sleeps, but only in snatches because she loses her breath entirely when she sleeps and awakes with a start and afraid. Father and the others do help out and comfort her, but most of her work falls on me, along with caring for her.

I did not get the teaching position in North Waldoborough, which is probably for the best now that Mother is ill, but still makes me angry. They gave the job to some man from Rockport. He spent two years at Bowdoin College but they say he's a hopeless sot. Father said that I should give up the idea of teaching because they will always hire the man first as they should. But Mother, sick as she is, tells me that I should keep trying. She said I have quality. I was so very tired and discouraged when she said that, it brought me close to tears. I am blessed with the best of mothers. I think also of my aunt, who would have said that I should not give up.

The town news is as slender as ever. Our church choir gave a concert with some fine patriotic songs as well as hymns. The money from the tickets went to the Schlesinger family because their son was killed at Antietam and they needed money for shipping his body home. Another man—from Damariscotta, I think—was killed recently but I didn't know him or anything about how he died. I suppose you grow more accustomed to such news in the army but people take it hard to lose our young, strong men. The town elections will be soon, and voting for state representatives too. Boss Reed and his kind, Father says, will sweep all the elections here, like always.

When you write, tell me what the army is like when you are not fighting. I will never know what the fighting is like but perhaps I can imagine your other times.

Yours,
Katherine Nash

CHAPTER TWO

✝

October 29, 1862
Near Warrenton, Virginia
Dear Katie—

I have yours of the seventeenth. I am sorry to hear
of your mother's illness and I wish for her recovery as
she has recovered before. I was on picket duty yesterday
a half mile or so from camp in a pine forest when I heard
some crows arguing and was reminded of home. Johnny
Baxter one of the younger boys in my platoon sneaked
away from camp yesterday and came back proud enough
to burst because he said he walked through the country
and heard a baby cry then he saw a woman doing chores
around her house and then watched a cat lick his paws
and stretch out on the ground. Seeing such home things
made the boy as happy as seeing the seven wonders of
the world. So there is part of the answer to your question about what life in camp is like—it is not like home
and we miss home.

My father writes that the tomatoes came in plenty this year. Have you all started drying apples yet? Last year was a good one for apples. You said the cider was good which is something I miss. There were apples here when we first arrived, but they are long since eaten; an army is like a pestilence on the land stripping it of anything that can be eaten or burned. The fence posts and rails go first because we don't have to chop them very much so after the war the richest man in this country will be one who can sell fences to farmers. Then we take the branches and windfall and then we cut down trees. We tell each other that we don't feel bad about taking all the wood and fences because these people started this war but it feels different when an old person or a woman who lives here sees us taking their fence and tree but we take it anyway because we need it. George calls it a war tax.

What do we do when not collecting the war tax? We drill and drill and drill some more. I have wrote how I think better about all the drills now than I did before but Colonel Ames is still like a person driven to madness. He screams about our extra left feet and weak minds and makes us ashamed and angry at the same time; he is pure savage once he gets started. We were going through motions of loading our rifles in a sort of a play-acting without using actual cartridges and balls since we have nowhere to shoot them except at each other. The colonel told Company G they were so hopeless that they might as well just charge with bayonets or use bare hands and rocks. We started to march better probably because we had to march on roads so much and know we need to stay in order. So many got lost marching to Antietam that the regiment was down almost to half-strength until the rest could catch up. The boys complain they will not need to do fancy marching with right turns and left turns out on the battlefield but I never let such remarks pass. The colonel wants us to know how to move as a group and follow orders during a fight and Yankees do not naturally follow orders much less when someone is shooting at you. A battlefield must be a fearsome place and nowhere to be asking reasons why you do things. I know I have a lot of opinions for a man who has never been on a battlefield except after the fighting is done but I think it must be about keeping your head. I do not know how you keep your head in a fight but I think maybe if you know how to move and handle your rifle and bayonet and if that comes natural maybe the fighting is easier.

There is one good thing happening. After supper of the evenings the corporals and sergeants and even the lieutenants and captains if they want to can go to class in the colonel's high-wall tent and he teaches us about drill and the military manual. He just talks to us, no shouting. We can get him talking about tactics sometimes which is how you fight against the enemy and set to meet his attack or organize your attack and how to work with the artillery so they shoot the other side and not us. Colonel Chamberlain teaches us too though I think he mostly knows things from books since he was a professor not a soldier. Those classes make for a long day so we lie down tired.

It is not as cold here as back home for this time of year but when you sleep out on the ground and sometimes in the open it is cold. We only just received new tents ten days or so ago which means we finally have some shelter. The tents are small and are divided in two pieces so you and your tent partner each carry one piece and then button them together to make the tent using posts at the ends and stuffing the ends with our rubber blankets to keep the wind and the rain out. My tentmate is a farmer named Flagg from Bristol. They say he snores like a cross saw but I've never heard him; I get so tired I sleep through it. We surround ourselves with brush and put it underneath us to soften the ground and keep us up off it.

The thing we think about most and talk about most is food which generally is only enough to keep us going and not always that. The basic thing we eat is hardtack which is a kind of cracker that has many of the qualities of rocks. We also get salt pork and coffee. Coffee is what we crave. Near the campfire we huddle close together against the wind and we talk and we talk both in the mornings when we have nothing scheduled and then again at supper time. Soldiers never stop talking and we often talk about nothing and certainly nothing that needs being talked about. We talk about the cold and about our feet and about officers. Mostly we talk about home. We tell each other small things we remember and funny stories and often remember things you would not think a person would remember. Some men talk about their sweethearts and wives but I do not talk about you. That part is for me to hold close in my mind not for anyone else. Sometimes the talk makes us feel better and other times we end up getting quiet and more homesick than ever and go into our tents. This is probably dull to read and my candle is getting low.

I got up early to finish this letter and the light is bad so I hope you can read it. The only thing I've left out is that the men are getting sick because we are out in the weather so much. They say they can hear their tentmates teeth chattering through the night and it all seems to end up with stomach sicknesses and you know how those are especially when you are living out of doors. The dysentery seems to be everywhere and that knocks a man down. It is a melancholy business to be visiting your friends in the hospital for sick soldiers which is just an old house taken over and then watching them die. And they die in a way that does not have the dignity of dying like a soldier or any dignity at all. We have lost four men in Company E already and the regiment has another score in the hospital. One surprise has been that it's the older men who seem large and strong who fall sick more. The skinny little men like Johnny Baxter—boys really who are smaller and younger than me—bear up better. I sat with an old salt from Wiscasset the other night named Johnson as his final breaths passed his lips. He had weathered voyages around the world through great storms and with adventures I can only dream up but he was felled by the Maryland and the Virginia hills. He commended his soul to our Lord and sent last messages to his family and friends which I made haste to write down. Then he was gone. We would prefer to get struck down in battle than to fall to a fiend-ish disease. We came here to preserve the best and no-blest government the world has known not get sick.

I will write more cheerful news in my next. Please write.

Yours always,
H. Overstreet

November 13, 1862
Waldoborough
My dear Henry—

I have yours of October 30 in hand and it made my heart sore. The sad fate of your poor Mr. Johnson from Wiscasset reminded me that the news from this place can only seem small to you who face so much hardship in a noble fight. I feel bitterly the limits of my sex, that I cannot carry a rifle and share your burden, the bur-den you all carry for the rest of us. I am embarrassed by my silly attempts to make myself a teacher. I pledge that you will not again open a letter to find the words of the silly woman who has been writing to you until now. I shall banish her and build something more wor-thy of you. You must take care to be safe and well and yes, you must learn all the ways of the soldiers so you can do your soldier's work and come home when that job is done. I know not how to advise that you do that, but I know you must.

The town voted Copperhead again in the late elec-tion, by a wide margin. It makes me sick knowing that Father did too. My parents send their best thoughts. Mother seems a little better.

Yours,
Katherine Nash

November 16, 1862
Near Warrenton, Virginia
Dear Katie—

I have had no letter from you recently but the mails have been poor. Because we march in the morning I write now. We don't know where we will go and must trust General Burnside to take us somewhere we can advance the war. On picket duty sometimes we see the enemy soldiers close enough to call to each other. Some trade with the rebels but I never have being a corporal which gets in the way of some things. Other times the pickets on the other side shoot at us so it is a strange war. We speak the same language and knew the same country as boys and yet we fight each other. A few weeks back we marched through Harpers Ferry where old John Brown started this war when he attacked there. The firehouse that he seized and where they took him still stands. Because of that old man and his hatred for slavery—or maybe his love of slaves—mighty armies tramp the roads he led a handful of men on.

Last week a boy on picket shot himself in the arm by mistake and lost the arm. Some say he did it on purpose to get out of the war but I don't think a man would give up an arm that way. In the shipyards bad things more often are caused by carelessness than by evil intent and I expect the same is true in the army.

The men are beginning to speak of Thanksgiving and even Christmas hoping that the army will have something special for us though it cannot be anything like we remember from our homes. Joe Maxwell a lumberjack from up past Bangor insists that he will bake a hardtack cake. That makes me realize that my last which described the life of the soldier in camp didn't describe enough how we feed ourselves. I think I said that it is the largest subject of conversation in camp and it is. Some general wrote that an army travels on its stomach or at least Colonel Chamberlain said that the other night. If that is true then this army travels on a sledge made of pure hardtack. In its natural condition hardtack is a harsh dish more like a stone than a food. It can be a trial for the teeth and jaws except for the soft worms inside that we sometimes disturb from their happy location between the dry layers. But the soldier will try almost anything to take these rocky things and make them into something that seems like food. Sometimes we shatter the hardtack into bits and soak the bits in water then fry the mush in pork fat we get from cooking down our salt pork. When we grow weary of this Burnside Stew we can mash the hardtack cakes into fine particles with rocks—nothing less than a rock will do the job—and again introduce water and bake the result over an open fire as flat cakes. This savory item answers to the name Washington Pie. One more approach favored by the desperate soldier is to plunge the hardtack into the fire and burn it black, then boil it in water to make Potomac chowder. The advantage of these different dishes would seem to be variety but that variety is an illusion since the basic nature of hardtack is not easily changed. We draw our rations every three days, an event we look forward to with real eagerness. We are awarded twenty-seven cakes of hardtack, nine for each day plus a little meat and three spoonfuls of sugar and coffee, one for each day. With these treasures the army leaves us free to try to make them into food in any way we wish.

Out on picket the other day I was invited to share the dinner of a poor widow woman who lived by herself. The meal was mean though I never enjoyed a potato as much as the small hard one that she placed before me. The people here suffer from the war but so do we. Still it was fine to sit down inside four walls and speak with a woman. When I got back to camp a fellow in Company F who plays the fiddle played a sad tune that matched my mood. A dozen hard soldiers sat and listened. When pleasures are few they become precious.

So are your letters to me. I know not when the mail will catch up with us but I will hope to find a letter from you soon.

Yours always,
H. Overstreet

CHAPTER THREE

†

December 16, 1862
Waldoborough
Dear Henry—

    The newspapers carry terrible accounts of the battle at Fredericksburg. Father has finally given up denouncing General McClellan as a worthless blackguard in favor of rants about the incompetence of General Burnside. Truly, even I wonder that from the millions of men who live in this Union the man chosen to lead our armies seems to have no idea other than to charge the enemy uphill and into the teeth of his guns. I know little enough of military matters and cannot appreciate what you and the others endure, but my thoughts are never far from you and my heart ever wishes you remain safe and well.

    My poor mother's troubles have taken over our house. She struggles for breath without complaint but is much reduced in energy and spirit while my father worries and worries, though his worrying can do no good. I have become a more competent cook and a grim harasser of lazy children who shirk their chores. I also have come to a decision. Since the good people of North Waldoborough do not wish to have me teach their children, then I will teach my own brother and sisters what they fail to learn in school. Somewhat to my surprise, they are willing pupils. I am reading to them in the evening from a recent book by Mr. Dickens called "A Tale of Two Cities," which is very thrilling and which they attend to. When I finish a chapter, we talk about what happened in the story—it is often tragic and sad and pulls at our feelings. They have come to look forward to our reading times. It's an odd thing that the sadness of the story takes our minds from the sadness we feel about our mother. Also, Mr. Dickens writes about times of turmoil and upheaval. Although Waldoborough is as dull as it has always been, the times in our country are anything but, as you know better than I. I decided that when we finish this book they shall write to the men from our town who fight this war. It will improve their penmanship and composition and also make them think about the struggles of these times.

An idea has recently taken hold of me that I might come to Washington as a nurse for the wounded and sick men. Miss Dorothea Dix of Hamden is reported to run the nurses for the Union Army and I admire her courage and determination. Her reputation grows in Maine. But my family needs me now and I have no claim to the skills of a nurse. If only the army needed arithmetic teachers and readers of Dickens.

I have saved for last the news that I am most proud of—you see, I am ever the teacher, testing whether you read to the end of this letter. I learned recently of a group of women in Rockland who have formed a Soldier's Aid Society. They sew clothes for the men in the army and roll bandages for the hospitals, then make up packages that they send to the soldiers. I have decided to start such a society here in Waldoborough. It is not the same as carrying a rifle, nor is it healing the wounded, but it is something I can do. Father opposed it, saying it would compromise my reputation because everyone would know I am doing it because of feelings for you. Then my mother spoke up. She said she would be proud to have a daughter who did such a thing for our men who fight for us. Father cannot oppose anything that Mother wishes, not now. I will speak about it at church on Sunday and hope to find others to join me. The minister said we can meet in church some mornings, every morning if we wish, but I doubt that will be necessary.

Our first package will be for Company E of Maine's Twentieth Regiment, you may be certain.

Yours,
Katherine Nash

January 4, 1863
Stoneman's Switch, Virginia
Dear Katie—

I have your last of the sixteenth. Rain drips on the tent as I set to write in this dim place with another board across my knees. We have had much rain here in our winter quarters so much we had to use our bayonets to dig a trench around the edge of our cabin to carry off water and keep it from running inside and making everything wet though most things are wet anyway. Christmas and New Years were not very happy but winter quarters means we should not be fighting for a while. It was strange to have Christmas and New Years with no snow or ice.

For winter quarters we have created our own town in the middle of a field—a town of soldiers—with streets and shops. Our regiment covers about three blocks of the town on both sides of a passage we named Lincoln Street. The army divides us into groups of four men each and each group builds a hut, about eight feet by eight feet. They had men come around to explain what to do bringing wood for us but not enough so we had to search for more. We built log walls and chinked mud between them to hold the rain and wind out. It's like our ancestors did when they came from Germany or wherever the Nashes came from. Our walls go up about three feet or maybe as far as my middle. Then we combine the tent pieces that each man has in order to make an oilcloth roof which drips a bit but you get to figuring out how to avoid where the drips are. The best part is building a fireplace with a chimney. We used a barrel to make ours. Having a fireplace means we have some warmth. When you combine that with the four of us in here breathing together it can get pretty snug as long as it isn't too freezing outside. We built four bunks using saplings which get us up off the ground and saves us from having to shape ourselves around the rocks and high roots you find even on ground that looks smooth

Being a joiner I used some hardtack boxes and scrap wood from other men's cabins to build a table so we can sit around it of an evening or when it rains. The men smoke and play cards especially cutthroat euchre. And we tell tales as I have wrote to you before. This cabin consists of me and Flagg who was my tentmate before, and Joe Maxwell a lumber man from near Bangor, and Teddy Meisner another lumber man but from farther north. Joe and I went through Fredericksburg together. Because everyone smokes we are always coughing but no one stops smoking. If there wasn't coffee or tobacco this army would up and walk home.

Most of our work now is standing guard, going out on pickets outside the camp, and chopping wood. Now that we have been on campaign we drill less since we know something about being soldiers. Even Colonel Ames doesn't scream at us much now. I heard him congratulate other officers for how we did at Fredericksburg which I did not understand. We did nothing except make ourselves targets but we did mostly get back which may be what he meant to congratulate. Whenever soldiers aren't marching or getting ready to fight they like to get into devilment and winter quarters is perfect for that. Some men have taken to dropping rifle cartridges down other men's chimneys which makes a fine pop and some very surprised men inside. They also like to get into fights over nothing or over card games which is the same. The devilment is not so bad. Since we have had no pay since we left Portland last summer nobody can lose actual money in a card game. And not many have figured out how to get whiskey which makes it easier for corporals like me to keep the peace.

Some men figure out how to go foraging which is a polite word for stealing from people who live nearby but we get hungry and these folks left the Union so most of the soldiers go ahead and steal anything they might be able to swallow so long as it is not defended with a loaded gun. When the men go forage and are interrupted by some poor woman or child they are pretty hard-hearted and usually say that they should just send the bill to Uncle Sam. Or that's what they say they say. I haven't done any foraging yet but I have eaten something that was foraged by someone else and I might sometime do the same. Right before Christmas we had a shipment of soft bread which eliminated grumbling around here for at least twelve hours in a row.

I read out to the other boys in my cabin about your Soldier Aid Society and they asked me to put in an order for socks lots and lots of socks because nothing is so miserable as wet feet for days on end which any soldier will tell you. And also blankets as ours become sodden and vile after only a few weeks of use in wet times when we can't dry them out and air them properly not to mention them becoming homes for hundreds of small critters with an appetite for our flesh who torment us through the days and nights. You can tell how long a man has been a soldier by his skill at plucking a louse and popping him with his fingernails by touch without having to look. And also they ask for tobacco which I know you can't make with a needle and thread but which makes the days as pleasant as they can be.

I am in good health with many thoughts of you. The fight at Fredericksburg was bad but we had little part in it and did nothing useful. Please write even if you receive no letter from me because the mail is so bad. Your letters remind me of what I miss and care for and am here for.

Yours always,
H. Overstreet

February 2, 1863
Waldoborough
Dear Henry—

Yours of January 4 arrived here only yesterday. It has been very cold. The river is frozen all the way across and the air feels quiet and still, especially at night. I am glad to learn that in winter quarters you and the other soldiers don't have to camp out . I am even more glad you don't have to camp out here in Lincoln County. However cold it is in Virginia, it is colder here. Our neighbor Mr. McDonnell died last week. They had no warning since he had not been sick and was still working at his wagon shop, although he was past fifty years old. Also old Mrs. Jennifer Smith died, but she was more than eighty. Father said about her that old folks often die right after Christmas and New Year's, that it seems like all the celebrating is over and they can't face another winter. I found that sad, but I think having you at the war and my mother sick makes me more likely to feel sad. The cold is hard on Mother's lungs, but she sits up much of the day now and has taken over the evening reading to my brother and sisters, though Theodore seems not to be listening much any more. I miss reading to them, but I am glad to see Mother better and glad they have the time with her. My time is filled up with housework now that I spend two mornings a week with the Soldiers' Aid Society.

So you see I did get it started. We began with eight women, all from the Methodist church, coming on Mondays and Wednesday mornings, though not everyone can make it every time and two of them have come only once. Nevertheless, I expect that we will have a package of shirts and socks for you and the other Waldoborough men very soon. I was sent very detailed instructions from some high official in Washington—Father was impressed that it came addressed to me, though I don't know how they knew we formed the society. It said that we are to send the packages to a central depot which will parcel them out to deserving soldiers, but we decided to send it to you direct and you can pass them out to the Waldoborough boys.

The women are older than me. Mrs. Long and Mrs. Sanborn bring their small children who play with yarn or thread or just run and shout. A couple of the other women have said they wonder that I've done this when I don't have a husband in the war. One of the things we do is bring letters in from soldiers and read them to each other, so we can share what we know and how we feel. It helps when you haven't received a letter from the soldier you worry about. I have told them only that you are a friend, since anything more is personal, but I imagine they know about you and me. It is not a big town and people talk. I shared with them the part of your letter about the food you make from hardtack—about Burnside Stew and Washington Pie—and they all smiled and laughed. It made the day easier for some lonely women. I number myself among them.

Yours,
Katherine Nash

February 22, 1863
Alexandria Virginia
Dear Katie—

I have yours of the second in hand but have not received any package from you and your ladies. That's as may be since I've been sick these last two weeks and have spent them in this hospital here in Alexandria which may account for not receiving the package which could be anywhere now. They thought I had the typhus at first but the doctors with the army are no good. Now it looks like it was just more of the dysentery what we call the Virginia quickstep and which I will not describe to a lady further. At least half the soldiers have it and others have measles or mumps instead. Even though it wasn't typhus it still made me miserable weak.

The food in the hospital is so good I have the pleasure of eating soft bread which is something I never appreciated before the way I should. I hate to think I might return to health and have to leave though any food anywhere would be better than what me and Joe and Flagg and Meisner put together every night. Also it's warm and indoors here which is a real advantage. Those of us not so very sick spend a lot of time talking about the war. We are a regular high command with nothing to do but read the newspapers and look at maps and show how the war has been fought wrong. None of us understands why the army did so little after Antietam and waited around until the rebels could march off and then attacked them like we did at Fredericksburg, which was pure murder like one of our men said. We agree that we left our homes to have this fight, which is a hard fight, so we need to have it now. So you see we should all be generals. One thing about this hospital is that the trains seem to run by all the time every few minutes day and night. They must be carrying more men and more supplies for the men, but it makes you realize how many others are working on the war more than just the soldiers.

Since I started feeling better, I have been noticing the darkies around the hospital where they work as orderlies and do the cleaning up and fetching and carrying. I tried to talk to one who is an orderly and whose eyes seem to take much in, but I had a devil of a time understanding his talking. The way of talking here is hard to follow even among white folks, but the blacks swallow and slur their words and come near to torturing the sounds at least to a Yankee's ears. I think it makes them seem more stupid than they are. I think that orderly is pretty smart except for how he talks.

Please keep writing to me even though we may be moving around.

Yours always,
H. Overstreet

CHAPTER FOUR

†

Challenged by guards who took their duties more seriously than most guards do, Henry and Joe Maxwell explained that they came to see a friend who got the pox from being vaccinated a few weeks back, at the end of February. "Him and me were lucky," Joe added, nodding at Henry. "We had the vaccination back home."

The guard with a mustache looked skeptical. "You got to show the scars." His partner nodded.

"It's cold, private," Henry said, hoping his corporal's stripes might give force to his objection. "We've got better things to do than undress out here."

"Not our idea," the mustache replied. "That's what the doctors said. Show 'em."

"Are those the doctors who're killing our men?" Henry answered. "You know they're a bunch of washed-up drunks who couldn't make a go of it back home. Three of our boys are already dead from this so-called vaccine. It's probably made from horse piss and donkey spit."

The mustache man was uninterested. "No scar, no entry. Those are orders."

Scowling, the Maine men unbuttoned their coats, then the top buttons of their tunics. They yanked the collars sideways, twisting around to display their scars.

"Go on," the guard without a mustache said. "Hope your friend makes it."

They found George Young in the third tent, which he shared with two other sergeants. His face shone with sweat. The sores Henry could see were scabbing. One scab sat on the side of George's nose, another next to an eye, two on his jawline. George opened his eyes and turned his head to his visitors.

"Hey, sergeant," Henry said. "How're you feeling?" There was nowhere to sit, which was awkward.

George groaned. "Poorly, I'll admit. Poorly. Then there's the humiliation of it all. Hard to know which end I'm going to leak out of next." He blinked. "How're the boys?"

"All right," Henry said. He and Joe had agreed not to tell George about the ones killed by the vaccine. "They're missing their sergeant."

"The way I feel," George answered, "I'll be lucky to get out of this tent alive. Goddamned army." He closed his eyes and took a breath. "Somehow, we get off that hill at Fredericksburg without the rebs killing us, or very many of us, so the army decides to do the job itself. It's like the doctors declared war on us."

Joe gave George a smile. "I woulda thought a man of your experience would know that about the army. And the doctors."

George groaned again. "I've made some mistakes in my life," he said, "but signing up for this army is at the top of the page."

"You'll be out of here soon enough," Henry said. He pulled a bottle of amber liquid out of his coat pocket, shielding it from the view of the other patients. "We thought this might take the wrinkles out of your day."

"Corporal," George said with new energy, raising up on an elbow. "I have always admired your initiative."

"It's just some old bust-head," Joe offered, "but it's what we could get."

"Where should we put it?" Henry asked. "Down in your pack?"

"God, no," George answered as he lifted his blanket. "You set it here next to Papa. Don't want those doctors making off with it while I'm crapping my guts out or having fever dreams about never wearing a uniform again."

Henry slipped the bottle under the blanket, where George cradled it. Then he looked up. "Don't mean to be a poor host, but maybe you boys should leave me to do some business with that pot down there, if you'd oblige me by leaving it next to my feet."

When Joe had moved the pot, he offered to help George sit up, but the sergeant shook his head. "Not dead yet, private. But thanks."

Henry put a hand on his old friend's shoulder. "Don't go confusing that bottle with the pot," he said.

George gave a slight nod. "Sound advice." Uncertainly, the two visitors backed up, then left.

* * * * *

"You sent for me, sir?" Henry stood at attention. It was a warm day in the middle of March. Captain Clark sat in a camp chair at the mouth of his tent, taking the sun.

"At ease, corporal." As Henry shifted position, the officer looked up from his paper. "You've heard about George Young?"

Henry's stomach tightened and he held his breath. "No, sir."

"The doctors're sending him home. Unfit for service." Henry breathed. "I know you two were friends. You've managed that well, both of you. Haven't heard any grumbling about him playing favorites."

"Thank you, sir. I'm glad George'll go home. The pox hit him hard."

"You may not be so glad," Clark said, "because you're the new sergeant for Company E." He handed a sheet of paper up to Henry. "This will be your badge of rank until I can get some new stripes for you. You can take Sergeant Young's tent. You know the job and the men know you, so I don't have anything to add." He continued to look into Henry's face. "Any questions?"

"I guess not, sir." Henry paused, prouder than he thought he could be. He would write Katie about this. "I'll try to do a good job."

"You do that."

Henry looked down and up. "One question. Would it be a problem if I stayed in my current tent? Me and Joe Maxwell and the others, we do all right." Henry didn't say that since the time on that Fredericksburg hill he had been shouting in his sleep, and he trusted Joe to keep him from running around the camp half-crazed in the middle of the night.

Clark sighed. "The army says no, but if someone complains about it, I expect I'll be surprised to discover that you failed to move despite my order that you do so."

"Yes, sir. Thank you, sir."

As Henry turned, Clark spoke again. "One other thing. As sergeant, you'll get some help from Rufus there." He pointed with his pen toward a dark-skinned man in rough clothes who sat on a nearby stone, holding a boot in one hand as he buffed the leather with a cloth. "He'll come by later. You'll be glad."

* * * * *

"What do I call you?"

"Rufus is fine, sir."

Henry, standing in front of his tent, winced. "I'm a sergeant. You call me 'sergeant.'"

"Yes, sir, sergeant."

"Are you in the army? I don't quite understand what you are."

"I'm a volunteer, sir—sergeant."

"So am I. But what *are* you?"

"Don't know beyond that."

"Who pays you?"

"Don't nobody, though the captain keeps me fed good and gets me clothes and stuff."

"You helped out Sergeant Young? Did he pay you?"

"No sir—nah, he didn't."

"What did you do for him?"

"What he needed, free him up for his other duties."

They were talking the same language, or close to the same language. And the man was nothing but agreeable. Still, Henry felt like the longer he talked to Rufus, the less he knew. There was nothing smart-mouth in the man's answers, just no information. He thought of a question. "What did you last do for Sergeant Young before he got sick?"

"Emptied his pot. Got him some water. And found him a bottle of corn liquor. He liked that. He wasn't particular about what kind I got."

"Yes, I imagine he wasn't." Henry thought for a minute. "Where do you come from? Where are your people?"

"Back at the Niles plantation, on the James River."

"Virginia."

"All the way through." Rufus smiled.

"You run off?"

"Soon's the army was close enough I could get to it."

"Why're you here? With the army?"

"For freedom. I'm dreamin' about it since I was yea big." He held his hand to mid-thigh level. "This way I can help out the ones that can't run, help 'em get their freedom, even if they got to wait longer."

Henry thought for a few seconds. He wondered how he would explain this to the folks back home. To Katie. "Rufus, I don't mean any offense, but isn't your life here—not being paid, taking care Captain Clark—isn't that like your old life, on the plantation?"

"No, sir."

"What's different?"

"I choose to be here. If I get the notion, I can leave. That's a whole world of difference."

"I see," Henry said, sort of seeing. "Tell you what, Rufus. I've never had someone to help me like this, so maybe we can have a deal?" Rufus nodded. "You concentrate on Captain Clark, make sure you do what he needs. If you see something that needs doing that I'm not doing for myself, and you can do it without much trouble, be my guest and do it."

"Yes, sir."

Henry figured he would have to get used to being called "sir."

CHAPTER FIVE

†

March 17, 1863
Waldoborough
Dear Henry—

Our days continue cold and full of bluster. I fear the weather presses on my mother's lungs. I was up until the dark hours of the morning with her. She now rests a little and I am alone with her during the days, feeling lonelier than ever.

It seems the winter has gone on too long. There's pneumonia in town. I helped with some of the sick through our church, which I do with old Mrs. Castle, who used to teach our Sunday School class. You may remember her: She's the very short lady with the long nose and the mole on her chin. We always feared her when we were children and sometimes we played mean tricks on her. Once some boys in our class sneaked into her house and tied her cat to a chair. Now I find that Mrs. Castle's head is filled with wisdom and her soul with compassion and I am ashamed of my thoughts and actions as a girl.

The snow and ice have forced the Soldiers' Aid Society to miss several sessions. We are falling behind what I hoped we could do. We also have lost some members. Mrs. Kissel asked why the government doesn't provide enough food and clothes to the soldiers and why citizens must send them at their own expense? I had no answer except that we must help if we can. Two of the ladies joined a group started by Mrs. Clark, whose husband is your captain and whose father-in-law builds ships, and that group helps the families of soldiers who have need while their soldiers are away. I'm sure that meeting in Mrs. Clark's fine warm home is more pleasant than in our drafty church, but theirs is also a worthy pursuit and I mustn't be small about it. The Clarks are patriots.

Though reduced, our society continues. These women who are yet with us—mostly Mrs. Chapman and Mrs. Benner—are older than me and know more of life. I am glad of the chance to know them. They also are skilled at knitting and sewing and teach me. We will send our first box when I post this letter. I will send it by special shipping, though, since I am not sure of the mails and delivery service. Your kind father helped raise the shipping costs by going to Brown's shipyard and a couple of the others but on strict condition that I accept no money from Boss Reed. He insisted that The Honorable Reed—his voice was full of contempt—would corrupt and befoul our noble efforts. Though you have said something about your father's political views, I was surprised to hear him criticize Boss Reed so openly and was not a little pleased. Your brother Ralph was here in Waldoborough and he also stopped at our house to make a contribution from his own funds which could not be very large. He reminded me so of you that it was both sweet and bitter to be with him and entirely bitter to see him go.

We hope not to have to beg for our money in the future. For next month, we are planning a concert of song with a piano accompaniment, led by the singer from

Camden, Alice Stimson, and then a strawberry festival in June. So you see that although I cannot be with you in body I am in spirit.

Yours,
Katherine Nash

March 20, 1863
Near Falmouth, Virginia
Dear Katie—

Just a quick line with two pieces of news. George Young got a smallpox vaccination from the army that made him sick. Several died from their shots. So the army is sending George home. I hope you will look out for him and be kind to him and his family who he may be a burden on because I'm not sure he will be strong enough to work either. As George is leaving they needed a new sergeant and Captain Clark made me sergeant which now I am. I didn't expect to be sergeant having never really thought about it but I feel like it is something to live up to. I allowed myself to feel proud for a short bit and since then try not to think that way. Maybe Overstreets are natural sergeants. Now there will be men depending on me especially new ones who know nothing about being a soldier. A sergeant can get his men killed quick enough—not as many as a general can but it is a sober thing to think.

Yours always,
H. Overstreet

April 15, 1863
Near Falmouth, Virginia
Dear Katie—

I have yours of March 17 in hand and also have received your blessed box of gifts. You have made me the most popular sergeant in the regiment. Were we to have elections for officers today, I would definitely beat out Colonel Ames and might come close with Colonel Chamberlain even though most like him because he isn't Colonel Ames. I have passed out the loot keeping a little for myself and preferring the Waldoborough boys. Captain Clark accepted socks with a smile. All of them ask to be remembered to you and the ladies who remember them. I will thank my father and brother when I write to them but I have made sure everyone knows that the wonders come from the Soldier's Aid Society of Waldoborough of Miss Katherine Nash.

You probably didn't know it but you sent your letter and package on one of the most dangerous days of the year in our camp—St. Patrick's Day. The Irish boys find liquor to honor the day and get themselves into a state where they are spoiling for a fight with whoever comes to hand. It's a good day for a sergeant to be away on picket duty which I assigned to myself.

We were visited again by Father Abraham who lets us know that he remembers us. The ceremony to receive him was an odd one. They drew us up in formation with clean uniforms and shaved faces and the men were pleased to look good. They take more pride now in their appearance and in looking like soldiers and not the rabble that Colonel Ames says we are. But the president is still a great tall man and the army again placed him on a sort of dwarf horse so that his bootheels nearly scraped the ground while his trouser ends raised up and showed his drawers underneath. It was comical the first time but this time it seemed mean. We see him for only a few seconds as his horse walks by; it's barely an eye-blink yet his gaze stays with you. He is not handsome but has dignity that is more powerful than any I have seen even the generals on fine horses with their gold buttons. The boys mock his horse and his outfit but they are devoted to him in a way that I feel too. We are reviewed pretty regular these days as generals trot by whenever you turn around.

We think there will be a fight pretty soon if our new commander Joe Hooker has anything to do with it. He is a fighting man which we saw at Antietam. I hope the regiment will give a good account of itself.

Your letters are dear to me. I read each one many times. We do sometimes as you ladies do and read passages of our letters to each other and I expect for the same reasons to hear of home things even if they are not your home things. I wish very much for a full return of your mother's health. That she recognizes your quality can only commend her more highly to me who knows that quality.

Yours always,
H. Overstreet

May 8, 1863
Waldoborough
Dear Henry—

I read now of another terrible battle in Virginia and find myself hoping that the problem with smallpox vaccine has kept your regiment out of it. I am sorry for any men who died or got sick from that but if it kept you safe then I would only thank those doctors that you think so poorly of. The news of the battle may have one good effect here in Waldoborough. The Soldiers Aid Society had dwindled to just Mrs. Benner and me but now two ladies have come back. It may be some weeks before we can again send something. All of us are busy with gardens and other chores of the season. There is good news, though. Mother came outside for the first time since last autumn. Father carried the large chair out for her and set it in the sunshine and then he carried her out. She closed her eyes and said the sun on her face felt divine. It warmed my heart so. Brother Theodore is beginning to talk of joining the army which my father insists he not do. On this I agree with Pa since Theodore is not even sixteen, but I fear he may run off and join as others have. The army doesn't seem too careful about soldier ages. I could not bear to have another in this fight. The sow had piglets again.

Forgive me, Henry, but I cannot go on prattling about this and that when so anxious about this battle. Write and tell me you are well and then I will write a proper letter.

Yours always,
Katherine Nash

June 27, 1863
Edward's Ferry, Virginia
Dear Katie—

For weeks since the unfortunate affair with the enemy at Chancellorsville we have not been where we could send or get mail so I have received none and have not written. I had many things to write but have forgotten most so I will write what I remember.

Company E missed that battle at Chancellorsville because of the smallpox that the army gave to us. Some said if we went into battle at least we could pass the pox to the enemy but we guarded telegraph lines instead.

It has been infernal hot for days now—hot beyond what Yankees from Maine could imagine. All the while we run after Bobby Lee trying to catch up with him but we never do. He must be moving fast because we march all day and do not catch him except for a short fight the other day that was mostly cavalry and settled nothing much. The boys start to talk about whether the generals march us in the wrong direction so they never face Lee and do not get whipped again. We are heartily tired of getting whipped. Everyone, including the newspapers which we have been able to read since we got here, think he is headed back to Maryland to try and scare the Union out of the war. He has the advantage because he knows where he is going and can decide when he wants to turn and fight while we just scramble after him and have to guess and stay on guard that when we come round the bend we'll be looking down the muzzles of a couple of hundred rebel guns or a half-dozen cannons. We know they are fine soldiers over on the other side but we are not going to give up our country. Two nights ago we camped on land that used to be owned by President Monroe which was something that made the men think. The secesh, they're trying to take that away from us and other history that belongs to all Americans.

It's been nearly a year we've been in the army and this regiment has not had a chance to show we can fight and we are on edge about that. Colonel Chamberlain took over for Colonel Ames and then we took in some men from the 2nd Maine regiment. That regiment signed up when the war started two years ago and a lot of them enlisted for two years and their time was up and they could go home so they did. Both others had signed up for three years like I did so they have another year even though they wanted it to be over which is only natural. Those men left behind refused to keep soldiering and it was looking like a regular mutiny which the army takes a sour view of. They sent some men from a Pennsylvania regiment to arrest the Maine men along with threatening that they would be executed in the army way. Colonel Chamberlain didn't want anything like that. He is different from Colonel Ames quieter and seems like more of a reading and thinking man though he can have an angry temper which we saw when he was arguing to get us into the fight at Chancellorsville. He gave the 2nd Maine boys some good food and treated them like men and said they had to serve so why not do it the right way. They came around and he spread a few into each company. They have been through plenty of fights and we still have little experience except for marching and getting sick both of which we are good at. We've got a few of the Second Maine boys in Company E and I am glad of it especially as sergeant.

Being sergeant brings me one thing I never expected. Now I get help from this contraband who has latched onto us here in Company E. He helps out Captain Clark mostly, but sometimes he even helps out sergeants. He ran off from his master somewhere near Richmond and has been with us for nearly six months. I used to see him around before but had no reason to know him. His name is Rufus Benson and he can set up a tent, get firewood, cook better than your ma and clean your rifle. He even boiled my uniform to kill the lice. The critters came back quick since they are sentimental sorts and don't like to be separated from us soldiers but it was like living in heaven to have twenty-four hours when I wasn't a meal for hundreds. The boys say if you sit quiet you can hear them chew. I still can't quite understand everything Rufus says the way he talks and he draws no pay but he seems like the best-humored man in camp. After being a slave even soldier life seems good. I almost asked him today what it was like being a slave but it didn't feel like I should ask. I think he wants to be a soldier himself;

he does not say so, but it's the way he handles my rifle when he cleans it; he knows it better than I do. I expect he would make a soldier. Lots of slaves like Rufus are running off from plantations trying to join our army and do what they can to help us. Women and children come now too because they want to be free too. They all figure we will protect them from their old masters and I guess they want us to win and end slavery and we can use the help. I wonder what will come of Rufus and the others when we win the war and they are slaves no more.

I have to stop now as we will head off after Bobby Lee in the morning and as sergeant I have to check up on the corporals and the other men. I don't know when I will write again but remain

Yours always,
H. Overstreet

CHAPTER SIX

✝

Henry felt like someone was driving nails into his forehead, or maybe like he had stared directly into the sun for an hour and the sun's rays melted everything behind his eyeballs, leaving a tangle of nerves and hurt. He hadn't known pain like this. As a sergeant, he didn't want to show it, even though he was getting tottery. He spread his feet and tilted his head down to ease the pain. He took off his cap and mopped his forehead with a sleeve.

He had no idea what was causing the searing headache except the heat and the sun and not eating much. Company E had stepped off three days before with forty men. It was down to twenty-five. Some lagged behind. Some went to the surgeons with sunstroke. Those men had passed out, though. They didn't seem to have this pain.

Covering thirty miles a day with a full kit, plus missing their rations, narrowed the men's horizons to their own misery. When the line of march neared a pond or crossed a stream, discipline dissolved. Men ran into water fully clothed and poured it over themselves with their hats. In seconds they stirred the bottom up, changing the water to muddy brown puddles that they drank down thirstily, indifferent to what might be floating in there.

Henry didn't stand between the men and water, which would get him trampled for sure, but he tried to move them along, calling out that other soldiers needed a drink too. So they hauled themselves up and started marching again.

When they passed a cherry orchard, Henry shouted at the top of his lungs to keep marching, holding his arms out to restrain them. Young Johnny Baxter sleepwalked toward the cherries. Henry grabbed his tunic and spun him back toward the road. Johnny stumbled to one knee and looked up, startled. A comrade helped him up. They resumed trudging. Usually such an episode would trigger insults and mocking for the wayward soldier, but no one had the energy.

On this, the third day, they crossed into Pennsylvania near noon, entering the real North but bringing Southern heat with them. It stuck to their clothes and got inside their minds, slowing their brains. They were too weary to marvel at the fertility of the local fields, which made the stony plots of Maine seem like penitentiary sentences, and the picked-over lands of Northern Virginia seem like the plains of hell. Waldoborough people talked about how German farmers had made Pennsylvania a garden spot. Henry would have to come back another time to decide if that was true.

What was new in Pennsylvania, though, was that people at roadside stands sold milk and buttermilk to the soldiers, along with baked treats.

"How much for that cherry pie?" Henry asked at one stop.

A young man—who looked to be of an age to march with them—said it was twenty-five cents.

The men around Henry made disapproving noises. To be overcharged by the people they were fighting for was a bitter pill, though none of them could pay even a fair price. They hadn't received their pay since leaving Maine nearly a year before. Henry picked up the pie and a pint bottle of milk. "Charge it to Uncle Sam," he said with a nod. He broke off half the pie and handed it to Johnny Baxter, whose eyes grew big. Henry swallowed the first bite almost without tasting it, his body's craving too strong to resist. He took another bite and made an effort to notice the flavor. It was bitter. The cheap bastards had skimped on the sugar. But it was wonderful.

The other men needed only his example. They greedily cleaned out the man's inventory.

"Those rebels pay cash money," the pie man shouted, his face growing red. "You're no better than thieves."

"Are you one of those Copperheads," Joe Maxwell shot back, "thinks we ought to give up and let those slave-whipping sons of bitches tear up our country?"

Facing a dozen armed men, the pie man chose silence.

Rufus walked briskly to Henry and offered him a canteen. Rufus wasn't quite Henry's height. Sweat beads stood out on his coal-black forehead and cheeks, but his smile was bright. "We sure could use ourselves some shade, sergeant," he said.

Henry couldn't help smiling back. "Rufus, I'm going to keep a lookout for some. You do the same, okay?" He handed the man his last hunk of pie and the remaining milk.

Stashing the canteen under one arm, Rufus took the pie. "I'm reckoning we're going to catch 'em soon."

"Unless they grow wings and fly, we'll catch 'em."

"Yes, sir. If you look over there," he pointed off to the west behind rolling hills, "I'm wondering if that sky isn't showing some of that dust from them marching. Or maybe it's cavalry."

"Could be ours."

"Could be, but I don't think so."

Henry squinted where Rufus pointed. It was hard to be sure of anything, much less whose cavalry it might be. Some stringy clouds were hanging on the horizon. He and Rufus started walking with the other men. Food improved the mood and the pace. "You may be on to something Rufus. You may need to go tell General Meade."

"Yes, sir."

They reached a field with horses and men sprawled in now-familiar positions of death in battle. It had been a cavalry fight, not long before. The company kept marching. Not far past, the men came upon another food stand and cleaned that one out too. When Henry got there, a woman in a faded blue dress looked up at him with tear-streaked cheeks. After passing the dead bodies, he felt no sympathy for someone who wept over food.

For the first time in days, the regiment stopped marching before sundown. Most dropped to the ground along the road.

Joe stretched out his long legs, leaned back on his knapsack, and closed his eyes. He was snoring in seconds. Johnny shrugged out of his pack and curled up. Two men from the 2nd Maine tried to eat hardtack, chewing and chewing and swallowing rarely.

Henry thought it might have cooled a little. There was a breath of wind. He turned in a full circle, searching for that shade Rufus had mentioned. Cornfields spread on both sides of the road. The closest trees were at least fifty yards away. Company C had claimed every scrap of shade, clustering shamelessly in the dark patches on the far side of the road. Turning to his own men, Henry realized that the corn was thriving, already thigh-high despite the searing temperatures. He admired the rail fences that lined the road. The armies had burned Virginia's fences months before.

He was counting the company when Captain Clark stopped by. Rufus held the bridle of the captain's horse.

"Thirty-seven, sir," Henry said. They both knew the number was laughable. The company had left Maine a hundred strong.

Clark grunted. "We picked up a couple."

"Yes, sir. There's more trying to catch up. They're game. They're just worn out."

Clark cocked his head. "You hear that?"

Henry tried to listen past the low conversation of tired men. He shook his head. "No, sir, I don't."

"Well, I can't either, but General Benson here can." He nodded at Rufus. "Seems they're fighting."

"They're going at it," Rufus said. "Yeah, they sure are."

"So this is it," Henry said.

"Or else it ain't." Clark tugged the reins away from Rufus and rode up the line, nodding at the men and probably hoping to find the colonel to see if he knew more.

Henry tried again to hear the fighting.

The regiment stayed there for an hour. Henry, his head on his pack, drowsed, happy to be off his feet. The thought floated through his mind that his head didn't hurt so much. A hoof stepped heavily next to him. Yeasty aromas of horse and leather wafted by. He scrambled up, grabbing his rifle.

"Ten minutes, sergeant," Clark said. "We're going through the night."

"Yes, sir."

"This is it."

"Yes, sir."

"Tell the men to eat what they can. This may be our last chance for a while."

Henry pulled some salt pork from his knapsack. Using his side teeth and yanking with his hand, he gnawed off a chunk. Saliva welled up to greet the salt. He began to chew and adjusted his pack. The word spread like wildfire as the bugles rang out, calling the men into line. Soldiers squared their shoulders and stood straighter. When the line started marching, Henry held the meat in one hand and his rifle in the other.

* * * * *

For a few hours, a tide of rumor and excitement swept them along. A full moon lit their way through clouds of dust. When the regiment entered a small town near ten o'clock, cheering people lined the streets. Some waved handkerchiefs or patriotic banners. Several women stood with buckets of fresh water and dippers for the men to drink their fill.

"What town is this?" Henry asked a dark-haired girl who handed him a dipper.

"Hanover, sir."

The water was cool. Henry handed back the dipper. "You've got a fine town, miss. And thank you."

She curtsied. "Thank you, sir."

A young boy ran alongside Henry and stared up with large eyes. Henry reached down and ruffled his hair. At the center of the town, a band—two cornets and a tuba and a drum—played "The Battle Hymn of the Republic". Then they broke into "Yankee Doodle". Henry looked over at Joe, who was smiling. All the men were, their faces glowing in soft moonlight. Henry thought about George Young and the others who never got to this night, who endured so much but never knew this rush of feeling. The regiment would fight now. They would show what they could do.

An hour past Hanover, the march began to fray. Men stumbled. Some sank to their knees. Eyelids drooped. Henry and Joe stayed at the rear of Company E, herding those dropping out. One of the new men fell out to adjust his pack. Henry helped, then pushed him back up to his place. No one spoke.

Shortly after midnight they came upon the army's rear. Other regiments were bivouacked. The Maine boys joined them, asleep as soon as they slumped to the ground.

Henry counted the men, then found Captain Clark leaning on a caisson at the end of a long line of cannon. A stack of rifles stood to his right. "Forty-one, sir."

Clark nodded. "Good, sergeant."

"We may get a few more."

"Every one helps. Colonel says there's been a bloody day, but we're not pulling back, not like before. We're going to have it out."

"What's the name of this place?"

"Gettysburg's what they say."

They stood for a moment in silence. Rufus approached and offered a full canteen. The man was a marvel. Clark and Henry each took a long drink. "Stay back here tomorrow, Rufus," Clark said, nodding ahead of them. "That'll be no place to be without a weapon." Henry wondered that Rufus was with them at all, now they were in Pennsylvania. He could run off to freedom any time. All he had to do was walk away.

Rufus held his tongue.

"Get some rest, sergeant," Clark said, running a finger along one side of his mustache. "We'll be up early."

Henry saluted. Turning to leave, the captain nodded at Rufus.

"We'll whip 'em tomorrow, sir," the black man said.

With men snoring everywhere, Henry found Company E by picking out Seth Flagg's raspy snuffle. The dew-damp felt clammy when he stretched out, his head on his pack. The heat had retreated, but he had no need of a blanket.

Reaching into his blouse, Henry touched the pouch holding Katie's letters. He meant to think about her for a minute, to share his fear and his eagerness with her in his mind, but he was asleep before he could.

CHAPTER SEVEN

✝

The sun, bright and brutal, began to rise as bugles blared. Company E straggled into the Fifth Corps formation, phalanxes of dusty blue uniforms in a barley field. Senior officers rode big horses along the front rank. The small, dark-haired man in the lead nodded solemnly, stopping every now and then for a word with a soldier or an officer.

"Who's that?" Joe whispered.

"Might be General Warren," Henry said, "but I've never seen him." How many of these men, Henry wondered, would see the next sunrise? Would he? His exhaustion was slipping away. The battle was near. He felt energy, anger, fear.

The regiment marched behind several others toward where the enemy must be. A hill stood between them and the front line. Orders came to stand down.

"What's the point?" Johnny Baxter asked as they stretched out on the ground. "Why don't we just go fight?"

Henry shrugged. They were all getting strung up, tense. "Hard to get everyone where the generals want them."

"And," Joe broke in, "maybe we'll wait for them to attack. Won't bother me none if they're the ones charging uphill." He pulled some hardtack from his pack. "Also wouldn't mind having another one of those pies from last night."

Henry walked around the company. The men looked all right, alert but not jumpy. They might not have the strength to get jumpy. He hoped they'd fight hard. They'd been on campaign so long and been at so many battles but still hadn't fought. He lay down against his pack and pulled his cap over his eyes. The sun beat down on them. He wasn't sure whether he slept. He heard gunfire at midday, but not for long.

After another two hours, the heat pressed like the heavy hand of God. Lying still, moving nothing but his eyelids, Henry felt sweat run down his ribcage. The stagnant air was a miasma of soldier stink. Henry was used to how the army smelled, but this was stronger. The smell of fear? His lips curled.

The ground trembled with artillery firing and the air exploded. The soldiers stirred. No one could rest while such massive upheaval rent their world.

Henry hated the cannon, the idea of cannon. He thought he could face rifle fire, even hand-to-hand combat. Those were human forms of fighting. They involved killing without obliterating. But he never wanted to face a cannon. He had seen the trunks of men whose heads or limbs were blown off, bodies that were pulverized. That terrified him.

The bugle calls began again.

"All right," Captain Clark called, "report to the ammunition wagon over there, then get back here!" He pointed.

Each man received twenty more cartridges, which meant sixty for the battle. They stuffed the extras into cartridge boxes or other pouches. As Company E lined up, Henry overheard a man who came from the Second Maine.

"Aim low, boys," the man said. "It's easy to shoot high. And remember to take the ramrod out of the barrel." He turned to a man who had snickered. "Don't laugh. We had boys leave 'em in, then fire. Doesn't work real good."

"Aim low," Johnny Baxter said back to the man. "Check the ramrod."

"That's it," the man said. "Doesn't hurt any to stop and think now and again. Don't always have time to, but if you do."

Henry counted again. Forty-three. Two more. He reminded the men to see to their personal needs. "Don't want anything on your mind but those Johnny Rebs."

A few stepped away to piss on the grass. One jogged off toward some trees. He was back soon.

They were the second of four regiments that moved to the left of the hill that stood between them and the battle. No one straggled. Henry felt no fatigue. Every sense was alert. His heart pounded as they climbed a second hill. His ears told him the fight was on the other side. Powder smoke drifted over them. They were on a lumber trail like the ones back home. Near the crest, artillery shells began to explode in the treetops. Each blast set off a shower of tree branches, some large enough to smash a man's brains out. The soldiers kept their eyes up as they crossed the summit. Colonel Chamberlain ordered a halt. Breathing hard, the column tried to look out through the smoke. They could hear everything now, not just the cannon booms. Rifle fire crackled in the spaces between. Screams came from men and horses.

They started down an incline, a rocky one with patchy woods that clustered without any pattern.

The Twentieth was the rear regiment now. Near the top of this last hill, Chamberlain rode up. He stopped them with an upraised hand, then stood in his stirrups and stared down the slope. After a full minute, he pivoted his mount to face the regiment.

"We're going to hold this line," he called out and pointed behind him, "to the left of these Pennsylvania boys." He pointed again. "We're the end of the line for the whole army, so we have to hold, no matter what!" With a stern face but without hurrying, he rode up to each company captain and pointed out the spot on the broken hillside for that company.

The boulders and trees on the hill would break up organized attacks. This wouldn't be a set-piece battle with precise movements by trim military contingents, but a melee in the woods.

The men jogged to their positions. Captain Clark brought Company E directly next to the Pennsylvanians, on the right end of their line. "All right, boys," he called out. "We're the junction. We can't allow rebels between us and those fellows there." He pointed over. "That'd be bad for both of us, and for the rest of the army."

The company spread out. Henry posted his men about four feet apart, taking advantage of cover offered by rocks and trees. "Step back here," he said, waving two soldiers from a clearing to some sheltering boulders.

After walking the line twice, Henry found Captain Clark, who nodded. "Sergeant, you manage the line from that oak tree over to the Pennsylvanians. Rearrange the men to fill in any gaps that open up. Listen for me or for any other captain. Orders may change."

Abruptly, the Confederate artillery fell silent. "That"—Henry cast his eyes up to the treetops—"that means they're coming?"

"I expect." Clark nodded.

Henry turned to the right third of the company, the part he was responsible for. He paced slowly behind each man, noting spots where he might find cover during an attack. He spoke in a low voice, one he hoped was louder than the hammering of his heart. "Just stay steady, boys. Keep track of your cartridges, your ramrods. Aim at your targets. Aim low. Keep steady. We'll show them what Maine boys can do." Henry touched several of the men on the sleeve, the shoulder, the back. When he got to Joe, he said, "This time, they'll be coming uphill."

"Amen," came back.

When Henry reached the end of the line, he asked Teddy Meisner where the Pennsylvania boys were. "Right here, sergeant." A man lifted his head from behind a low bush and waved at Henry.

"Glad to see you, friend, but that bush won't be much cover."

The man nodded. "That's a fact," he said, then pointed to a nearby tree. "I may move over there once the balls start flying."

"You two know that you've got to hold, stay connected?"

"Do or die," the Pennsylvania man said. "That's what my sergeant said."

"Always listen to sergeants."

Henry returned to the middle of his stretch of the line. He saw no sign that the men were spooked, that they might run.

The rebels would have a hard climb up that slope. They'd be shooting uphill, which should make them fire high. They'd be exposed. They'd get tired. But they'd have some cover. The regiment was spread thin, at least Company E was. If a few of the Maine men got hurt—when they got hurt—the line would have holes. Still, he'd rather be up here than down there.

A brown toad hopped near the man in front of him. Find some cover little fellow, Henry thought. This is no place for a toad.

He looked back uphill. If this regiment really was the end of the army's position, taking this hill would give the rebels control of the battlefield. Cannon up here could scour the Union lines. If the rebels won here at Gettysburg, they could choose their next target—Philadelphia, or Washington, or New York.

He heard a breeze in the treetops but couldn't feel it, not on the ground. In a clearing down the slope, some high leaves stirred, shimmering with reflected sunlight. He took a breath and slowed his pulse. He gazed intently into the trees.

Where the hell were they?

Bullets began slashing through leaves and branches. Every man dropped his head. The Pennsylvanians on the right fired a volley that stunned Henry with its crash, then another. Next came a high-pitched sound that started out like angry dogs howling, on the far edge of insane. Not dogs, but hellhounds. Couldn't be human voices. Except it wasn't dogs. The rebel yell. Some claimed the yell made the boys in blue run. Underneath that high-pitched screech surged the thunder of the Confederate artillery, blasting the Pennsylvanians to Henry's right. His pulse leapt. He saw men in gray—a sun-bleached gray that ran to yellow—running across an open field and starting up the slope on his right.

Why weren't they attacking here?

"There they are!" Joe, staying low, pointed downhill. "There's a pile of 'em, looking to circle around us. See?"

Henry stepped forward. Yes. Straight down. The light-colored uniforms flashed through the leaves. They were moving across the regiment's front. They meant to come up on the left.

Henry looked to the center of the regiment's line. Chamberlain stood atop a giant boulder, facing down the slope. No man was ever a better target. The colonel was shouting to his left. Henry looked back downhill. Joe was right. There was a load of them. More every second. "Steady, boys," Henry said. He walked his end of the line. He repeated himself, then added, "Load!"

The men twisted on the ground or turned where they knelt. They bit open cartridges, poured powder down the barrel, shaking the barrel to help gravity. They rolled the balls down. Shoved the ramrods in. Set the ramrods close to hand. Twisted back into position. Thumbed the hammers back to the click of half-cock. Fished out the caps. Placed them in the trays.

"Wait on 'em," Henry said. "Make 'em come to us. Steady now. They won't move us. We don't go back."

Henry looked over to the colonel. He was waving troops back from the left, then pointed across his body. He was remaking the line into an "L" shape, turning a right angle with the corner in front of him, where the regimental colors stood.

"Sergeant!" Captain Clark shouted. "Spread the men. Shift to the left. You have to cover more of the line."

That was crazy. They were already spread too thin. He started with Bill Starrett, a new man from the Second Maine. Starrett grabbed his cartridge box and ramrod. He scrambled left about five feet, stopping at a thick locust trunk.

"More," Henry said. Starrett gave him a look. "Company I ends way over there." Henry pointed. The soldier scrambled again, stopping at a rock. Henry nodded and hurried to the next man, who was already sidestepping in a crouch. The next dozen moved on their own. Henry left Teddy Meisner where he was. They had to hang onto the Pennsylvanians.

The shift took no more than a minute. The insane screaming started again, closer now. Hairs rose on the back of Henry's hands. He stood to peer down the slope. They were coming.

CHAPTER EIGHT

†

The tattered uniforms flapped as the attackers ran to the base of the hill. There were hundreds of them. They slowed when they started to climb. They moved steadily, confidently.

Henry's skin tingled. His men shifted—a leg here, an arm there. Muscles twitched. Holding a single position was unnatural. The screams kept coming. Like banshees. He scanned his thin line. They looked steady.

Some rebels crouched and aimed. Bullets whined overhead. They were within range. "Now!" Henry screamed.

The crash of gunfire wiped out other noises. Muzzle flashes streaked down the slope. A bullet clipped a leaf next to his head. "Aim low. Steady fire." The boys were loading. They didn't need him shouting.

Henry stepped behind a tree. On one knee, he leveled his rifle barrel. Powder smoke obscured his view. He swung the barrel slowly in search of a target. A man ran uphill without swerving. Henry fired, the recoil digging into his shoulder. He loaded. Smoke rose on his left, then cleared. He found another target. Fired again.

The attackers slowed about fifty yards from the line. Some walked, hunched low. Some dove for cover. Henry looked over for Captain Clark. He was there. Henry paced behind his men, crouching when he remembered. He looked the other way for the Pennsylvanians. The smoke hid them, but he could hear them. The tang of burnt powder filled his nose. A bullet hit a nearby rock, spewing fragments in the air. Something stung Henry's cheek.

Blasts came from behind. Union cannon. More blasts. Then more. Unhearing, Henry stared down the slope. The rebels weren't climbing anymore. Henry started back down his line. "Find a target, boys! Don't waste your fire. Aim low. If you see one, get him." He sounded far away to himself.

He found Teddy at the right end, reloading. The Pennsylvanians were fighting. Henry slapped Teddy on the leg and shouted, "Good man," then slid back along the line.

The Union cannon kept booming, but not at these attackers. Henry glanced to the left. More muzzle flashes. Smoke cloaked much of the Union line. Chamberlain was still on the boulder, still a perfect target.

The enemy was advancing again, thirty yards away now. Henry jumped next to a rock to load, then fired. A rebel spun from the impact of a bullet. A shout came from Henry's left. It was Seth Flagg. Lying on his back, his hand gripped his right thigh. Crimson showed through the pant leg. Henry ran to him. Flagg, grimacing, had his kerchief off. Henry tied it around the leg above the wound, yanked it tight.

"Can you get back there?" Henry pointed up the slope.

Flagg shook his head. "I can still shoot." He rolled onto his belly, then fired. Henry loaded his own gun and fired. The enemy was closer, darting from tree to tree. Twenty yards. Less. Two attackers fell awkwardly. They were madmen, Henry thought, charging into the mouths of guns.

There was a thud, a wet sound. Henry looked over. A piece of Flagg's skull was missing, brains oozing. What was left of his head, eyes open, rested on the ground. Henry froze.

A shriek came from his other side. A grayback stood over Henry's man. Henry gripped his rifle by the barrel, not noticing its heat. In three strides he swung. The heavy butt knocked the man down. Henry smashed the butt into his face. Again. Again. More screams to his right. The Union man at his feet moved, grabbing for his rifle. Henry jumped back to Flagg's spot in the line. No gaps in the line. No gaps. He pulled his bayonet from his belt, crouching as he moved, and fumbled it into the socket at the end of the barrel. Fewer bullets whizzed through the air.

A rebel, coming from nowhere, smashed his rifle into Henry's knee. Crumpled, Henry watched the man rear up for a second swing. Henry drove off his bad leg, lunging with the bayonet but falling short. The man staggered back down the hill. Henry rose, ignoring his leg, looking for someone to kill. To the left, Joe was grappling with someone. Both were barehanded. Henry rushed over and stabbed with the bayonet. The rebel grunted. Henry pulled back then stabbed again. He pulled the man off Joe, then rolled him down the slope.

Gasping thanks, Joe found his gun.

Henry moved back toward Flagg's body. No gaps. No rebels coming. Fewer gunshots. He moved down the line to the right, stepping over a gray-clad body. He clapped Bert Humphrey on the shoulder. "Load," he shouted. He ran to Teddy Meisner. Teddy lay on his back, moaning, his tunic bright red in front. Henry knelt, calling Teddy's name.

The man's eyes focused, but he said nothing.

"We'll get you back to the docs." He waved for help from the rear, not knowing who he was waving to.

Teddy's eyelids drooped and his breath rasped. "I'm shot through, Henry. I'm done for."

A man arrived. Henry turned. "Find someone and take him back." Teddy's hand grabbed Henry's arm, his eyes desperate. Henry found his canteen and unscrewed the cap. His hand trembled. Supporting Teddy's head with the other hand, he tilted the canteen to his lips. Teddy swallowed once, then his eyes closed.

Henry stared at him. The gunfire seemed far away. "Sergeant," came a voice, "he's gone." Henry nodded, then straightened. He took a swallow from the canteen, then offered it to the other man. It was Bert Humphrey. Henry never thought much of Bert. He seemed like a complainer.

"Take his cartridges," Henry said. "Set up here. You need to stay connected to those boys over there." He pointed to the right where the Pennsylvanians were. "No gap. Can't have a gap." Bert nodded. Henry headed back to the left. Maybe Bert was all right.

The grays had dropped down the hill but not far enough. They gathered just out of range. They weren't through.

The men were spreading into the gaps. Two dead already. Joe Maxwell had his cartridges on the ground. He jammed his ramrod into the dirt next to them, staking his claim. Other men did the same. No going back.

Henry took Flagg's cartridges to the men on his left. Their lips and mouths were black from powder. Henry would cover the gap left by Flagg. There was no one else. They needed another company to hold this line. They needed another regiment.

The werewolf screams started again. Not as strong now. The company fired down the hill. Bullets flew back up, but the rebels came on slowly, more cautious. Maybe the reckless ones were dead. Henry darted left behind a rock. Joe crawled to another rock on his right. Powder smoke enveloped him. Henry could see nothing. He blinked and turned his face down. Tears came. He looked up and saw a man carrying a sword. An officer. He swung the barrel that way, fired blind. Smoke made him wince again.

The firing kept up. Henry fingered his cartridge box, cursed. They were running out.

This time rifle fire was enough. The enemy never reached their line. They backed down the hill. They weren't running. They weren't licked. Henry's hearing started to come back.

"Joe," he shouted, "get that reb's cartridges."

"Already did. Wasn't but a dozen."

Henry went looking for more dead. They needed ammunition. A man in blue, carrying a musket, ran up to him. "Where do you need me?" he asked.

Henry pointed toward Bert Humphreys. "Hold that corner. You have a full cartridge pouch?"

The man nodded. Henry recognized him as one of the lead mutineers from the Second Maine. He had been scheduled for court martial. "Share them out."

Henry thought he saw Chamberlain through the smoke, down off the boulder now, shouting. The color sergeant cradled the regiment's flag in the crook of an elbow. He seemed to be holding himself up with it. Bodies lay in heaps over there. It looked like the line was pulled back on the left. The rebels were pressing hard there.

Rifle fire picked up but no rebel yells. *We don't scare off*, Henry thought. *You know that now. You have to kill us.*

He ran back to Joe, who was shooting. Henry left some cartridges there, then started shooting himself.

The rebels came on slow, using cover, moving back and forth, always uphill. There were so many.

"Sergeant," Captain Clark's voice rang out in a space between shots. Henry turned. Clark waved his arm up the hill. They were pulling back.

Henry jammed his cartridges in his pouch. "Up the hill, boys! We'll be back! Up the hill! Now!"

He didn't want to stand upright, not with the rebels coming on like that, but he did. He waved down the line in both directions. He turned his back on the enemy, teeth clenched, waiting for a ball to slam into him. He held both arms out and pushed air up the hill. "Back ten paces! Everyone! Go! Go! Find new cover."

The men scrambled up. To his left, two didn't move. Two more down. He couldn't see who. "New line here! Make every shot count!" Joe stabbed his ramrod into the earth again. There was blood on his sleeve.

Henry moved left to fill the new gap. A grayback ran at him, shouting as a musket fired nearby. The man clutched his side and fell over. Rebels were crossing their line. Henry swung his musket again, connecting with a man's legs. When he fell, Henry dropped on him with his bayonet. The man screamed. Henry screamed. The other man fell silent.

Joe was shrieking. He swung his gun one-handed but missed his target, a rebel who was lifting his gun to fire. Henry jumped on the enemy, his hands searching for the man's windpipe. His fingers slipped on sweaty skin. He had to let go. Henry drove his knee up as he slid off the man but connected with nothing.

The rebel staggered back. Henry ran at him, reaching blind for a handhold, something he could break or twist or throttle. They fell, knocking the wind from each other. Neither could stand. They stared at each other. The rebel's face was six inches away, unshaven, bad teeth. Henry's brain said to move, but he had no air. With a gasp, he inhaled. The rock there. He grabbed it and smashed it into the man's face. Into yellow teeth.

"Come on, boys!"

It was Joe, leading the men down the slope. Henry rose to follow. The rebels were running. This time they were running.

Henry grabbed his rifle and ran after them. Joe was past where their first line had been. Two others followed. They found a rebel trying to slip away and tackled him.

"Stop!" Henry called. "Back to the line! We hold the line!" He threw a ramrod into the ground. "Right here."

Joe hauled the rebel, now empty-handed, up the hill with him.

"What the hell you gonna do with him?" Henry shouted. Joe was breathing too hard to answer. Henry pointed to one of the others. "Take him back and dump him with the first man you find, then get back." He turned to Joe and nodded. "Get some water. Find cartridges. They'll come again."

Henry caught his breath, then headed to the right end of the line. "You're still here," he called to Bert Humphreys. They exchanged grins. "Cartridges?"

"A couple."

Henry gave him all he had. "Strip the pouch from anyone who falls."

He moved left. The smoke was rising. Henry had started with eighteen men. Four were gone that he knew about. Fewer than fourteen were left. He shifted the survivors as best he could. Captain Clark still stood. They waved at each other. He could see the colonel too. More bodies lay near the colors. As bad as it was for Company E, the others looked to have it worse. The regiment's left wing was bent back nearly double. Chamberlain was ordering his men forward.

The next charge wasn't as bad. They never got closer than twenty yards. When they pulled back, Henry sat on his haunches. He thought he'd lost another man on the left. He didn't want to go look. He stood anyway.

"Hey, Henry." It was Joe. Henry stopped. "What's wrong with those boys? Still coming on like that. It ain't normal."

"Cartridges?"

Joe shrugged. Henry paced the line. Six men to his left. None with more than six cartridges. Henry jogged over to the captain. Clark's face was flushed, smeared with powder and sweat. "We're down to throwing rocks," Henry said.

Clark grunted. "Simons!" he called. A man from Bristol stood and turned. "Tell the colonel we're almost out."

Sliding back to his end of the line, Henry wondered about the artillery. They kept firing, but it didn't help. There was more fighting on their right. His leg started to throb. He touched his neck and found blood there. He felt a cut there.

A man came from behind. He asked where to go. Henry pointed. "Left of Maxwell. Try to keep him from charging by himself."

Henry paced some more. The men in gray were massing again. They'd taken losses, but they weren't done.

Henry felt the rage build. They were going to hold this line. They weren't going back. His hand went to his bayonet. No one liked a bayonet. Let the rebels see it. Let them feel it. He scanned his men, black powder on their faces like war paint. They didn't need to be led, not by the likes of him. The time for tactics was over. It was just pure murder.

"Bayonet!" Colonel Chamberlain shouted the word over and over. Captain Clark picked it up. So did Henry. The men fumbled for the wicked-looking blades, then jammed them into sockets. Henry helped a couple of them. The socket on Humphrey's gun was twisted. Henry found another gun for him.

The graycoats started back up the hill. They were about halfway, less than a hundred yards away. Bastards. To his left, Henry saw a sword flash. A man in blue, an officer, rose up and shouted. Bayonets glinted in the dappled forest light. Others rose, picking up the shout. Not the rebels' high-pitched screech, but a deep roar, a bellow of rage and bloodlust. The left wing started moving downhill.

Henry looked to Captain Clark. Clark held a hand out, palm down. Henry understood. They were the right corner, the anchor for the others to swing around. Company E would charge last.

He walked the line. "Hang on, boys. We'll be going down. Stand ready." The men could see the rebels slow. They were wavering. Henry looked back to the captain. *Now*, he thought. *Now. Now.*

Clark swung his sword, and Henry started the shout. The men joined. This was their hill. No slave-whippers would take it. "Steady!" Henry shouted. "Don't run! If you get a target, shoot the bastard."

He took his own advice. His target doubled over. The rebels were backing away. No one liked bayonets. He started the shout again, and the men picked it up. Captain Clark swung his sword overhead. Joe broke into a trot. The others matched his pace. The line was moving. God help anyone in their way.

The rebels broke. They ran like rabbits. Some sprinted, showing the soles of their shoes. Some tripped and fell. They dropped their guns. They ignored officers who were screaming themselves hoarse. One with a fine uniform stepped out from behind a tree and pointed a revolver at Henry. It misfired. Henry charged him with his bayonet. The man turned in fear. Henry knocked him down with his gun barrel and straddled him. He snatched the man's revolver and jammed it in his belt.

"You're my prisoner, general." He stood and stomped his heel on the small of the man's back, hearing the groan he wanted to. "Don't go anywhere."

He called a man over. "Start a prisoner camp right here. He's your first. Kill him if he moves."

Henry resumed the pursuit. The others were twenty yards ahead. Three rebels held empty hands up in surrender. Henry pushed them over to the new prisoner camp. A sharp volley sounded off to the left. Henry crouched. Were the graycoats making a stand? He needed cartridges.

He shifted to the left, through patches of light. He caught up to Joe, who had five rebels at bayonet point, their hands up. "What was that?"

"Ours. Some of the boys were out ahead, and we ran the bastards right into 'em."

Henry straightened and took a breath. "Over there"—he pointed—"that's our prisoner camp." Henry rounded up another half-dozen.

Some rebels sat on the ground. Others sprawled. Their faces were haggard. They were spent.

Captain Clark walked up. "Prisoners over there," he said, pointing uphill. "Sergeant, get your men together, sweep the front for more prisoners, then back up to our line. We still need to hold it." He nodded at Henry. "Report when you're on the line."

Henry ended up sending two soldiers to the rear with about forty prisoners. He found Captain Clark. "Thirty-one men still with us, sir, counting the two taking prisoners to the rear."

"Counting you?"

"Yes, sir."

"Good men."

"Yes, sir. Sir, we'd like to bury our dead."

"Not now. We've got orders. We're supposed to take that hill." Clark nodded at the dark mass that loomed opposite them, even higher than the hill they'd been defending.

"Are there rebels up there?"

"We'll know soon enough."

"When do we go?"

"Any minute." Clark started to tremble. He sat down abruptly. He fanned himself with his hat. Perspiration beaded his forehead.

"You all right?"

"Fever. Can't shake it." He pointed. "Hand me that canteen." After drinking from it, he offered it to Henry. "Careful now. It's brandy with quinine. It'll cure what ails you."

Henry took a swallow. It burned at first, then made him shudder. Clark laughed softly. "I keep thinking I'll get used to it, but not yet." He cocked his head. "Hear that, sergeant?"

"What?"

"The quiet." He stood with a groan and a grim look. "I had no idea these men were so splendid."

"Yes, sir," Henry said.

CHAPTER NINE

✝

July 4, 1863
Waldoborough
Dear Henry—

    I write when you are again in the midst of a battle and all I can do is hope and feel terrible fright. Writing this, even though you don't know I am doing it, is the only way I have to reach my hand out when you face peril. You should know that I think of you and hope only for your safe return while the worst danger I face is the pack of dogs that seems to run through this part of town whenever I have wash to put out. They carry no guns but their teeth are sharp. They bit a boy of ten recently. The town should do something about them.

    Instead, the town readies its Independence Day celebration, featuring our local Copperheads. I will enjoy the band concert and the fireworks, but I don't know that I can bear to hear Boss Reed deliver the Declaration of Independence. My friends in the Soldiers' Aid Society feel the same way, especially Mrs. Benner, though the group has begun to fall away again. Summer is a busy time for farmwomen. We think we should be the ones reading at the ceremony because we are the ones who make sacrifices that Boss Reed would never consider— not me so much, but the women with their husbands gone away, the children with their fathers gone, and the families of the poor soldiers who gave their all. Through the ceremonies, my thoughts will be with you and I know the other women will feel the same about their men. We don't speak of our fears, but we know we share them. I will look for your friend George Young at the ceremony but they say he has not regained his strength.

I had a surprise the other day. I passed by the Clark shipyard and Captain Clark's brother stopped to speak with me. He spoke of your regiment and asked after Sergeant Overstreet. You see how word has spread of your promotion. No Clark has ever spoken to me before, as the Clarks have had little enough reason to know of Katie Nash or her connection to Sergeant Overstreet. I was proud for you, Henry.

Yours always,
Katherine Nash

July 29, 1863
Near Warrenton, Virginia
Dear Katie—

I have just received yours of July 4 and it has been a balm for my heart. You seemed to be here with me speaking in your own sweet voice. That's how I read your letters—in your voice, speaking into my ears.

Truly we passed through a crucible at Gettysburg and left fine men there though none from Waldoborough. Like other regiments we bury our own but at Gettysburg they sent us away from the field right after we fought but we went back on our own. We made head boards from ammunition boxes and carved their names on them so their families will know where to find them and will know they were cared for when they died. We have lost other men who had to go to hospitals and we don't know when or even if they will return. In all we have lost about a third of the regiment and are down to about two hundred men. But we stood fast. I know now that this is God's war no matter how stupid our generals may be, no matter that we sometimes fail in the face of the enemy. As part of this army and in this cause we are worthy and we have shown it and the men know it.

The rebels retreated after the battle as the newspapers say but we haven't done anything so sensible as to follow them. Instead we tramp across Maryland and Virginia hills to no purpose that I can see. We have been in this place for two nights which has allowed me to receive your letter and to start this one. Yesterday we found a blackberry patch which made the day bright and last evening's rain brought a rainbow. Those are moments that make us remember God's grace which is not often on our minds. In truth our minds are most often on our stomachs or on when we might be able to sleep or get out of the rain. There is a strange state that comes over us when we march for many hours and our rations don't keep up. The mind retreats and we plod forward mostly silent but for occasional grumbling over this or that which is like an itch that breaks out in many men at once and must be scratched but then it ends. Then our minds retreat again and the quiet returns.

You may think from this that I have become a man of religion or philosophy which I never have been and am not now. This war has shown me things that may change me I hope for the better. It does not change my feelings about Katie Nash.

Yours always,
H. Overstreet

August 20, 1863
Waldoborough
Dear Henry—

As I just received your letter and for once I have read no recent news of any terrible battle, I will try to write an ordinary letter without filling it with my fears and worries. The crops look well for this time of year, something I can see for myself with the corn and wheat nearby, but which some of the old farmers down at Winslow's were talking about the other day. You know how they are. It would kill them to say it is a good year. They say they've seen worse. Or that it might turn out all right, you never know. Then they remind each other about terrible years in the past. For a Maine farmer, not complaining about the crop is the same as jubilation.

My brother and sisters and I went to the launching at the Clark yard. They call the new one the *Edwin Clark* after the brother of your captain. It's a large ship. They said it was over 700 tons though that doesn't mean much to me. I could see that it is large and will have three masts when fully rigged. You have seen many launchings, but this was my first for a long time. The river is so tight where the Clark yard is that you know they wait for full high tide, which meant they launched early in the morning and slid it down on its side, so it rolled over onto its other side when it first entered the water with a great crash. It was exciting. Then they hooked up a steamer to pull it out to where it won't get stranded when the tide leaves. There was a sad part of the launching. One of the workers, a man everyone called Jerry, got his foot caught in a rope loop just as the ship was dropping into the water with all its force. They say that the rope pulled taut and sliced his foot right off, though I didn't see that. Father says that ship orders are still strong so the yards are doing well. It seems wrong for people back here to prosper while soldiers face such hardship, but I don't wish hardship on my neighbors either.

I must tell you the news that is most pressing on me. There's a school down below Sampson Cove that needs a teacher for when classes begin next month and they have asked if I would be interested. They have fourteen students between ages five and thirteen, so it's not so big. Mother thinks I should, that my sisters are able to take care of themselves now and that Theodore would prefer I not be around. She may be right about them but she also says that she will be fine without me, and I am not sure about that. I worry about times when school will be in session and Father will be at work and she may take a bad turn. Father says nothing about the teaching position but I know what he thinks. I will decide next week whether to meet with the school director, but I expect I will.

Yours always,
Katherine Nash

October 1, 1863
Near Beverly Ford, Virginia
Dear Katie—

It has been a quiet camp of soldiers over the last day because no one wants to talk about what they made us watch yesterday morning. The entire Fifth Corps which has to be close to ten thousand men was drawn up in formation on a shallow hill that allowed us to see what was going to happen which was the execution of five deserters who were shot like dogs. It was a solemn and awful thing. No man in this army will speak up for de-

serters who enlist for the bounty and desert and enlist
for another bounty and desert again and keep the game
going on as long as they can. We know that men do that
though not in this regiment but each of those five men
was a child of God and all the men were sad to see them
die like that. We see too much death that is necessary so
we hate death that is not. I could not help but think of
my brother as well and am glad he is safe.

I had no intention when I picked up my pencil to
be so gloomy. We may not have defeated the secesh yet
but we did get paid last month only for the second time.
Most spent the money on food as soon as the sutlers
showed up and some spent it on drink. I bought paper
for writing letters and stamps and food. We have had
one treat from the company cook who perfected the
making of doughnuts when he can get flour and when
he has saved the fat from boiling salt pork. When he
starts the doughnuts the smell is enough to draw men
from miles around all of them desperate to pay ten cents
for a hot doughnut and he even lets the sergeants buy
first. His doughnut business is prospering according to
the cook because of a paper battle the Union has started with the South as part of the war. The cook says he
buys flour from merchants here in Virginia and pays
with counterfeit Confederate bills that are being printed up in New York and sent down here in order to ruin
the Confederate currency. He says the counterfeit bills
look better than the real ones so it is easy to spend them
though the Confederate bills are worth so little to start
with it seems a lot of trouble to counterfeit them which
is probably why the merchants here in Virginia take the
counterfeits. We can thank those false bills for other recent delicacies the cook has bought like sweet potatoes
and eggs so I am all in favor of this paper form of war.

You may remember that I wrote about Rufus Benson, the contraband who was working for Captain Clark
mostly but also looked after me a little. He is an able
man and always seemed to want to be a soldier himself
to end the infernal slave system that held him in bond-

age. While we were marching here and there to no particular purpose Rufus heard about a new regiment of colored troops being formed in Baltimore. I didn't know about it but the colored men talk to each other about things they don't talk to us about. He is an honorable man and told both Captain Clark and me that he wished to go fight and we could only wish him good luck and thank him for his help. My life isn't near as easy as Rufus made it but he will be a fine soldier and I will be proud to have him part of our army which Captain Clark says the same.

Yours always,
H. Overstreet

November 12, 1863
Waldoborough
Dear Henry—

I have just completed a second six-week contract teaching in the Sampson Cove school. I will not renew for the coming semester because the cold weather is setting my mother back. She suffers in her breathing and I am not willing to leave her for so long. Mrs. Castle comes over now with a few of the concoctions she has used over the years, which we don't tell the doctor about. She also prepares plasters that seem to help for a short time, but not long enough.

I find that being a schoolmistress is not easy, but I like it and think I am good at it. At least I was good enough in Sampson Cove and can get better. I had to remember again to be very strict inside the schoolroom and to be sure to see nothing outside of it where young scholars should be free to do as they wish. What happens outside is not the concern of the schoolmistress. Each of the different ages of the children presents its own problems. The very young ones need mothering. If I was reading a story to the class—and you will guess that I read Mr. Dickens to them—the young ones sometimes want to climb up on my lap and I permit it. A child of five is entitled to a warm lap when she is tired. We had two boys of nine and ten who were full of mischief. Three times other children came to me to complain of their tricks and I had to say that they must resolve such matters themselves, and all the time I would have to stop myself from grinning. I will confess to some irritation when the boys hid my boots on a rainy day, but they seemed truly sorry when they saw me in my good shoes in the muddy schoolyard calling them in from recess. There were three older children. Two of them were bored to be in school and restless to begin working. By springtime, I expect they will no longer come to class. But the third, a girl named Joanna, is such a bright thing. I had to try very hard not to play favorites with her because she is so eager and quick-witted. I expect she will be a farm wife but she will be a clever farm wife who helps her husband and reads interesting things and raises intelligent children. I gave her additional assignments and loaned her books to read. I will miss her.

The town has voted Copperhead again but the state is strong for the Union. Sometimes I wish I lived in a place I could be proud of but then I know these people and that they just vote as Boss Reed tells them to. Mrs. Benner in the Soldier's Aid Society recently shared with me a call that came from the Women's Loyal National League, which was formed in New York to support an amendment to the Constitution to end slavery. I think my father would take vapors if I was to join that League but I would like to. Certainly I would if it would end the war sooner and release you from the army.

Yours always,
Katherine Nash

December 10, 1863
Rappahannock Station, Virginia
Dear Katie—

We are in winter quarters and disappointed to realize that we will have another year of war though we
already knew that was true because the rebels are not
licked. They are devilish fighters and hard men and
their women and children must be hard too. We all
hoped after Gettysburg that we might drive on to Richmond and end this. We had some fighting in the fall but
nothing that could end the war no matter how it turned
out. Our generals sometimes seem to want to avoid losing men more than they want to win the war. Worrying about having the men killed is right and proper and
generals should not get us killed for no reason, yet every soldier knows that he may not return home until we
beat the enemy and we cannot beat him without fighting whether it happens this year or next year so why not
this year? Not fighting only stretches out the time we are
away from our homes. We have just learned of General
Grant's great victory in Tennessee. That is a general that
is not afraid to fight and who wins to boot.

We have built our winter cabins as we learned to do
last winter which I was hoping never to do again. We are
on Meade Street now. The boys don't exactly love General Meade they call him an old lady sometimes but they
are proud of Gettysburg and he was our general there.
The best part about these winter quarters is that we are
next to a train line so our rations and supplies should be
regular. Since Gettysburg things like that have not been
regular. We had almost no tobacco anywhere in the regiment this fall which is hard. Tobacco can get a soldier
through a day better than food though by the second day
there better be food. The only worse thing would be not
to have coffee as most soldiers would give up their rifles
and tents before they would give up coffee. In a mag-
ical way a few weeks ago suddenly there was tobacco
to be purchased from a sutler who sold right out of the

regimental headquarters tent. It seems he was an agent for one of the colonels—not Chamberlain—who got the tobacco from some political connection in Washington. When the men grouse about the officers making money from them I don't say a word to silence them. If I was not sergeant I would grouse about it too.

Unlike how I feel about that colonel I am glad to serve with Captain Clark who recently won the men's love when we were facing a line of Confederates across a farmer's field. With both sides behind breastworks, a sheep unwisely walked between the lines. Captain Clark shot the sheep and jumped out on the field in front of hundreds of armed men to drag him back to our works. Out of respect for other hungry soldiers the Confederates ceased firing to allow him to complete the exercise before commencing to fight again. You may not believe it but it happened.

Yours always,
H. Overstreet

CHAPTER TEN

†

January 8, 1864
Waldoborough
Dear Henry—

    I can write about nothing except the passing of my mother from this earth, which occurred just five days ago, making the new year no cause for celebration. She left as quietly and kindly as she dwelled among us. I am glad she will not have to shiver through another winter struggling for air and worn to the bone, though I miss her keenly and am so sorry she won't greet spring with us. If there is any justice she knows a much better world, one where she can take full breaths for the first time in years and lie back and sleep calmly. She was the best of mothers and I shall think on her example every day that I have left to live.

    We buried her yesterday. Father and Theodore burned a fire on the gravesite for a full day and then dug the grave themselves. We have cried ourselves dry and then we cry more, even Father. The lumber mill brought a coffin and didn't charge him. The minister says it's a sin to abandon myself to my grief and to neglect my father and my brother and sisters but I care little for his words. It can be no sin to ache for the one who gave me life and whose love overlooked my faults and ever warmed my heart. Her loss makes me hurt. I will not be able to teach this winter but at least I know that you are in winter quarters. Please, Henry, be safe.

Yours always,
Katherine Nash

January 30, 1864
Rappahannock Station, Virginia
Dear Katie—

Yours of January 8 and its news about your mother have made me sad. I knew her but little but saw much to admire and know that she raised the best of daughters and could have been of no less quality. The loss of an excellent mother is as hard a thing as I have known but I also know that the pain will grow less though it never ends entirely.

We have had quiet times here in the land of solid cabins, soft bread, and daily drills. The men amuse themselves with jokes and pranks that may not seem funny if you haven't been in the army for months on end with nothing but other soldiers around you with their rough sense of humor. Here is an example. A new recruit arrived—we now get them inserted into the regiment to make up the losses of men in battle and to sickness. He said he was troubled by the prospect of having to stand on a picket post and the boys realized he did not understand that it refers to serving as a guard who watches for the enemy. The men kindly offered to set up a picket post for him to practice standing on. They planted a post in the ground with a sharpened point at the top and allowed him to climb up on it and balance there for nearly two hours, to the hearty compliments of all his comrades who admired his nimble abilities. Some still laugh over that one.

I just broke off writing for a while because we were visited by a sing which is when a group of men goes from tent to tent and sing good old songs sometimes hymns too. We join in whether we know the songs or not and the singing can keep us warm and help us remember home. I favor the sad ones which seem to take away my low feelings. I am not proud of my singing but I joined in on Johnny is Gone for a Soldier and Just Before the Battle Mother which moves all who have been through those moments. We finished with Gay and Happy Still so the men tried to put smiles on their faces.

I have real news for you that I have been saving through all this palaver. The army has started granting two-week furloughs to go home. The word is that if we reenlist for three more years then we can get the furloughs plus another bounty. The reenlistment can't happen until a soldier has served two years which I will reach in the summer so I hope I will come see you in the summer. The thought of it makes my feelings light. Serving three more years is not my favorite thought but the war certainly cannot last that long since both sides will run out of men before then. I know I must see the war through no matter how long it lasts so I might as well reenlist. Our army looks better every day which the other side must know and now we will have General Grant to lead us and he is a hard-fighting man of the kind we never had.

Yours always,
H. Overstreet

March 3, 1864
Waldoborough
Dear Henry—

I fear I have neglected our correspondence because my spirits have been low and I did not want to inflict those on you. I am ashamed to say that I have done nothing these last two months with the Soldiers' Aid Society. It has been all that I could do to look after the family that my mother has left behind. The cold of the winter has not let up. Last week the mercury was so low that no one went outside for two full days. I notice the days grow longer and my spirits rise with the additional light. At the end of the day I look outside and think it is better that the world is still lit.

The news of your furlough is the finest I have received in ever so long, but I don't want to rely on it until you know for sure it will happen. I don't want to be disappointed but I hope you can come home. I have just been thinking that I should try to find a teaching contract in the spring to rouse myself from this sadness and become a worthy companion by the time you return.

Yours always,
Katherine Nash

April 8, 1864
Rappahannock Station, Virginia
Dear Katie—

I have yours of March 3 and am glad to hear that you are considering teaching this spring which will be a tonic for you as your young scholars will not allow time for sadness. Joe Maxwell says that here in the army we do so much drilling to prevent us sitting around and thinking gloomy thoughts but I think maybe that is simply what Joe would do and maybe not what others would. It may be from all the drilling but the army looks better. New recruits arrive all the time and bands play music of an evening. The music is sweet and stirs us so Joe and I go to listen.

Some of the boys are demon baseball players and knock each other about pretty brisk but I never got the hang of the game and this seems an odd place to start on it. We are now having target practice three times a week after serving almost two years in the army. I always puzzled that the government would give us rifles and send us off to shoot our fellow men but never help us become marksmen. We compete with each other now in shooting contests. The city men from Boston and New York have trouble keeping up because this is the first time they can learn shooting though I hear some of the New York boys are good with knives especially the Irish. I'm a pretty good shot though some from the woods who hunt squirrels and other small things are better.

We know General Grant means to fight and to win this war and we are behind him. I hope we can do it this campaign season. We know the other side will fight like madmen as they always do but we also know that we fight for liberty and must prevail.

Yours always,
H. Overstreet

April 30, 1864
Waldoborough
Dear Henry—

The newspapers say that your army will begin the great drive to Richmond. That news excites me because our hopes go with you and, as you say, the sooner you win the war the sooner you can come home. But the news also makes me fearful that you and your fellows will suffer more.

There is talk around that General McClellan will run for president as a Democrat against Mr. Lincoln. My father says that Boss Reed is probably the source of such talk and he says it with disgust. It is the first time I have heard him speak of Boss Reed in that way and I wonder at the changes the war makes in all of us. Father also is still sad about my mother. I hope it is not true that General McClellan will be a candidate, as it seems disloyal for him to oppose the war that you are fighting and he did not win. Since he could not win it, it's as though he wants to be sure no one else does.

I have been teaching at the Sampson Cove school which has been the tonic for my spirits that you suggested. I was pleased to see all of the children again but especially the girl I wrote about, the one named Joanna. She came back for the term when she heard I would be there and we are reading a new book by Mr. Dickens called Great Expectations which is very long but full of heart. I hope you will come home soon.

Yours always,
Katherine Nash

May 20, 1864
Waldoborough
Dear Henry—

The reports of your battles are terrifying and I grow frightened when I know I should be strong. We are all on edge hoping that victory will come but fearing the terrible price being paid. Mrs. Benner and I have revived the Soldiers' Aid Society and I am teaching another term but I care about none of it. I must hear from you. Write to me.

Yours always,
Katherine Nash

June 10, 1864
Waldoborough
Dear Henry—

I am coming undone without news. Such blood-shed and battles are described in the newspaper. Every day they say more thousands have been slain but I hear nothing about you. I asked Mr. Edwin Clark at the shipyard and he said that he had word from his brother your captain that the fighting has been vicious and that you have all been in the thick of it but he had no news of you. Why do you not write? I am unable to concentrate on anything and disappoint my scholars daily. This afternoon I washed the same shirt of my father's three times and this evening I burned the biscuits. Theodore has signed papers to serve as a sailor on a schooner in the coasting trade. Father disapproves because he thinks sailors are mistreated by their masters but I think he will consent as it will keep Theodore out of the army. I could not bear having both you and Theodore in peril. However ill or wounded you may be I must hear from you or I shall go mad.

Yours always,
Katherine Nash

June 24, 1864
Waldoborough
Dear Henry—

I can bear this silence no longer. If I have no letter from you by Independence Day, I have resolved to travel to Washington City and find you. I have told no one of this plan but I have saved the money. Write to me.

Yours always,
Katherine Nash

TELEGRAM

From: H. Overstreet

To: K. Nash

Have two-week furlough. In Waldoborough July 1 or thereabouts.

CHAPTER ELEVEN

✝

Mostly free of lice and wearing clean underclothes for the first time in a month, Henry stood at the steamboat rail to take in New York's harbor. The voyage from City Point in Virginia had been much rougher than his southward journey two years before. Over the last two days, thunderclouds gathered in late afternoon, then erupted in shattering booms and rain that drummed on the ship's decks and roof. Henry gloried in the storms, their natural power so impersonal and majestic. Mostly he loved being sheltered and dry while the heavens raged. Since his hospital spell eighteen months before, he hadn't been under a solid roof during a storm. Even tossing on a ragged sea, he felt snug and secure.

The harbor swirled with activity on the muggy morning. Small steamboats belched smoke. Wooden sailing vessels slid with quiet majesty. A brown haze hung over Manhattan Island. Henry brushed debris from his tunic and straightened it.

"Aye, it's a dirty place, it is," said a lean, red-faced private next to him, "but it's home."

Henry nodded at him. "You live in the city?"

"Bang in the center, sergeant. Over near the East River." He tilted his head to the right. "I had to go to war to find out how much space there is in the rest of the country. When I was coming up, we had no idea."

Henry squinted at the island before him. Buildings filled the shoreline and stretched into the island as far as he could see. To the right, another shoreline looked the same. The shore on his left had more green. "You back for good?" Henry asked.

The man turned his torso, revealing an empty sleeve on his right side. "Not much use to the army anymore." He looked back at the city. "But I'll only stay long enough to say hello to my sisters, buy regular clothes, and head out west."

"West, you say? To do what?"

"I'll be figuring that out when I get there."

Henry smiled and gave his name. The man—Patrick O'Neill—took Henry's outstretched hand with his own left. "I guess," Henry said, "we've all got some figuring out to do."

When Henry reached the end of the gangplank, he found O'Neill waiting for him. "Can I help with where you're going?"

"I need the trains to New England. The New Haven railroad—that's what they said I should look for."

"You sound like a man in a hurry. Must have a girl to see." Henry felt himself blush, which brought a smile to O'Neill's face. "We're right at the bottom of the island here," he said. "The Bowery's there." O'Neill pointed his chin. "Broadway's the ticket for you, straight uptown to 26th Street. There's an omnibus that'll take you up there for a dime, or you can walk if you have the time. It's a bit over two miles. Not even three."

"We're used to doing that much before breakfast, aren't we?"

O'Neill grinned. "Have a care, sergeant. You know what they say about the evils of the city. It's mostly true." He waved, shouldered his bag, and strode off.

Henry hoisted his knapsack and started for Broadway. The street overflowed with people of all ages, sizes, colors. They all hustled and carried and pushed, walking with purpose. No one looked Henry in the eye or wished him good day. They had business that needed attending to.

Despite the tumult, the city didn't impress him the way it might have before the war. Just weeks ago, he'd seen more men on the battlefield at Spotsylvania. He saw so many corpses at Cold Harbor that he could have walked for a half a mile without his feet touching the ground. Four bloody battles in the last eight weeks. Company E had buried ten more soldiers, most of them recruits. One hadn't been new—Joe Maxwell, half his face shot off at the Wilderness, then singed in the fires that roasted both lines through a hellish day. After Joe died, Henry became a sleepwalker, seeing only two types of soldiers – haunted ghosts like him or new faces that knew nothing. He shook his head to push those thoughts from his mind.

Henry wrinkled his nose as the air grew ripe. Buildings were blocking the shore breeze. New York could match the vile smells of army camps. A large pig, snuffling and snorting, brushed his leg. Three more trotted past. Even the pigs had business to attend to. Henry stepped carefully over cobbles, edging around piles of manure, toward a wooden walkway that could be reached only with a leap across a garbage-choked gutter.

At the corner of Broadway, he stopped. A shapeless older woman with white hair stood at a low table that held a basket. A sign offered meat pies for a nickel. The aroma assaulted him. He bought one.

Henry groaned with pleasure with his first bite. The flavor was rich. She must have used lard for the crust. Gravy and meat juices filled his mouth. He chewed slowly, relishing every flavor. It was still warm. He couldn't remember anything tasting so good. The second bite was better. Sooner than he thought possible, he was licking each finger and sidling back toward the woman. He saw that she'd been pretty once.

"Another?" she asked.

Henry nodded and reached for the coin. "I've never eaten anything like it."

The old woman smiled, revealing a dimple in one cheek. "You soldier boys are easy pickings. None of you's eaten anything but hardtack for years."

He eagerly took the pie. She reached out and touched his arm. "You go straight home, now, dearie. I'm sure there's people waiting to see a fine lad like you."

He nodded and said around a full mouth, "Yes, ma'am." He swallowed. "On my way."

Broadway held more people. Many looked ill, pale, down on their luck or worse. Some wore fine clothes and stepped into black carriages. He paused at the famous Winter Garden Theater. He had read in the newspaper that Edwin Booth, the great actor, performed there, but a sign said it was closed for the week in honor of Independence Day.

Sweat soaked into Henry's uniform. The crowds and buildings made a warm morning warmer. He started to feel queasy, off his feed. A trace of irritation came into his mind. All these people, all with somewhere to be and something to do. It looked so normal, as though great armies of men weren't slaughtering each other a few hundred miles away. His irritation mounted and came close to anger.

He wasn't being fair, he thought. Most of these people couldn't be soldiers. They were too weak or too old or too young or too sick. But still it stuck in his craw. Not so much that they weren't with the army, but that they didn't seem to know the army existed. Some of these people were probably in the riots just a year before, when thousands rampaged through the streets in a fury that they might be drafted into the army, but no one here seemed angry. Just busy. And indifferent. Henry was glad to pass through.

* * * * *

The hand on his shoulder wasn't unfriendly, nor was the voice. "Waldoborough's right there."

Opening his eyes on fading daylight, Henry focused in stages on Storer's yard. A lantern shone in the office for Clark's yard, next to the town wharf. The deckhand was lowering a sail to slow the mailboat as it neared the town wharf. Henry reached into his knapsack for the letter Captain Clark gave him. He slid the letter into his tunic.

Business looked to be good. Several yards held the upside-down skeletons of ships under construction. He filled his lungs. Waldoborough might be a backwater, but its air was sweet.

Henry pulled his tunic away from his skin, then did the same with his pant legs. After three days of hard travel, he must look as worn as he felt. He had shaved on the mailboat, leaving the imperfect mustache he had recently raised. He wasn't sure it was an improvement. He'd let Katie decide. He certainly stank, just like he had for the last two years. He thought he should go home first and see his father, but he wasn't going to. He smiled to think of Katie. What would he say? What would *she* say? He emptied his mind. They'd think of something.

He dropped the letter off with Edwin Clark, who was working late. Wearing spectacles now, though he couldn't be past thirty-five, Edwin asked after his brother, then caught himself. "I'm sure," he said, "you've got people you'll be wanting to see."

Walking to Main Street, then down to the river, there was no denying it. Nothing had changed. The Fish Block yet stood on the corner, graceless but solid. Winslow's, buttoned up for the evening, still filled most of the first floor. Henry could recite the businesses on the floor above: seamstress, dentist, two lawyers who didn't like each other. The Medomak Hotel was next door, high windows refracting the gas lights of the parlor.

A team of tired horses pulled an empty wagon across the bridge and up towards him. The farmer on the seat let his head droop. His team probably knew the way home as well as he did.

The Nash home looked no different when he got there. Mr. Nash opened the door, holding a newspaper and his pipe in the same hand. He smiled and held out his free hand. "Henry, come in," he said.

Katie flew from the kitchen and into his arms, spinning him partway around. He held her, aware that Mr. Nash was close but not caring. He couldn't speak. He felt her tears on his neck and feared he would weep too. Her sisters stepped out from the kitchen, noting every detail. They were inches taller now, becoming women.

Mr. Nash spread his arms to herd his other daughters. "Why don't we see to matters in the kitchen," he said.

Katie said his name over and over. His cheeks were wet. He cleared his throat and leaned back to study her face. "It feels like a dream," he said.

She moaned, low, and looked up, then hugged him again.

"You're my dream come true," he whispered into her ear. She said his name. He had never liked the sound so much.

After another minute, her grip began to relax. She leaned back and rubbed her eyes. "I don't seem to control my feelings very well."

"Thank God for that, Katie girl."

Hands clasped behind his neck, she gave him an appraising look. His skin, usually fair, was red-brown. The mustache was new, scrawny. His expression, his features, were spare, hard. His body was thinner and harder too. But his eyes, those pale blue eyes, they were the same. And it was Henry behind them. She was sure of that. "I've been trying to meet the boats like a ship captain's wife," she said, "but I had to make dinner, and then Theodore argued with father and spilled the potatoes and stomped off." Henry put his finger to her lips. Then he kissed her, gently. Then more firmly. They embraced again, not as desperately.

"I'm really very angry with you," she said. "I had no letter for nearly three months. Every time I saw a newspaper, there was a new battle, a new list of casualties. I thought I would lose my mind."

His smile was tight.

"Why didn't you write?"

He shook his head. "I couldn't." He looked away and then back. "You have to be my place away from it." He looked toward the kitchen. "I should say something to your father."

She made a face. "After two years, you can't wait to speak to my father?"

"I should say something about your mother. Then perhaps you would go for a walk with me?"

Surprised by Henry's focus on her father, Katie couldn't think of an objection. As she stepped away, her hand ran down his arm, then her fingers twined with his. "I'll send him out here and finish cleaning up."

When they were out on the road, holding hands as they walked, Henry apologized for being so dirty. He promised to clean up at home.

"Have you seen your father?" Katie asked.

"Not before you."

She smiled. "Do you know what a nice thing that is?"

"I'm not so dense as you think."

"I'll marry you, Henry. If you want."

He laughed out loud. She grabbed his tunic and shook him. "Don't laugh. That's a very impolite response to a lady who has just offered herself so shamelessly."

He took her in his arms again. "It's a lucky thing I just asked for your father's consent."

Her eyes grew wide, then narrowed. "I don't need his consent. He's not marrying you."

"That's a burden off my mind."

They laughed and embraced again, then kissed with energy Henry didn't know he had.

"When?" she said.

"Tomorrow." He gazed into her eyes. "I have to go back."

She nodded, instantly near weeping. She touched his mustache with a fingertip. "When did you grow this?"

"Stopped shaving altogether about a month ago. Looked like a beast according to Captain Clark. I shaved off everything else for you." He cocked his head. "You decide if this stays."

"No, I won't. It's your face and your lip."

"But you're the one who has to look at it and kiss it." His smile looked sad to her. "As long as you can stand to."

CHAPTER TWELVE

†

His father's voice was soft. "Henry," he said. "Son, it's a poor idea to sleep through your wedding." A hand shook his shoulder.

Henry stretched in the bed, luxuriating in how dry it was, how it yielded to his body yet cushioned it. What a brilliant invention a bed was. What genius it embodied. After rolling on his side, he squinted up.

"It's after ten," Lewis Overstreet said, "and there's a few things need seeing to." Henry groaned and sat up. "Well, since you ask," his father continued, "so far this morning—and it's after ten, did I mention that?—you've had three callers. First was Mrs. Castle, who promptly seized your army uniform, which was lying on the floor where you dropped it when you stumbled in last night and requested a bath. She promised to freshen it up in time for the ceremony. I would describe her conduct as high-handed but well-intentioned.

"Then there was George Young, who used to work with you? He expressed a strong wish to get you roaring drunk before the ceremony, insisting it would improve your future happiness. I promised to convey his message but not to endorse it. He said he would return by three with a jug.

"Finally, Theodore Nash, the brother of my future daughter-in-law, said that you and the young lady are to meet with the minister of their Methodist congregation, Mr. Jenkins, at noon at the church on Friendship Road. Because you should look respectable so as not to embarrass the soon-to-be Mrs. Overstreet, I thought to intrude on your sleep."

Sitting up, Henry accepted the mug of coffee that his father offered. The hot acrid liquid brought his mind alive. His father believed in strong coffee. "I need to go to Ralph's and tell him."

"No time for that, but as luck would have it, your brother and his family are planning to come to Waldoborough for the celebration of today's holiday and to see their ancient relative—that would be me—and in the hope that you would have wandered home by today. They may not be dressed exactly as they would prefer for a wedding, but they are a presentable family. I expect a scolding from Lucy for the lack of warning, but I withstood worse from your mother."

Henry looked up and nodded. "I should go see her."

"Katie will be at the minister's."

"No, I meant Ma."

His father sat on the chair against the wall across from Henry's bed. His expression didn't change, but his voice did. "Yes. I've been thinking of her."

"I'll stop on my way to the church." Henry stood and stretched. "I thought we'd get married with about three people there. How did all this hubbub happen? It was only last night she said yes."

"Folks have been expecting you since your telegram. You should know that army telegrams are hardly secrets. More like public announcements." He passed a hand through his hair. The white had spread up and back from his temples. His cheeks seemed heavier, the lines beside his nose and mouth deeper. He still moved and spoke as he always had, quietly but quickly. "Mrs. Castle claims she's expected this for several months, which reflects a female way of thinking. Perhaps the Soldiers Aid Society ladies have had the same expectation."

"I'm not sure I've ever spoken to those ladies."

"They dote on your future wife. As they should." His father

stood and smiled. "Now, I'll start the water on the stove for your bath. You can wear your old suit to see the minister. I pulled it out. It may be a bit roomy on you now."

"Thanks, Pa. I'm sorry to bring this on so fast."

His father smiled. "That's the silliest apology I ever heard. This is the best day I've had in some time. You know you've caught a prize, not that I'm surprised. Overstreet men marry up. Now you need to get a move on."

Henry left Cricket to crop the grass at the edge of the burial ground. No Overstreet rested in the German cemetery. A few of them might have been able to pay for plots on the lowest level there, with no view of the river. They might even have put up stone markers. But they'd always left that ground to the shipyard owners, the merchants, the strivers. The view from this smaller cemetery, which had no name, was of fields on three sides and the road before it. It was quiet.

Taking off his hat, Henry stopped at a stone on the righthand side, at the back with the more recent graves. The chiseled letters carried his mother's name, the dates of her forty-one years. It said she had been a cherished wife and mother. He wished there was more. He remembered so much about her. She was always knitting or sewing or gardening or fixing something. She often hummed to herself. His father would rest at the end of his day's work at the shipyard, reading or staring into the night, watching the trees sway in the breeze. But his mother was always busy. He remembered her touch on his cheek. She often smelled wonderful. Probably, he thought, kitchen smells that a hungry boy would love.

He jumped and turned at a bang, his heart racing, reaching for a rifle that wasn't there. A wagon on the road had bounced through a deep rut. Drawing a breath, he turned back. What could you tell of a life on a piece of stone?

She liked a party, especially a family party. Her face lit up when there was music. He stood for a long while, trying to hear her voice.

Stepping inside the heavy doors to the whitewashed church, Henry instantly disliked the minister. The man had an angular build. His mouth curled up at one end, a smile or a sneer, or both. He greeted Henry by inclining his head. Neither of them extended a hand.

"I understand," the minister began, "that you and your family are not regular members of any congregation."

"Nope," Henry said. "When my mother was alive, we went to the German meeting, but then we lost the habit." He looked at the man. "I haven't had much chance to attend services for the last couple of years."

The man nodded and let the silence settle. He was either a Copperhead, Henry figured, or in thrall to the Copperheads in his congregation. Henry said he'd wait outside for Katie. The minister said he would be in his office.

Henry smiled when Mr. Nash drove up in their wagon, Katie on the high board next to him. She was worth it all. For her, he could survive anything.

The minister warmed slightly for the Nashes. He asked Henry about his plans for church attendance following the wedding.

"Parson," Henry said, "in a week I'll be back with my regiment. That occupies a man's mind. Plans'll come after the war."

"Men in the army should be especially concerned about the state of their souls."

"There's parsons in the army. Some are brave, stay close to us, near the fighting." Henry and the minister locked eyes. "They've left safe places far from the war."

Mr. Nash cleared his throat. "Katie," he said, "had some ideas about a hymn we might sing before the vows. She'd like things simple."

When Henry walked Katie back to the wagon, she asked if there was something between him and the minister. Henry shrugged. "I won't be so ornery later," he said. "It'll be fine."

She squeezed his hand. "I know who I'm marrying, Henry Overstreet. You show up and say the right words, and I'll get the ornery out of you."

Henry grinned and put his hat on.

* * * * *

Through the service, he concentrated on Katie, barely aware of anyone else. She wore a cream-colored dress that had been her mother's. His eyes lingered on the snug bodice and flaring skirt. Her dense hair, dark against her fair skin, was parted in the center with a braid that crossed the crown of her head, leaving her neck exposed. She carried roses provided by Henry's father—he had removed the thorns from the stems. Henry was transfixed by the slight tremble in her hand, the single tear that formed at the corner of her eye and slipped slowly down her cheek as the minister droned on. Henry had no ring of his own to give her, so he presented one of his mother's. It was silver, not gold, and hadn't been her wedding ring. His brother used that one to marry Lucy. But Katie proclaimed it perfect. He vowed to replace it when he could.

His focus on her broke once. The minister began wishing the couple a life of peace and happiness and then extolled the virtues of a peace that spread throughout the land. Henry felt his hackles rise. He was wearing his army uniform, a sergeant's chevrons on the sleeves. He was a man of war. George Young stood nearby, a husk of his former self owing to his military service. Was the minister inserting a Copperhead dig? A veiled reference to Ralph's desertion?

Henry looked over to the pastor as the man continued his praise of peace. Henry made himself listen to the words. They echoed slightly in the nearly empty church.

"The Scriptures say through Isaiah that you will go out in joy and be led forth in peace; the mountains and hills will burst into song before you and all the trees of the field will clap their hands. But we know also about the shadow that lies over this land, that today's generations know troubles that have not been visited on many generations, have suffered from them, and will continue to suffer from them. Men have been torn by shells and charred by fire and laid low by pestilence. Hate and rage have seized hearts and divided families. They have set neighbor against neighbor. As we celebrate this union and as we join with the trees of the field in clapping our hands for Katherine and Henry, may we also wish that they and their issue will never again know such evils."

Amen, Henry thought, his hackles descending. He was just tetchy, he decided. He wouldn't resent paying the man's tip.

"So, lad," George Young said in front of the church as he pumped Henry's hand. "You giving up your independence on Independence Day. I'm not sure that's what Washington and his men had in mind."

"Now, now, George," brother Ralph broke in. "Think of the advantages of having this wedding day. Henry'll never forget what day he was married, and every year the whole country'll set off fireworks in celebration. I think it's very shrewd."

Three of the Soldiers Aid Society ladies assembled the wedding supper at the Nash home. Henry laughed to see his father's succotash on the table. "Pa," he said, "am I never to escape it?"

"Just try it," his father said. "I've changed it."

With a shrug, Henry did. He took a second bite and shrugged again. "Maybe two years in the army has killed my taste sense."

"You see, Katie," Mrs. Castle spoke from a corner chair, "how easy it'll be, married to a soldier? Everything will taste good to him."

George Young produced two jugs of home-brewed whiskey and passed them around to the gentlemen. "In this state," he proclaimed, "this form of contraband should be in the widest circulation!" Frowning, the minister stepped from the room.

Mrs. Castle asked for some of the brew. "If it has the power to spare us that man's fish-eyed looks," she confided to George, "then it has considerable virtues."

Soon, those two were leading the party in song, Mrs. Castle mildly tight and George thoroughly so. Henry shared his whiskey with Katie. She handled it easily. Perhaps, he thought, she wasn't entirely Methodist.

When the singers took a break and Katie left for the back of the house, George draped an arm over Henry's shoulder. Before the war, that arm would have been heavy, connected to a powerful trunk.

"Now, Corporal Overstreet," George began in an intimate whisper that doubtless carried farther than intended.

"Sergeant Overstreet, George."

"*Sergeant* Overstreet, well, would you be surprised to hear that this town has started paying a two-hundred-and-fifty-dollar bounty to each man who enlists?"

Henry was surprised.

"It's true, ask anyone here. And do you think they're going to give any of us that two hundred and fifty dollars, even though we answered the call of our country two years before? Not a chance, my good friend, not one chance in the world." He stared down at Henry. "And don't it just make your blood boil."

Henry forced himself to smile, though his blood was rising above its normal temperature. "I suppose virtue is its own reward," he managed to say.

"Ah," George picked up again, "speaking of virtue, perhaps you'll confide in your old friend about those sweet Virginia belles. I never had the chance to know them, yet I hear they're becoming more receptive of Union boys."

Henry slipped out from under George's arm and gripped the man's shoulder to be sure he remained upright. "They're not so desperate yet as to spend time with any boys from Maine," he said, "not so's I noticed."

"Ah," George said, laying an index finger beside his nose, "wrong time and place. Mum's the word."

"George Young," said his wife, placing a firm hand under her husband's elbow. She had been quiet much of the afternoon. "It's time to leave these people to their wedding night." George began to object that the sky was still bright, but Katie's emergence in her traveling dress confirmed Mrs. Young's sense of timing.

In the wagon, Katie held Henry's arm and rested her head on his shoulder. They passed a few remarks about the day. The wedding night would be at Ralph's farm, while Ralph's family stayed with their father. Then Lewis Overstreet would leave his house to the newlyweds until Henry returned to the war.

It was dark when Henry and Katie neared Rockport. When the half-moon showed the outlines of Ralph's house, Katie sat up. "So have your father and brother given you advice for tonight?"

"Tonight?"

Katie extended a hand to the house. "Tonight."

"Oh. Not the old man. He's pretty proper."

"Not like George Young."

"I didn't think you could hear him."

"He's easy to hear." She gripped his arm again. "And your brother?"

"He said I should resist any temptation to make a joke."

"Really."

Henry pulled on the left rein to encourage Cricket through the opening in the stone wall that bordered the road. "Says he nearly ruined the night. It may have had to do with the special circumstances of their wedding, but he was emphatic."

"All right, then. No jokes, though I hope we can smile."

"And what advice have you received?"

"Without a mother or an older sister, I had only Mrs. Castle."

"I'd take advice from her."

"She said we should relax. The animals of the fields manage it, so we should do fine."

Henry pulled the horse up, then leaned over to kiss her. "Smart woman."

* * * * *

The days sped by. They followed Mrs. Castle's advice. Henry slept heavily at night and napped some days. He felt lightheaded much of the time, drunk on Katie, on her touch and her warmth. Entering her, knowing her, was the greatest thrill. When they finished, he wondered how soon they might again. Why would they do anything else?

In truth, he did little else. On the third day, they walked into town from his father's house because they had eaten everything in the kitchen.

Henry waited for Katie on Main Street, leaning back against the wall outside Winslow's. Several men stopped to wish him well, then asked about the war. Henry pushed their questions aside. One man persisted. He asked about the long casualty lists in the newspapers. "How can there be so many?" he asked. It was driving up the price they had to pay in bounties for new soldiers. What was going on?

"It's war," Henry said, speaking slowly. "The longer it goes on, the better we get at the killing part."

The men nodded, waiting for more. Henry suddenly wanted them to know.

"Take Cold Harbor," he said. The men leaned in. "Before one of the charges, in the regiment next to us, the men wrote down their names and their hometowns on pieces of paper and pinned them to their breasts, so their families could be notified of their deaths. Then they marched off and charged uphill into the guns just like they were told." He was suddenly angry. "But we enlisted early, so you got us at a bargain price, before the bounties went higher, so we're not so much of a loss."

The men shifted uneasily, looking at their feet. Two of them touched their hats and began to walk away. The persistent one leaned toward Henry. "Friend," he said, "I didn't mean anything by it."

Henry brought his eyes back to the man.

"Mr. Embry," Katie said as she came out of the store. "How are you?" Henry took her parcel from her.

"I'm fine," the man said to her, lifting his hat and forcing a smile. "I wish you both much happiness."

The newlyweds walked back up the river in silence. After a ways, Katie said, "Mr. Embry riled you."

Henry kicked a rock. "People should let me alone about the war." Katie kept walking. "Do you know," he asked, "how many of us are left in Company E—left from when we started?" She shook her head.

"Sixteen," he said, "out of a hundred or so."

A large, mud-colored dog ran at them and barked furiously. "Duke!" a deep voice called from inside a nearby house. "Duke! You get your sorry ass in here." The dog retreated slowly. "Duke! Don't keep me waiting."

"You see," Henry said, "it's just luck. Every time you face the guns you use up some. It runs out. We all know it." He looked off ahead of them. "No point talking about it."

He left on the eleventh of the month. If he'd missed any of his travel connections, he might've been late getting back to camp, but he wouldn't mind coming back late. Some soldiers didn't come back at all, which Henry thought about when he lay with Katie on that final morning.

She didn't cry or carry on when the packet boat to Boston began to load. He didn't think she would. Her cheeks were red. Her eyes were full of feeling. Her voice faltered once, but then she got it back. "Come home as soon as you can, Henry," she said when the gangplank was laid.

"Yes," was all he said. Then he kissed her. From the stern rail, he watched her form on the wharf grow smaller and smaller. Then she disappeared behind a turn in the bay.

CHAPTER THIRTEEN

†

July 13, 1864
Waldoborough
Dear husband—

It made me smile to write those two words. We are so fortunate to have come together. I thought our marriage might make the waiting easier but it's the reverse. Now I know more of you that I miss. I do not complain. It's what Shakespeare called "sweet sorrow." But know that this heart on the Maine coast beats only for you.

I have little news. It feels peculiar to be back in my family's house, in my old room, with my old chores. The only difference—and it is a difference—is that everyone calls me Mrs. Overstreet. My father does it with a smile and my sisters and brother do it with a smirk and the people in the town do it while tipping their hats. I enjoy it. I've just been to see Mrs. Castle, who seems to have come down with the grippe. Her chest is wheezy but she waves off any expressions of concern. She is so small and yet so strong. She is marvelous. I wonder if when you get to her age you just expect to survive the things that bring other people low.

Now that I am a wife, I find the prices being charged to be scandalous. Slocum was asking eight dollars a pound for bacon the other day, which should be a crime, like the fifteen dollars a pound he wants for butter. Your father dropped some butter off that he brought back from your brother's farm, which was a treat for all of us. He is a dear man.

I have decided to seek another teaching contract for the fall. The war cannot go forever but it seems sure to last through then, and father has agreed that any money I earn should be saved for us to start our own home. I'll buy some food for the family, of course, but I'll also hold out some for you and me.

Please write, Henry my husband.

Yours always,
Katherine Overstreet, your wife

August 6, 1864
Before Petersburg, Virginia
Dear wife—

I have yours of July 13 which is even more precious to me as it comes from my wife. The last few days have been quiet. We sit in trenches across from rebels who are dug in too. Neither side shoots much by silent agreement among the soldiers. It has been hot and dry which makes the trenches dusty especially when the wind blows and raises swarms of flies which afflict us especially when we eat which is when the flies also wish to eat.

It seems our generals are trying to find a way to attack that doesn't include sending us across open ground against the fortified enemy which is what we did through May and June and which was not successful. Nearly a week ago there was an explosion under the rebel lines that some men thought was an earthquake. It sent men and guns and wagons and dirt up into the sky as though it was the end of days. It came from a tunnel that our men dug underneath the enemy and it must have blown hundreds to kingdom come. The noise was enough to make you deaf and it left a giant hole in the ground they call the crater. We were some distance away in a trench and had no idea it was going to happen. Other regiments attacked the rebels after the blast but they tried to go through the crater and got stuck at the bottom which turned into a regular turkey shoot for the rebels looking down on our poor men so that's another idea that didn't work out.

There are some signs that maybe the rebels are having their fill of fighting. Last night we received ten deserters from their side and Captain Clark says the rebels are having trouble with that. We sometimes have the same trouble but I think it's worse for them. With Sherman invading Georgia and with us having them cornered here before Petersburg they must be starting to wonder how they can win, at least I hope they are. But as the minister said at the wedding there is a lot of hate loose in the land and that hate can overpower men's thinking.

There is good news which is that we got paid. As a newly married man and inspired by your plan to teach this fall I am saving some for us and spending only a bit on doughnuts and tobacco and coffee and sugar which are close to necessities at least some of the time.

I have now wrote everything in this letter I could think of to put off this moment, which is the moment when the new husband writes proper sentiments about his new wife that will reach across the miles between us and make her smile and wish for him to be close by, as near and as gentle as the morning fog coming from the sea. I fear you have struck a poor bargain in this marriage while I have made off with the prize. I spoke little about the fighting part of the war which I don't want you to know and which I don't know if I can keep on with now with my mind and my heart always with you. I have more to fight for—for your good opinion of me most of all—but also more to lose. I understand better how

Ralph chose how he did. I swear you will never have to say or think your husband lived or died a coward and you should know that your smile and grace were in his mind however the battle raged.

Yours always,
H. Overstreet, your husband

September 4, 1864
Waldoborough
Dear Henry—

I have no letter from you since you left Waldoborough but cannot fail to write on the occasion of the fall of Atlanta. This is news of the finest kind. I now wish for General Sherman and his men to sweep all the Confederates from the field while your army sits somewhere very peaceful. My father says, however, that General Grant will never sit quietly anywhere and that the war cannot be won until Lee is defeated. I hope he is wrong.

I have secured a teaching position in Bremen which pays slightly better than my last. It is farther to travel in the morning and home in the evening but the extra money makes it worth it. With prices so high, I may not save much. I am sorry not to have the chance to teach Joanna, who was my fine scholar from last year's classes in Sampson Cove, but have been so pleased that she has come to several meetings of the Soldiers Aid Society. She has a brother in the war in the Twenty-First Regiment and is skilled with a needle and thread for one so young. I have thought of introducing her to my brother Theodore when he comes back from his voyaging but you know that the life of a sailor is unpredictable and I'm not sure he is worthy of her. The only man in town I would deem worthy of her is one H. Overstreet and he is firmly taken.

I am writing nonsense here, I know, because writing to you makes me feel better and you say you like my letters. Write to me soon, Henry.

Yours always,
Katherine Overstreet, your wife

October 4, 1864
Before Petersburg, Virginia
Dear Mrs. Overstreet—

You should receive this letter by hand from my brother, Edwin Clark, who I believe has made your acquaintance. I send it by him in hopes that it will get to you more quickly than otherwise. I am sorry to inform you that your husband, Sergeant Henry Overstreet, has been injured in the vigorous fighting at Peebles Farm several days ago. As has always been the case with Sergeant Overstreet, he was performing his duties with great bravery. Shot from an enemy cannon struck him in the side. It is a serious wound. He was taken to a field hospital and will shortly be removed to a hospital in Washington City. I have not seen him since his injury but have a report that he bears his wound with courage. I pray for his swift recovery and equally swift return to you and others who care for him.

Respectfully,
A. Clark, Captain, 20th Maine Volunteers

BOSTON DAILY ADVERTISER

OCTOBER 3, 1864

THE ADVANCE ON RICHMOND

GENERAL WARREN LEADS FIFTH CORPS

SUCCESSFUL ATTACK TOWARD THE SOUTHSIDE RAILROAD DEFENSES

IMPORTANT OPERATIONS OF THE ARMY OF THE POTOMAC

THE ENEMY'S LINE AT PEEBLES FARM CARRIED

Before Petersburg, October 1st. Details are still emerging about a major advance under General Warren with troops of the Fifth and Ninth Corps to the west below Petersburg in the continuing effort to cut off rail traffic to the Confederate capital. Griffin's brigade began the action yesterday with another move to the left toward the Boydkin Road and beyond it to the Southside Railroad, which has become the lifeline of the Confederate Army dug in at Petersburg.

The army's advance encountered a line of resistance at a place called Peebles Farm, which is a large open area surrounded on all four sides by the pine woods that cover most of the land in this part of the South. The enemy had built fortifications on the western edge of the area at the crest of a gentle rise. A brigade of the Fifth Corps commanded by General Griffin formed a line across the field and began a half-mile charge on the far fort, which included artillery as well as infantry defenders.

With whoops and shouts and flags waving, the soldiers set forth gallantly, moving quickly across the field in a sight that would stir the most jaded heart. The lines of brave men paused in a slight ravine at the center of the field, then with cheers charged up the rise into the mouths of cannon and the teeth of enemy musket fire. The firing by both armies was furious and blood was spilt on all sides and many a bold man in blue fell. Owing to the audacity and valor of the charging brigade, they carried the works and overwhelmed the defenders, who turned and ran.

Ninth Corps units under General Parke took up the advance and moved out smartly toward the Boydkin Road but ran headfirst into a spirited Confederate counterattack, which sent the troops moving smartly back toward whence they came. General Griffin positioned his men and cannon on a small prominence within the woods and was able to stop the enemy advance in a sharp engagement that was not decided until the two foes grappled hand to hand and bayonet to bayonet. The fight was a stern test of will between the armies. Ultimately, the men of the Fifth Corps sent the enemy streaming backwards, ending the counterattack.

General Grant and General Meade performed a horseback review of the victorious troops the next morning, hailing their achievement and spurring them on to further flanking moves across the rebel railroad lines. The soldiers cheered lustily for their chiefs. There can be no question that General Grant intends to continue this campaign until General Lee and the Army of Northern Virginia crumble, or he runs out of soldiers, whichever comes first.

The War Department will not release casualty lists for these engagements for several more days yet.

CHAPTER FOURTEEN

†

"**I**'m looking for Sergeant Overstreet with the Twentieth Maine." Katie was relieved that her voice came out steady. Travel fatigue made it difficult to calibrate such things. A middle-aged man with thin hair and spectacles looked across the desk at her.

"How do you spell that?"

Katie spelled Henry's name.

"When was he brought in?"

"It was after Peebles Farm. He was wounded on the thirtieth. How long does it take to get here from Petersburg?"

"Ma'am, anywhere from two days to ten, depending on how long they held him at the field station. I'll start with October second."

The man ran his index finger down successive pages of a leatherbound account book, stopping to lick the fingertip each time he needed to turn the page. The General Office of the Armory Square Hospital was a drab place. Only blocks away, the massive new dome of the Capitol loomed over the city. In the other direction stood the red brick complexity of the Smithsonian Institution. The hospital, however, had the style of a building put together quickly for as little money as possible.

Katie had left the day after reading Captain Clark's letter. Both Henry's father and her own produced money for the journey and then for her to stay in Washington City. No one said that the money could be used to ship Henry's body home, but they all feared it.

Katie had started her search at the War Department office next to the White House, which referred her to the medical service, which gave her a printed list of nearly thirty soldiers' hospitals in Washington. When her eyes filled with tears, a sergeant asked about Henry's wounds and where he was coming from. The wounded from Petersburg came in by steamboat, he said, so her best bet was Armory Square. It was closest to the wharf and dealt with the most injured men, which an artillery casualty would be.

"Overstreet, you say?" The clerk was looking up from his register.

"That's right."

"We've got him. Got here on the eighth." He gave her directions to Ward K and the name of the nurse there, Miss Starrett.

Katie stepped out into a light rain, trusting her cape and bonnet to keep her dry enough. The office building faced a line of unadorned hospital pavilions, perhaps a dozen, built with whitewashed planks. Ward K was at the north end. Katie walked past grass and flowers planted between the wards. When she came through Ward K's door, she faced another desk, this one occupied by a severe-looking woman in a gray dress. Beds extended down both sides of the long ward. Two large stoves stood in the center, stovepipes extending along the ceiling to vent through side walls. A square piano squatted near the stoves. With many windows and gas lighting, the ward was not as dingy as it might have been on a dreary day.

When Katie explained her business, the woman said, "Yes, he's number twenty-two." Katie didn't understand. "I'm sorry," the woman added, "you're new. We use bed numbers to refer to our soldiers. Yours is in number twenty-two. It's on the right-hand side."

"May I see him?"

"Of course. Are you his sister?"

"His wife." She held out her hand. "I'm Katherine Overstreet."

The woman stood and took her hand. "Diana Starrett, nurse for this ward. These are my boys. Number twenty-two is weak. He was badly hurt, and erysipelas may be developing. Please don't agitate him."

Katie wasn't sure where to look as she passed down the rows of beds. On her left men played cards. One sat in a rolling chair. A man in another bed smoked a pipe, his eyes fixed across the room, his hand holding the stump of his other arm. Another walked toward her carrying a bucket. Katie nodded and tried to look pleasant. Number twenty-two. That was all she should think of. She quickened her pace as the numbers climbed. But she didn't need numbers. She would know Henry.

She stopped. Her eyes sought the number, just to be sure. He was lying still, eyes closed. He was shaved, his hair short. One cheek and eyelid were bright pink, almost crusted. She hurried over and knelt, breathing his name softly. Then again. He turned his head and opened his eyes, though one didn't open all the way. He looked at her evenly.

"Are you real?"

She nodded. "Completely." She gripped his arm, letting the tears come.

His eyes closed. He breathed deeply.

"I came as fast as I could. I got the news three days ago. Captain Clark wrote." She stopped herself and reached over to touch his good cheek.

"I thought," he said, looking again through his good eye, "I might've dreamt you."

She leaned over to kiss his forehead. He was hot. "I'm here and I'm not leaving. Then I'll take you home."

He nodded and closed his eyes. She rose and perched a hip awkwardly on the bed, trying not to disturb him. She took his hand.

"He had a pill this afternoon," the nurse said from the foot of the bed. "For the pain."

"How bad is it?" Katie spoke softly, without looking away from him.

"He doesn't complain. They mostly don't. But you can see it in his face."

Katie swiveled to the woman. Mrs. Starrett, she was. "I've cared for the sick before. I'd like to look after him."

"Of course, dear. You might take that cloth on the stand and keep it damp and on his forehead. For the fever."

When Mrs. Starrett brought milk toast for Henry's supper, Katie was at the window, watching the day darken. Low clouds reflected the city's lights. The nurse explained that he was on a special diet because his wound was hard on his insides. Also the opium, which kept those insides from working too well.

"Can you tell me about the wound?"

The nurse sighed and looked at a card that was tied to the end of the bed. "It's his right side." She indicated with her hand, running it from rib cage to hip. "It was a cannon. They jam them full of metal balls—grape, they call it. To do the most damage." She reached and patted his foot. "He had to have been at least a little ways from it or it would have killed him sure. The surgeons dug out as much metal as they could, but the field hospitals are rushed. There may be more. Inside." She sighed. "Cannon wounds are the worst."

"I think he's cooler now."

"Yes. He's lost some of the glow."

"What about the dressing?"

"The cadet surgeon will be by in the morning. That's his job." Mrs. Starrett pushed a strand of hair behind an ear. "I must bring supper to the others. See if he'll eat when he wakes."

"Sleeping is good, right? I haven't waked him."

"Yes. I don't think he knows day and night. I'll ask the orderly to find you a chair." She took a step away and stopped. "Do you have a place to go tonight?"

"I'll find something tomorrow. I'd like to stay with Henry tonight, if it's all right."

"The privy's that way." She pointed. "And if you step to the end on the right, there's a dining area. I'll have them set aside something for you."

At around seven, a soldier rose from the bed opposite her and struggled onto crutches. He made his way to the center of the ward and sat on a stool, then picked up a melodeon that Katie hadn't noticed. He played a few airs, drawing others to him. Some sat on nearby beds. Others leaned against the stoves or walls. Orderlies paused in their duties. With a nod, the melodeon man began "Home Sweet Home," and they all joined in. Then came "Shining Shores," a hymn Katie loved.

"I dreamed you."

She turned and smiled. He looked more like himself. "And here I am." She helped him raise his head to drink water. "Isn't the music fine?" She lost track of the music as they stared at each other. "You must be hungry." She reached for the plate and tore off a piece of milk toast. He opened his mouth for it and seemed to chew and swallow it. She tried another piece, but he was drifting off. She freshened the cloth on his forehead and stroked his hair.

The music had finished when Mrs. Starrett came by and introduced Victor, the night watcher for that half of the ward. He left a blanket for Katie.

Henry cried out in the night but didn't wake. So did others. Katie kept her hand on Henry's arm. She was resting her head on the mattress when he stirred. He was awake. He took some water and another bite of food. When the night watcher came by, Katie smiled at him and said things were fine.

When Katie jolted awake, it was still dark. A wall clock said it was four-thirty. Henry was wincing. His breathing seemed short. He moaned once and raised his right side slightly. "What can I do?" she said. She reached for his side, then stopped her hands, afraid the wound was tender, that her touch would make him howl with pain. He seemed to want to raise the injured side from the bed. She took a towel hanging on the bedstead and folded it, then wedged it under his right hip, trying not to trouble the wound. She grabbed another towel from the next bed over and put it under his right shoulder. His face relaxed and his breathing slowed.

"Better?" she asked.

He nodded. "Thanks, miss."

She leaned over to his ear. "That's missus, Sergeant Overstreet. I'm Katie."

He grunted. "I like you to talk to me like that."

She pulled the chair over with her foot and sat, still leaning in to his ear. "I've missed you so, Henry."

He nodded. "I'm sorry about this."

She stopped the tears. "You can't help being brave and true, Henry. I'm just so glad to be here with you."

He nodded. "You know I dreamt you."

"I know. Now you need to dream that you heal quickly so that will come true too."

He smiled. "Tell me about your trip. Tell it to me like this."
She spoke into his ear. He was soon asleep.

* * * * *

"See here," the surgeon said as he opened the door for her. Katie carried a basket of dirty sheets and shirts for the laundry, where she was helping out. "We have nigras to do that."

"I've always washed sheets," Katie said as she stepped outside. It was a cool day in early November. "How else do they get clean?"

Victor, the heavyset orderly who carried another basket of laundry, grinned over at her as the surgeon let the door slam behind him. "Ma'am," Victor said, "don't most folks talk back to that man."

"Perhaps he'll have me fired."

"I suppose Mrs. Starrett'll settle him down. She the one runs things." Victor hoisted the heavy basket on a meaty shoulder and opened the door to the laundry with his free hand. "How's old twenty-two doing? I saw him eating."

The laundry's damp warmth welcomed them. "I think it's a good day, Victor. This last fever was hard, but his eyes look better."

"That's good, ma'am. Having you look after him'd make any man get healthy fast."

"Why, Victor," she said, "I'm a married woman."

The man laughed, his teeth bright against his dark skin. "Ain't no man as married as I am, but I ain't blind nor deaf either."

The laundry was hard work, but Katie liked it. There was always hot water, so with enough scraping over the washboard, the sheets and shirts got mostly clean. Even bloodstains and shit stains disappeared as she and Victor scrubbed and hauled. Sometimes he sang in his rich baritone. Katie felt cleaner after laundry work.

She was surprised by the care at the Armory Square Hospital. The surgeons were a mixed lot. Dr. Spurgeon, the one she had just passed by, was fussy and indecisive, sometimes carrying liquor on his breath. But Dr. Spencer was smart and cared. Mrs. Starrett couldn't have been more dedicated. Men like Victor swept and built fires. The ward could be noisy. The patients talked too loud, and the staff argued and scolded them; patients moaned and groaned, and instruments and trays and buckets clattered.

Sometimes it sounded more like a train station than a hospital. All that noise couldn't be good for the patients—definitely not the nervous ones. The other day, number nine climbed up on his bed, swinging his stump of an arm and shouting that his hand at the end of that arm was paining him.

Some died. From the new arrivals that week—the newspapers called the fight the Battle of Burgess Mill—three died the first day. Their wounds were terrible and their suffering so great that Mrs. Starrett said that death blessed them. Katie almost agreed.

"Victor," Katie said as he pulled shirts from the tub, squeezing them out before running them through the mangle. She envied his strength. "What about that steward, Mr. Holmes?"

"What about him?"

"The food, I mean. The men complain they're hungry. Not Henry, of course, I'm still waiting for him to be hungry. But the others. You must've heard them."

"Missus, you got to understand, those fellows been through hell, and they don't want to think a second about that mess. And part of that hell wasn't having anything decent to eat. So they get in here and eating and thinking about eating and talking about eating are the things they want to do most."

"Still, Victor." Katie realized the shirt she was scrubbing was clean and began to wring it out. "What about the packages from home that the men say never arrive? They think he's stealing them."

Victor put a finger to the side of his nose and resumed his singing. So it was like that, Katie thought.

After nearly two hours of work, she and Victor were hanging the sheets and shirts on the lines next to Ward K. "Look there," he called over. He nodded toward Seventh Street. A cavalry company, crisp in deep blue uniforms with bright yellow trim, escorted a black carriage. The officer in charge kept his drawn sword against his shoulder. "That's Mr. Lincoln. Wonder if he's coming."

"He does that?" Katie couldn't keep the excitement from her voice.

"Done it twice I know of. They're his boys."

She hurried to Ward K's entrance, where Dr. Spurgeon and Mrs. Starrett stood. "Is Mr. Lincoln coming here? Is he?"

Mrs. Starrett smiled. "They say so. We never know if he'll get this far."

Katie hurried into the ward. She found a rolling chair and pushed it to bed twenty-two. "Mr. Lincoln's outside," she announced.

"I heard," Henry said. "I put on trousers."

Katie beamed. He was as excited as she was. "Let's get you out where you can see him."

Shifting Henry into the chair was awkward, but she did it. She draped a blanket over his shoulders and another over his legs, then muscled him through the ward and out onto the wooden entryway.

The president was stepping out of the hospital's office. He walked to his right, straight toward them, his long legs covering great stretches of ground, his tailcoat flapping in unpredictable directions. His pant legs rode up, and the tails of his necktie streamed over one shoulder. His tall hat perched on the back of his head. Aside from his mismatched outfit, he had an ordinary, everyday look. In different clothes, he could take a place on the walk in front of Winslow's, Katie thought, or stroll into Waldoborough's custom house to complain about a tax bill. She waved and smiled at him, but he strode by to Ward L.

"We'll be next," Mrs. Starrett said. "He's very methodical. He'll work his way down the line until someone comes to make him leave." Other patients began to step through the doorway and sidle along the platform. Katie kept Henry at the front, so the president couldn't miss him. Victor stood to the side with the other black workers.

In a few minutes the tall, dark-coated figure bore down on them, now holding his hat. Dr. Spurgeon greeted him, but the president moved past, saying, "Fine, doctor, but I'm here to see your work." His voice was high for such a big man. He held his hand out to Henry.

"Bless you, soldier, but I'd've come inside to see you."

"He's a sergeant, sir," Katie broke in as Henry took the man's large hand.

The president glanced up at her. "Well, sergeant, you have a fine advocate here."

"I do, sir. This is my wife, Katie." Henry held onto the president's hand as Mr. Lincoln turned to her. "I want to say, sir, I just voted for you even though we come from the rottenest Copperhead town in Maine. There's a lot of us Maine boys here, and we're all for you." Other patients murmured agreement.

The president allowed himself a small smile. "I'm grateful for your vote, sergeant, but you've given me something to take up with Mr. Hamlin. He assures me there aren't three Democrats in your entire state." Through the laugh that passed through the group, he added, "Bless you for your bravery. I hope you mend quickly."

Without seeming to hurry, the president exchanged a word with each man, then stepped inside. Katie pushed Henry's chair through the door so they could watch. Mr. Lincoln worked down one side of the ward and up the other, pausing longest with the soldiers who had strength only to look up at him. He spoke softly to those. He skipped no one, even the ones with vacant looks and no words. He wore a look of care until he turned from a patient who Mrs. Starrett had said wouldn't make it to tomorrow. Katie could see pain in that long, weary face.

When Mr. Lincoln had worked his way back to the front of the ward, he turned to face them. "Thank you all," he said in that high voice, "for your sacrifices. And for reminding me that we must reward those by uniting and healing this good land God has seen fit to give us." With a wave of his hat, he wheeled and strode out.

When Katie had Henry back in bed, he closed his eyes. She held his hand and sat. "That was wonderful," she said.

He smiled without opening his eyes. "Not worth getting shot up for."

"Of course not, but he's a great man, I'm sure of it." She straightened his blanket. "Did you see how sad his eyes are?"

Henry looked at her and nodded.

"Won't this be something to tell people. Your father'll be impressed."

"And Boss Reed. We'll tell him too."

CHAPTER FIFTEEN

†

Henry pushed with his legs to sit up in the bed. Twisting carefully so he didn't set off the pain in his chest, he adjusted the pillow. Katie, he knew, was with number six, a new head wound case from a New York regiment. The man's headaches were bad. He could sleep only if someone rubbed his temples. With Henry improving, Katie was helping other patients.

Mrs. Starrett approached Henry's bed. A man hobbled next to her on a single crutch.

"Sergeant," she said, "Mrs. Overstreet thought you might wish to meet Otto Krause, from a Pennsylvania regiment. He just got here."

Henry gestured to the chair next to him, the one Katie used. "I'm not going anywhere."

As Krause maneuvered between the beds, Mrs. Starrett added, "Mr. Krause is recently from Germany, and Mrs. Overstreet said you speak German, so you might help him." She bustled away.

Krause dropped into the chair with a groan. He was a spare, long-limbed man with fair hair and a spade-shaped beard. Not the sort of beard that could be maintained on campaign. Henry wondered if Katie had shaped it for him. She had learned how to shave Henry when he was at his lowest and now applied that skill to others. They liked to get cleaned up. Getting out of filthy uniforms and into the hospital shirts and trousers raised their spirits, no matter how much they were suffering.

In German, the man greeted him and asked how he fared. Henry understood that much. The problem came when he had to answer. Nothing came. He looked away and tried to remember words his father used when talking to his grandfather. Still nothing. It was more than ten years since his grandfather died, since Henry had heard the language in the house. He shook his head. "Sorry. I know what you said, but I don't remember how to answer."

The other man held out his hand. "Otto Krause. I must get better English, so we try that." He crossed his bad right leg over the other knee. He had no foot at the end of the now-dangling leg.

"How did that happen?" Henry pointed.

"Many *dummkopfs*, one of them me." He used his hands to adjust his leg. "In artillery, Pennsylvania Fourteen?" Henry nodded. "Artillery is no place for *dummkopfs*. Big cannons. Big horses. Big cannonballs. Big powder." He waved alternate hands with each item on his list of large things. Henry suspected that this performance had been staged before, but the man was doing it well. "So. I have horse—*big* horse who pull cannon—I hold by bridle, no?" Henry nodded. "And other *dummkopf*, he carry powder keg while smoking pipe." Otto offered a disbelieving look. "Very big *dummkopf*. I shout at him not to do. He... surprised. He reach for pipe"—Otto acted out each step—"he throw away. But he not can carry keg with one hand so it fall." He spread his hands wide. "I duck. Get low. Much afraid. Horse afraid too. Horse jumps. I not ready. Lose balance. Fall. No boom from powder but horse pull cannon wheel over leg." Otto pounded his fist into his hand, then shook his head sadly and pointed at his leg. "Crush."

Henry didn't want to laugh at the man's misfortune but found it hard to control himself after such a lively narration.

Otto smiled and spread his arms wide. "No believe, no? What need for rebels to kill us? We do it for them!"

They laughed together. Otto pointed at Henry and raised his eyebrows. "How? You?"

Henry pointed to his side and began the story. How they spread across an open field to charge the enemy. How he realized halfway there that they were charging cannon and he had sworn he would never do that. He didn't say how he had realized at a stroke that it was the day he would die and how that wasn't as big a thing as he thought it would be. He had seen so many dead, had walked over them, had added to their number by shooting and stabbing and clubbing. It was his time, which he didn't say to Otto.

He told how the wave of men in blue kept on, charging cannon. They started to run and shout and Henry with them, and then the cannon roared and swept him and others off their feet like they were leaves in the wind, and how it was only last week—more than two months later—that he'd been able to stand, his two legs holding him up for the first time since then. He didn't say that he didn't know why he was alive. That it had been his day to die but he hadn't. He woke up in the middle of some night knowing he should be dead. Why wasn't he dead?

"Leaves in the wind," Otto repeated, nodding his head. "You are poet. They say a poet comes here sometimes, with the men. You and he must talk."

Henry shrugged. "I never talked to him, that poet." He shook his head. "Because of my wife, I think, he stays away from me."

"Ah. I see." Otto twisted around and pointed. "She? Your wife?"

Henry nodded.

"She is angel. I see that. She is, no?"

Henry nodded again. "I suppose so."

"Ah." Otto shifted back in the chair. "That my reason to live. Even on one leg. Find angel for Otto." He grinned again.

"I hope you do."

Katie walked down the aisle toward them. Henry smiled at her, looking like the Henry she knew in Waldoborough. That new man was smiling too. Who was he, number fourteen?

"What are you two grinning about?" she asked.

The other man rose on his good leg, the crutch under his armpit. He looked conspiratorially at Henry, then cocked his head at her. "Men see angel. How not smile?"

* * * * *

Katie was enjoying herself. She had hung flags between the windows and baskets of flowers from the rafters. With Victor's help, she was strewing evergreen boughs on every bare surface, beginning with the square piano that was being tuned as she worked.

That evening, musicians were coming to play a concert. Vice President Hamlin was bringing them, and also taking credit for the Christmas turkeys shipped from Maine. The vice president was supposed to give a speech as well. Mrs. Starrett had browbeaten a local baker into contributing a dozen pies. Two were mincemeat, Henry's favorite. It wasn't Christmas like home. There was little chance of snow, and so many of the men still suffered. But it would be a holiday. She would make it one.

The preparations kept her mind from the special examination that two surgeons would perform that afternoon. Henry was improving. He still had waves of pain, sometimes low fevers, and he wasn't strong, but he walked on his own now. She could see him starting to get restless. Recently, several patients who recovered from their wounds had been sent back to the war. She dreaded that Henry might be sent back, too.

The surgeons had him stretch out on a table in the dining area. Katie stood well back as each looked at the wounds, still an angry red in places. Much of the bruising had faded. Henry's ribs seemed ready to burst through his abused skin. Dr. Spencer, evidently dissatisfied with the pale wintry light from the window, held a lantern close. He sat back and looked at the other doctor. "Well?" he said.

Spurgeon nodded assent and left the room. Spencer helped Henry off the table. He pulled out a cigar and bit off the tip while Henry pulled his shirt on. The doctor lit the cigar, drawing on it as it flared. Katie realized she was holding her breath.

"Sit down, sergeant, please." Spencer looked over at Katie. "You too, Mrs. Overstreet, since you're something of a medical person by now."

Katie sat, remembering to breathe. Henry sat erect.

Spencer puffed on his cigar. "Sergeant, your war is over." Henry didn't react. "You're healing. You're not healed yet, but you're coming along. We have no idea what's still inside you."

Spencer gestured to Henry's trunk. "The surgeons did their best, I'm sure, but you know what those field hospitals are like. Your fevers tell us they probably missed something. Maybe a few things. We don't know what that'll mean for you. Men have walked around with bullets in them for decades, mostly feeling fine. Or you may keep getting sick, as you have been. Or it may kill you. We don't know. But I couldn't send you back to fight, not how you are."

"Can't you take out what they missed?" Henry asked.

Spencer blew a mouthful of smoke up at the ceiling and pointed at Henry with the glowing cigar. "Now that, sergeant, that would very likely kill you. No surgeon would try that."

"Can he go home?" Katie asked, unable to keep the joy from her voice.

"Not yet." The surgeon looked over at her, then turned back to Henry. "We can't send a man in your condition back to winter in Maine. We want to keep you until spring. See if your wife can fatten you up. Then you can go back to whatever peaceable life you had before."

Henry took a deep breath. "There's no chance I can go back to my regiment?"

"None, sergeant. Your war is over."

After Spencer left, Katie threw her arms around Henry's neck. "Did you hear that? I'm getting you back, Henry. We'll go home." She sat. "What a wonderful Christmas gift."

Henry nodded absently. No emotion showed on his face.

Katie grabbed his hands between hers. "Isn't it grand?"

"Yes," he said in a monotone. "Grand."

She sat back. "What is it? What's wrong?"

He winced. "The war isn't over. I signed up to see it through. Of course I want to go home. But I can't leave before it's won."

"They won't let you fight, Henry. For heaven's sake, you fought for years and then got shot by a cannon. No one could ask for more, not even the army."

He shook his head. "It feels wrong. I don't want a discharge. I should be with my men."

She squeezed his hands. "Henry, dear, your men aren't there. You told me yourself. Most have died or gotten hurt or sick and gone home. You've done more than most. And the war's ending, isn't that right? That's what everyone says. The South can't hold on much longer."

"Katie—"

When he didn't say anything, his face frozen in a gaze like horror, she said, "What? What is it?"

"I don't know why I'm here. I shouldn't be here."

"Where should you be?"

"You know."

She sat upright. "I don't."

"I don't feel right—"

"Of course you don't, you've been terribly hurt."

"That's not what I mean." He pulled his hands away but still didn't look at her. "I'm not…me anymore. I don't know who I am. I can pretend for a while, being some kind of me, but then I get worn out by the pretending."

"What does that have to do with going back to the war?"

He looked up into her eyes, "Don't you see? *That's* me. There at the war. There's nowhere else I can be me anymore."

"Henry, your place is here with me, and then it's back home with me and your father and brother and all the people who love you."

He grimaced and nodded but said nothing.

* * * * *

"See here, look!" Otto's voice was strong as he leaned on his crutch, pointing at the map of Petersburg spread on his bed. He and Henry had studied it since morning, when Katie gave it to them. Now, she had announced, they could work out the military strategy and get word to General Grant, who was eager to hear from them.

Otto placed his finger on the map. "There, that is where your commander, Griffin, should have been for Hatcher's Run. He could have attacked there. Why cannot these fools see? It's plain on the paper."

"Otto, Otto," Henry shook his head. "How many times do you have to hear how things look different on the ground. The map doesn't show trees, how the land slopes, whether the road is sunken so it can be defended easily. You gunners just set up on the nearest hill and blast away, safe and warm."

"Safe and warm! I take you to Pennsylvania fourteen some time and show you safe and warm! By God, we lose men all the time. Those sharpshooters, the other cannons, they shoot at us extra special."

"Look over here," Henry pointed. "What about the right flank, coming through on Gordon's left? They didn't try that."

Katie loved to hear them argue about the war and politics and the weather and whatever else came up. Otto, with his bright eyes and fractured English, brought Henry back to life in a way that Katie couldn't. And Otto's English improved with every argument. He was a printer in the old country, he explained, and worked for a German printer outside Philadelphia. Not until he was drafted did he have to learn English. Even then, Pennsylvania's Fourteenth was mostly German speakers. With Henry and Katie's help, he said, he was mastering English so he could become a printer of English after the war. He was eager to heal enough for the surgeons to fit him with a false foot. It didn't need to be a good false foot, he said, since printers don't walk very much.

In the mornings, the two men traveled up and down the ward, pausing to talk with those men who would talk. They watched card games but never joined. They spent much of the afternoon reading the newspapers, never getting past the war news. Henry took it personally that Grant and the Twentieth Maine were stuck in the mud before Petersburg, unable to budge Lee's army, while General Sherman rampaged through the Carolinas, seeming to win the war on his own.

Sometimes the two men nipped from Otto's cache of bootleg brandy, the source of which remained a mystery to Katie and Mrs. Starrett. Katie suspected Victor. Really, the men of Ward K had little to spend their pay on except tobacco, newspapers, and smuggled liquor. When Congress adopted the constitutional amendment to ban slavery, Otto passed one of his bottles around the ward to celebrate, then produced three others.

In the evenings, if there was no music, Katie and Henry visited Otto's bed, which was next to a stove, so she could read to them from the novels of Scott and Cooper. Otto sometimes interrupted to ask what a word meant. Other patients listened in. Henry's fevers were less frequent. He ate more.

Katie's days had changed too. With Henry's recovery and this new friendship, she wrote letters home for men who couldn't write or were too weak. After the Hatcher's Run battle in early February, a dozen new patients swamped Ward K, so she helped Mrs. Starrett with them.

Katie sat with the ones with the worst wounds. They often calmed at a soft touch and a quiet voice. They were frightened, of course. So was she. One night she sat with a man whose arm stump was infected. The amputation had been botched, or perhaps he was doomed from the start. Fever and chills were wearing him down, clouding his mind, yet at the end he quieted. Shortly after midnight he asked Katie to tell his mother that he died well, then he died with a sweet smile on his face. Katie lost track of time as she sat with his hand in hers.

"Mrs. Overstreet." The voice was the night watcher's behind her. "Number twenty is poorly. Mrs. Starrett was called away."

Katie stood and the watcher carried her chair to bed twenty. The boy there—next to Henry—was shot through the lung. Mrs. Starrett had said he wouldn't make it. Katie touched his brow. He had red hair, wild blue eyes that seemed to vibrate in their sockets. Every breath seemed to be torture, his chest heaving, groans coming as he breathed in, then as he breathed out.

"Does it hurt much?" she asked, leaning over to speak in his ear.

He turned his head abruptly to her. His eyes filled with tears, and he nodded, then winced to inhale.

"The pain will end soon," she said, stroking his head. "Very soon. No more pain."

He closed his eyes and nodded, then groaned. She spoke into his ear that his father and mother loved him. That God loved him. Whatever she could think of to fill his mind that wasn't the pain. It was nearly thirty minutes before he stopped in mid-breath, his eyes wide open. The pain was over.

Katie stayed there, feeling hollow. Her breath came so easily as she looked down the dark line of beds. A few smoked in the dark. One at the far end of the ward called out, then subsided. She walked to Henry's bed and looked down at his face, mouth slack in unguarded sleep. Soon she would take him from this place.

CHAPTER SIXTEEN

†

K atie tried to talk them out of it, but Henry and Otto insisted, even though two days of pounding rain had turned Washington into a marshland. "When else," Henry had asked her, "will we see a president sworn into office?" The men put on uniforms, new ones. She made them wear capes against the cold and damp of early March.

Thousands jammed the streets. They were late to the parade route, but some people made way for Otto's crutch and missing foot, letting them advance to the curb where they could see. Military bands played. A company of Negro troops marched. The crowd cheered when the president's carriage passed.

They hurried after Mr. Lincoln to the Capitol building where the ceremony would take place. In the middle of Fourth Street, Otto's crutch slipped, and he went down in the mud with a squawk.

Henry looked down and shook his head. "Drunk again, eh, private?"

"Blast your hide," Otto sputtered. "Get me up and we race to the Capitol. I win easy, you see." He turned to a man who was reaching down to help him up. "Did you see? That man push me down! Some sergeant, eh? Of course Lee still holds Petersburg."

Henry and the other man lifted Otto by his armpits while Katie tried to knock the mud off his crutch without getting it on her gloves. Otto and Henry were grinning when they reached the other side of the street.

"This uniform," Otto said, "when I wear it I always have wet feet. It's part of the uniform, I think."

"Quit complaining," Henry said. "You've only got one wet foot."

They joined the mass gathered before the Capitol. Under a stony sky, people buzzed with eagerness to see Mr. Lincoln. Negroes mixed among whites. Katie held Henry's arm with both her hands and rested her head on his shoulder.

"Are you all right?" he asked her quietly.

"Look," she said, pointing to her right. "Isn't that Mrs. Starrett, with number four?"

Henry grunted his agreement, then added, "Promise you'll never call me number twenty-two."

"But you're such a twenty-two."

The crowd's murmuring rose as black-suited figures emerged onto the Capital porch. The president, arriving last, was unmistakable, the tallest man with the tallest hat.

Lincoln stepped forward. Sunlight burst from the sky, bathing the scene. They could see him, hatless now, with his hand on a book, taking his oath and kissing the Bible. They stood on tiptoe, shifting to see past heads in front of them. The people around them wore expressions of awe and delight. Katie closed her eyes and felt sun-warmth on her face.

When the president began to speak, the crowd grew even more respectful. The only sounds were the breeze in Katie's ear and Mr. Lincoln's high-pitched voice. She couldn't make out the words. He was too far away. She knew the words were important, that he had thought about them for a long time.

When his short speech ended, cannon boomed and cheers erupted.

"Well," Otto said as they started back to the hospital. "In the newspapers tomorrow we read the speech."

* * * * *

On a single day, the pneumonia struck six patients, including Otto. Mrs. Starrett ignored her own symptoms until Dr. Spurgeon heard her coughing. After a private examination, he insisted she remain in her room. Only he and Katie saw her. He directed the orderlies to move the six patients to the end of the ward. The move scrambled the patients' numbers, which confounded some of the staff.

Two days later, a major asked for Henry. From the look of him, Katie doubted he had done any fighting. She left him in the dining area and brought Henry. With Mrs. Starrett sick, she couldn't stay for the interview. An hour later, she found Henry on his bed, looking grim.

"What was it?" she asked.

"My discharge papers. Effective in two days."

She clasped her hands together at her breast. "We can go?"

He smiled. "If you can bear to leave all this."

She sat with him, her hand on his leg. "We'll take the cars to New York, then by water?" They had money from his last few paydays.

He agreed. "There's something else."

"Yes?"

He held another paper out to her. Signed by Colonel Spear and Captain Clark of his regiment, it announced that Henry Overstreet was promoted to lieutenant, U.S. Army, Fifth Corps, Third Brigade, Twentieth Regiment of Maine Volunteers.

"Henry. Did you know this would happen?"

He shook his head. "Not that I did anything to earn it."

She held the paper out to admire it. "Now you'll outrank that old sergeant major of yours."

Henry smiled. "Maybe so." He shrugged. "I guess I did my part."

Katie was up that night with Mrs. Starrett. She sent the night watcher for Doctor Spencer, who arrived when Mrs. Starrett was ten minutes dead. Katie felt as empty as she could remember. Next morning, the patients of Ward K wore black armbands. When Mrs. Starrett was carried from the ward, the stronger ones formed a line to honor her.

Katie told Henry they would stay until the ward had a new nurse, but that took only a day. When it was time to leave, they went from bed to bed saying farewells, saving Otto for last. He was sitting up, recovering from the pneumonia.

"I don't suppose you'll be coming to Maine any time soon," Henry said.

Otto shook his head. "Why would I go? So many Yankees there. And to see a damned officer like you?"

Henry sat on the bed. "You'll go out west?"

"I think so."

"That's exciting," Katie said.

"I will see this country. Maybe I see it all." He gestured at his leg. "After I get my new foot."

Katie handed him a paper. "That's where to send mail to us. Tell us where you are. And how you are. And about all the little Krauses you will have."

"Ach, first I need to find an angel who prefers a man with one foot." He nodded to them. "Maybe you come west. It's your country too."

"Maybe," she said, "but first I'm taking this lieutenant home as fast as I can."

They stepped out of the ward into a glittery spring day. The Capitol looked huge, the sun hanging over its right shoulder. Buds showed on trees along Seventh Street. A sharp wind blew. A dog barked close by. She sighed. "This is the place," she said, "where we've been together the longest. Five months."

Henry shook his head. "I promise you, Katie, things'll be better." He gave her a small smile.

She kissed him.

PART III

CHAPTER ONE

†

Katie was awake that Monday morning when the steady gong of church bells began. She and Henry had been in Waldoborough for only a week, staying in the converted workshop behind the Overstreet home. More bells joined, inserting jarring new rhythms, each pitch slightly different, drenching the town in joyously discordant noise. She gripped Henry's arm. "Something's happened," she said.

He rolled on his back and smiled. "We won."

Katie climbed on top of him, nose-to-nose. She kissed him. "It seems the celebration has started without us, lieutenant."

With a surge of energy, he reversed their positions and tugged her shift up to her waist. "Let's catch up," he said.

A pounding came from the workshop door, then the jubilant voice of Henry's father. "Coffee's almost ready. No time for lollification today! It's over! The war's over!"

Henry groaned and rolled onto his side. "Poor lieutenant," Katie said, kissing him quickly as she rose. "We'll celebrate tonight."

When they reached the kitchen, the coffee was ready and Lewis Overstreet eagerly reported. "Fred Huber rode by," he said.

"Lee surrendered yesterday. The news came over the telegraph last night. The Army of Northern Virginia is no more." They clinked coffee cups. "*You*"—he pointed at Henry—"beat that man, and he's one tough bird."

Henry smiled. "I had help, Pa."

"So," Katie said, "after I cook us a delicious breakfast—"

"Flapjacks?" Lewis broke in.

"I made those two days ago."

"Henry?" his father asked. "To the victor goes the spoils."

"Flapjacks," Henry said. Katie looked bewitchingly disheveled from the morning's interruption. Evening couldn't come soon enough for him.

Katie gave him an impatient look. "All right, but only because you won. Then we go into town and join the fun."

"Absolutely," Lewis said. "Put on the uniform and cap?"

Henry shook his head. "I don't have to wear them ever again."

Katie placed her hand on his. He was still hospital-pale. People commented on it. But he was better, much better. "You don't mind if I get gussied up a bit?" she said.

"Not a bit. Makes the other fellas crazy."

She made them wait while she dressed, the church bells now punctuated by explosions that could be muskets or maybe fireworks. She felt a bone-deep joy to be home, even in the converted workshop. They were out of the war, out of Ward K. The wind coming off the river made her feel alive in a way that she never felt in Washington. So many had been swept away over the last years, yet here she was, with Henry, where they knew the people and the sky and the hills. They'd been lucky, to be sure, but maybe Henry was wrong when he said that sooner or later you use up your luck. Maybe their luck was just starting.

She emerged in a bright red frock with a square neck, topped off with a lace-trimmed bonnet she had bought when they passed through New York City. "Oh, my," Lewis said. He shook his head, for once groping for words. "I've become a sentimental old man," he said, "but I can't help but think how much your mother would have loved seeing you two."

As they neared Main Street, joyful noises piled high in the dazzling sunlight—horns and clanging cowbells, school bells, sleigh bells, plus the occasional bang of a musket. Red-white-

and-blue bunting fluttered on storefronts and at the collars of
dresses and jackets. Men shouted hurrahs and threw their hats
in the air, then scrambled to retrieve their headgear. Wagons,
jammed with shouting children happy to be out of school, rattled
up and down Main Street, then over to Jefferson Street. Then the
wagons turned around to cover the same ground while celebrants
jumped on and off.

Lewis pulled off his hat and scratched the back of his head.
"Will you look at those damned Copperheads," he said. "It's like
they beat the rebels all by themselves."

Henry smiled. "They're probably happier than the rest of us,"
he said. "Now they can get back to sucking up to the Southerners."

"You two," Katie said, hands on her hips. "This is a celebration,
not a grouching contest." She took each by the arm and pulled them
down toward the river. Soon Henry was being hugged by male and
female alike. Edwin Clark pumped his hand and thanked him for
looking after his little brother. George Young dragged Henry away.
Henry gave Katie a helpless look and followed George behind
Winslow's, where a dozen men laughed and hooted while passing
around a jug.

"Attention!" George called out. The men straightened as best
they could, arms straight down at their sides. Henry clasped his
hands behind his back and stalked among them, examining their
outfits through squinting eyes.

After a full ten seconds, he shouted, "Who's got the damned
jug!"

By noontime, the hilarity was flagging. Word spread that the
town would stage a formal ceremony at the Customs House at
four, then an evening illumination. On Saturday night, there would
be a dance at the German church. Worn out by morning revelry,
Waldoborough went home for dinner and a rest.

Katie rode on Cricket, with Henry and his father on foot on
either side. Henry was quiet while she and Lewis chatted about
the people they'd seen. At the house, she waited as Henry tied up
Cricket, then gave the old horse an affectionate nuzzle.

"Something wrong?" Katie asked him.

He gave a small shrug. "They say the Twentieth was there. At
Lee's surrender."

"Isn't that wonderful?" She turned him to face her. "They were
there for you, so you were there too."

"Not really." He took a deep breath. "I know I couldn't be there. But it must've been quite a moment for the boys."

"Yes. It must have."

"They say Chamberlain—he's a general now—he's the one received the surrender."

"You've been with the great men of our time, Henry, including the president." She embraced him, then leaned back. "I'm so proud."

He nodded. "I was thinking of Ralph."

"Do you think he'll move back to town?"

Henry shook his head. "Nah, they've got their life in Rockport, but maybe this'll make him feel, I don't know, freer. Let's go see him tomorrow."

Solemnity prevailed at the afternoon ceremony. Ministers prayed for those who were lost, and for the wounded. The mayor read the name of each man who served. Katie squeezed Henry's hand when he was called. Now, the mayor said, was a time for forgiveness and loyalty to the Union. He added in his strongest voice, "The cruel war is over." A deep roar rose. Many sang with the band's version of the "Battle Hymn of the Republic" and "Tenting Tonight." Henry couldn't command his voice well enough to join in.

After a picnic supper along the river, Lewis went home to fix the windows for the illumination. When he returned, the bonfire revealed that a woman held his arm. As they approached, Lewis bowed slightly and said, "You know my son Henry, and daughter-in-law Katie." It was Mrs. Beckett, who lived down the road. "I didn't want Amanda to be alone tonight."

After the hellos, the older couple walked on. Henry whispered to Katie, "What happened to Mr. Beckett?"

"Killed down at the Storer Yard last spring. I guess I didn't write you about it."

Henry wore a half-smile as he watched them climb Main Street in the direction of Boss Reed's mansion.

"Do you mind?" Katie asked.

"No. Pa's been lonesome a long time. I don't wish lonesome on anyone." He began to walk, pulling her along. "While those two lovebirds sashay around town, why don't you and I try the same?" They walked out onto the smaller roads, then into farmlands, admiring the flickering lights in each window that gave each home a smile. A sliver moon allowed the stars to sparkle across most of the sky. He saw the soft light in Katie's eyes.

"Sometimes…" he said, then thought about the stone fence they were passing, which might have stood there for a hundred years. The thought ran through his mind that on the Maine coast, an invading army would have to look long and hard for something to burn in their campfires. They had been lucky that Virginia had both trees and wooden fences.

"Sometimes?" she prompted him.

He dredged up the thought. "It's that—that sometimes I can't accept it. That I'm here. That there won't be reveille in the morning, before our twenty mile march. That I'm not eating hardtack and salt pork and water." He looked over at her. "Maybe now I can."

"We've got our whole lives, Henry."

"I've been thinking, and talked to my father too, about us. You know that land over near the river, the last part of the old Mayflower Hof where the Overstreets first settled?"

She nodded. Henry and she had walked by it before he enlisted.

"Pa, you know, he divided it into one piece for Ralph and one for me. Ralph sold his to old man Schreiber, to raise the money for the Rockport farm. I can build us a house on the other piece."

"How can I help?"

"With what?"

"With building our house. Hammering nails and sawing boards."

"You don't know how."

"I didn't know how to make socks or reach school, or even nurse soldiers. I can learn." When Henry was quiet for a minute, she added, "There's no school this summer. No more Soldiers Aid Society. I won't have anything to do."

"You're taking care of my father and me." When she kept her eyes trained on the ground, he added, "You can plant a garden,"

"I can do those things and help with our new house too. Your father may not take much looking after, what with Mrs. Beckett in the picture."

* * * * *

Five days later, on a Saturday morning, the news arrived that President Lincoln was dead. People gathered on Main Street again. This time they were quiet. Most wore black or black armbands. They read to each other from newspapers. When the packet arrived, people rushed for new editions from Boston or New York.

Black draped the windows of shuttered shops. Flags hung at half-mast. Hard words passed between those who had supported the war and those who had opposed it. A scuffle broke out but was quickly quelled.

A requiem service was set for the German church the next day. Henry didn't go. He didn't want to display his grief to everyone. While Lewis took Katie and Mrs. Beckett down to Main Street, and then to the memorial service, Henry made drawings for the new house, starting a list of materials he would need. He walked upriver and studied the property for the spot that would provide the best drainage, the best light, a view of the river in winter when the leaves fell.

He felt tears on his cheek three times that day. Each time, when his eyes cleared, he went back to work.

CHAPTER TWO

✝

Henry leaned against the Customs House as the hands tied up the Boston boat down the hill and across the river. George Young offered his bottle of whiskey, but Henry declined. Not in the morning. George had no such rule on a July day under a warm sun with a gentle breeze.

At the wharf, the town band struck up a patriotic number, almost all on the beat. Blue-coated figures clustered on the boat's deck, then came ashore. Avoiding military formation, they crossed the bridge over the Medomak and started up the hill. Henry was glad they didn't march. They didn't have to march ever again. He didn't have to count them. There were eleven, the Waldoborough men who signed up for the Twentieth when he did and lasted all the way to Lee's surrender. Eleven out of maybe fifty.

A small group had assembled at the Customs House: family and friends of the eleven, plus former comrades like Henry and George, who went home with wounds or sickness. He was glad to greet them, glad they were safe, but also unsure of his ground. He hadn't seen them for nearly a year. They had experiences he couldn't know—different battles, different fields, different comrades, and the surrender. For him, that moment outweighed any honor he might claim. He didn't want to be jealous, but he was definitely uncertain. Also, weighted down with memories of Joe Maxwell and Meisner and Flagg and others who never left the battlefield.

The eleven approached. Henry stopped George. "Let the families go first."

"Sergeant!" Henry turned his head. It was Dexter Brewer, who had lied about his age to sign up. A middle-aged woman who had to be his mother had a death-grip on his arm, but Brewer waved with the other one.

"I'm just Henry these days," he said as they exchanged a warm handshake. Brewer looked impossibly young for all he had been through. Was he even twenty yet? Others stopped for grins and back slaps and congratulations. Henry kept saying he wasn't sergeant anymore. George's whiskey was popular.

When the musicians recovered their wind from scaling the hill, they struck up a march. Katie appeared next to Henry. He had told her not to come, that he wasn't sure how he would feel. There was no ceremony when he came home, and now this one wasn't for him. That nettled, though he didn't think it should, since he got to come home early. He was glad to see her. Also, that these boys were home.

When the tune was over, the mayor waved the eleven forward. The mayor didn't say it, but Henry thought it. Now the cruel war really was over.

* * * * *

"You always said you'd never work for old man Storer," George shouted over the wind-roar and sail-flap of his small boat. "Now I hear you're building boats for the old crook."

George, who seemed to have an inexhaustible supply of homemade hooch, had kept drinking after the ceremony and now was several sheets to the wind. So far, he was managing the tiller well enough, but Henry was watching him closely.

"The way times are," Henry called back, "a fellow can't afford to be choosy. I get a few days here, a few days there. I feel like a hen scratching the ground for seeds others have missed. Anyway, old Storer's turned patriot, gave me the day to greet my old comrades." He smiled. "Some of us still try to work."

George gave an exaggerated shrug. "Can I help it that Dorrie and me raised fine sons who support their ailing father who gave his best to these U. S. of A.?"

"Don't you worry what happens when they have families?"

"They have family, Dorrie and me. Oh, I suppose they might think about cutting me off, but never their dear old Ma. So I just have to stay in good with her."

"The woman's a saint."

"Amen to that." George oversteered when he brought the boat back to the wind. Correcting the mistake, he sat up straighter. Henry needed to take over the tiller soon. Still, the boat was old, slow, and stable. Sinking her would take grim determination.

The story had been that Henry would help George with his fishing business today, but Henry didn't care for fishing and nothing about George was businesslike. Henry expected they'd cast a few lines out, chew the fat, maybe wedge in a nap. Only a fish with poor judgment would gasp his last in George's boat.

The peninsula ahead held the village of Bremen, treeless like the rest of this coast. Scalped was the word that always came to Henry's mind. The Indians may have taken scalps in their time, but the settlers got even by cutting down every scrap of forest where an Indian might live, a vengeance upon the land. Henry smiled at the biblical-sounding phrase. Something stuck from those dreary Sunday mornings. He wondered what the land looked like when the forests were thick and dark, filled with wild animals.

After George found a likely spot for pretending to fish, Henry struck the sails. He baited a dozen lines and tossed them in. Clouds lingered in the eastern sky, but they were thin and flat, no threat. The boat rocked in the wave-swell. The lines trailed behind. Henry settled in the stern, sitting at right angles to his friend.

"You know, George, I don't have a good feeling about the yards," he said, "beyond old man Storer." He shook his head when George offered the bottle. George took a long draw, then looked off at the horizon. He pointed the boat's nose into the swell.

"Those bastards down at Bath up to their old tricks, eh?" George said. "Still underbidding, then piling on extras?"

"Sure, they're always a danger, but it's more than that. The Navy work's dying out. There's only one thing the Navy wants— ironclads—and we can't make them. And for steamers, anyone with a lick of sense wants to build 'em where they make the engines too—which also ain't here. Shipbuilding's getting played out, like the land."

"Remember how bad things were before the war," George said. "I scrambled every day to keep you boys working, I'm here to tell you."

Henry grabbed George's knee and squeezed it. "You made it work, George. We didn't appreciate it good and proper. The thing is, I'm trying to look at it like I was some rich son of a bitch. Suppose I want to build a spanking new boat, but I don't want to just piss money away. Why would I come up to this far corner of the country?"

George laughed and pointed the bottle at him. "There's your problem."

"What's that?"

"Now you've seen some of the rest of this fair land, seen how big it is and full of people and machines and whatnot, you know what a little corner we're sitting in."

Henry sat up straighter. Despite a half-day of steady drinking, George—bluff old George—already knew what was taking Henry so long to work out, what was bothering him every time he tried to plan out what his life with Katie could be.

"That's it," he said. "That's exactly it. You know how my brother, Ralph, settled into that farm over in Rockport. He's happy as a pig in shit. He and Lucy're working on producing a baby every year or two and they've got the hang of it."

George snorted.

"Well, Ralph says he's happy. Except for having all those children, he might as well be a damned monk. Put aside his six weeks at the army camp, he's never been off this coast, much less out of Maine. He's not seen what's out there."

George looked at Henry out of the corner of a squinted-up eye. "What do you think's out there?"

"George, it's the whole wide world. This country—I could feel it when I traveled between here and the war, every time I talked to men from other places, even the Irish boys and this German fellow at the hospital—this whole country, it's bursting at the seams. It's getting taller and bigger and faster, laying railroads from one end to the other, building towns where there was nothing, whole new places jumping right up out of the ground. But Waldoborough just keeps getting smaller. The yards lose more business. The land around here'll never be good. Winter's still long. My hands are cold. They never get warm, even in summer. We've got no way to build ourselves up, so we watch other people do great things."

George took another long swallow. "So what are all these great things you've got it in mind to do?"

Henry shook his head, "Katie asks that. I don't know, not yet. I'm just another journeyman joiner sitting in his backwoods town doing the same things my father did and his father before him. I know what I *don't* want to do, and that's a pretty fair description of it." He pulled his lips tight together.

"So, for you it's 'Go west, young man!'?"

"Why not?"

"You mentioned Mrs. Overstreet. Does she have an opinion about this?"

"I haven't talked to her about that part yet, about going west."

"Women will have their opinions."

"If I could get out where people try new things, where it's not just the same rich people owning the same places, then I can figure it out, I'll know what the right thing is. But I can't do that here.

"I'll tell you, George, I get out on that piece of land where we're building the house." He shook his head. "I'm leveling off the land with a pick and shovel. I swear it feels like I'm digging my own grave. Digging a hole for myself that I'll disappear into and never get out of."

A swell caught the boat sideways and rocked it. Henry caught his balance by grabbing George's leg. George grunted and his eyelids fluttered. He had dropped off while Henry was talking. As gently as he could, Henry stretched his friend out in the bottom of the boat and shoved a coiled rope under George's head. Then pointed the boat back into the swells.

Henry wasn't much of a sailor, but every boy in Waldoborough spent time on the water. Henry figured he'd be all right as long as the wind didn't swirl. After a while, he pulled in the lines and headed home, making a couple of clumsy tacks. Then he recovered the knack of crossing the wind. Coming up the river, he dropped their speed too early, so they limped to the dock at an agonizing creep. He hoped no one was watching. He had to pull the boat over to the dock before jumping off to tie on the bowline. When he turned back for the stern line, George threw it up to him.

"You old scoundrel," Henry said. "You've been playing possum."

"Just the last mile or so, while you were sneaking up on the wharf here. You did pretty well for a joiner. You wouldn't consider going in the fishing business, would you?"

Henry smiled. "I couldn't afford the liquor bill."

* * * * *

During a dinner of Ralph's sausage combined with cabbage she grew in the garden, Katie tried to get Henry to talk. Lewis was having supper with Mrs. Beckett, which he was doing more often. Katie asked about the day on George's boat. What had they caught? What were prices like at the wharf? She brought up the ceremony for the eleven other men of Company E. Wasn't it good to see them again? They seemed glad to see Henry. She asked about their new house, how it was going, and what she could do to help. Nothing produced actual conversation, the type with spontaneous remarks and reciprocal inquiries. She let the silence stretch between them.

"I thought you were going to teach some more," he said. "The money would be good."

"I heard about an opening right in Waldoborough. But it's weeks before school starts. With you down at the yards, we only work on the house on Sundays. I'm not sure when we'll finish. Show me what I can do during the week, then we can get out of this shed a little faster."

"I'll get it done."

"I can help."

"You don't need to do that." He stood and grabbed his hat from the hook at the door.

"Where are you going?" she asked, but the door was closing behind him. She stayed in her chair, tracing patterns on her plate with her fork. She missed that passionate, cheerful boy she fell in love with. What she had now was a quiet man growing quieter. Not angry or bitter or surly, but aloof, numb to human interaction. She couldn't remember when she last heard him laugh. She wondered if he laughed with George.

It's the war, she thought, as she always did. When they got married, in that week's mad swirl, he said there were things he wouldn't talk about. They must be awful. When she first got to

Ward K, she wasn't surprised he didn't talk much. He was hurt and so were all the others. Terrible times might naturally dry up your talk, make it seem unimportant, like the buzzing of flies or the rustling of leaves. Then again, he seemed to find it easy enough to talk to an old souse like George Young. Just like he'd found it easy to talk to Otto Krause back at Ward K. Maybe it wasn't the war or his wound or the months in Ward K. Maybe it was her.

"Not much happening since I left." Henry was in the doorway. She hadn't heard him approach.

"Just me being lazy again."

"Not again!" He smiled as he sat. "Katie bug, you're the least lazy person I know."

"You know I never liked being called that."

"You never mind when your father uses it."

"He's my father."

Henry put his hand on hers. "Then I need to find other words to tell you."

"Tell me what?"

"Just how much I want you not to do these dishes and to come with me to our shed."

"Your father'll get back here and find this mess; then he'll think ill of me, especially compared to the excellent Mrs. Beckett."

"My father thinks I'm not worthy of you, and it's one of the things he's right about."

"Henry," she said, baffled by where this person had just arrived from. The one she loved. She dared to look into his eyes and there he was, completely there, looking back. "I'll carry these out and then we'll go."

He held her hand down as she moved to stand. "I'll get you a better place. Soon."

"That's not what we're talking about now, is it?"

He smiled and tilted his head. "No, ma'am. Not at all."

CHAPTER THREE

Late March 1866

Henry stepped into Winslow's on his way up from the river.

"We're closing," Anna Winslow called from behind the counter. She had the cash drawer out. Three stacks of greenbacks stood next to a pile of coins. "Grab what you need quick now."

Henry rubbed his hands together and stomped snow off his boots. His hands ached from the cold. "I just need some of your fire. I'll go whenever you're ready."

"My heavens, Henry, that time in Virginia's made you soft. It's not that cold today."

Henry smiled and hurried to the pot-bellied stove. The fire had dwindled, yet standing there felt wonderful. Henry gladly would have knelt and embraced its iron warmth. "Not cold when you're working in here all day. Over at the yards, though, there's a genuine nip in the air, especially after the first eight hours."

Anna looked up at him. "Well, you have a point there. How's the baby?"

"Thomas? He's a corker. Strong and noisy like all the Overstreets."

"Maybe that's like the Nashes."

"Don't you fall for that line that James Nash is peddling. That boy is Overstreet through and through, from the cold blue eyes all the way down to the evil temper."

Anna was counting two-bit pieces, then jotted something down. She smiled at him. "You sure know a lot after only a few weeks."

"Don't tell me you can't hear him down here."

"I'm glad for you and Katie."

"Say, do you have any bread I could bring home?"

"There's a pumpernickel, but it's seen better days."

"How much?"

She waved her hand and reached back for the dark loaf. "I can't sell it. Tell Katie I said to warm it first."

"Thanks." He accepted the loaf, then turned back and set his hands on the stove for one last moment. He pulled his hat down tight over his ears. "You're right about one thing, Anna," he called over his shoulder from the door.

"I suppose it's the law of averages."

"I definitely forgot how cold it gets around here." He closed the door behind him as he stepped into the street.

Henry hunched his shoulders and drove his hands into his jacket pockets. The air felt cold enough to shatter like glass if he swung a fist into it. The shrill crunch of his boots on the snow ran up and down his spine. Any breeze seemed to curl under his collar, then seep through his clothes. His breath-fog formed and vanished. He picked up his stride to get home quicker. It was late March. This had to be the last cold snap of the year.

He loaded his arms at the woodpile near his father's house. He'd split more before supper, but it could wait until he'd warmed up.

"Close that door," Katie said as he stepped in. He shut the door and set the wood down with a bang next to the stove.

"Sorry," he said. "Cold fingers."

"Henry, this little place gets completely chilled if you open the door for a second. That's hard on Thomas." She was sitting across the bed, leaning back against the wall and cradling the baby's head as he sucked. She rocked him gently.

"I know, I know. But you and Thomas can stay in the main house during the day."

"I don't want to stay in your father's house. I want to stay somewhere that's ours."

He held out the loaf to her. "Pumpernickel, from Winslow's."

"What do you expect me to do with that now? Put it on the shelf." The baby pulled away from her and made small coughing noises, then a thin cry. "Oh, baby," she crooned, "you know you're hungry. My sweet baby."

"Maybe it's gas," he said.

She had lifted the baby to her shoulder and was patting his back. "It's like this every time. He eats a little, gets angry, then eats a little, then falls asleep. Then wakes up angry that no one fed him better the last time."

"Ah, we're a bad lot, aren't we, Katie girl?" He sat in the chair and smiled at her.

"Did you get butter? We have none."

"Sorry, no. I'll get it tomorrow."

She stood, leaving her blouse up but pulling her shawl tight across her and Thomas. She started walking across the small open space. The baby made mewing sounds. His head bobbed. "That's it, sweet boy," she said softly. "That's it."

Henry watched her walk back and forth three more times. "Are you going to build up the fire?" she asked sharply.

"Yes, of course."

When flames leapt up in the stove, he leaned back on his haunches and looked over to her, now back on the bed.

"Henry," she said.

He knew that careful, measured tone. Like she was tiptoeing over broken glass. It signaled something she'd been thinking how to say. It never led anywhere good. He raised his eyebrows in answer, awaiting the blow.

"I never meant to raise our family in a shack, a shack where there are still tool racks on the walls from when it was a workshop fifty years ago, a shack with so many gaps between the wall planks that there isn't enough plaster in the world to keep them stuffed. Your son and I deserve to be treated better than you treat hammers and chisels."

"I know, I know. But what can I do? I work ten hours a day in the cold, and I can't build the new place in the dark even if I had the strength. And on Sundays by the time I get out there and get set up, I need to find a little warmth myself. I don't know why you won't stay over in the house, just for this winter."

"I don't want to start our life like that. All I've ever done is live in other people's houses. My father's, my uncle's, your father's, Mrs. Starrett's room. I won't keep doing that."

Henry rubbed his hands together and jammed each into the opposite armpit. "It's got to warm up soon. Then I'll make some progress, get Pa out there to help. Maybe George."

"George," she said with disgust. "Really, Henry."

The baby grew fretful again, sliding into a full-throated cry. "I need to split some more wood," he said. He cut her a slice off the loaf and held it out.

"How many hands do you think I have?" she said as she sat on the bed. "Put it over there."

When he returned with a fresh load of wood, he quickly closed the door behind him. Katie and the baby seemed to be dozing. The flickering light from the oil lamp glowed across her skin. He set the wood down piece by piece. Thomas took a sudden breath and caught it, then drifted off again.

Henry picked up the slice of bread where he had left it and took a bite. Anna hadn't lied. It was tough. His eye fell on an envelope propped against a jar on the table. It was littered with postmarks. One from Hartford. Another from Cleveland. A faint one that looked—when he held it next to the lamp—like Chicago. It was addressed to him in a precise hand. He tore it open.

Two pages bristled with the same fastidious writing, the words marching across the page along straight lines that had been exactingly measured. He looked for the signature. Otto Krause!

March 15, 1866
Chicago
My dear Henry—

I imagine you have long since forgotten your one-legged friend from Ward K but I have remembered both you and the angelic Mrs. Overstreet. I trust that you and she have produced at least one cherub or seraph by now. You see that I am showing off how many English words I have learned. I work as a printer for a newspaper that persists in printing in English, even though German is a far more expressive and morally correct language. Therefore I have learned a great deal of English words in a very short time. I still do not always put them together the way they should go, but that will come.

I now have an artificial foot which allows me to walk only with a cane. Indeed, I can walk fairly quickly now, though I am not yet ready to compete in races. Perhaps in races with turtles and tortoises. Such fine words those are!

Chicago is an amazing city to live in, much different from Germany or from Pennsylvania—although there are many Germans here, so that is one thing that is the same for all three places. But here in Chicago the spirit is bold and large. Men walk down the street looking for a way to make money, as though they will find it seated on the corner waiting for a man with the grit and gizzard to grab it. I am very proud to use gizzard. I just learned it yesterday. It is such a good word that it is almost German.

There are railroads that run down almost every big street carrying people and so many things to the stockyards and grain elevators where the food of the country comes and then goes. Whole neighborhoods seem to be built overnight. It is something that every man should see. I hope that you and Mrs. Overstreet and your cherubim and seraphim may someday come to this place and look up your old friend from Ward K, although my wish also is that you all are sampling heavenly delights that a one-legged printer could never imagine.

Your good friend,
Otto Krause

Henry read the letter a second time and then a third.

"Who is that from?" Katie asked.

He looked up. "How did it get here?"

"Your father brought it. Who wrote it?"

"It's from Otto, you remember, from the hospital." Henry's eyes were shining. He held out the letter. "Here—read it." As she pulled the blanket around the baby more tightly, Henry said, "I'll take him."

She sat in the chair while Henry paced with the baby. After a minute, she said, "He's quite the writer."

"Yes," he smiled. "He already knows more words than I do."

Katie moved her chair closer to the fire, then closed her eyes. Henry decided to wait, though an idea was bubbling so powerfully inside him that he felt he would explode. He would wait until they had had some supper.

The meal was simple. Katie warmed slices of pumpernickel on the stove and melted cheese on top. She opened one of the last jars of applesauce she had put up in the fall, and they drank ginger beer. She sat on the edge of the bed as Henry pushed the table in front of it. He sat in the chair. She forced herself to eat through her weariness. It was a relief to have Thomas out of her arms for a few minutes, though she knew it would be another long night. If he would only eat more, maybe he would sleep longer.

Henry got up to feed the fire, then sat again, leaning on his forearms. He reached over to take her hand. She managed a small smile. She knew he was trying. She couldn't help being cold and tired.

"What did you think of Otto's letter?" he said.

"What I said. He's a fine writer. I wish I could have written such letters to you."

"I didn't want Otto's letters. I wanted yours." She gave his hand a small squeeze. "I meant what he wrote about Chicago, what it's like out there."

With her free hand, Katie pulled the shawl more tightly around her shoulders. She stole a glance at the baby, who was still quiet. "He sounded excited by it. It sounds exciting."

"That's it! That's how it sounded to me." Henry stood abruptly and stepped across the shed, then back to the chair.

He gripped the chair back and leaned on it. "What he wrote, it matches what I've been reading in the papers, what I've been thinking and feeling, for a long time now. Katie, there's a whole new country out there. Out west, in places like Chicago, there's opportunities, real opportunities, ones that a man with nothing can grab onto. They're building a railroad all the way across the country that'll open up everything. You read his letter—they've got railroads on the streets in the city. Here, the trains don't even come to Waldoborough yet!"

He started to pace, really an elongated twirl since he had to reverse direction every two strides. "Don't you see? I could feel it sometimes in the army—maybe you saw it in Washington. This country is so much bigger than here, full of places where what matters is what you can build and what you can do, where no one cares if you're German or English or Hottentot but only if you can get done what needs to get done." He stopped and waved behind him. "I feel it every day when I go down to the yards and back, scrounging for a few days' work here, a few days' there, never sure how we're going to pay for what we need. You can see it. It's right in front of us. Just look at this place. All the trees cut down. The river dammed in a dozen places, every stream too. Farmers've been pulling rocks from the ground for years and they haven't made a dent in them. You can't even get a legal glass of beer or a drink of whiskey." He sat in the chair and leaned forward to her.

"Maine, all of New England—it's played out. Look around. We're a hundred years too late. Out west we can build a life in a new world. For Thomas and for all his brothers and sisters. Look at the men who've been heading west. Joe Weber left for Wisconsin last fall. Josiah Turner took his family to Iowa. The West is full of people like us, people who need a chance." Henry realized she had shrunk back against the wall. He pulled himself up and ran a hand through his hair. He took a deep breath. "What do you think?"

"I don't know. I know it's been hard for you. I do. The yards not being busy and all. But I didn't know you felt this way, that you wanted to throw it all over. How long have you been thinking like this?"

"Months. Since I got a good look around. The war's made it worse. The rich—the Storers, the Clarks—they're doing fine. The rest of us scratch for pennies." He reached for her hands. "I need this, Katie. I feel like I'm being strangled. I don't want to end up like George."

"Henry, this is our home. Both of us. Our fathers, my sisters and brother. Your brother. How could we leave them all?"

"Mrs. Beckett will take care of Pa, and everyone else will be all right. Maybe they'll want to follow us out, be part of this adventure. We can send back for them. Katie, we can't build a new life without leaving the old one."

"Haven't we had our lives turned upside down enough, with the war? We've never had normal times, just living, being a family."

"Can't you see?" he said. Katie raised her hand in warning and pointed to the baby. Henry lowered his voice but couldn't keep his feeling out of it. "Can't you see? What's normal here in Waldoborough isn't enough. It's smothering me."

The baby began to stir. The accusation came in the way she reached over to pick Thomas up, glad for the distraction. She wrinkled her nose. "I'm going to need to clean him up. Can you warm some water?"

Henry slammed more wood into the stove, banging the fire door with a clang that made Katie wince and Thomas cry out. "Henry!" she said. "What's got into you?"

Without a word, he grabbed his coat and hat and left, leaving the door hanging loose. When he returned, she was in bed, Thomas cradled against her. She could tell Henry was trying to be quiet. When he climbed in, the cold coming off his body made her shiver. He was asleep in minutes.

Katie took a deep breath and tried to think. Some things made more sense now. When she'd been feeling that he was far away from her, that he didn't care about her and their life together, it was this. He had been far away—far from Waldoborough, from Maine. He made no progress on their new house because he didn't want to. He must hate the whole idea of it. But she didn't want to leave. Her sisters were becoming young women she liked. She had friends from the Soldiers Aid Society, knew young people she had taught. She hadn't ever thought about living somewhere else, somewhere strange, completely new.

In Washington City, she rarely noticed the city around them. She lived in Ward K, never left it, not even in her mind.

It was her home, an odd one, but no less a home than anywhere else. Wasn't that because Henry was there, because she should be where he was? Could Chicago be a home? Was everything that she'd leave behind more important than this family they'd started—Henry and Thomas and her? She thought of the Bible story of Ruth and the phrase she loved as a girl: "Whither thou goest, I will go." She hadn't understood it before. It wasn't only an expression of love and loyalty, but also an acceptance of loss, what you have to give up.

What choice did she have? She was his wife. She couldn't watch him become George Young. Talking about Chicago and the West, his face had lit up. He hadn't been so animated since he marched off to war. Not even when they met the president. But what did she know about Chicago? Her eyes filled with tears.

When she woke in the morning, Henry was sitting up with the baby in his arms. He brushed a knuckle against the baby's warm cheek, then let Thomas grab a calloused finger.

"You're sure this is what you want to do? Chicago?" she asked.

He looked up, surprised. "Oh, yes. Yes. I am."

She nodded and looked away. She didn't trust his certainty. Her stomach knotted. "Shouldn't you go and look at it first?"

"Sure. That makes sense. I can look for work and for a place to live, and then I can send for you and Thomas."

"If it's not what you want, you could come back."

"Yes, sure. Of course."

"We're talking about Chicago, not anywhere else out west?"

"It's the center of it all. And we know Otto there, so that would be a help. You always liked him."

She smiled. "I liked him because you liked him." She looked away again. "Thomas and I might move in with your father while you were away, while we were waiting to hear from you. It would be easier. Do we have the money to do all this?"

"We've never touched my army bounty."

"How far will that go?"

"We could sell the land where the house is going up. That's what Ralph did."

"We could, I guess. Your father wouldn't mind?"

"Ralph did it." He shrugged. "If I have to, I can come back and work long enough to get us started out there."

"That's if Chicago turns out to be what you want."

"Yes."

She looked down at the baby and stroked his head, then shifted her gaze back to Henry. "I thought there was something…something that was wrong…with me," she said, "but I didn't think of this." The baby began to fret. Katie felt her milk start. She reached for the baby. "I suppose you might as well go soon."

"If I have to come back, I can work here through the summer. With any luck, the yards'll be busier then."

His eyes looked so alive.

CHAPTER FOUR

†

Carrying a worn grip borrowed from Katie's father, Henry entered a cloud of engine steam after dropping from the last step of the train car. A few strides revealed that the shed for the Lake Shore & Michigan Railroad lived up to Chicago's reputation for the grand and the oversized. It was the largest structure he'd ever been inside, including terminals where he changed trains in Boston, New York, Pittsburgh, and Cleveland. Trains on other tracks belched steam and smoke. The grinding journey had consumed forty-eight hours, but Henry was too excited to feel fatigue. The West began here. The future beckoned.

Henry ignored the men who offered to carry his bag, to drive him in their wagons, or to show him the way to the horse-drawn omnibus. He trusted none of them. Back in Waldoborough and again on the train ride, he was warned to mistrust such offers. The big city types, he was assured, lived to swindle small-town refugees like him, pick their pockets, swipe the clothes off their backs.

Henry was resolved not to fall victim to any sharpers. He had too little money to trust a face that seemed honest but might cloak a larcenous heart. Most of his dollars were stashed inside his union suit, in a location where he would notice an intruding hand.

He had Otto's address on a piece of paper. A fellow passenger had advised him to cross the river to the north, then walk west on Kinzie Street and cross another arm of the same river. The hubbub in the depot unsettled him. Everyone seemed to know where they were going. The ones who walked slowly, their heads swiveling, were plainly newcomers. Henry tried not to look like them.

Henry emerged from the terminal's din. The day was brisk. Water trails snaked from piles of melting snow. Thick clouds thwarted his plan to orient himself with the sun's position in the sky. He asked someone where a bridge crossed the river to the north, but the man seemed not to understand. He found another who pointed and rushed on.

Swinging his grip to his other hand, Henry headed in the direction indicated, trying to take in this new place with surreptitious glances. Ship masts on his right were reassuring. The river was where he expected it to be. He must be heading west. He started thinking about the differences between Chicago and New York and Boston, cities he also walked through.

The wood-planked sidewalk rose well above the street. Frequent patching showed in the shades and grains of the planks. More patches were needed. Signs clamored from rooftops while others dangled over sidewalks, hazards to tall men. They touted hair tonics, purgatives, tobacco, whiskey, clothing, dry goods, and remedies for ailments Henry did not know. Building fronts bristled with posters testifying to the excellence of a certain canned pork or beer. A banner drooping over the street proclaimed that the finest haircuts and shaves in North America were just steps away. Rooms were for rent around the corner. Chicago seemed obsessed with objects and services that could be bought or rented.

Despite the cold wind, storeowners had claimed portions of the sidewalk to display their wares, braying extravagant claims of price and quality. Henry had to concentrate to breast the stream of passersby while steering around vendors and holes in the planking. His progress was halting yet exhilarating.

After several blocks, he turned right to reach a bridge that spanned the river. Wagons, carriages, and men on horseback pounded by with no regard for foot traffic. Crossing the irregularly paved street required sharp timing and a wide range of vision. With a start, he realized he had passed almost no women.

He stopped at the bridge's threshold to view the swarming river activity. Men unloaded lumber from two cargo ships. Small craft powered by engines or sails or oars skittered between larger ones. Further down the river, another bridge had spun sideways to allow a fat steamer to pass on one side. Wagons and walkers were backed up on the streets on either side of the water, waiting for the bridge to rotate back.

In the other direction, a four-story brick building announced that stoves were built within. A taller building with few windows belonged to a grain merchant. An uproar of engine sounds washed over the scene. Voices shouted greetings and instructions and warnings. Wooden wheels stuttered over heavy bridge planks while hooves thudded hollowly. The wind carried a sour odor from the river. The water was dark, clotted with boards and litter.

Across the bridge, he stepped over train tracks and turned west on what he hoped was Kinzie Street. He jumped at the sound of a shrill whistle, followed by the pounding of a locomotive. He collided with a man in dirty work clothes and a cloth cap, who cursed him without conviction. Others brushed by in both directions. At the edge of a street corner, Henry paused. Not fifty feet away, a locomotive plowed through the street, sparks shooting from its engine and wheels. Hundreds of people paid no notice. How, Henry wondered, could it stop in time to miss a reckless rider or wagon driver?

Around him the city shouted its ambition, its energy, its happiness and its anger, all spiraling up to the flat gray sky, heedless of nature or weather. America's future would be written here.

After crossing the river again, the train tracks veered to the center of the street. He shifted over one block to resume his westward walk. A horse-drawn omnibus slowly passed him on its own tracks. With each block, the city's intensity slackened. Spaces opened between buildings. Traffic thinned on the sidewalk and in the street. He had trouble finding street names. Advertisements obstructed some. Others were faded and indistinct. At several corners he never did find one.

Shifting the grip to the other hand, Henry began to feel weary from the way Chicago hammered itself into his head. He stopped people to ask for Rose Street, winning a range of responses from clueless shrugs to convoluted directions that flew by faster than his tired brain could absorb them. He tried a tall man in a long overcoat, who leaned back against a building while smoking a cigar. Henry concentrated on remembering the first two turns the man described. When he had completed those, he stopped another man and tried the same gambit, hoping he would draw ever closer to Otto's address. When he turned a corner, he saw the same tall man leaning against the same building, smoking the same cigar. Henry ducked back around the corner, put his bag down and leaned against a building. He closed his eyes. He felt ridiculous.

"Who might this lazy fellow be?"

Just what he needed, Henry thought. Some wiseacre looking to have fun at the expense of the bumpkin from Maine. He sighed and opened his eyes, then straightened in surprise. "Otto!"

"You walked by my boarding house two blocks back. Are you looking for someone else?"

Laughing, Henry pumped Otto's hand and confessed his confusion.

Otto's boarding house was a rickety affair of unpainted wood panels. Walking as quietly as his wooden foot permitted and holding a finger to his lips, Otto led Henry up to the back room on the second floor. Inches separated five narrow beds, leaving space for the unnaturally slender to slide past sideways. Four beds held snoring bodies. Otto placed Henry's bag under one of them, then tiptoed out and downstairs.

"But that bed is taken, isn't it?" Henry asked when they reached the ground floor.

"You get it for twelve hours, from 6:00 p.m. to 6:00 a.m. You sign in at six." Otto shrugged. "Since I work at nighttime, which is when the newspaper is written and printed, the empty bed you saw is mine."

"Why aren't you in it?"

"I am meeting an old friend from Ward K. Also, I don't sleep so good. The foot, you know. We may see each other not so much, because of my work times."

"How long have you had the false foot?"

"Since summer."

"You walk well on it. I barely notice."

"Yes, It is not bad for a foot of wood and leather. But there's pain where it rubs. It's lucky that printers mostly stand, not walk."

After Henry paid the pudgy landlady for a week's stay on the night shift, she issued him a sheet and pillow and a towel that resembled a well-used handkerchief. Breakfast, she said, was at 6:00 a.m. sharp. Coffee and oatmeal, the same for everyone. After stashing the linens with his grip, Henry joined Otto on the street.

"How long have you been in that place?" Henry asked as they set off.

"Here"—Otto pointed to a spot on the walk—"is where we wait for omnibus to North Side." He pulled out a pipe and began to fill the bowl with tobacco from a paper bag. "Mrs. Ryan's place," he shrugged, "it is lousy to be sure, but cheap."

"In Ward K, at least we had our beds for twenty-four hours." Henry leaned out to peer down the street. An omnibus was about two blocks away. "You've got a good job. What're you doing with all your money?"

Otto smiled around the pipestem as he lit the tobacco and sucked in air to help it catch fire. "Ah, that is the secret."

"Wine, women, and song?"

"Some on wine and song, as you and I will do now. Not women, though. I still look for the woman."

"Well?"

"What do German people come to this country for?"

The omnibus was still one block away. It would be faster to walk wherever they were going, but then Henry remembered Otto's false foot. "Not for the beer, right?"

Otto raised a finger. "For land, sergeant. For land. So I save my money and already have a payment down—no, down payment is it?—on a lot about a half-mile to the northwest. I take you there another day. You can see."

"You're building a house there?"

"Not yet. When I find the woman. And make more money. For now I have the land. It is a start."

They ate sausages and drank in a beer hall where voices all spoke German. After an hour, an apple-cheeked brunette in a flouncy dress sat at an out-of-tune piano and led the customers in thumping renditions of songs that were new to Henry. During a lull, Otto fixed him with a stern look. "You say you're German, but you know no songs."

"My people were German. A long time ago. I guess we're American now."

Otto gave a theatrical sigh. "I will teach you songs."

After another hour, Otto led him to a building next door that was labeled Turner Society. In a large room, young men engaged in violent-looking exercises. In another room, swimmers thrashed through a pool, leaving frothy wakes. "These places, these Turner Societies, they were political back home," Otto said, "part of our revolution against the princes. But our revolution failed, and now they are for health and strength. We don't need revolution. You had revolution for us. But is for men with two good legs, so you might like it."

* * * * *

Henry spent several days walking through the city, marveling at it, trying to figure out how he and Katie and Thomas might fit. He spent an afternoon at parkland along the lakefront, dawdling on beaches in cool April sunlight. Telegraph wires lined the streets, supporting alarm boxes for calling police and firemen to emergencies. At night, gas lights sparkled on poles.

The wonders seemed endless. Henry goggled at the brick building on the river where McCormick built his reapers. He saw Irish workers emerge from a six-foot-high tunnel they were digging under the lake to draw clean water into the city. After the tunnelers filed out, bricklayers entered to line the tunnel walls. Because parts of the city were too low for water to run off to the lake, they had to raise the streets by as much as six or seven feet. One afternoon he watched a thousand men use thousands of jackscrews to raise a hotel while customers entered and left the building undisturbed. The lifting created odd sights. A building's foundation might rise several feet higher than its neighbor's, along with the sidewalks in front of it, which made walking difficult. He watched elevators scoop corn from railroad cars and carry it high up into huge storage buildings where it was weighed and sent down chutes into ships that plied the lakes. Everything was big. Most things belched smoke. Men never spoke, but shouted.

He spent a morning examining the ship models at Col. Wood's Museum, along with a rifle that belonged to Daniel Boone and the skeleton of a whale. He never tired of the swing bridges over the river that rotated to let ships pass. Compared to Chicago, he decided, New York looked lazy, Boston sclerotic, and Waldoborough purely dead.

After a week, he realized—and Otto confirmed—that Chicago was full of men like him, uprooted by the war, footloose, looking for a new place. Jobs could be hard to get. Henry pressed Otto about it.

"But you have skills, no?" Otto said. "As a carpenter? There's so much building here. You have no problem finding work. As a printer, I find plenty of work."

Henry wasn't so sure. Shipyards lined the river, churning out boats for the bustling traffic on Lake Michigan and its sisters. But his skills mattered little for the ironclads that were taking over. And Otto's assurance about the house-building industry began to ring hollow on the day Henry went to see Otto's lot at the western edge of the city.

He passed dozens of lots where houses were going up— slapped together, in Henry's opinion. The house frames were spindly two-by-fours. Over these, men nailed raw, thin paneling and laid floors of simple planks. Only nails held each house together. No self-respecting carpenter in Maine would build such a flimsy structure, much less live in it.

At one site, he passed a heavy-set carpenter who was taking a break. "What do you call this way of building?" he asked, waving at the house frame.

"This crap, you mean?" the carpenter gestured over his shoulder with a thumb.

"These, yes. I'm from New England. We don't build like this."

"Nor in Pennsylvania where I come from. Good wind might blow these bastards down. Build 'em fast and cheap, sell 'em to the suckers. That's what the boss wants."

"But what's it called?"

"Balloon frame is what I've heard. Not sure why. About as solid as a balloon, I guess."

"Huh." Henry ran his eyes over the structure. "We use mortise-and-tenon, mostly. Brick and stone are too expensive."

"Don't talk to anyone here about some other way to build. Fast and bad, that's what we do."

226

"The work must pay well."

The man gave a short laugh as he stood to resume his task. "If it did, then the houses wouldn't be cheap, would they?"

So that posed a problem. Henry wanted to remake himself, to build a new life. He wanted to have his own business, maybe end up rich and powerful like old man McCormick. If not carpentry or joining, what should he do? Moving through the city, he searched for an idea.

It came to him one evening when he was finishing his dinner, a hefty beefsteak that cost fifteen cents at a café near Mrs. Ryan's. A moaning sound came from the street. Dust filled the air. The café owner a noisy Bohemian named Dvorak who already was greeting Henry by name—stalked past tables full of customers to shout outside the door. Henry followed him.

"—don't bring those filthy animals through this street ever again." Dvorak was screaming, waving an arm, red-faced. "What's the railroad for if not this?"

From one sidewalk to the other, the street was a river of slow-moving animals. The cattle did the moaning, responding to prods by mounted riders, the first cowboys Henry had seen. Behind the cattle came a sea of hogs, snuffling and trotting, careening off each other.

"Ach," Dvorak appealed to Henry, the only person near him, "see how they stir up the filth, then they make their crap everywhere. By the time they are done, it will be a carpet of shit. You make a face. How much you want to eat my food with people coming in with that on their shoes? And what if these beasts—if they become scared? They trample everything!" He turned back to a cowboy passing by on horseback. "This is a decent place! Why you bring these beasts here!"

The cowboy touched the brim of his dusty hat. "Sorry, doc. Train broke down. Boss said to get these critters down to the stockyards, chop chop. He's not a man to reason with."

"They used to do this all the time," Dvorak sputtered to Henry, "but the railroads were supposed to change all that." He shook his head and turned to the door. "Filthy. Filthy."

After settling his dinner bill, Henry came back out to watch the livestock parade. Here it was, he thought. Meat. That's what was special about Chicago. He had never eaten so much of it as in the last two weeks. It was good, and it was cheap. Back home, there was fish, being on the ocean. Even here you could get fish from the lake. But Chicago people were used to meat. It came into town on dozens of trains every day. He decided to investigate meat.

Next day, he walked to the Union Stock Yards, acres of pens for cattle and pigs and horses. Trains came and disgorged oceans of animals. Back home, people butchered their own livestock, one at a time. Henry needed to know a lot more about meat.

At a nearby beer hall, Henry sought out men who worked in the stockyards. They explained that some cattle were kept in Chicago and sold as fresh meat, but most were shipped east to be slaughtered and sold there. The hogs stayed at the yards, but the hog slaughtering happened in the cold months—that season was ending. Then pork was cured so it could be shipped anywhere and would stay good for months. The smells around the yards were foul. They clung to clothes and skin and drifted through the beer hall, but the work of feeding Chicago and the nation went on all day and all night.

By the end of the day, standing on a railroad platform that overlooked the stockyards, Henry felt it. Chicago was a sprawling brute, a natural place for the meat business, harsh and simple, an indispensable business. A fire flared within him. This was what he'd been looking for. People would never stop wanting meat, and Chicago would provide it.

He would provide it.

CHAPTER FIVE

SEPTEMBER 1866

"I'm not going to watch," Katie said. "Thomas and I will be inside with Lucy and the others, staying warm."

"Suit yourself." Henry grinned at her as he coaxed Cricket to pull them into his brother's yard in Rockport. Two other wagons were already there. "They say old man Webb's an artist with a saw and a cleaver."

"No, thank you."

"But you'll help with the sausage?"

She sighed. "Of course. I did that with my mother."

Henry jumped down and accepted the baby, then handed him back when she was on the ground. Ralph unharnessed Cricket while Henry fetched his knives from the wagon. After leading the horse behind the house, they joined the others near two tripods, an iron kettle suspended from each. Bright fires licked at the base of each kettle.

"Henry," Ralph said, "this is Elias Webb, the man I mentioned."

A small man with an aggressive white beard glared from under a broadbrimmed hat. They shook hands.

"You've got a mighty reputation, Mr. Webb," Henry said.

"There's worse things to know how to do than slaughterin'. This here's my boy. Knows all I do and twice as strong." The younger men nodded to each other. "So you want to be a butcher out west?"

"Yes, sir. I know I've got some learning to do, though I worked a few weeks at the stockyards there. I won't often be starting with a live animal like this, but I want to know the whole business, start to finish."

"By the time we're done, we'll use everything but the squeal." He put his hand into the water. "That's coming along. Let's get to it. Now, we don't bang 'em on the head like the big yards do. We cut 'em and let 'em bleed out. Makes for less wrestling."

Ralph pointed out the pig to be butchered, one that had been born a month after Thomas. The pig had grown faster. After six months, he looked to be nearly two hundred pounds. The younger Webb climbed into the pen with a wicked-looking knife and casually herded the animal into a corner. The older man followed. A quick move under the pig's throat brought a spurt of bright blood. After a minute of startled squeals, then gargled ones, the pig staggered and toppled over, his blood soaking the dirt. The Webbs hauled him to a trough with two chains spread across it. After heaving the pig onto the chains, they poured the scalding water on him.

Webb pointed to Ralph and Henry. "This part is for you young folks." He showed them how to rotate the pig by his legs through the water to loosen the bristles. Then they used Webb's scrapers to remove the bristles and everything else on the hide. Following Webb's instructions, they moved a tripod off its fire and hung the pig on it.

"This here," Webb said, "is the part you want to get right. You got to slice open the belly, starting down here and working up, one clean motion. But not into the bowel. You cut that and you've got a world of trouble—have to crack that bone down there, get in quick with twine and tie off the bowel. Messy." He pointed to the spot on the pig's belly where Henry should start, showed him the right grip to use, pantomimed three movements, then jammed twine into Henry's pocket.

"How deep?" Henry asked.

"Deep enough, but not too deep." The other two snickered. "Also, watch your fingers. Them's as play with knives usually end up slicing themselves."

Henry placed the blade against the pig and took a breath. "Shoot, Henry, he's dead," Ralph said. "He's not gonna feel a thing."

Henry made the first cut clean, had to fight his way through the bone before cracking it. He almost dropped the twine tying off the bowel. When he stepped back, shaking muck off his hands, Webb said, "All right, I've seen worse. You'll get better."

Henry realized he'd cut his thumb, not too bad. He went to suck the wound, then thought better of it. Webb gave him a sardonic look. "I've seen worse of that too."

Henry knew more about the rest of the butchering—stripping the hide to sell to a tannery, cutting up the carcass, boiling the scraps for sausage and scrapple, and rendering the lard. He'd done or watched those before.

When the hard work was done, weak sunlight brought a measure of warmth. The day turned sociable when Lucy and Katie came out with potatoes for chips, slicing and dropping them into the bubbling lard. While Webb counseled Henry on cutting the carcass into pieces, the women mixed the chips with fresh-cooked pork. Everyone took a plateful and washed it down with home-brewed beer. They filled scrapple pans and sausage sleeves. Henry set aside good cuts from the haunches for the Webbs.

On the road back to Waldoborough, with a set of ribs in the back, Henry was feeling good. The baby was tugging Katie's hair, then decided to taste it. After four difficult months, Thomas had discovered the joys of eating his fill every chance he got, a discovery that transformed him into a charming little fellow. His eyes stayed pale blue and his hair sparse and flaxen, though Katie said it would darken. That's what happened in her family. Henry wasn't so sure.

"Did that go how you wanted?" she asked. The front right wheel banged through a hole. The wagon rolled on. It seemed to be okay.

"Guess so. That Elias, he knows a lot. He said he'd send a few people to me that need help with their butchering, so I can practice. He said he always gets more business than he and his son can handle. I hope to do a cow. Out in Chicago they have a real taste for beef. We talked about the ways they're different from hogs."

They rode in silence. "Henry," she said, "are you sure this is what you want? Pull up all our roots, walk away from the trade you know and are good at, start something completely new in a place where we don't know anyone?"

"We know Otto."

"Since you've been back, you've been finding work at the yards. Enough anyway. Being a butcher seems so savage, not like you."

He smiled. "You didn't think it was so savage at dinner back there." He adjusted his cap. "Katie, when I get you to Chicago, you'll feel it. You'll know what I mean. Maybe that whole town's a little savage. We're all there to make out the best we can, and going hard at it. Meat just seems the perfect way to do it. It's a river of meat goes through every day and more people pouring in all the time. Every day, the world wakes up hungry. There's no better place for this."

She sighed and spread her cape over the baby. "I know you've thought about this, but what do you really know about butchering, compared to what you know about joining?"

"What did I know about soldiering? I did all right."

"It's also that it's so…so *far*. Our families are here. We'll never see them. We won't have days like this with Ralph and Lucy. Thomas won't know his cousins. I won't see my sisters or my brother get married. And Chicago, from what you say, it sounds like a wild place."

"The future's a wild place." He snorted impatiently and waved at the land around them. "There's nothing for us here. Do I want to spend every winter freezing my fingers off at the shipyards, if I'm lucky enough to find work? Which still isn't regular."

"Of course it isn't regular. You went away to Chicago for three months. *You* weren't regular. What would you expect?"

He waited before responding. "I've got to do this, Katie. It's a new world. I want to make a place for us there. I want Thomas to know more than this worn-out speck on a rocky coast."

She chewed the inside of her cheek and sighed. "So when? When do you want to go?"

"After the new year. I'll get more experience butchering, find a place for us to settle. Prices there, I'll tell you, they're going up. The longer we wait, the harder it'll be."

"I don't think I can go then. Not that soon."

"Why not?"

"I'm pretty sure we're going to have another."

He looked over with a quizzical look, then smiled. "You're sure? I haven't noticed anything."

She nodded. "No, you wouldn't. You've been tired and thinking about ribs and haunches."

"Katie."

"I've missed twice now, and Lucy asked if I was, just from looking."

"So when—when will the baby come?"

"May? May, I think."

He smiled at her. "It's a pretty time of year. For a birthday."

"Even in tired old Waldoborough?"

"Even here."

She reached over and put her hand on his arm. "It's another mouth to feed, I know."

"That's my problem."

"Do we have enough money to move? With the land on the river not selling."

"Doesn't that tell you everything? No one wants land here in Maine. Pa thinks we'll sell it to Schreiber, the farmer next door, but the old fox is waiting to knock down the price. So we have to wait him out."

"I'm sorry about the baby, Henry. I know it's the wrong time."

He pulled up Cricket and set the brake on the wagon. "That's silly, Katie. Do you think I'm sorry about Thomas? All right, we're not going to start out with much. No Overstreet ever did. And we may not finish with much. But we'll be part of it, that's what this is about." He pulled her to him. "This is just another reason to go. One more Overstreet who needs a future."

* * * * *

Katie's sister Alice came inside waving the letter. She had moved in when Katie didn't bounce back from the birth of baby John. Alice recognized Henry's hand. Katie held her breath as she took the letter.

"Watch Thomas, will you?" she said. He was crawling toward the kitchen at top speed. She shifted John to her other side; he accepted the move placidly, as he accepted most things. He was as mild as his brother had been querulous.

Katie sat down as her heart sped up. The future lay in her hand. It was the first letter she'd gotten since the war.

November 10, 1867
Chicago
Dear wife—

The time has come. I have worked the last two months for a butcher named Svoboda who has a mean temper and only eight fingers and is as close with a nickel as any farmer in Maine but he knows his business and I have learned. I also discovered the truth in what Mr. Webb said as all too often my blood mingles with that of the beasts. Every Sunday I walk through the city looking for a home for us but they build small houses here on small lots, more like cottages. And then they build a second cottage behind it with the privy and well in between and it is very close quarters. I saw one cobbler who had acquired both cottages on a single lot and had his family behind and his shop in front on the street and it looked like a smart way to go. So I have been looking for something like that and found it on the southern side of the city on a place called Polk Street. They named all the streets there for presidents in order so this is pretty far down. The closest butcher is at least four blocks away, so I want to get established soon before any other moves in. I have been working on the cottages in the evenings by the light of a kerosene lamp which is not the best way to work and also on Sundays when I fix my mistakes and they will be ready when you and the boys come out. I know this is right for us and I need to do it right and proper and with all that I have in me.

I will be in Waldoborough some time next month. Please let my father know our plans so he can sell the land in time as we will need those moneys for getting started. I hope you and the boys will like it here; it has been lonesome without you.

Your husband,
H. Overstreet

She closed her eyes. It wasn't a surprise, but now it was real. Before this day her life was Maine, their families, what she had known all her life. After today it would be—she had no notion what it would be.

"What's he say?" Alice asked.

"We're going. He's found a place."

"Oh, Katie." Her sister called out Thomas's name and dashed into the kitchen. She came back with him and sat across from Katie. "When will I see you?"

Katie shook her head. "Please don't." She sniffled, then boosted John on her shoulder. "We'll write. Long, wonderful letters. And we'll see each other. Somehow." She nodded.

"Of course we will."

CHAPTER SIX

JANUARY 1868

On both sides of the clangorous train, with both sleeping boys on her in different postures, the land stretched out—flat, immense, an endless gray in the gradual morning light. The world beyond the smudged window looked cold and dismal, a reflection of the dull ache that settled behind her eyes after a second night of fitful dozing seated upright. She tried to imagine living on those treeless plains, where patches of snow alternated with yellow-brown stubble and scrub, lone trees looking embarrassed and regretful.

Back in Ohio, Henry had pointed out one of the new reaper machines standing next to a barn. Those, he said, were changing the world, allowing a single man to do the work of six or eight. Much of that land looked too wet for crops, though reaping and plowing would be easy on ground that never rose or fell, that held few cattle or hogs and no forests. The leaden panorama dragged her spirits down.

She twisted her head to be sure that Henry still was wedged between the seat back and outer wall. He must be cold there, so far from the stove in the car's middle, without any warm boys against him. He had stood, arms folded and head drooping, since Ohio. Other men held worse spots, crammed into every corner and against every wall that allowed them to remain upright without much effort. Katie's muscles ached from two days on the pinched seat cushion, flattened and tilted by innumerable backsides. The seat seemed to bruise her bones, but at least it was a seat. Passenger comfort was not a priority for the railroad.

She felt the iron wheels slow. A few rough dwellings came into sight. Henry's hand squeezed her shoulder, and she placed hers on it. His was cold.

She gave him a tired smile over her shoulder as he reached for Thomas. They had worked out the station stops. While Henry guarded her seat, Katie had five minutes to get the boys off the train, washed up and in clean linen if there was any left, then she handed them back for her dash to the privy. Henry got any remaining time for his own privy run and the purchase of food or drink, while Katie defended his space against the wall. In such cramped quarters, conversation focused on the tasks at hand.

When Henry climbed back into the car, he handed over a meat pie that was cold, glutinous, and salty. She fed pieces to each groggy boy. John got mostly crust and congealed gravy. Henry leaned down and spoke into her ear. "This is Illinois. Only a couple hours more."

The approach to the great metropolis began with a proliferation of parallel tracks carrying trains that slammed past in the other direction, sidetracks where freight cars stood empty, other tracks that merged and spread in dizzying patterns. Then came sheds and work buildings, warehouses with murky contents. Teamsters on wagons waited for the train to pass. The buildings multiplied. More had windows now. People walked on the streets that stretched away from the tracks. Katie roused the boys. "Look," she said, pointing out the window. "We're coming into Chicago, our new home."

"Will we get off here?" Thomas asked. "For good?"

She smiled. "Yes, sweetie. For good." The prospect of liberation from the punishing journey submerged her anxieties about Chicago.

Climbing from the train into the cavernous terminal, their goods loaded on a cart, Katie gawked at the soaring ceilings, then at the waiting room that seemed to reach for miles. The scale of the place put her on edge. What race of people required such immensity?

Reality intruded when they reached the street. Henry reached into his pocket for money to tip the porter but found nothing. He had warned Katie about the pickpockets and thieves who preyed on travelers, never expecting to be a victim himself. As a precaution, he had divided their money into several different packets. One was in his left boot, another in Katie's purse, the largest inside his union suit.

"Must've got me at that meat pie stand," he said darkly.

"You planned for this," she reminded him as she handed over the money from her purse. "And you must be exhausted from standing all that way."

Loaded into a wagon, Thomas and John revived, taking in the city with wide eyes. The older boy couldn't stand being held any longer. Struggling to get out of the wagon and run through the teeming streets, he broke into anguished wails for the last twenty minutes of the ride. Oppressed by Thomas's cries, Katie could form only jumbled impressions. Everything looked temporary or half-finished, especially as the wagon lurched farther away from the terminal. It didn't feel as cold as Henry had warned it would be, nor was the wind as raw. Even Thomas couldn't drown out the raucous city noises—peddlers' cries, traffic clatter, the cacophony of construction.

Their new home on Polk Street was as raw and unfinished as everything else in the neighborhood. Henry carried their things into the back cottage, then built a fire in the stove from wood he had left in place. He kept looking over at her, eager to gauge her reaction. She walked through the front room and was glad it had two windows, even if they would let in the cold. They needed curtains. Men never thought of that.

Thomas, unsteady on his legs yet determined to run every-where, caromed off the door into the small back room, landing on his bottom. Back on his feet, he strained to climb on the solid bed in the corner, which nearly filled the room. It was a used one that Henry had rebuilt. Katie had wondered who owned it before, what had happened in it. Had they been happy or miserable? Had someone died, right in that bed? Or been born there? Had the last owners prospered so in the new West that they cast it aside with little thought?

Henry boosted the little boy onto the horsehair mattress, where he rolled from side to side and giggled. Henry joined him there, then Katie added John to their melee. She perched on the edge. The baby stared in wonder as Thomas spun nearly out of control, Henry grabbing him by a leg before he plunged off the side.

"Come, Mrs. Overstreet," Henry said, "there's more to see." Scooping up John, with Thomas keeping up at a steady half-run, he led them out past the well and the privy to the front cottage. He pointed proudly at a board next to the door. It announced:

FINE MEATS

BEEF A SPECIALTY

H. OVERSTREET, PROPRIETOR

"Otto made it at the newspaper where he works."

"Proprietor," she said. "That sounds very distinguished, Mr. Overstreet."

"Otto insisted. He said butcher sounded common, and that owner sounded lazy."

"I quite agree." She kissed him on the cheek. "You must show me."

The tour of the two-room shop, replete with his plans for improvements, took little time. When the boys were settled on the bed for proper naps that they desperately needed, Henry fed the stove in the front room, then warmed his hands over it. "Well?"

"We'll be fine here," she said, smiling through her fatigue. "It's ours."

"That's it, Katie. It's our start." He took her hands. "Finally, I feel like I'm going to do what I've chosen to do. During the war, the newspapers were full of how we were fighting for freedom and liberty for the slaves, but then I came home and I wanted freedom and liberty for me. Now, out here, I've got the chance to grab them for all of us. This is just the beginning. I know you've got your doubts—"

"Henry, that's not—"

"No, no, I'm not blind. Don't tell me what's not so. I've got doubts too. But let me tell you this. If I can get it for you and for Thomas and for John by working hard, then you'll have it, whatever it is."

She put her arms around his neck and rested her head on his shoulder. "I know, Henry." She wished she felt happier.

Henry was as good as his word when it came to working hard. Most mornings he rose at three to get the best carcasses from a nearby stockyard. He had them cut in half, then hauled them in a cart he pulled himself, sometimes making a second trip. Then he trimmed the meat and cut it into portions for sale. He did some of the butchering in the yard between the houses, some in the back room of the shop. Katie worried about the boys being near so many sharp edges. Once she screamed across the yard when Thomas reached, on tiptoe, for a cleaver. Her cry brought Henry at a trot and made Thomas cry.

When the weather warmed, the smells of the trade asserted themselves. The yard, already burdened with the privy, turned noxious. Flies massed. Katie started hanging the laundry along the side of the house, even though the sun rarely penetrated there, to protect the clothes from the scents of dead animals.

The trade through Henry's shop proved steady, though rarely heavy. He acquired a reputation for fair prices and an honest scale—the last being a sore point with many butchers—and for not selling spoiled meat even when he had to throw it out. But he was too small an operator to have a wide assortment of cuts, and he sometimes ran out. His manner in the shop was correct, matter-of-fact, sometimes impatient.

Katie helped when she could. In the morning, Henry told her what to chalk onto the slate of offerings and prices. The less expensive cuts sold more quickly, so she listed those at the top. When she greeted customers, she praised their hats, or inquired after their children, bemoaned or celebrated the weather. When she urged Henry to make such talk, he became exasperated. "I have a thousand things to do and you want me to sit around and babble with every old biddy. Who'll cut the steaks? Or clean the blades? Or wash out the back room?"

To preserve meat in the warm weather, Henry needed a steady and affordable source of ice. Back home, ice was cut from the Medomak during winter and stored in sawdust underground. Anyone could have enough so long as he was willing to put enough away.

But Chicago's river and lake were foul. Ice had to come from fresh lakes and ponds that were miles away. Ice prices made Henry grind his teeth. Three different ice men served customers on Polk Street. All, Henry insisted, were thieves. When a block of ice from Flanagan melted into an evil-smelling pool of fetid water that spoiled the meat rather than preserve it, the supplier list shrank to two, which did not improve prices.

Henry had been open for several weeks when Otto Krause came by on a Saturday afternoon. The two men planned to reinforce and extend the counter he used for butchering in the yard. A stout, red-faced woman with a kerchief over her hair was staring at the slate of prices. Three cuts had sold out, and Katie had wiped off those listings. Henry had learned to dread visits from this woman, Mrs. Schmidt. She came late and haggled for lower prices, alternately understanding his English but failing to understand it when she disliked the prices. She strained his patience. He posted the prices—and he set them fairly—so he wouldn't have to haggle, and certainly not in pidgin English and half-German. Moreover, Mrs. Schmidt had no reasonable claim on his charity. Henry knew that her husband turned a good dollar at his beer hall on a corner of Harrison Street.

"*Verzeihung bitte*," Otto said to Mrs. Schmidt, then rattled off a few sentences that Henry couldn't follow. The woman brightened. After a few more exchanges, Otto said she wanted two pounds of chuck roast for stewing and as many pig's trotters as he had. She had, Otto explained as Mrs. Schmidt beamed at him, family coming from Milwaukee.

Assembling her order, Henry could barely keep his mind on it. He had been stupid. Though he remembered little of the German he once knew, he still had a feel for how the words should sound, what the rhythms were. After the woman left, Henry called out the back door for Katie. She arrived with John on one hip. Thomas marched around the shop, marking time with a stick.

"We must sell in German," Henry said, looking from Katie to Otto and back. "I know only a few words, but we need to know them all. Otto, you'll help us?"

Otto nodded.

Henry wiped his hands on his apron and tore off a sheet of butcher paper. He handed the sheet and a pencil to his friend. "Give us the German words for each of these." He began to rattle off cuts of meat from loin to shank, from flank to round to ribeye to pot roast, from rump roast to brisket. Otto held up his hand to slow Henry down. The final list held almost thirty terms. Otto provided German terms for most, though he stumbled over T-bone and sirloin, saying with a shrug, "We never ate such cuts."

Henry tore off another sheet and asked Otto for some friendly phrases, questions like, "How is your health?" and "Are your children well?" The answers that came back didn't matter, Henry said. If the woman's tone of voice sounded negative, he could cluck and shake his head. He would greet good news with a smile and a quick "*Wunderbar!*" In either event, his next question would be the most important one: "What would you like today?"

He turned to Katie. "So, now we do two slates every morning. One in English, one in German. Okay?"

"Of course."

He held his hand out for the sheets. "Now, Otto, how do we say these things so it doesn't sound like we're insulting our customers?"

"It's late for you to discover you're a German."

Henry grinned. "I never had such a good reason before."

Katie rose to go start supper. "Henry can teach me what you teach him," she said. Halfway through the door she added, "And if you can explain to him that we shouldn't extend so much credit, that would be better."

"*Vas ist?*" Otto said after she was gone.

"Pay no mind," Henry said. "Women, you know, can be hard at business. If a woman's been cursed with a drunken husband, or if a man fought in the Union Army and hasn't found his way, why can't I give them a poor cut of meat that I may not sell anyway?"

"She has a point," Otto said. "Vanderbilt didn't get rich by giving out free rides on his ships."

Henry shrugged. "She thinks I'm a dreamer, that I don't know that they won't pay off their credit. But I know. Now, teach me the words."

Within a week, the new words slid easily out of Henry's mouth as the local Germans discovered the Overstreet shop. Henry visited shops run by German butchers and noted their popular items. He found a sausage maker on the North Side and arranged to sell the man's bratwurst, bockwurst, and Thuringer. He didn't make as much on those as on meats he butchered himself, but they brought customers in. He lost the trade of some Irish women who felt excluded by the foreign palaver, but the Bohemians had no such reservations.

By the end of summer, neighbors greeted Henry in the street in German. He had hired the Novotny boy—only twelve, but strong for his age—to help on the predawn run to the stockyard. The carcasses were hard on Henry's war wound. He was all right pushing the cart, but heaving the carcasses in and out could set off waves of pain that came near to blinding him. Tramping through the quiet, dark streets with the boy, he imagined Thomas and then John joining him. Perhaps then they would drive a horse-drawn wagon, one with their name painted on the side: Overstreet & Sons. The idea warmed him on cold mornings, when the old ache in his hands threatened to come back.

CHAPTER SEVEN

OCTOBER 1871

"Just look at that," Bessie Grove sputtered. She pointed at a cluster of cabbages and boards that washed against the shore. A passing workboat's horn shattered the Sunday morning quiet. "It's not decent, Katie. These people don't care how they live."

Katie and five-year-old Thomas had joined Bessie, who lived on Clark Street, for services at the Methodist church, a whitewashed building six blocks away. Henry, insisting that Sunday morning was his best chance to sharpen and clean his knives, was keeping an eye on their younger boy, who—like Henry—squirmed during sermons. Bessie, whose husband was off on a lumber boat that ran to the Wisconsin forests, was glad for Katie's company. The women had New England backgrounds in common, along with a shared dissatisfaction with Chicago. That morning, Thomas had begged to walk along the river.

Bessie's tirade prompted the boy to take a closer look at the river trash. "Mama, look," he called, "It's a rat! There's two of them. They're swimming." He pointed with a stick.

"Come back here, Thomas," Katie cried. "Don't you go near them." The rats looked as big as bobcats. Heaven only knew what animal they really were.

"I think they're drowning, Mama."

"Well, good riddance," Bessie said. "Come, Thomas, we can find better companions elsewhere."

As the boy reluctantly moved from the river, Katie asked, "And how's your water?"

Bessie sighed. "Ah, my. The well's no better. The Curran girl— they're the people behind us—she's still sick. They say it's not the cholera, but I don't know what to believe."

"Have you taken milk from Hellman lately?"

"No, the lord and master won't abide milk in the house."

"I swear, Heilman's has more alcohol than a bottle of whiskey."

"Ach, that swill milk."

"I fear it, I do. They say Heilman feeds his cows from the brewery slops, so you're the second creature that drinks the beer. He says no, but what else would he say?"

"We don't drink the stuff, nor the water from our well. It all smells wrong and who knows what's in it? The washing smells worse when I'm done than when I started."

"You drink only beer?"

"What can you do? Mrs. Curran's started giving beer to her children. It seems an evil habit to start in ones so young, but I don't know if I blame her. Better to have them be souses than meet an early grave."

"Thomas," Katie called. The boy was poking a stick at a pile of indeterminate refuse. "Come along. We need to get ready for our picnic."

When they reached the yard behind the shop, Thomas ran to help his father with the cleaning up. "Do you have the ham?" Katie asked. Henry gave Thomas a long-suffering look.

"We're butchers, Mama," Thomas called back. "Of course we have the meat."

Henry held out a paper-wrapped package. "Carry this to your mama," he said, "with our compliments." Crouching next to John, who was trying to get a top spinning with a string, Henry showed him again how to start it.

It was a perfect day for a picnic, bright and warm. High, wispy clouds scudded across blue sky.

Henry and Thomas, who was trusted with the smaller knives, deliberately placed them in the racks that Henry had designed to shield the blades from moisture and to protect small children from the blades. He stepped back and looked over the room. Order pleased him. He was ready for the coming week. He placed a hand on Thomas's head, feeling the lank hair that Katie had washed the night before. "Picnic time, mister," he said.

Henry carried the dinner basket as they walked toward the lakefront park. Katie rode herd on the excited boys. The morning walk had reminded her of the city's filth. It seemed dirtier every day. They had to watch every step on the decaying sidewalks. So many boards were snapped off or rotted through. Crossing the street was not as terrifying with the lighter Sunday traffic, but on Sundays the manure from horses and wandering pigs was even more treacherous. On other days, storekeepers paid sweepers to clear off the crossings near their businesses, but on the Lord's Day the detritus lay undisturbed. And the gutters—who knew what might lie in wait there? Even the pigs disdained them. She always lifted John over gutters. The streets were flat and dull. Except in the rich neighborhoods, many buildings looked ready to fall down as soon as they were built. Henry had reinforced the wall struts in their two cottages. Many buildings never knew paint. Bare wood swelled and rotted in wet times, then bleached and dried out in sun or cold. She had found Washington City a graceless place, but it seemed an Eden compared to Chicago.

The way to the lake took them through rough neighborhoods where Katie held each boy's hand. Drunks and bums, unshaven and belching, loitered near the city's numberless saloons and gambling halls. Even the children on these streets looked hard and mean, their faces pinched with hunger and smudged with dirt that no one was sober enough to wash off. She assumed they were Irish, because everybody did.

A pack of mismatched dogs trotted down the street toward the river, bouncing on their paws, tails high. Katie tightened her grip on each boy. Light Sunday traffic emboldened the packs to emerge from backyards where they held sway.

Katie's mood lightened at the park. Henry spread their blanket on the last grass before the beach began. She helped the boys off with their shoes and socks. They splashed into the lake, halting when the water was no more than ankle high. Henry shed his footwear and rolled up his trousers. "Coming?" he asked.

She smiled and shook her head. "It's my day off too."

Thomas shouted from his wading spot. Laughing, he threw handfuls of water high in the air so the drops fell back on his head. He reared back to kick the water as far as possible, not incidentally splashing his brother. John didn't react, his focus on the lake bottom. He had bent from the waist for a better look and was in immediate danger of tipping over when Henry grabbed his hand. The rescue was short-lived. Within five minutes, Henry and Thomas were wet to mid-thigh and John, to his great pleasure, had achieved full immersion.

A half-dozen families sat on either side of Katie, a few more behind. Conversations drifted around her—where was something packed, or who left what behind. The lake was thick with waders, but only to a depth of a foot or two. Some shouted. Many stood and gazed at the point where sky and water merged. They thinned out quickly as the water deepened. Few turned to look at the land. A cooling breeze brushed Katie's hair. She took off her hat and unfastened the top two buttons of her blouse.

Despite the carnival atmosphere, Katie couldn't shake her wistful mood. Her world was so crowded. Voices came at her all day – from neighbors' yards, from streets and shops, from the children and from women in the shop. She missed quiet. Sometimes she woke when Henry left for the stockyards in the middle of the night. She would pretend to sleep until he was gone, then rise to look at the night sky and know calm interrupted only by a barking dog or a drunken man. Her boys, she feared, would never know much quiet. They'd have few chances to lie on their backs and watch clouds blow by, forming and reforming into fantastic shapes. They wouldn't follow the zigzag path of a butterfly down a country path.

Her task-filled days didn't leave time to puzzle over how Henry had changed and kept changing. That sweet, happy boy who worked at Waldoborough's shipyards had become almost grim, devoted to duties that he seemed to multiply for himself. He rested less and less, sometimes waking in bug-eyed terror of horrors he refused to describe.

"Mama, look!"

It was Thomas. He and John were crouching, ready to race back into the lake. She waved and Thomas said something, then they ran in, falling into the water with gales of laughter. Katie couldn't resist. Barefoot, she followed them, lifting her skirt. The cool wash spread around each toe and lapped at her ankles. John ran against her leg and grabbed her hand to drag her out deeper, but she stayed where she was, moving her eyes between their basket on the shore and the splashing boys.

When they were ready for food, she wrapped each damp boy in a corner of the blanket. She tried to peel their wet clothes off, but Thomas resisted, his sense of modesty fully engaged. John imitated his brother. They cheerfully ate their bread and ham and cheese and pickles.

By the time they were following the setting sun to Polk Street, a brisk wind whipped dust clouds up from the streets. Away from the lake, the air felt brittle and dry, charged with a nervous energy. It had been weeks since it rained—not really since July. Henry carried John with one arm, the boy drowsing against his shoulder, and held the blanket and basket with his other hand. Thomas staggered along blearily, too tired to resist holding his mother's hand.

"I think it's time," Henry said to her in a quiet voice, "for a horse and wagon."

"We can pay for it?"

"I think so. We're about clear now, no credit with anyone."

"Where would we keep them?"

"I can put up a shed on Landis's lot. He's agreed, and we'll split the cost—the shed, the horse, the wagon." Robert Landis was a grocer three doors down from them. He already had bought the properties on either side of his original shop for expansion.

"You think you can share with him?"

He shrugged. "It's not forever. But a horse and wagon will make things a lot easier. Maybe Thomas could start coming to the stockyard with me in the morning."

"He can't lift those heavy carcasses, Henry, and you shouldn't lift them either. I saw you the last time. You were staggering."

"Maybe I could find someone at the yards to help with that."

"And after this year Thomas should start school. It's required, you know."

"I know, I know. But he needs to know about the business too."

"He's only five, Henry." She reached down and grasped Henry's hand around the handle of the basket. "He'll have his whole life to work."

A sharp wind blew up, then spiraled at them, throwing dust into their eyes and mouths. The desiccating blast crackled with electricity, sucking the moisture from the air, clogging noses and mouths and ears and eyes.

"Mama," Thomas said, holding his forearm in front of his eyes. "Mama, I can't see."

Katie knelt, blocking the wind with her body. "Just wait, Thomas," she said into one ear, her own eyes tearing from the dust. "Close your eyes and your mouth. Be patient, sweetie. When the wind stops, you can open your eyes a little bit at a time." A hanging sign banged against a nearby post.

Henry suddenly was on his knees next to her, coughing hard. He pivoted to shield the younger boy from the wind, then set him on his feet. As the wind relented, his coughing intensified. He lurched forward onto his hands. Blood spurted from his mouth. He gasped.

"Henry!" Katie cried, reaching for John and pulling him to her. She had no more hands. "Henry, dear God!"

The dying wind dropped dust and grit back onto the walks and street. Henry's hacking spasm slowed, though his chest and back heaved with his breaths. Katie held the boys' heads against her, trying to keep them from seeing.

"What can I do?"

He shook his head, then straightened to his knees. His face was glowed scarlet. He had pulled out his handkerchief to wipe off his lips and chin.

He nodded his head and took a jagged breath. "I'm all right. I'm all right."

"Here," Katie said, fumbling in the basket. "There's some beer left. Get the dust out of your mouth."

After Henry drank, she picked John up with one arm and the basket with the other. "Take Thomas's hand?" she said.

They walked the rest of the way in silence. Katie didn't want to scare the boys, so she swallowed her questions. Coughing like that, hacking that brought up blood, Katie had seen that with her Aunt Tess. Henry's mother died of consumption, just as Tess did.

And consumption was everywhere in Chicago. There were at least four cases on Polk Street that she knew about, probably more. Henry wouldn't even turn thirty for another few months. He must be too young for consumption. But if he had it, what would she do, how could she care for him, stranded with two young boys in this brawling city she didn't like and with a butchering business she liked even less?

After the boys were asleep, she asked him. He'd had a few fits like that, he said. This was the worst. It was the dust. He said it wasn't consumption. He didn't have the fever, the way his mother had. Katie thought back to Tess. He might be right.

"So what is it?" she asked.

He shrugged. "I think it's from my wound, the war. The doctor said they didn't know what I had inside, something might happen later."

"You should see a doctor."

"What's he going to tell me? That I cough sometimes. That it was stupid to run in front of a cannon? That I shouldn't try to do too much?"

"What brings it on?"

"I've never had anything like today. It's mostly when I carry too much, too big a carcass. It goes away."

"Get the wagon and the horse with Landis."

He smiled. "All I had to do was spit blood to persuade you?"

"I don't mind if we owe money. The boys need their father."

He took a deep breath, then smiled. "See? All better."

Henry fell asleep quickly that night, his breathing not different from other nights. Sometimes he snored, but not as loudly as other men had in Ward K. She was used to his angry dreams. When she tried to wake him, he often didn't know her, even when he seemed to be awake, his eyes open.

She thought again, as she had in recent days, how she missed his touch at night. They were together so rarely. She wondered if it was natural after the years being married, becoming used to each other, taking each other for granted, having the boys around—underfoot and on her mind, worrying about the water and the milk and the dogs and the gangs of tough children who rampaged through the streets, them both working so hard that they fell into bed at night, drained and empty.

The only times Henry seemed to enjoy himself were when Otto came by. They drank beer and talked about the army, sometimes lapsing into long silences that didn't bother them. And today. He had fun with the boys today, before his coughing. She thought back to it. She had grown used to his coughing, too used to it. Now that was one more thing to worry about.

She got up for water. The wind was picking up again. She absently scratched her forearms, leaving long stripes with her nails. It was so dry.

CHAPTER EIGHT

†

For seven more days, the parching, enervating wind swept the city. It blew the stink of stockyards and steamboats, of garbage and privies and gutters. It blew the loosened soils of the prairie and of unpaved streets. It blew cigar stubs and newspapers and leaves that fell early from thirsty trees. It blew clouds that never fattened but raced overhead, eager for more restful skies, skies where moisture might gather and grow and bless the earth. But no rain fell on Chicago.

Everything dried. Not only the people, slack-jawed and cotton-mouthed, but also the hay piled in yards to feed livestock through the winter, the elevators jammed with wheat and corn, the pine-built houses, the fences around pig sties and corn cribs, the lumber yards and furniture factories and ships on the river, the sidewalk planks, the woodpiles next to each home for cooking and the wood chips meant for tinder. The world was bone-dry.

Katie sat in the front room in the late night, fanning herself as she read a newspaper by kerosene light. The wind blew overhead. It was impossible to keep anything clean. Three times that day she swept out the dust. Henry and the boys slept. He had started on the shed where he and Landis would keep their horse and wagon.

Autumn was late, walled off by the relentless western wind. Katie longed for the brief golden days between the furnace of summer and the numbing winter. The *Tribune* reported a fire the night before in the western part of the city, across the river. Her eyelids sagged.

A shout came from outside, then several more. The wind blurred the words. Standing at the window, she still couldn't make out the voices, so she stepped into the yard. A scent filled the air. Smoke. She walked quickly to the street. Her eyes went to a flickering light in the southwest sky. Her hand went to her mouth. Fire. It must be across the river. That couldn't reach them here on Polk Street.

A powerful gust brought a shower of sparks and embers, stinging her hand, smoldering on her dress, burning holes. A flame flared across the sky like a meteor. Was it a burning stick? A windblown piece of wood? She watched for moments more, transfixed, not believing it. The fire wasn't across the river. It was here. When the wind eased, she heard jumbled voices, then a low boom. Her breath quickened. Terror seized her.

Henry came awake fast. He ran into the yard in his shirt. The sky was brightening. Embers danced like fireflies. A low rumble surged, either fire or wind, then panicky voices.

He told her to get the boys and pack valuables in their trunk, then ran to the shop. She hurried groggy boys into pants and shoes. Through the window, she could see Henry digging in the yard, his knives and cleavers and tongs piled on a rag next to him.

She threw good clothes into the trunk, along with the blue and green afghan her mother made, their letters during the war and their few photographs. John brought his top and string. Thomas offered a stuffed dog and a hoop and stick. She pushed them in and sat on the top to force it shut. The boys climbed on too. The latch finally caught.

Henry ran in, cash box under his arm. Sweat and soot streaked his face. He opened the trunk and forced the cashbox in. The hinges and latch groaned but finally clicked. He jammed keys in his pockets. Together, Katie and Henry hauled the trunk into the street, the boys close behind.

People were crowding into Polk Street. Some strained to see the blaze. Others pressed to the east and the north, carrying or dragging their belongings. Henry grabbed the handle on one end of the trunk. "It's too heavy for you," Katie said, jostled by people passing by.

"Hang onto the boys," he shouted. His face was hard.

Holding a boy with each hand, she followed him. Henry went east, bumping the trunk over the plank sidewalk. It snagged where boards were missing. When they reached Michigan Avenue, they joined a northbound river of humanity that filled the street. Henry lifted the trunk into the street. The going was smoother there.

The smoke was thickening. Screams flew through the air. Flames cast long, dancing shadows. John started to cry. Katie swept him up with one arm. She and Thomas trotted to catch up to Henry.

The low roar—it had to be the fire—seemed closer. Sparks swirled to Katie's right. John wailed again. His grip tightened.

"Mama." Thomas's voice cut through the din. She realized she was dragging him. She paused so he could get his feet underneath him.

"You have to keep up, darling," she said, then started after Henry. She was dragging Thomas again. The smoke. Henry's lungs. Her own were raw. His legs kept pumping. She strained to keep up.

Henry stopped abruptly at a corner. She swerved around the trunk. He was breathing hard. Sweat beaded on his forehead and temples.

"The talk is to head for the lake," he shouted. A man bumped into the trunk. He cursed Henry. "The fire jumped the river. Moving fast. The wind."

"We can leave the trunk," she said. "They're just things." He was already lifting the trunk handle, pointing east and nodding. He set off again.

They joined the human wave. Katie heard distant sirens and bells. What chance would the pumpers have against an inferno?

They couldn't go as fast on this street, not through the clogging throng. They passed a man with a parrot on his arm. A woman on Katie's right clutched a cat with terrified eyes. The crowd slowed, piling up in front of a haberdashery where the door was smashed in. Men climbed through the door carrying away shirts and collars. One clutched a full bolt of cloth. Henry stopped. "Wait," he said.

He pushed into the store, then came out with two blankets. He wrapped one around Katie from her head down. He draped the other over his head and shoulders. He started again, pushing through the crowd with his free hand.

A wagon was stalled in front of them. Henry shouldered his way into the stream of people to the right. Katie and the boys kept in his wake. Two well-dressed ladies, jewels sparkling in the firelight, sat in the wagon, which held framed paintings, trunks, furniture. Further on, the crowd struggled to get around four pianos that sat in the street. In front of each piano, a man stood with folded arms.

The light from the fire behind them was growing. Like midday, Katie thought. She was sweating. She shifted her grip on Thomas's arm.

Others dragged trunks. Some carried books. Some held loose clothes in folded arms. A box fell to the ground, spilling out letters. A woman and fell to her knees to gather them as they were trampled.

"Henry!" Katie shrieked. Thomas's arm had slipped from her. Red fear surged through her. Henry stopped. She passed John to him—nearly hurled the boy through the air. She screamed Thomas's name. A man pushed into her. She pushed back, shoving him to the side. A woman shrank from her. She screamed Thomas's name again, her arms flailing like a blind woman's, bursting through the arms and legs of these maddening people. He couldn't be far. It had been only two steps. Maybe four. She saw a gap in the crowd. She turned sideways, leaned in to push more stupid people away. "My boy!" she shouted. "My boy, Thomas!"

A man was crouching, holding Thomas's hand. She called his name again and reached for him. Her knee caught the man off balance, knocking him down. She snatched Thomas up. He was crying. She started crying. "I'm sorry," she said to him. "I'm so sorry. Stay with me. You must."

The man. He was still on the ground. She reached a hand to him. "I'm sorry. He's my boy." The fleeing people yielded a little space as he rose unsteadily. "Thank you," she said. "I'm sorry. I'm sorry."

It was easier to return to Henry, moving with the crowd. He had John on the trunk, holding him with both arms. Henry's mouth hung open. His eyes were shadowed in the stuttering light. Black soot covered his face. She nodded. He nodded back.

"You must walk again," she said into Thomas's ear as she crouched to set him down. "You're the bravest boy in this whole city. But Mama needs you to walk."

"Yes, Mama," he said.

"Grab my skirt and don't ever let go, no matter what happens."

She set him down and reached for John. Henry started.

A half-block farther they neared a saloon with its front window smashed in. The sidewalk had collapsed under the thirsty men scrambling to get inside. In the brightening firelight she could see them swarm the bar, turning their heads under beer taps, passing bottles around. The drunken men created eddies of disruption when they plunged back into the crowd. One drinker staggered into Henry's path. When Henry brushed him aside, the man grabbed a heavy woman for balance. They both fell without a sound. Henry didn't stop. Neither did Katie.

A bird cage smashed into Katie's shoulder from above, just missing John's head. She looked up. Someone was throwing things from a window.

The wind pushed more dust at them, more smoke. The people kept shuffling forward, beating out the embers that fell on their shoulders and arms and heads. The fire moved faster than they could, leapfrogging buildings, jumping across streets. Katie could feel heat on her back. A slash of flame flared into the sky on her right. Two blocks away from the park? Only one? Trapped. No one could move faster. How could Henry keep going? How could he breathe? "Breathe through your nose," she said to John, then shouted the same words down to Thomas.

A group of five men in dark suits trudged on their left. Each hugged a coffin to his chest. They took a few steps, then stopped and set down their cargo. They took a few breaths. One mopped his forehead with a sleeve. Then another few steps. A red-haired girl carried a doll by one leg. No one held the girl's hand. Katie tightened her grip on Thomas. She could feel his hand tug her skirt. An old woman carried a grunting pig who looked to be half her size. Another woman squeezed a quilt to her chest, eyes fixed on the quilt, brushing off any embers the moment they fell.

Explosions came from behind. Katie turned her head to look. A rocket of flame soared up. Close. The fire, voracious, all-powerful, was sprinting to them, gorging on the brittle wood of homes and abandoned possessions, racing to consume stables and sheds and plank sidewalks, fed by highways of fire-fuel.

Another explosion boomed, louder but farther away. Barrels of kerosene or oil, she thought. Maybe paint. Maybe grain elevators. They sometimes had explosions, even without fires like this. Another terrible noise, a crumbling, screaming crash. A building collapsed, walls tumbling amid cries of surprise. Animals screamed. John burrowed his head into her neck. Her arm ached. She wanted to switch the arm that held John but couldn't risk losing either boy. She held Thomas's tight.

Across the street, a horse was kicking and screaming. People scrambled to get away, some slipping to their knees as they scurried from the hooves. Dogs howled as they butted through the human legs that blocked their path.

Katie felt heat on her back. Smoke stung her eyes and scraped her throat. It was black, coal smoke. The fire had found another fuel. She saw movement from a stable on her right. Rats, big ones, scampering from dark places. A bird exploded in mid-air, reduced to a black thing that dropped to the scalding earth.

Glancing back, Katie gasped as a building ignited. The fire didn't start in one corner or on its roof. It didn't spread, step by step. The whole structure simply flared like a giant matchhead; one moment it was solid, the next moment it was an exultation of flame that released blazing cyclones into the sky. She squinted against the glare of red and orange.

They shuffled on. Henry shifted his grip on the trunk from his right to his left hand. He never lifted his head. Twenty feet ahead, an untethered cow plunged into the crowd, knocking people over, bellowing its fear. A man punched the animal in the side of its head. Startled, the cow froze. The man punched it again. Other people began to bludgeon it with whatever they held. The cow fell to its knees. More people kicked it. Henry dragged the trunk by as the cow gasped and moaned.

"Don't look, Thomas," Katie called down. "Look up at Mama."

Thomas looked up. Behind him on the street lay the body of a child, broken and twisted. Katie grabbed Thomas's collar and pressed him against her leg.

Henry grunted and stopped. He kicked something on the ground to one side, then to the other. He shifted to grab the trunk with the other hand, then started with a glance back for Katie and the boys. Stepping forward, she walked on blankets and linen. They were fighting for their lives, not for sheets and towels.

Henry stopped again. He set the end of the trunk down. His chest heaved. A man nearby shouted. "May the Lord deliver us from this firestorm we so richly earned! This is the curse of heaven that raineth down upon our heads for our sins." The man wore a battered hat and stared straight ahead. Ash smudges covered the hat and his shoulders. He seemed unaware of the cinders or the chaos around him. "As the Lord did with Sodom, as He did with Gomorrah, as He did in the time of Noah, so He does tonight with this sinful place! Repent all of you! Repent your wickedness and open your heart to the Lord, for the end of days is upon us!"

More shouts and cries mingled with the roar of wind and flame, with far-off whistles of tugs in the harbor, with the deep concussion of explosions and building collapses. "Henry, are you all right?" Katie shouted over the clamor.

He nodded. He pointed ahead.

Katie's heart leapt. The buildings ended a hundred yards before them. It was the park. Lakeside. She could see sky there. She looked over her shoulder. The fire was flying north to gobble the timbers of other neighborhoods. The air felt cooler. The smoke was thinning. The fire-roar was less.

Beyond the buildings, the throng of refugees stopped. No one could move. The wind swept fresh sparks and smoke over them. Henry climbed on the trunk for a look. Back on the ground, he pointed south. "Have to go that way," he yelled. He heaved up the end of the trunk and lowered his head. By inches and then by feet, he wedged into the mass of people and through it. Katie stayed so close behind that she nudged the trunk forward with her knees and thighs. After ten minutes, the street began to open up. After another thirty minutes, Henry stopped at the lakeshore. He leaned against the trunk. His head sagged. He let the blanket fall from his shoulders. Katie put both boys on the trunk, hugging them through tears. "Henry," she said, turning to him. "Sit."

He dropped onto the trunk and coughed once, lightly. Katie took his hand and squeezed it. He coughed again, a few times, then shook his head. "I'll be okay," he said. He looked up at her. "How are you?"

"With my family," she said.

"It'll all be gone."

"There's insurance."

"This many houses? The whole city?" He shook his head. "They'll never pay."

"It doesn't matter." A shower of cinders came down. A large one landed on the blanket draped over Katie's shoulders. Henry brushed it off, then lifted the boys off the trunk. He used his hat to pour lake water over the trunk to shield it from the embers. He coughed again, a few times, then controlled it.

The flickering firelight showed frightened faces around them. When the wind shifted and smoke blew down the shore, exhausted people stumbled into the lake to escape the choking billows. Katie and Henry carried the boys out until they were waist deep. Katie, turning to make sure no one was after their trunk, missed her footing and slipped into the lake, then came up coughing and gasping for air. They held each other, the four of them, for long minutes.

The fire-glow transfixed every eye. A hushed groan rose when a tornado of flame broke above the horizon, another house or factory or gas line or oil depot consigned to oblivion. A few people waded up and down the shore, desperately calling out names. The mocking flames danced before disbelieving eyes.

The crowd's energy leaked away by degrees. One woman, her dress nearly burnt off, skin blistered, held a crucifix before her, praying aloud. Most stood in silence, mouths open and eyes squinting at the horror that barely passed them by.

They stayed there through the night. The boys slept in their parents' arms. They never stirred, not even for the explosions.

CHAPTER NINE

†

As daylight stealthily reclaimed the sky, weary fugitives emerged from the dingy lake water. Many shivered as they absently stamped water from their shoes and squeezed it from skirt hems and trouser legs. Most found a scrap of ground to collapse on, wrung out by cold water, lack of sleep, the terrors they'd seen. The fire glowed to the north. Smoke clung to the lakeshore, stinging eyes, searing sinuses, and roughening throats. To the west was a dispiriting tableau of charred hulks amid unrelieved blackness.

"I think it's done," Henry said as he lifted the boys onto the trunk. Both curled up there. He stroked John's knotted hair. "I don't think it can turn around on us—nothing left to burn down this way."

Katie nodded and leaned against him. They stank of smoke. Henry coughed. She could feel his chest shudder, but then he mastered it. He had never regained the weight he lost in the army. "We're alive, thanks to God," she whispered up at him, "though only He knows what we do now."

He leaned against the edge of the trunk. "We didn't survive that hell to do anything but go back and rebuild what we've lost."

His words made little sense to her, but she was too exhausted to say so. He helped her sit on the ground. She leaned against the trunk and slipped into a dozy sleep.

Movement startled her awake. People were talking nearby. Henry still perched on the trunk, staring west at the ruined city. She rose awkwardly, muscles knotted and stiff. The boys slept, Henry's arm across both of them.

"I've been thinking," he said. "It looks all right to go back. I'll see what's left, see what we can do next." She looked at him, trying to sort through the things in her mind. Where else could they go? What would they eat? Where would they sleep? "I buried some food with my tools," he added. "It shouldn't take too long. I'll come back and find you here."

"No," she said. "We're not splitting up. We'll never find each other again. What if something happened to you? Or to us?"

He shrugged. "Okay."

"Did you sleep?" she asked.

He shrugged again and looked down at the boys. "I think John can walk much of the way; give yourself a break."

"What'll we do with the trunk?"

"Take it."

"Henry, you'll kill yourself."

"I'll manage."

"You're no good to us if you wear yourself out doing something foolish like that."

"Well, I didn't drag it here just to leave it for the jackals. You saw them last night."

"Hire a wagon. There were some last night. There'll be more today."

"Do you know what they'll charge?"

She glared at him without answering.

He nodded. "All right. Wait here."

Katie took Henry's seat, her arm over Thomas and John. Their mouths hung open as they slept. What would they remember of the night? What would life be like in this filthy, devastated city? She didn't fight the tears that slid down her cheeks. A woman walking by reached out and patted her arm. Katie looked at her. She was too thin, with wispy, white-blonde hair. A little girl clung to her smudged skirt. Katie would love to have a little girl like that. She smiled at the woman, who walked on.

Katie woke the boys when Henry returned. They drank doubtful-looking water from the lake. The wagon driver, who looked as tired as everyone else, grunted as he and Henry lifted the trunk. Katie placed the boys in the back and climbed up after them. She didn't ask what the wagon cost.

When they left the park, the fire-blackened city lay around them, scorched into silence but for the grinding of the wagon's wheels. Heat came from smoldering timbers. They passed a yellow dog who whimpered as he licked his singed hide. He looked up at them with a half-burned face. "Mama," Thomas said, "look at him."

"I know," she said.

"Can we help him?"

"Not right now, Thomas."

A dozen pigs trotted down a side street toward them, rooting in the charred gutters. Even the garbage had burned. A horse approached from behind them, hooves pounding the street. The animal passed by, riderless, the eye on the side of his head white with confusion. In the next block, drunken men with ash-smeared faces sprawled against piles of debris. A woman stood and howled at a vacant lot that held only cinders.

"Sir," Katie leaned forward to speak to the driver. "How can you find where we're going? I can't recognize anything. The signs all burned up."

"Don't worry, little lady," came the tired answer. "I've been on these streets all night."

"Where are we? What street is this?"

"Well, you can see—we're passing..." his voice trailed off. "We're going west," he said.

"Henry," she said, pulling on Henry's sleeve. He started awake. "Isn't that the river? We don't want to go all the way to the river." She repeated her questions.

Henry straightened and looked ahead. "Yeah, you're right." He pointed to their left. "We should be south, Polk Street."

The driver sighed and turned the wagon south.

Katie wanted to cover the boys' eyes but there was no point. This world was black, a landscape of negation. Remnants and corners of boards or furniture stood in a few places, somehow passed over by the apocalypse. Windblown ash left black specks on their clothes. A few coal piles still burned blue, sending more smoke into the gritty air. The people were gone. The animals were gone.

262

At a cross street, the driver pointed toward the river. "Bridge burned up there. Three others too. Gonna be hell getting around."

"Slow down," Henry said to the driver. He was turning his head from side to side, looking for a landmark, something that might tell him where they were. Chicago had neither hills nor valleys. No stream marked out neighborhoods. No familiar buildings or signs rose anywhere.

A lone figure walked slowly toward them. He wore the billed cap of the Chicago fire department and carried his jacket over one shoulder. He, too, scanned the damage from one side of the street to the other.

The wagon stopped as the fireman approached. "Sir," Henry called out. "We're looking for Polk Street."

The fireman stroked his thick mustache with a finger. "Ain't easy getting a fix on where you are." He turned and pointed behind him. "You know the post office at Post and Campbell?"

"Yes," Henry said.

The fireman looked back at him. "It was mostly brick, though the insides burned. That'll be your best landmark. Count the blocks from there. Most everything else is gone."

As he turned to leave, Katie asked, "Where are the people?"

"The parks," the driver said. "Some of 'em didn't get burned much."

They found the ruined hulk of the post office and counted the blocks until they reached what had to be Polk Street. Katie stared intently at each lot, trying to recreate what had stood where now there were half-walls, ash and debris piles.

"Look," Henry said, pointing to the side. "There's Butler's barber pole." The striping had burned off, but the distinctive shape survived. Their shop and home were across from Butler's. Or had been.

On their lot, burned planks leaned at unnatural angles. The tree to the right of the shop was a black skeleton, its branches pushed northeast by all-conquering wind, then frozen by flame. This was a dead place, Katie thought, like Carthage after the Romans finished with it.

The driver refused to do more than lift down the trunk with Henry, who dragged it onto their lot. They could see the outline of the shop's foundation. Using a knife from his belt, Henry began to stab through ash and dirt. After a few minutes, he hit something and began to dig. When the boys whined that they were hungry, Katie gathered them to her. "Papa's getting something," she said.

Watching him claw at the ground, Katie made up her mind. They would return to Maine. She had given Chicago a fair try. More than fair. She had done everything Henry asked. But she couldn't let him work himself to death in this bleak, rootless place. She had to find a way to explain this so Henry would accept it.

After an hour, he had excavated the tools and two bundles of food. He handed the bundles to Katie. She left an ash fingerprint on a half-loaf of bread. "The well?" she asked.

He sighed. "Should be over there. But I won't have it open for a while."

She wiped her hands on her skirt and told the boys to wipe theirs, then passed out bread and cured pork.

"When I was in the army," Henry said to Thomas with a smile, "this would've been a feast. We used to dream about actual bread."

"What did you eat?" the boy asked.

"Bugs and rocks, mostly."

"Henry," Katie scolded.

"It's true! We ate hardtack, and it tasted like rocks and sometimes had bugs in it."

John held out his piece of bread. "I want hardtack."

"What a stout fellow you are," Henry said. "But your father wishes that you never have hardtack." He put down his bread and started to gather a few boards and random objects that had survived.

"What're you doing?" Katie asked.

"Starting to rebuild. I was a joiner, you know. There's a lot to do. Come on, Thomas, lend a hand."

"Finish your food," Katie said to the boy, then looked back to Henry. "We can't stay here. It's…it's all black. The children can't be in a place like this."

Henry stopped and thought for a minute. "Then I guess you should take them to the park, like the fireman said. Lincoln Park would be closest. I'll come tonight. Take the food."

"What will you do with the trunk?"

He thought again. "Guess I'll take the things out and bury them. Can't stop anyone from stealing the trunk, but it's pretty heavy to haul around, even when it's empty."

"At the park—how will you find us?"

"Katie girl, I'll always find you." He had a kind look as he said that. She couldn't help but smile back. She reminded herself that all the things he did, even the stubbornest and most wrong-headed, were for her and the boys. *Especially* the stubbornest and most wrong-headed.

The park overflowed with refugees, many from the lakefront. The terror and astonishment were wearing off. They shared stories of flight and escape and loss. Treasures saved from the flames littered the ground—bedsteads, carpets, rolls of cloth, shoes, boxes holding keepsakes, clocks, framed items, even mirrors. Some had been saved for sentimental reasons, some because they would be useful, and others because they came to hand in the panic. Occasionally an ember fell as the fire flickered uncertainly to the northeast, throwing quarter-lit shadows across the people.

Katie found an open spot at the park's east end. She spread the blankets that Henry took from the dry goods store the night before. A nearby family shared their water, so Katie offered them the last of their bread. She was relieved when they declined.

She sang the boys to sleep, then settled down to wait. The wind blew clouds that covered the moon and stars and reflected the dying, far-away fire. She heard Henry before she saw him. He was whispering apologies to those he stumbled over. She called his name softly and soon he was there, dropping onto the blanket with a groan.

"I saved some for you," she said, handing him the remains of the food bundle. He fell on it hungrily. When nothing was left, he took a breath and leaned back on his elbows. She put her hand on his chest and spoke very softly. "You must be so tired."

He nodded and replied in the same tone. "I am that." He waved at the rest of the park. "All of us."

"They say there'll be food kitchens tomorrow, for those who've been burned out."

"I don't like that."

"I don't like being burned out either, but we are."

"No, I mean taking charity."

"Sometimes you give, sometimes you take. The boys have to eat."

"We have some money. Let's see how it works out."

Katie decided not to have that argument. She wanted to talk about something else. "We can't take the boys back to that place."

"What place?"

"Where our house was. It's nothing but filth and wreckage. Smoldering nails and everything burnt. It's no place for them."

Henry closed his eyes, then opened them. His face suddenly looked harsh. "I suppose you can stay here at the park."

"You mean sleep out in the cold?"

"Just for a few days. I'll come up at night and bring food."

"Henry." He closed his eyes again. She wasn't sure if he closed them from fatigue or to gird himself for her words. "Henry, there's no good reason for us to stay here in Chicago. If we have some money, if you were able to save it, then we should use it to go home to people we love and who love us and will take care of us. You can work there, you know you can. The boys will have cousins and friends and be out of this filth."

"You want to give up?" The fatigue was gone from his voice.

"It's not giving up. It's facing facts. We've been here three years. You've worked so hard, and so have I. And here we are sleeping in the park with thousands of strangers."

"We've had bad luck just now. We still have land."

"A single lot with a well whose water I don't trust, surrounded by wild children and animals, on a dirty street."

"We're here, Katie. We've survived. We're making our way. This city will rebuild and thrive. Its spirit is too strong not to. And so is ours. We're going to rebuild and thrive too."

"It doesn't make sense."

"Dreams don't have to make sense. They're what matter."

Her heart sank. How could he be so practical and so impractical in the same moment?

"We're staying," he said.

She dropped her head and pulled her hand back. She heard him lie back, and soon his breathing slowed into the rhythm of sleep. She would try again, sometime when he would listen to reason.

She couldn't be sure when the rain started that night. At first it felt like a benediction. The people on one side of them stood up to hold out their arms and let the water wash over them, carrying away ash and anxiety. They wrung out their soot-stained clothes. They put out a pot to catch the water.

Katie didn't have the energy to join them. She wrapped one blanket around the boys and the other around Henry, though they were already wet. They didn't stir. The last of the fire had almost vanished from the northeast sky.

After twenty minutes, the rain had become one more misery, drenching, depressing, cold. Katie lay down with Thomas and John and took them in her arms.

The rain had stopped when Henry's movement woke her up. Using a bar of soap and his knife, he was shaving.

CHAPTER TEN

✝

On their second evening in the park, a crisp one that foretold the changing season, Katie and the boys walked at a leisurely pace from their thin supper at the soup kitchen. The fire had blistered some of the paving stones into chips, shiny like glass. One end of an iron fence had melted, leaving a thick wad of metal. Only bricks survived the blaze intact, but everything around and behind them had vaporized.

Thomas picked up a charred stick to tap on the ground, so John did too. Katie let them be, even though the sticks were making their hands filthy and the tapping frayed her nerves. They passed a yard where two men were laying out wood planks, preparing to rebuild. Such fools, she thought. They were all fools.

She realized what was missing—in addition to the buildings and the people and the animals. The smells were gone. The putrid reek of rotting garbage, untended privies, animal shit and horse piss—all were submerged in the lingering smoke that clung to the black ruins. Small blessings.

Seated back on the blanket that marked their spot in the park, she used a pencil to write a letter home, to report that they had survived. The words came slowly. And were the mails even running yet? A shadow fell across her.

"Mrs. Overstreet, how are you faring in this terrible business?" Otto Krause bowed his head slightly. In the twilight, Henry grinned broadly from behind the taller man.

"Mr. Krause," Katie nodded from the blanket she sat on. She turned to be sure she could still see Thomas and John, who had fallen in with a band of savage young children. She extended one hand at the parkland teeming with refugees. "You can see how we fare."

"Ah, yes. But your clever husband and I have been talking about an approach to the situation. Not exactly a solution, perhaps, but an improvement." She looked the question at Henry, who stepped forward.

"Otto's neighborhood escaped the fire," Henry said. "You three can move in there until I've got the cottage ready."

"I thought," Katie said to Otto, "that your house isn't finished yet."

"Unfinished, Mrs. Overstreet, is better than nonexistent."

"He's got walls and a roof and some of it's floored. I'll come out and finish it enough so you and the boys can be out of the weather. It'll turn cold soon."

"Where will Otto stay?"

Otto looked away so she turned to Henry. "We can't ask him to leave his house," Henry said. "I'll come out every chance I can."

Katie stood awkwardly. "Henry, let's walk over to see the boys," she said. "We'll be back soon," she said to Otto with a gesture for him to sit on the blanket. "Make yourself at home."

When they were a few feet away, Henry started. "He's a fine fellow, you know, and wouldn't take advantage—"

"I'm not concerned about Otto Krause," Katie said, wheeling on him. "I'm concerned about Henry Overstreet. Why didn't you mention this to me? When I tried to ask you about what we were going to do, you just said we'd think of something. Then you go ahead and make this arrangement without even talking to me?"

"It occurred to me today as I was working. His job is going on just as though there wasn't a fire at all—the newspaper's printing in some temporary space—so he'll be gone much of the time. I stopped by there and he's willing." Henry took her hands. "Katie, you're right that you and the boys need to be inside. It'll be for just a few weeks, but it's a good solution."

"Henry, you know the solution is that we put this cursed place behind us and go back where there's people to help us in hard times. We should be using what money we have to get back to Waldoborough and not throwing it away on this crazy dream."

"Otto's a good friend. You've always liked him."

"I haven't wanted to live with him."

"It's not really living with him. You're just going to share the same building for a few days. I'll be there some too."

"But not every night?"

He clenched his teeth. "I need to get the rebuilding done before winter. I'll be working into the night."

She looked away, searching for the words. "Henry, we shouldn't be separated at a time like this."

"And we won't be for long. You and the boys are going to get sick staying out here, and look how they're running wild."

"Yes, but you're here at night."

"And I'll be there all I can." He squeezed her hands. "Katie, I have to insist on this."

She felt something snap inside. "You have to insist? You have to insist? When do I get to insist on something?"

"Katie, your voice—people…"

"I don't care, Henry. I've overheard a dozen arguments in this park today. That's what people do when they're stuck in a terrible situation and one of them won't listen to reason. They argue."

"Look, you and the boys can come to the house during the day and check up on the progress, even help me out. There's a lot to do."

Tears came to her eyes as she dropped her head. "Henry, why can't you be reasonable?"

He pulled her to him. She rested her head on his shoulder. "I can't run away," he said. "You know that about me."

She reached up and gripped his shoulders. "But it's what we should do," she said into his shirt.

* * * * *

"Uncle Otto!" At a full run, Thomas led his little brother through the open space of the house and collided with the man's leg. John crashed into the other leg. "What'd you bring us?" The boy reached for the man's jacket pockets, then his pants pockets.

Smiling, Otto patted each boy, then pulled two small bags from his back pocket. "Peppermint drops for you," he said to Thomas, peering into one bag and handing it over. "And gum drops for you." He delivered the other bag to John.

"Thank you, Uncle Otto!"

"Yeah, thank you!"

Katie came in from the yard where she was washing clothes. She pushed a lock of hair behind her ear. "You don't listen to me any more than Henry does," she said. "These boys don't need candy."

"We all need candy. There must be something sweet in life, no?"

"Yes. That's right." She gestured to the two crates that passed for chairs in the half-built structure. "You can sit a moment? I don't have long—I'm in the middle of a wash for a very impatient railroad worker who's leaving this evening."

Otto stayed on his feet. "I should not detain you hardly at all. I was hoping that the boys and I might go down to the park and watch the kites that fly on this windy day."

She turned to the boys. "Would you like that?" she asked.

"Yes!!!" they cried in unison. "Kites! Kites! Kites!"

"But first, we must stop for vaccination for smallpox. They have set up a station with nurses and I think this is a good idea, no?" He looked at Katie, who nodded. "They do not charge. For now, though, you boys should play in the yard while I talk with your mother." They left, chanting about kites.

"Otto," she said as he sat down on a crate, "you really must come back and live in your own house. Henry and I never meant to drive you out. We've taken such advantage of you."

"It is my great privilege to help my friends. And you should not forget everything I get from this. I receive the companionship of two young gentlemen with excellent dispositions. I learn carpentry skills from a man who never sleeps. He really should be in the carnival show, you know. *The Man of Awakeness!* And Henry and I are able to relive the pleasures of our soldier days, sleeping outside and fending off enemies by night." He pantomimed swordplay.

"What enemies?"

He shrugged. "The occasional pack of dogs, mostly. Some have become most arrogant about their place in the natural order of things. Not, I think, what Mr. Darwin taught us."

After a nervous silence, Katie said, "How is Henry?"

"Mrs. Overstreet, he is a man possessed. I leave for work at four in the afternoon, and he is working. I return at four in the morning, and he is working."

"Does he rest at all?"

"A few hours. When his mind becomes clouded with being tired, he knows he must stop. Scientists, you know, have tried for years to invent the perpetual motion machine, but your husband has nearly achieved it."

"And?"

"Please, would you bring the boys by the house? Henry would stop for you and for them. You could make him stop."

"Otto, I can't make him do anything."

"Yes, I know. Completely unreasonable. I believe now his family really was German. But he needs to see you."

"He knows where we are."

"The house, it's coming along. The roof, that is the part that's the problem. And, of course, he wants to build it very well. No shortcuts for Mr. Overstreet." Otto wagged his finger. "You know he tore down a wall he had built because he said it was not—what was it—plumb? I think to myself, no, is not a plum, is not even a peach or apple. But I do not say it. Your husband has no laughter about walls being plum."

Katie smiled in spite of her anger with Henry.

"Another thing," Otto went on, "he has trouble getting lumber. Everyone wants it whenever a train or ship brings it in. You have to sneak in and trap it before everyone else knows it's there. He waited at a lumber yard a whole day yesterday and came home with nothing. I could not help."

The man looked down at his hands. He was knotting and unknotting the fingers. "I must ask, Katie. What do you know about his coughing?"

"How bad is it?"

"I cannot be sure. I go to work for many hours, and I—not like Mr. Overstreet—must sleep. But I hear coughing. Loud and long.

Sometimes like opera." He looked up. "I see there's blood. He tries to hide it, but I see. I think this is never good. You are a nurse. That is true, is it not?"

* * * * *

Lowering clouds looked ready to spit cold rain the next morning. Katie led the boys to the omnibus that had resumed service to Michigan Avenue. It slowly crept through the streets. The boys, impatient to see their father, chattered in their seats.

The city still presented mostly desolation. The burned bridges looked like biblical catastrophes. Stores were gutted. The trains from the South Side stopped far short of the former depots, unloading their cargoes onto wagons. Yet there were signs of rebuilding on many lots, banging hammers and shrieking saws, the loud commands of workmen. Derrick hoists rose, tall and powerful, poised to recreate the city's downtown. Enterprising men sold from carts or roughly built stands.

Katie held tight to the boys' hands as they walked toward Polk Street. A small company of blue-uniformed troops marched past, their commanding officer swinging his eyes from side to side, alert for disorder to quell. Hand-painted signs marked the streets, but nothing was familiar. When they turned onto Polk, Katie took a sharp breath.

"What is it, Mama?" Thomas asked.

She pointed. "Look. See what your papa's been building."

The cottage on the rear half of the lot was framed in, the wood panels in place. Henry balanced on the half-built roof. A crude hoist ran from a pole planted in the yard. Otto was hauling on a rope to lift a packet of shingles. The boys began shouting for their father. Katie let them run to him, though the street was thick with ash. When Henry heard them, his face lit up.

Otto left on an errand, and Henry conducted a tour of the emerging cottage. He showed off the improvements he hoped to make over time, but stressed that at first it would be only basic shelter. "A few more days, Katie girl," he said. "Maybe a week." He took her hand. "You're a sight for sore eyes. What a beauty you look."

She knitted her brow. "That's the first compliment you've paid me in over a year."

"Then I'm a fool." Their eyes met for a moment. The boys were watching them. Henry rubbed his hands on his pants. "Did you see Kincaid's begun to rebuild the saloon?"

"That's hardly the first need for the neighborhood."

"Now don't get all blue-nosed about it. Kincaid's'll liven up the area, make people want to come back."

"I saw Flanagan's funeral parlor is rebuilding too."

"We'll take the bad with the good." He coughed, but only once. "Boys, boys. Put those down. Here, Thomas, pick up that hammer and give your brother the other one. There's a wall needs some nails in it. Come with me. I'll show you how."

Once the boys started pounding with their hammers, Henry returned. Katie nodded toward them. "They ask after you. All the time."

"I know, I know. Everything takes so long. I'm pushing as hard as I can. Did Otto mention, the insurance is going to pay twenty cents on the dollar! It's a raw deal, of course, but better than some. It should give us money to finish the shop."

"He didn't mention it, but he did say you're killing yourself with work."

"That's what he said?"

"Not those words. But yes."

"Look at this," he said, spinning slowly in place, his head tilted back to drink it all in. "It's better than it was before. Stronger. I learned from last time. It's for us. All of us."

"No, Henry, it's for you."

He looked at her with sad eyes. "Katie."

"I don't want to be here. I'm sure you've done the best job a man could do, but it's still going to be in the middle of this wasteland in this crowded, smelly city. I want our boys to grow up safe and clean, in a place that won't burn up their lives with no warning."

"Don't you think I'd use brick if I could afford it? I can't afford that—"

"Henry, I'm not talking about brick or wood. I'm talking about what we're doing here. Why we're here and not home." Henry leaned against the front wall of the cottage. His face wore no expression. "This is insanity. Take us home. Our families will send train fare. Better yet, we can sell this cottage, use the money to get home and make a fresh start there."

She stepped closer to him. "Henry, I've been thinking about this. It's almost all I think about. I could teach school again. I'm good at it. I'd like to and my sisters could look after the boys. Out here there's no one to help and you need me to work in the shop, anyway. And Henry, you're a good joiner. You know that. Even if the yards slow down, there'll always be work of some kind. You're not a butcher."

He shook his head. "I thought you understood. I don't want just to scuffle from one job to the next. I want to build something, to have a business. Something that lasts. We'll be together soon, here in our own place. A week at the most. Things'll be better then." He straightened and stared at her. "I need you to trust me, Katie."

She closed her eyes and clenched her teeth. "I've done everything you've asked, Henry. Everything. Came halfway across the world to this, this, this *place*," She spat the word. "Now *I'm* asking."

His pale blue eyes looked tired. Her vision had gone blurry with tears of anger and frustration, but now they cleared. She wasn't expecting to say what came out next. "We need money, Henry, the boys and I. You need to give us some."

He looked like he'd been slapped. "Otto said you were taking in wash."

"It's not enough. There's three of us."

He pounded the wall with his fist, his face turning red and the cords of his neck standing out like cables. "If I had any money," he said in a low tone, "you'd have it. I've had the lumber to pay for, the hauling to get rid of the debris, the well-digger. And then there's the shop still to go, and we don't have anything coming in until I get the shop open and get it stocked."

Katie looked at him. The boys had stopped pounding their hammers and turned to stare. She held out her hand, palm up.

"Christ, woman, haven't I given you everything I have?"

She didn't feel angry when she answered. "No, you've given me what you wanted to give me. I've given you everything I have."

CHAPTER ELEVEN

WINTER 1873

"**D**earie, don't you know?" Mrs. O'Brien called over as she knelt by her wash tub in the frigid air. Katie was in the same posture in her yard. "Chicago's become the divorce capital of the world." She wrung out the union suit she'd been working on, then draped it over the rope that was strung a few steps from her tub. It would freeze before it dried. Or maybe not. "Not that divorce means anything to me, what with how the church is."

"I never heard it was easy." Katie flexed her aching fingers in water that had long since turned icy. She had to finish this load before she could allow herself a fresh tub of hot water, and even that would stay hot only for minutes. "I know it takes a lawyer."

"Oh my, yes. But then the courts just zip 'em along, long as the mister consents or don't bother to show up. Women come from hundreds of miles and pay a pretty penny. Seems like a powerful lot of bother when you can just throw a bad one out of the house, but I suppose it's mostly women that want to marry again. If you ask me"—the florid woman, bundled against the cold, let out a yip of amusement—"the odds ain't any better the second time as the first, but we all live on hopes and dreams." Mrs. O'Brien turned to look behind her. "You there, Rose! What's that I hear? Don't make me come in there." The sound of crying from inside the one-room shack brought a sigh from the woman. She buried her wet hands in her coat and trudged through the shallow snow to the shack.

Helen O'Brien wasn't telling Katie anything she didn't already know, hadn't already taken the trouble to find out. Of course, it was no coincidence that the woman raised the question of divorce. Since the five O'Briens had moved onto the lot next door, they'd had plenty of chances to notice the tension at the Overstreet house. Katie and the boys had the cottage. Henry slept in the shop. Meals were awkward truces with clipped conversations. The boys had grown subdued except for Thomas's nightmares.

During his fits, Katie couldn't calm him. He sat upright, one shriek after another tearing out of him. They poured out like a dam had burst, sometimes with his eyes open but never really awake. She tried singing and stroking him, rocking him, hugging him. She whispered about how fine the world was and how wonderful he was and how much she loved him, but none of it worked. He kept wailing, wordless, terrified.

Then Henry would be there. She never heard him come in. It was the only time he came inside without knocking. He would place a hand on the boy's sweaty head and murmur a few words. Slowly, the boy would quiet. Henry would drape an arm over Thomas's shoulder. The boy sometimes gasped for breath, exhausted. Henry would lower him back to bed, then sit and pat John's head too, because the little one was frightened for his brother.

Katie hated it. She hated being useless. She hated the boys needing him. She hated being grateful to Henry. She hated being so small-minded that it made her angry when her husband loved her sons and they loved him back. And she hated living in this non-marriage.

He had opened the shop by Christmas time, even with boards still covering the windows because glass was scarce. Trade was light. On Sundays and Mondays, Henry built other people's homes.

Which meant that on wash day, Monday, Mrs. O'Brien could feel free to bring up divorce—only in passing, of course.

A breeze brought the smell of smoke into the yard. A few of the grain elevators along the river still smoldered from the fire. Henry had been right that Chicago would rebuild quickly. Not even four months after the fire, it was leaping out of the ground. What bothered Katie was that the building was just as careless and shoddy as before. Rickety shacks, like the O'Brien's, came first. Then more pine cottages, like the Overstreets'. Nothing was built to last. Nothing could last.

Mrs. O'Brien groaned as she plunged her hands back in the water. "Jesus, Mary, and Joseph, but I'll be glad for the warmer weather," she said. "And how's your little one? I saw him out the other day. He's over the flux?"

"Almost, I think," Katie said. "He's pretty chipper today."

"That's good, that's good. The little ones, they're the ones that give you the scare."

Thomas showed up at Katie's side, carrying a basket of clothes. "They're Mr. Schultz's," he said. He turned to feed the fire under the water that was warming for Katie's next batch. Then he straightened a shirt on the line that she had bunched up. He was too quiet for a boy of six. He was too good a boy.

"How's your brother doing?" she said, forcing a smile.

"He's all right. He filled the pot again."

"I'll take care of it, Thomas. Don't worry about it."

"I've been reading to him."

Katie smiled. Thomas pretended to read to John by making up stories as he turned the pages of a book. John had to know that was what his brother was doing, but he played along. "And what was the story this time?"

"It was about soldiers attacking a train to keep it from getting through."

"And what do you know about that?"

"Uncle Otto and Papa were talking about something like that. You know, about the war. I want to be a soldier like they were."

"I hope you never are. You know they were both hurt in the war?"

"I know. Sometimes Uncle Otto lets me touch his wooden foot."

"Don't you think that hurt him a lot?"

"I know. He was a hero, like Papa."

Katie bent over and hugged him fiercely. She held him too long. He twisted out of her grip. She turned and wiped her eyes with a sleeve.

* * * * *

Henry hurried through the streets that evening. He squeezed his hands into fists inside his mittens. One of the many things he hadn't missed about Waldoborough was the winter days working outside at the yards, but now he was doing it in Chicago. Old Warner didn't care whether the house was built well, so Henry had to set his mind to cutting corners. He was getting better at it. The city had new rules to stop people from building firetraps, but city rules were no match for men like Warner, who knew every city inspector and what kind of liquor he favored. The old pirate liked to say that he was a friend to poor families who couldn't afford fireproof houses.

The shop wouldn't be any warmer than the street until he got the stove going, but within an hour he'd be able to shed his coat and begin to feel his fingers and toes again. He envied men like George Young who could warm themselves with liquor. It seemed to work faster than building a fire. But Henry never cared for the taste and hated how it made the world spin. George always said that was because he didn't drink enough so he never got used to it. That seemed a dumb thing to say—that if you didn't like something, you had to take it more to get used to it. That was George. When Henry next wrote to his father, he'd ask how George was doing.

The streets weren't crowded. Much of the fire debris was gone. It was quieter than before, though people moved back in every day. Butler soon would reopen his barber shop, which should bring more foot traffic. Of course, men didn't buy meat. Women did that. But anything that livened up the street would be good.

"Hey!" The shout came as he stepped into Clark Street. A speeding coach pounded down on him. He hopped back, the horses' hooves narrowly missing him. That was one good thing about when the streets were more crowded—the coaches had to go slower.

He didn't mind the work for old Warner. It ended at sundown, leaving Henry with some time and energy to fix up the shop. He wasn't working through the nights anymore. It wore him out too much, and Katie didn't seem to care what he did. He had another coughing bout today, bad enough for Metcalf to ask after him. He couldn't shake this cough. Maybe warm weather would help.

Though the fire had set back his plans by a year, maybe more, it had brought him back to working with wood, and he was glad for that. He had missed the sawdust smell, the firm feel of a plank or timber that he could shape into something that might last, shielding out the rain and sheltering a life. And it produced ready money. He had enough now to buy the first load of bricks. He was going to replace the walls of the cottage, one wall at a time, as the money came to hand. He had never worked with brick, but how hard could it be? Then, with brick walls in place, let the fires come and let Katie try to complain about what a flimsy place they lived in.

Going back to carpentry reminded Henry how brutal butchering was—not that it had ever been a secret. There was an art to it, carving the carcass, making sure to distribute the fat and bone evenly to provide value to each purchaser. And, he had discovered, there was an art to getting along with the customers, all those women. Polite, respectful, concerned about their troubles. After hearing him wait on Mrs. O'Connor a few weeks back, Katie had looked at him with wonder. "You're never like that with me," she said. As though she was like that with him.

But the butchering itself, there was no way around it. It was taking something that had been alive and hacking it into pieces, leaving mess and fluids and smells, which sank into his clothes and wedged under his fingernails and never went away.

He lit the lamp in the shop, then went to the stove. Soon, flames danced behind the heat shield. He held his hands as close to the warming metal as he could stand. Keeping his mittens, he shed his clothes, piece by piece. He pulled the chair in front of the stove and filled a pipe. He took off his shoes and rested his stocking feet and his hands on the stove at the same time, an awkward but gratifying position. He wiggled his toes in pleasure, then reached for a match. When the pipe was lit, he took a long drag, then gagged. He started to cough, spitting out smoke. The cough took over, spasms throwing him back and forth in the chair, tears flowing. The blood came. Not that much, but he'd have to clean it up. His head hanging toward his knees, he groaned.

"Are you all right, Papa?" It was Thomas. Henry nodded his head. "Mama sent me to ask."

Henry sat up and held his arm out. The boy stood next to him, too big now to pull up on his knee. He was sturdy, not big, an Overstreet. "I'm fine, son," Henry said. "How are you?"

"I'm all right. John's better now. I read to him." Thomas walked behind the counter and looked at the knives and cleavers.

"That's good."

"Mama sent me with your supper too. It's up there." He pointed to the corner of the counter.

Ah, Henry realized. They hadn't waited supper for him. He sighed. "Thank you, Thomas. I'll come say good night to you boys."

"Okay." Thomas left.

Henry tossed his pipe onto the counter when he fetched the plate. Smoking might be another pleasure he would have to forego. Henry smelled the cornbread on the plate before he bit into it. The woman might be a trial, but her cornbread was wonderful.

"I'm glad you like it," she said.

He almost dropped the plate from his lap. "I didn't hear you come in." He stood. "Sit here, I'll fetch a crate for me."

"No, no, you sit down, Henry. You've been working all day."

"So have you." He nodded at her reddened hands. They both worked in the cold.

"Henry, I can't keep on like this."

He put the cornbread down and placed the plate on the stove. He swallowed the mouthful he'd taken but didn't taste it.

"Married but not married. Feeling beholden to you but angry with you. You know we have no marriage now. It's been more than a year like this, since before the fire. The boys can see."

"I'm trying, dammit. I'm working hard to make this business—"

"Working hard, Henry. Working hard. That's all I've heard from you since we got to Chicago. What happened to caring for each other?"

"There was a fire, Katie. Remember? We have to claw our way back."

"You know that's not it. Otto doesn't live like you, dragging himself from one job to another, no joy, no pleasure."

"Otto didn't get burned out. Otto doesn't have a family to support."

"Henry, I need to go home. I want to take the boys back home. If you'll come, that's fine. Or if you want, we can divorce, end this pretending."

Henry stared through the stove grate. He reached to feed the fire. As he closed the grate, he started to cough. The seizure gripped him, squeezing his chest then letting go, then squeezing it again. He rocked back and forth again. His face turned purple. It backed off slowly. No blood came up that time. He took a deep breath. She was looking down at the floor, a tear running down one cheek.

"What happened to us, Henry?"

"I don't know about you, but I ran in front of a goddamned cannon." He threw his plate, hitting her in the shoulder. She didn't flinch as it clattered on the floor. He sat down and stared at the stove grate again.

"You can't go," he said to the stove.

"What do you mean?"

"You can't take my boys. You're not that cruel. I'll give you the divorce. You can tell the court anything you want. Say I beat you or drink all night or run around with women. I won't deny a thing. But you stay in the cottage. I built it for you and the boys. It's yours. My boys have to stay. They need a future where there is a future, not back where there isn't one."

"You won't fight it?"

He stared at her. "You've always been the only thing I care about."

"Don't, Henry."

He turned back to the grate. "You can go off with Otto. I don't care. I know it's him, he's why you want the divorce—"

"Henry, what are you saying? He's your friend, not mine."

"He isn't a bad fellow. He's nice to the boys, though I think he favors John, but you know"—Henry shook his head—"he really isn't a hard worker."

* * * * *

The July sun beat down on Henry's head as he set the brake and stepped down from the wagon seat. He'd forgotten his hat because he left before the sun was up, but this was going to be another hot one. This was when he needed the Kolinsky boy, who was supposed to be helping him. The boy hadn't showed up that morning. Henry reached into the wagon bed from the back and dragged the carcass to the edge. It was larger than he usually bought, but he got a good price and business was picking up. He figured to sell out by mid-afternoon.

He turned his back to the wagon and crouched, pulling the carcass onto his shoulder. With a groan, he stood, wobbled a moment, then started back to the yard. Halfway there, he started to cough. He wobbled again. Lost his balance. Then sank to the ground. He twisted so the carcass would roll off, but it stayed, like it was glued on. He coughed more. Then more. The blood came early this time. It wouldn't stop. He couldn't stop it.

The shriek from Mrs. O'Brien brought them into the yard. Katie ran to Henry, whose face was in a pool of red-brown blood. "Stop, Thomas, John!" she shouted. She turned to Mrs. O'Brien. "Grab them! They shouldn't see!" The woman ran to the children and took them in her strong arms.

Katie knelt to Henry. His blood soaked into her skirt and stained her hands. She could see he was gone. She leaned down to kiss his temple and brush his hair back.

"Dearie." It was Mrs. O'Brien. "I left the boys with himself." She knelt next to Katie and held her. "I'm so sorry."

Katie nodded. There was so much blood. An ugly sound came out of her, deep and angry and honking all at the same time. She held her hands to her face. She rocked back and forth and howled and cried.

"Away with you," Mrs. O'Brien yelled at people gathered in front of the shop. She waved with one hand. "You dirty jackals, go!"

"What have I done?" Katie moaned. "What have I done?"

"Not a thing, dearie. You haven't done a thing."

Katie slumped in the woman's grip. She pulled her hands from her face, leaving blood smears. She sniffled and took a breath. She felt the panic come again but fought it off.

"I can have my big girl go call for Flanagan." Mrs. O'Brien said.

"No, I'll wash him. Then the boys can say good-bye." She turned to the woman. "Can your husband help me carry him inside?"

"You and I can do that. But you're sure you don't want the undertaker?"

"Later." She started to stand. It was hot in the sun and her head hurt. "I'm his wife."

CHAPTER TWELVE

†

"**U**ncle Otto! Uncle Otto!" John, the fair-haired younger boy, ran across the yard toward the man with a full mustache. Thomas, feeling the weight of his seven years and his role as the man of the house, approached more slowly. His smile was shy. "What's in the bag?" John asked as he reached toward the brown paper sack with visible grease stains. He stopped just short of grabbing it.

"Ach," Otto said, raising his eyebrows and an index finger. "Where is your mama? Mamas are in charge of such things."

"She's behind you." Katie's voice came from the rear door of the butcher shop. "You walked right past her."

"Such a goose I am," Otto said as he spun around. She looked tired. Thinner. He shrugged. "The sign is down for the shop, so I didn't think to look in."

"Mama's closed it." This came from Thomas in a sullen tone.

"Of course she did," Otto said. After an awkward silence, he gave a low chuckle and held up his bag. "But I have never answered John's very intelligent question."

"I know that smell, Otto." Katie wiped her hands on her apron as she crossed the yard. "You've been to Heffelfingers, haven't you?"

"A man must eat," he said, "as must a woman and so with young boys, as well. Is that not right?" He addressed the question to the boys.

"*Kreppel*!" John shouted. "We've got *kreppel*! Can we have them now, Mama? I love them!"

"I see no way around it," Katie said. She stepped over to the pump and ran water over her hands. "I'll start some coffee." Her voice turned commanding. "You boys wash your hands, then you"—she looked at Thomas—"draw some water in the bucket and bring it in." She reached for the pastries. "I know I look a fright...."

Making low noises of denial, Otto followed into the cottage on the rear of the property. Thomas was manning the water pump. Otto noticed an unmended chip in the door frame above the latch.

Katie let each boy have two of the jam-filled pastries, which they swallowed very nearly whole while Otto asked them questions, especially about the school Thomas had begun to attend.

"Sit up straight," Katie said, "and don't speak with your mouth full of food." They used to have better manners, but she lately hadn't been as vigilant about reminding them.

"But, Mama," John said, "what if it's my turn to talk and my mouth is full?"

"Then you finish chewing and swallowing before you answer. Uncle Otto will wait. He knows how to behave like a gentleman, not like you two barbarians."

When Otto had exhausted his questions for the boys—and had been exhausted by Thomas's one-word answers—Katie had them wipe their hands and faces on a towel, then released them into the October sunshine. As they ran out, she felt again the uncertainty that had come over her when she saw Otto walking past the shop window.

"You're very nice to come by," she said to Otto. She reached for a shawl that was draped over the rocking chair. "They need a lift."

"I should have come before. I'm still working the graveyard shift, you know, and I never have enough sleep. It seems so far to come here, which it isn't. I should have come."

"The boys have missed you."

"They seem good."

She shrugged slightly and drank coffee. She knew Thomas was too serious, too sad, but she didn't want to say so. That would make it more true, harder to change. And it would be disloyal.

"And their mother," Otto said. "How is she?"

Katie let a smile cross her face and reached to the serving plate. "She might just have a second doughnut."

"It's a *kreppel, mein frau. Kreppel*!"

She smiled. "The boys are never going to learn much German from me."

Otto snorted. "They weren't going to learn much from that make-believe German father of theirs. He could barely say '*guten morgen.*'" He watched her chew for a moment. "I asked how their mother is." She looked away from his bright blue eyes. They stared too hard. She shouldn't have been thinking that he wasn't a bad-looking man, that he was a kind and agreeable man. "Have you sold the equipment?" He nodded across the yard toward the shop, then noticed Thomas setting a piece of wood on a chopping block, a hatchet in one hand. "Can he handle that?" Otto sat forward and pointed.

"Of course he can. He cuts the kindling." She sighed. "Henry wanted to get a coal stove. He said the heat was steadier and lasted longer, but we can't do it now."

Otto cleared his throat and leaned back. "So, are you staying here? In Chicago?"

"I don't know." She still didn't look at him. "Henry insisted that the boys must grow up here, not back home."

"Yes, I know." He ran a hand through his graying hair. "He said that you…you don't agree."

Katie smiled and turned her head to Otto. "Very diplomatic."

"And now?"

"And now?" She shook her head. She had to say it. "Now, Otto, I feel like a monster who watched a man work himself to death without offering a word of sympathy."

Otto waited for what seemed like a long time. "I wouldn't allow anyone else to say such things about my friend's wife, so you shouldn't say them either."

"It's true."

"It certainly is not true. A cannon killed him. It took a long time killing him, but that doesn't mean anything else killed him."

"The way he worked is what killed him—look how he died!"

"The way he worked may have kept him alive extra years. It may have made him strong enough to keep going. What do you know? What do doctors know? Very close to nothing."

She twisted the cloth napkin in her hands. She liked the idea that all that work might have kept Henry alive, not killed him. That had never occurred to her. It didn't make a lot of sense to her, but…

"Katie." Otto's voice was low and direct. "He was not an easy man, not at the end. He worked as he worked because he had to. He could not be any way other. He could have the stiff neck."

"Be stiff-necked?"

"Yes, and you stayed, after all that…what had happened, you know, between you two. You stayed." Quiet settled around them as they watched the boys through the window. Thomas was lining up another piece of wood. John was wrapping a string around a top. "That top John has." Otto had a small smile on his lips. "Henry bought it, didn't he?"

Katie nodded. "John loves it." She kept facing the window so Otto wouldn't see her eyes glisten. "It's the first thing John picks up in the morning and the last thing he puts down at night." She turned to Otto. "I'm all right, Otto. Thank you."

He cleared his throat and gestured around the room. "If you need help, if I can do something, something for the house or the shop. I can even help you pack if you decide to leave. It would be my honor."

Katie smiled at him. "Such a nice way to say it. 'Your honor.' How would you say it in German?"

"*Es wäre meine Ehre.*"

She nodded. "Well, we'll be staying through the winter, I've decided that much. Decisions are hard now. I'm not certain about most things."

"Really, through the winter?"

"Yes, the winters in Maine are no easier than they are here, and, you know, people here have been nice. Very nice. Mrs. O'Brien next door—I used to think she was a tiresome, ignorant busybody. But she's been as kind as she can be."

"That is good."

"You said Henry could be difficult?"

Otto nodded.

"I would have said something much worse about him, before. But then for days after, people came by, bringing food and gifts, small things, things they couldn't afford to give away. And they'd tell me how he carried them on credit for so long, or gave them meat when they had no money. He wouldn't even write it down." She shook her head once. "I scolded him for that."

Otto said nothing. He wanted to put his hand on hers, to comfort her, but he didn't know if she would welcome his touch, not while talking about Henry. He nodded. He had known that man too, the one neighbors described.

"So. You stay in Chicago, you and the boys."

"Through the winter. Then, we'll see." She kept tracing a finger around the rim of her coffee. "Otto. Did the war change you?"

"What do you mean?"

"Were you a different man after the war, from before?"

"I don't think so. I am just Otto, always Otto. Too simple to change."

She reached over and patted his hand. "No, not simple."

"Very simple," he said. "Do you mean that Henry changed?"

"I felt like he did. I still think that." She stood next to the window that faced the yard. "It was as though the war squeezed the boy out of him. That charming, charming boy I knew."

Otto took a long breath. "He had a hard war."

"He talked so little about it. Did he tell you?"

"Not so much. Here and there. When we, we soldiers, when we talk about it, sometimes we lie." He shrugged. "Many times we lie, to ourselves too. It's easier than to say we were so scared that we wanted our mamas."

"Did you?"

"Oh, yes. Most of the time. I was lucky, though, to lose that foot, that foot that wasn't ever much good to me—"

"Otto—"

"No, you hear me. Because then I meet a fine man named Henry and his wife who worked in the hospital like an angel. And then I get to know his family, so now there are boys who miss me. Can you imagine that? That was so very lucky for me."

Katie was saved from speaking when Thomas burst through the door with an armload of kindling. He set it in a basket next to the stove.

"You do a fine job, Thomas," Otto said. Thomas nodded without turning around, then left. "You raise fine boys. Thomas, he is like his father."

She smiled, "He has the same bad manners?"

Otto smiled back at her. "Over this winter, how will you pay…? I can help. It would be my honor."

"Your *'ehre'*?" Katie smiled.

"Exactly. Already you have more German than Mr. Overstreet ever did."

Katie sat forward and began to lay out her plans. She would take in wash, like she had after the fire, when she and the boys had to stay with Otto. Chicago had so many single men with dirty clothes. They had no time to get them clean and still go to the saloons, so they needed laundries. The only local competition, she explained, was Sam Wah, a Chinaman around the corner. She thought there were lots of people who would rather have their clothes washed by a white woman. Helen O'Brien was already talking up Katie's laundry among the Irish in the neighborhood. And her sister could come out to Chicago and help with the house and the boys and the laundry.

"You would work from the shop?"

"If I can ever get the smells out of the wood. That's what I was doing now, scrubbing the counter. People won't want their clothes to smell like wurst."

"That could be very delicious."

They both smiled.

"Thank you for coming by, Otto. It's been good to talk."

"I will go in a minute, but if you pour us each a small bit of coffee, then we can drink to your new business."

When she handed back his cup, she made a face. "Not much of a celebration, toasting with coffee."

"Ah," Otto said. "Next year, champagne."

CHAPTER THIRTEEN

AUTUMN 1876

"Thomas." Katie's voice came out just as hard as she meant it to. "Put down that paddle. I told you to go study." She stopped cranking the mangle, leaving a shirt hanging out both sides of it. "Now, mister."

Rather than answer, he kept stirring the tub filled with soapy water and dirty clothes. He stood up straight to grip the wooden paddle with both hands, then pumped it up and down for the churning effect Katie had showed him. Though only ten, he was a good worker—by far the best she had at the Overstreet Laundry. Using her wrist, she pushed some hair away from her face.

"What did I say." She raised her voice and resumed cranking the handle. "Schoolwork first, young man. You know the rule."

"I need to get this done, Mama. Just one more load after this. It should be a good dry night so we can leave everything on the line."

"Who's in charge here? Chrissie will do the next load." The girl from next door was out in the yard, hanging wet clothes on the lines that crisscrossed what used to be open space.

Thomas didn't answer right off. Then he pointed out that the next load was a pile of coveralls from Mr. Maracek, who worked at the machine shop for the Illinois Central. Katie acknowledged the information with a grunt. Chrissie, a cheerful girl with a rich supply of younger siblings, would never apply the elbow grease required to deal with Maracek's oil and dirt stains, even though she was two years older than Thomas and four inches taller.

"Right after Maracek's load, then," Katie said.

"Yes, Mama. There're some sheets she can do."

She appreciated that Thomas was smart enough not to gloat over winning his point. The sunlight was almost gone by the time Chrissie finished the last load. The girl stumbled while carrying it to Katie, who steadied her, then took the soggy linen. To save on kerosene, Katie always put off lighting the lamp, but now she got it started. "Well, now," she said to the girl, who was close to her height but still in a girl's body, "how many hours?"

"Four, ma'am."

Katie nodded and wrote the number down on the sheet she kept on a tack for the hours of those who helped out. It hadn't been more than three and a half, Katie knew, but Katie didn't pay enough— and the O'Briens didn't have enough—to argue over it. She realized that Chrissie hadn't bolted for the door as she usually did, but was standing just behind her. "Yes?" she asked.

"I don't mean to be butting in on anything, Mrs. O," the girl started, "but I couldn't help but hear you and Thomas—"

Katie nodded.

"You shouldn't worry about how he's doing in school. Not ever. He's really smart. All the kids in his grade say so."

Katie smiled, allowed herself a moment of pride. "Thanks, Chrissie. That's nice of you to say."

"It ain't nice at all, Mrs. O. He just is."

"Okay. I'll see you Wednesday?"

She was gathering the sheets after running them through the mangle when Thomas came back into the shop. Without a word, he took them outside to hang. With a sigh of gratitude, she lifted the ledger book down from the high shelf where Henry had kept the cleavers. Sitting next to the lamp, she entered the day's work. They would make it through the month, but she couldn't be sure about the winter. Business always dropped in the cold weather. Men didn't worry so much about wearing dirty clothes in the winter, since they wore so many.

She leaned back in the chair and packed her pipe with tobacco. She took in its fresh smell before lighting up. She drew in a lungful of smoke and let it out slowly. It calmed her in a way that beer or liquor never did. She watched the smoke rise from the bowl and allowed her thoughts to drift. She thought again, as she had a hundred times before, that they'd stayed too long in Chicago. They couldn't go back home now. Every month there had been another reason to stay—something with school, something with the laundry or the season or one of them getting sick. She kept putting if off until they had stayed without deciding to, five years now. Even after the second fire, the one in the summertime that came within blocks of their house, she stayed.

Had she done it out of duty to Henry? She hadn't thought so, but lately she'd been thinking that maybe he was right, that Chicago was such a bustling, exploding place that it was the best place for young men like John and Thomas—like they would be so soon. Because they'd got halfway to being men without her even noticing. And here a young man with wits and drive could make his way a lot faster and farther than in Waldoborough. She took another lungful of smoke.

"Mama," John said as he opened the door. "I'm hungry."

"Come over here, you sweet thing." He stood next to her, the cold of the evening coming off his clothes. "Have you done the kindling?"

"Of course, Mama. What's for supper?"

Knocking the ash out from her pipe onto the floor, she smiled. "Why don't you and I go see?"

* * * * *

Katie didn't recognize the Chinese man who waited patiently while customers picked up and dropped off. The only Chinese she was sure she could recognize was Sam Wah, who had been pointed out to her on the street. Walking by his shop, she saw him presiding at his counter with an air of command that she admired. This man, though dressed well in a vested suit without a cravat, did not have the same imperial posture. It was cold enough for a topcoat, but he had none. He stepped aside several times so newcomers could approach the counter ahead of him. He plainly wanted to speak with her privately, which was not so easy at the end of the day.

When the last customer left, she looked at him and raised her eyebrows in question. He removed his bowler hat and gave a shallow bow. "You are owner? Overstreet?"

Katie nodded.

"I am Hong Fat."

Katie nodded again. His speech was clipped and accented, but she could understand him. "What can I do for you, Mr. Fat?"

He smiled and bowed again. "I am Mr. Hong. For Chinese, family name comes first."

That seemed odd, but Katie saw no reason to pursue the matter. He evidently knew enough English to understand that calling himself Fat Hong would be a mistake. She began to straighten up the counter. "I must get to my family and supper, Mr. Hong."

"Yes, of course." He took a step toward the counter. "I want to speak business to you. We can do another time."

She stopped. "What business?"

"Our business, you and I. Washing clothes."

"Did Sam Wah send you?"

"No." The man paused and took another step toward the counter. "I work for him long time, but I'm here for Hong Fat, not for Mr. Wah."

"He's not Mr. Sam?"

The man smiled. "He change name to American style, so he's Mr. Wah. Confusing, no?"

"I really must see to my boys."

"Missus, I come to see if we go into business, you and I."

"Together?" Katie shook her head. "We don't even know each other."

He leaned forward. "I watch your business. I see customers here. Steady customers. They like you."

"We do a good job for them."

"No, missus, you do not. You have children wash clothes and they do job that is, what, okay? But not good. Sam Wah, he laugh about how you wash, say that you work only for poor people with dirty, not for fine people with fine, who pay more for fine job that you cannot do."

Katie drew in a breath and raised herself to her full height, which was slightly above that of this pumped-up little foreigner.

"No, no, missus. Please do not be angry. I don't mean this is bad business. I not come here if it was." He waited for a moment, then plunged on. "I know how to do fine. I'm strong to do washing. And I use iron like artist use paintbrush." He gave a flourish with a hand. Katie smiled despite herself.

"If you're such an artist, why not stay and do fine with Sam Wah?"

"Mr. Wah and I, we not friends. I not wish to work there anymore."

"He fired you."

Hong Fat said nothing, his face locked in a neutral expression and his posture rigid. He repeated that he didn't work for Wah anymore.

"Why?"

"Why?" Hong Fat echoed her.

"Were you stealing? Did you do a bad job?"

"We argue. I tell him how to make business better. He not listen. I tell him other ways to make business better. He still not listen. I see another way to make business better and he get mad, shout all kinds of things." The man gave a small shrug. "I shout back."

"And he fired you."

The man said nothing.

"So why would I want you to work for me? To argue with me?"

"Not work for you. Be in business. Together."

"I have a business. I'm not looking for a partner." John came into the shop through the rear door.

"Mama," he said, then stopped when he saw the man on the other side of the counter.

Hong Fat bowed again. "Missus, might we speak again? Then I tell you why?"

Katie agreed that he could come back the next evening after supper. He placed his bowler back on, then spun and left. She wasn't sure why she had agreed to see him again. She wasn't looking for a partner, certainly not some Chinaman who had just been fired.

* * * * *

When Katie lit the lamp in the shop, Hong Fat was outside the door, wearing the same suit. He rubbed his hands against the cold. Katie let him in.

"Let's sit next to the stove," she said, gesturing to two stools she had placed there. "It's banked for the night, but has some heat left." That afternoon she had asked Helen O'Brien next door what she knew about Hong Fat, or Sam Wah's business. If there was anything to know about the people on Polk Street, Helen knew it. When it came to the Chinese laundrymen, though, Helen came up dry. They keep to themselves, she had offered in explanation, which was something Katie already knew. When Helen asked why Katie wanted to know, Katie changed the subject. No need to set tongues wagging. She was hardly likely to go into business with this Chinese stranger.

"Thank you." The man shivered slightly while she pulled her shawl up over her shoulders. "I talk business now?"

Katie nodded.

He reached into his jacket and pulled out a folded paper, then spread it for her. "You do well here, missus. I see. But winter is bad time. We see that with Sam Wah. So you need more. More laundry, more better laundry, the kind that pays more."

"You said that yesterday."

He gestured to the paper. It was the layout of her laundry. The counter and stove looked to be in the same places, but...she looked again. The counter was actually closer to the front door. There were outlines of two mangles and two tubs for washing clothes, and an ironing board between the stove and the back door.

"I don't need those," she said. "We can keep up the way we are. Can't pay for them either."

"I pay." He reached into his trousers pocket and pulled out a purse. When he shook it, a jaunty clinking sound rang out. "One hundred dollars in gold. From work for Sam Wah. I put into business."

Katie sat up straighter. She held her hand out. "Not only gold coins make that noise."

He handed over the purse while moving his stool so she couldn't be seen from the street. "You look."

She poured the coins into her hand. Five double eagles glinted in the lamplight. She had held Henry's greenbacks from his army bounty, but never so much in gold. She slid the coins into the purse and handed it back. "Okay, so there's money. But what do I need more equipment for?"

"We get work from hotels. They have people, stay there short time. People stay there need clothes washed, fine clothes. Need fast. They have money. So we work with hotels. Like Sam Wah does."

"If they have a laundryman already, why would they come to us?"

"I see these hotels. I pick up and take back the clothes sometimes. I see they not like me, not like me to be there. If they see pretty American lady who can do laundry, do fine wash at same price as Sam Wah, they will use her."

"The closest hotel is three blocks away. I can't be traipsing all over Chicago carrying clothes." It wouldn't be decent.

"You have boys. I see. Strong boys, no?"

Katie nodded, uncomfortable that he had been watching Thomas and John. "Boys pick up and take back, use cart. Hotel men like having strong American boys do work." The man scanned her face for her reaction. Then he said, "Also, inspectors, police, aldermen, all would rather deal with you, not with Hong Fat or Mr. Sam Wah."

Katie was quiet for a minute. She wasn't thinking about his business ideas. They were good, she knew that. She was thinking about this strange man sitting with her. He smiled at her, his face dissolving into crinkles that seemed to consume his eyes. Could she trust him? How could she decide that?

"How do I know you can do fine?"

"I come early morning, before you open. I bring iron. You have fine clothes—your dress, or someone else's, I not care. And I show you. Easy. Fast." He leaned forward for emphasis. "Better than Sam Wah."

"What do you want? I don't plan on giving up my business to you."

"No. I need you. You need me. We be partners. You run business, Overstreet Laundry. You manage, talk to people, hotel men, police. They like you. I work here. I do fine and teach how to do it. When I have idea, you listen. We talk. If idea good, we do it. If not…" He tilted his head to one side.

"What about money?"

"We partners. Money even Steven. But you own more of business, enough more. And we use my money"—he held up his purse—"for business. Tubs, washboard, maybe new sign outside. We make deal and write down. Both sign."

Katie nodded. Her stomach was tense, empty. She hadn't been able to eat all day, worrying about this Hong Fat, this odd man. He knew so much more about her than she did about him. "Where do you live?" She hadn't planned the question.

"On Clark, near Van Buren. Some Chinese there. We cook together."

"How long have you been here?"

"Three years."

"All with Sam Wah?"

He nodded. "We meet on railroad. Work together four years. He save money better than me and start business. So I learn. Now I have money."

Katie allowed herself to think about the great distances Hong Fat had traveled. From China, then across the ocean, then from California east to Chicago. He was so far from his home. "You've seen half the world," she said. He said nothing. "Is there a Mrs. Hong?"

There was a sadness around his eyes. "No Mrs. Hong. No Chinese woman, not for us. They all in China."

"I didn't know. None?" He shook his head. "Is there a sweetheart back in China?"

"I'm here seven years. She marry now. Have babies."

He didn't make a joke about it, or smile, or pass it off as unimportant. He looked sad. She made her decision. "Come with your iron in the morning," she said. "Seven-thirty."

CHAPTER FOURTEEN

SPRING 1884

"Hello, Thomas!" Chrissie's voice was followed by a giggle that was nearly womanly. "You'll not be putting on airs with us, will you—you being the biggest toad in the puddle and all?"

Thomas, wearing his good jacket, stopped and looked over. Chrissie, grinning merrily, stood with a tall, slender girl with dark hair, a pale complexion, and a quiet air. Both girls wore the square-necked frock and blue apron required for barmaids at The Shamrock, the saloon on Jefferson Street that catered to the Irish trade. It was impossible not to smile back at Chrissie. He bowed slightly, tipped his snap-brim cap, and stepped toward them.

"I trust," he addressed the other girl, "you know Miss O'Brien well enough not to believe any of the lies she has told you about me."

"Listen to him," Chrissie broke in. "The college man in his fine jacket, with his highfalutin ways, accusing me of telling untruths!"

"There we have Exhibit A of the shameless way this woman traduces known facts," Thomas said to the quiet girl. "I take evening courses in the business college. Not exactly a college man." He turned to Chrissie. "Are you going to introduce us?"

"I'm Brigid Shaughnessy," the girl said. "I can introduce myself." The Irish inflection in her speech sounded like music.

"Miss Shaughnessy, I'm pleased to meet you. I'm Thomas Overstreet, next door neighbor to your charming friend and fellow graduate of Overstreet's Hand Laundry, a punishing sweatshop that's managed by my sainted mother." He gave her a severe look. "All my Irish friends have sainted mothers, so I must have one, as well."

"Ah, 'tis not something I can speak of," Brigid answered, "as I've neither mother nor father."

A troubled look crossed Thomas's face. "I meant nothing by that stupid joke. I'm sorry   "

"Of course you meant nothing by it. Perhaps my mother was a saint. I'm inclined to doubt it, but it would please the sisters where I live."

"Brigid lives over on Taylor Street," Chrissie said. "With the Sisters of Mercy." She smiled. "Since you two have a lot to catch up on, I'll go run my errand. See you tomorrow, Bridg!"

The dark-haired girl looked at Thomas. "What is it that we have to catch up on?"

He grinned. "I'll think of something. If you're going somewhere, it would be my pleasure to serve as your escort and protector against the many dangers of this evil place."

"I was just going home. As she said, it's over on Taylor Street."

"That's an especially hazardous route. Cutthroats, alligators, trolls and ogres, not to mention the odd constable looking for a handout. It'll take all of our cunning and courage to get there in one piece." He held his arm out for her. With a very light touch, she set her hand on his elbow.

"In the face of such dire risks, I suppose this is my lucky day to come upon you."

"Miss Shaughnessy." Thomas placed his free hand on hers and looked into her large hazel eyes. She didn't look away. For a moment, they were the only people on the street. "I know this is my lucky day."

* * * * *

"I liked the buffaloes best," Brigid said after swallowing some popcorn. "They have such majesty and sense of themselves."

"Oh, there you go," Thomas said, leaning on his elbows on the fence between the boardwalk and Lake Michigan, "confusing size with presence and dignity. They're just big. Trust me, they've nothing on their minds but the grass they're chewing and the gurgling of their bellies. The whole world confuses size with understanding."

"And your opinion is based on your extensive exposure to the American buffalo in your explorations of the Plains?"

"Exactly right." He held the popcorn box out for her, and she took some. "While fighting off Indians and discovering gold."

She smiled. "So much you've packed into so few years." She leaned her shoulder against his. "So are those adventures you're going to have? Go explore the great West?"

Thomas shook his head. "I don't think so. I like Chicago. It's my home. They bring the sights of the great West here to Lincoln Park for us to stroll through on a Sunday afternoon." His eyes were following a coal steamer off in the lake. "My father was restless, insisted we come here from Maine. He and my mother argued about it. I don't remember much about him, but I remember that."

"I wonder what that's like, parents arguing."

"It's scary. Or it was for me." He was quiet. Brigid put her hand on his shoulder. "He had a quiet way of arguing. It drove my mother 'round the bend."

"What's a quiet way of arguing?"

"I don't know—not getting angry but not changing your mind, not ever."

"He sounds stubborn."

"Yes, I guess so. Both of them."

"So that's how you got to be."

Thomas smiled. "I suppose if I deny it, you'll just say I'm being stubborn."

"Stubborn's all right by me, Thomas. It means you care. Caring's important."

He cocked his head. "The things that come out of you, Miss Shaughnessy. You think about things. Is that from living in the home, back in Ireland?" He traced a finger along her jaw line. Her skin was smooth.

"Might be. Living with all the other kids, there's some that spend all their time with others, playing and tussling and talking."

"And then there's Brigid, watching and thinking."

"Was you there?" She pulled back to give him a skeptical look. "Do you think you know about it?"

"I wish I had been there."

"No, you don't."

"No, I mean so I could have known you."

"You'll be tired of me soon enough."

"No." He turned to face her. "Not ever."

"Oh, Thomas." She rested her forehead against his. "You shouldn't say such things. I'll make a fool of myself."

"I can't help it."

They stepped back from the fence and started down the walk. The breeze off the lake filled their lungs. The cloud-filled sky showed little interest in raining.

"Thomas! Thomas Overstreet!" Thomas grinned to hear the voice. He stopped and turned to see Otto Krause waving one arm and using his cane to bear down on them at impressive speed. "Aren't you a sight!" Otto cried as he grabbed Thomas by the shoulders. Otto's hair was entirely gray now, but he was fit enough in his Sunday suit.

"Otto, you look grand." Thomas turned to Brigid and introduced them, adding, "Otto fought in the war with my father."

"Ach, I did no such thing," the older man said. "I was no kind of hero like Henry Overstreet. But I did become his friend in the hospital." Otto beamed at them for a moment. "You are such handsome young people. But, here, you must tell me the news, Thomas. I haven't seen your mother in, I don't know, it's months now. How is she? And John? And you?" Otto laughed and fell into step with them, making sure the girl was between them, included in the exchange. After Thomas told his news, Otto learned of Brigid's long journey from Ireland, alone.

When they neared the depot for the streetcars, Brigid excused herself to use the ladies' washroom. As soon as she disappeared from view, Thomas wheeled on Otto.

"You must say nothing of this to my mother."

"Of what? I run into you on a beautiful day in the park. It reminds me that I have not seen my friends on Polk Street for too long."

"Nothing about Brigid. I haven't told my mother about her."

"She is a lovely girl. What reason could there be not to tell of her? You should be proud."

"I don't want to deal with my mother about this, not now. Brigid is wonderful. I'm going to marry her. But it's too early to subject her to my mother." When Otto just stared at him, Thomas added, "Look, I've never spoken to my mother about your secret. I'm just asking you to do the same for me."

"My, my secret?"

"Yes, I've always known. John does, too. Why don't you just do something about that, anyway? You know she likes you."

Otto's face flushed red. He shook his head several times. "Thomas, your mother, she's never stopped being married to your father."

"That's crazy. She hated him at the end. I was old enough to see. I remember."

"She was just angry. You can be very angry with someone without hating them. While still loving them." Otto threw up his hands in frustration. "Which she does. I can see this with my own two eyes."

Thomas stared at him. "I thought she was just being cruel to you."

"Katie is never cruel. She misses my old friend. I miss him too. A good friend cannot be replaced any more than a good father or a good husband can be."

Brigid, stepping out of the washroom, stopped while still several steps away and began to adjust her collar, then the cuff of her sleeve. Otto caught sight of her and smiled. "Come, come, you two must be on your way. Otto Krause does not stand in the way of love." After saying his good-byes, he winked at Thomas and set his uneven stride back toward the lakeside.

CHAPTER FIFTEEN

†

Even though the tulip bouquet was wrapped in wet newspaper, two of the blooms had wilted by the time Otto turned onto West Polk, on his way to Overstreet's Hand Laundry. He still had time to back out. He could just drop the flowers into the gutter, act like he was distracted by something across the street, then turn on his heel and reverse his direction. No one would know he had embarked on this hopeless errand, a ridiculous errand on a Saturday afternoon for a man of his age, of his lack of position, and of his chronic one-footedness.

"Hey, Uncle Otto! What's the occasion?" It was John Overstreet, pushing through the street behind a cart filled with packages wrapped in brown paper, the laundry's evening deliveries. Otto had no idea how the boy got so tall. He was nearly six feet, yet barely seventeen. His older brother was more the size of their father.

Otto stopped and gave a half bow, dropping his hand holding the tulips and turning sideways to conceal them. "I might ask the same of you, young sir. What's going on with you and your family?"

John had to pull on the cart to stop. "I suppose the only real news is that Thomas is getting to be a lost case over that girl."

"The Irish one? What's her name?"

"Brigid Shaughnessy." John gave him a reproachful look. "You've met her, Otto. He told me."

"Ah, yes, the great secret love, never to be mentioned to your mother until Thomas gathers up his courage in both hands."

"That's the one. The secret may be about to get out. Mrs. O'Brien next door saw them, and you know nothing's a secret to her." The boy's expressive face lit up. "Those *are* flowers, right, Otto? For my mother?"

"Every woman deserves a touch of beauty in the spring."

"So, talk about finding your courage. Are you finally going to risk it?"

Otto tipped his bowler hat and gave the haughtiest nod he could manage. John gave a quick whoop as he set off, then called back, "Don't start till I get back, okay?"

When he reached the laundry, Otto peered in the front window. One of the Chinese was behind the counter. A handful of men waited for their wash. Otto skirted the shop, passing down the side into the courtyard. Katie was bent over an account book, squinting against the smoke that rose from her pipe. Another worker was wrestling sheets through a mangle board on the yard's far side. Closer to Katie, a short man hunched over a shirt collar with a charcoal iron. Otto knew that man, Hong Fat. Katie called him a genius with an iron. She liked that one. He had been the first of her Chinese. She said they were honest and worked hard, but they had no women. Otto knew that situation.

As Otto approached, Katie took out her pipe and gave him an appraising look. "Have you been picking other people's flowers, Herr Krause?"

"Katie, you don't give a fellow much credit, you know."

"You paid for them?"

"Shall I produce the receipt?" The laundrymen were listening intently. When Katie stood, Otto held out the bouquet. "Mrs. Overstreet, I present these with all the compliments of the season, to brighten your day."

"They're lovely, Otto. I'll find something to put them in." She took the bouquet and turned to enter the house. "Boys," she called back, looking up at the sky. "Why don't you put all that away and we'll call it a night?"

After he followed her into the cottage at the back of the yard, Otto said, "I thought they didn't speak English?"

"They don't talk it so good, except for Hong Fat, but they understand it just fine. Especially quitting time."

She handed him some dried-out flowers from a vase. "Toss those in the yard, will you?" She pumped water into the vase, then sorted the flowers to blend the reds and yellows. "So, what do you know about Thomas's Irish colleen?"

"Katie, really now. You can't expect me to carry tales."

"I'm not asking you to carry tales. We both know the boys tell you things they'll never tell me, so help me prepare for this, would you? It's not gossip I'm after. Just information."

"And what, pray tell, is the difference?"

"From Mrs. O'Brien, it's gossip." She gave him a direct look. "From you, I hope, it'll be information. Sit and talk to me."

He took off his derby and set it on the kitchen table. Katie put the flowers in the center and sat. "Well, she's a slip of a thing, you know."

Katie sighed. "We all were, once."

"She's well-spoken. With an accent, of course."

"Of course. I hear she works as a barmaid."

"The girl must work. She's an orphan. Came over all by herself, with nothing but the address of St. Aloysius's Church and the name of Father Beckett."

"I hadn't heard that. Well, then, she's a brave girl. But I won't stand for some girl from the wrong side of town holding Thomas back, giving him baby after baby and trapping him in this neighborhood forever."

"Why, Katie, you sound a hard woman."

"If you'd washed as many shirts as I have and seen your bright boy all the way to business college, you'd fight to keep him moving the right way too."

He reached over and put his hand on hers. Startled, she looked up at him. "You've done a wonderful job with both of them, Katie. They're a great credit to you."

She nodded once. "She'll need to get respectable work."

"You can help with that."

"I could. If it was the right thing to do, and so long as there's none of this popping babies out every year."

"If you have a way to manage that, you're even more of a wonder than I think you are."

"And how much of a wonder is that?" She nodded down at his hand, which still rested on top of hers.

Otto thought to pull his hand back, but didn't. Instead, he squeezed hers. "Katie, I would like to ask you to control your natural fierceness now."

"I'm fierce? What makes you say that?"

He paused to choose his words carefully, but decided not to. "I've been knowing you for nearly twenty years, while you nursed us all, then built this home and this business and raised those fine boys. But now you have to rely on me and that Mrs. O'Brien to find out about Thomas and this young girl." Katie looked down at hearing those words. He squeezed her hand again. "It's taken me all these many years to get past that fierceness."

"Now, Otto, don't—" she started to pull her hand away, but he held on.

"I have to say these things. If I don't say them now, I'll grow even older and more full of regret. I have thought of you as my friend's wife. Long after he has been gone. I think—I think always, that you keep acting like Henry's wife. That you do things to make him proud of you and I know he would be."

"Otto, I don't know what you mean."

"I think it's time. We still have some time, Katie, you and I. We have some little time now, when we can have some life with each other. You don't need to tell me about my limitations. I know them all. But I have been a good friend to you and always will be. No one will ever be a better one." He cleared his throat, where his feelings seemed to have stuck. He kept his eyes on their two hands. "You see, Katie, I have always loved you." He looked up. "That's all. That's what I came to say today."

They sat silently. Hong Fat stuck his head in the door. "All closed, boss, okay?"

Katie looked over at him. "Yes. See you Monday."

When she stood, Otto rose and faced her. "So?" he said.

"Oh, Otto," she said in a low voice. "I've taken terrible advantage of you."

His shoulders slumped. John burst in from the yard. "Hey, you two," he said. When they looked over, he stopped, then took a step back. "Oh, sorry. I'll see to things out here."

Katie followed John out the door. She sat down and picked up the account book, turning to the page she had been working on. She tried to concentrate on it as Otto walked by.

* * * * *

"How do you get the skirt to drape that way," Katie asked over her shoulder, "sweeping up like that?" She poured hot water into two teacups that she carried to the table. Brigid Shaughnessy sat with perfect posture, a tribute to the nuns who raised her. Katie had laid out milk and cubed sugar and teaspoons. Thomas had said that he loved this girl and would marry her. He would rather do it with his mother's blessing, he said, but he would marry her without. The way he held his head had reminded her of Henry. That pigheadedness. Not even pigheaded. That certainty. How could Thomas have that, with Henry gone so long?

"One of the girls at The Shamrock, where I work, she's clever with a needle, ma'am. She helped me with it."

"Do you like working there?" Katie gestured to the milk and sugar. Brigid took only a little milk.

"It's all right. It's hard being on my feet, and the men can be cheeky. But I cover my rent and meals at the house where I live with the Sisters."

"You live with nuns?"

"I do, ma'am."

"That must be very quiet."

"It is, ma'am, though they're not above a good laugh now and again. It's not a bad way to live. I've a room of my own. Up at the top." She took a sip of the tea. "They've been good to me, coming with nothing like I did."

"How did you come to meet Thomas?"

"It was through Chrissy O'Brien, your neighbor here. We both work at The Shamrock. She's a friendly one, I do like her. And we were walking one day, and Thomas came by. He greeted Chrissy and spoke to us all three and walked me home. He has very fine manners, ma'am. He's a gentleman."

"And?"

"He came to the bar one day—"

Katie fought the urge to interrupt. Thomas had promised he wouldn't frequent saloons until he was twenty-one.

"—not like that, ma'am. Not what you're thinking."

"What am I thinking?" Katie drank some of her own tea. When she put her cup down, she made more of a clatter than she intended.

"That he was there to be drinking beer and hanging about with the other lads. It wasn't like that, not at all. That's not Thomas. He just came by to ask if he could walk me home after my shift. And"—the girl cast her eyes down at her hands, then looked up with those large eyes—"I said yes. He was most polite."

"Yes."

The girl was quiet. She put her hands in her lap and straightened. "The thing is, ma'am, I don't know what to say here. I've no idea at all. I think you believe I'm not worthy of him, just some barmaid with no family, and he's a fine man and will be an important one someday. I know it. But I am worthy of him. I have some education, the sisters saw to that back home, and I still work on it here. And I love him. I love him very much."

"How long have you known him?"

"Five months now. Almost five months."

"And you know him well enough to know you'll love him forever?"

"I do, ma'am. He's the heart of my heart."

"Yes," Katie said. "Yes." She remembered that.

"Thomas told me how his father died so young. That must have been terrible."

"Yes. Yes, it was." Katie fought off the memories, the hard ones and the soft ones. She forced herself to look at this young girl. She seemed gentle, but Katie knew that was just how she seemed. Thomas could have done worse for himself, but that wouldn't have been like him. She knew she couldn't change this romance, however much she feared it. It would be foolish to try. Thomas would not love another. His father never had. Nor had his mother.

"Miss Shaughnessy—"

"I'm hoping you'll call me Brigid, ma'am."

"Yes. Your church is important to you?"

"It is, ma'am. It's been like my father and mother, in a manner of speaking."

"And you'll want to raise your family in that church."

"Yes, ma'am. Thomas and I have spoken of it."

"And he agrees?"

"So he said."

"I'm glad he agrees."

Brigid smiled uncertainly. She tilted her head slightly, her eyes showing the question but convent-bred manners too engrained for her to ask it. Katie saw no reason to answer it.

* * * * *

Next day, at the noon break, Katie put on her good dress and left Hong Fat in charge. As she walked to the streetcar, she tried to remember what the block had looked like on the day after the fire. Not a scar remained from that. She never would have believed it.

She was proud now of her small part in Chicago's roar of recovery. Laundry work was the bottom of the ladder. She cleaned up other people's filth. It was work fit only for Chinese and women. But she'd made something of it, she and Hong Fat. They didn't hobnob with Colonel McCormack or Andrew Carnegie, but they made something good from the opportunity they had.

The streetcar ride to the West Side was slow, hampered by wagons and people on foot who walked with as little care for the traffic as a blind man would have. The slow pace matched her mood on an overcast day. The city wasn't as filthy as it used to be, nor as rough. Though mostly men walked the streets, more buildings were stone and brick now, more streets were paved. Fewer people shouted in public.

No one answered her knock at Otto's house. She knew his lodger worked a day shift at a nearby factory that made men's suits. Because Otto still worked overnight at the *Tribune*, she had thought he would be home now. She stopped a workman who carried his jacket over one shoulder and swung an empty lunch pail. In response to her question, he mentioned two nearby beer halls.

"Which," she asked, "is the one where they sing?"

That, the man explained, would be Mueller's, only a block away. He pointed the direction.

She could hear the singing from several doors down. The air inside felt moist. She could make no sense of the song. It must be German. She stood for long minutes just inside the door, scanning the men who sprawled at long tables. Loud conversations blended with the music. A piano player in the corner pounded his keyboard, but the sounds vanished in the din.

Her heart began to sink. She didn't see him. None of the barmaids came by to urge her to take a seat. She would be the only female customer. She took another step into the cavernous, rollicking room for a last look around.

She ignored the touch on her arm. When fingers closed around it, she turned. Otto was beaming at her. She smiled back. He waved his hand to suggest that they step outside. She leaned forward and said, "Why don't we get a beer?"

Still smiling, he led her to a side table where the clamor was slightly less. Katie found she was the object of furtive glances from around the beer hall. She flashed a wide smile to the other men and nodded. Her seat was an empty beer barrel.

"I had no idea," she called over to Otto, who was waving for service, "what a spectacle this would be."

The weary-looking barmaid paid no attention to Katie as she took their order from Otto. Katie removed her gloves, finger by finger. After so many hours in wash water, the skin was rough, and her hands usually felt cold. She resumed her viewing of the scene. A long bar of dark wood stretched along the wall on her left. Across the room was a stage draped with curtains, for formal performances. Tobacco smoke rose to a cloud that hovered at the ceiling.

"I didn't expect you," he said, leaning his head close to be heard. "How did you know to come here?"

"Henry spoke of it. He liked it here." She looked around. "You're here with friends?"

"Yes, over there." Otto gestured toward the end of a table where a half-dozen middle-aged men clustered. One waved at Otto, beckoning him and Katie to join their group. The other men made the same motions. Otto waved noncommittally.

Their beers came in ceramic steins. After saluting each other, they drank the cool liquid. Katie licked her lips like a child. The singing fell off when the piano player stopped. He rose from his seat, hoisting a large mug and drinking deeply. She leaned toward Otto in the sudden quiet.

"The other day, you said we might still have some time, for each other. Well, I agree."

He raised his eyebrows and gave her a wary smile.

"In fact, I'd like that." She patted his arm and nodded toward the rest of the room. "Maybe you could introduce me to your friends."

OVERSTREET

FAMILY TREE

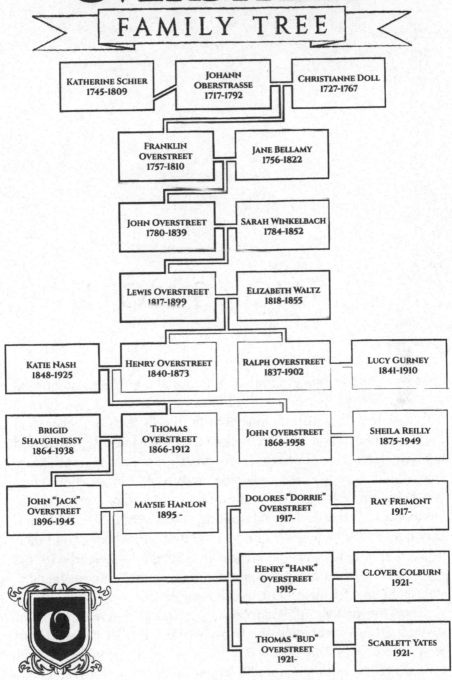

Katherine Schier 1745-1809

Johann Oberstrasse 1717-1792

Christianne Doll 1727-1767

Franklin Overstreet 1757-1810

Jane Bellamy 1756-1822

John Overstreet 1780-1839

Sarah Winkelbach 1784-1852

Lewis Overstreet 1817-1899

Elizabeth Waltz 1818-1855

Katie Nash 1848-1925

Henry Overstreet 1840-1873

Ralph Overstreet 1837-1902

Lucy Gurney 1841-1910

Brigid Shaughnessy 1864-1938

Thomas Overstreet 1866-1912

John Overstreet 1868-1958

Sheila Reilly 1875-1949

John "Jack" Overstreet 1896-1945

Maysie Hanlon 1895 -

Dolores "Dorrie" Overstreet 1917-

Ray Fremont 1917-

Henry "Hank" Overstreet 1919-

Clover Colburn 1921-

Thomas "Bud" Overstreet 1921-

Scarlett Yates 1921-

AUTHOR'S NOTE

The Overstreet family is a fictional construct, established in the first of my Waldoborough books, *The New Land*. This volume, however, was inspired by the lives of Sergeant (and brevet Lieutenant) David Overlock of the 20th Maine Regiment and his wife, Katherine Nash. Both, my great-great-grandparents, were from Waldoborough. They married on July 4, 1864, while David was home on furlough. After returning to the war, he was seriously wounded at the battle at Peebles Farm. A few years later, Katie and David and their young sons moved to Chicago, where David died of his war wounds. As a young girl in Chicago in the early 1920s, my mother visited her great-grandmother at the Chinese laundry she ran in an African-American neighborhood.

For the history of Waldoborough, Maine, I have drawn on several sources, including the two-volume work by Jasper Jacob Stahl, *History of Old Broad Bay and Waldoboro* (1953); Samuel Miller's *History of the Town of Waldoboro, Maine* (1910); and both volumes of Mark W. Biscoe, *Merchant of the Medomak: Stories from Waldoboro Maine's Golden Years, 1860-1910*. I also reviewed the collection of the Waldoborough Historical Society, and one of the society's trustees, Bill Blodgett, showed me his town and answered questions that were doubtless annoying.

Published sources about the Twentieth Maine's service during the Civil War are especially rich, due in part to the unit's inspired defense of Little Round Top at the Gettysburg battle and in part to the high reputation of the regiment's second commanding officer, Joshua Lawrence Chamberlain. I benefited from John J. Pullen's *The Twentieth Maine: A Volunteer Regiment in the Civil War* (1991); Thomas A. Desjardin, *Stand Firm Ye Boys from Maine: The 20th Maine and the Gettysburg Campaign*, (1995); and Alice Rains Trulock, *In the Hands of Providence: Joshua L. Chamberlain and the American Civil War* (1992). I also studied primary sources written by soldiers in the regiment, including Theodore Gerrish, *Army Life: A Private's Reminiscences of the Civil War* (originally, 1882); Abbott Spear, Andrea C. Hawkes, Marie H. McCosh, Craig L. Symonds, and Michael H. Alpert, eds., *The Civil War Recollections of General Ellis Spear* (1997); William B. Styple, ed., *With a Flash of His Sword: The Writings of Major Holman S. Melcher of the 20th Maine Infantry* (1994); and Roderick M. Engert, ed. *Maine to the Wilderness: The Civil War Letters of Pvt. William Lamson, 20th Maine Infantry* (1993). For an understanding of General Oliver O. Howard, I turned to William S. McFeely, *Yankee Stepfather: General O.O. Howard and the Freedmen* (1994).

For accounts of Chicago in the late 1860s and the Chicago fire, I drew on several websites that provide eyewitness accounts of the blaze, including www.greatchicagofire.org and www.hiddentruths. northwestern.edu, as well as Karen Sawislak, *Smoldering City: Chicagoans and the Great Fire, 1871-1874* (1995); Perry R. Duis, *Challenging Chicago: Coping with Everyday Life, 1837-1920* (1998); and Donald L. Miller, *City of the Century: The Epic of Chicago and the Making of America* (1996).

For essential critiques of the work in progress, I am indebted to Gerard Hogan, Garrett Epps, and my wife, Nancy, always the reader I care about most. I'm also grateful to my editor, Roger Williams, and his colleagues at Knox Press.

ABOUT THE AUTHOR

After many years as a trial and appellate lawyer, David O. Stewart became a bestselling writer of history and historical fiction. His first novel, *The Lincoln Deception,* was about the John Wilkes Booth Conspiracy. Sequels include *The Paris Deception,* set at the Paris Peace Conference in 1919, and *The Babe Ruth Deception*, which follows Babe's early years with the Yankees. Released in November 2021, *The New Land* began the Overstreet Saga.

David's histories explore the writing of the Constitution, the gifts of James Madison, the western expedition and treason trial of Aaron Burr, and the impeachment of President Andrew Johnson. In February 2021, Dutton published his *George Washington: The Political Rise of America's Founding Father.*

For more information visit davidostewart.com.

The

RESOLUTE
LAND

CHAPTER ONE

WASHINGTON, D.C., JANUARY 1942

✝

When the taxi stopped at the White House portico, a uniformed attendant immediately pulled Lorrie's door open. Denied any time to collect herself, Lorrie took a breath and stepped out. She took a moment to smooth her coat and square her shoulders in the harsh glare of electric floodlights, then climbed the few marble steps. More uniformed men, upright and hard-jawed, walked briskly through the small lobby. The country was at war.

Lorrie paused, hoping to gawk for a moment around this sacred space. A colored man in a black suit interrupted her, gesturing toward a young woman at a desk to the side. After checking off Lorrie's name on a typed list, the woman instructed the colored man to take Lorrie to the dinner.

"Could we stop for a second?" Lorrie asked after a couple of strides. When he looked the question at her, she smiled. "My first time here. I just want to drink it in. The flowers. All the marble. The red carpet."

The man allowed himself a small grin. "Of course, Miss. When you work here, you get used to it."

Turning slowly in place, Lorrie noted signs of wear under the surface grandeur. Carpet threads showed in high-traffic areas. Gouges marked the chair molding along the corridor. The walls could do with some touch-up paint. Lorrie decided to like the signs of neglect. The United States was limping out of a decade-long depression and plunging into a global war. The Roosevelts faced more pressing matters than interior decoration. "Thanks," she said.

To Lorrie's relief, a dozen people were already gathered in the reception room, smoking and chatting. She was neither early nor late. Lorrie's last-minute invitation to this Australia Day dinner recognized no merit on her part; she had been invited, Mrs. R's social secretary had explained, to serve as the unattached female needed to fill out the table, an honor that was rotated among Mrs. R's staff. Some of these people, she thought, must be Australians, now key allies after the Japanese attack on Pearl Harbor, especially with all the bad news coming from the Philippines. The only familiar face was Mrs. Roosevelt's, looming over several people in a small circle. Lorrie headed in their direction, then waited for the First Lady to acknowledge her.

With a toothy smile, Mrs. Roosevelt introduced Lorrie to an Australian couple and an older gentleman. "Miss Overstreet," she explained, "works with us at the civilian defense office. Don't be fooled by her youth. She has a precocious gift for organization, and has got us all marching in rows – myself included – in a matter of days."

Lorrie's embarrassed denial of any such talent was drowned out by the noisy arrival of the president in a wheelchair pushed by an aide. By his side were a man with a ruddy face and a tall, leggy woman who Lorrie recognized from news photos as Princess Martha of Norway. Even in his seated position, the broad-shouldered Roosevelt seemed to fill every corner of the room with his beaming smile, his big chin, and his booming shout that the cocktails would be martinis. "I have been accused of mixing stiff ones," he exulted in plummy tones, brandishing his cigarette in a long black holder, "so I advise that you take up your courage in both hands!"

With giraffe-like elegance and calm, Mrs. R joined the president at a wheeled drinks cart. She left Lorrie with the older gent whose name had flown past her during the introductions. "That man can certainly make an entrance," the gent said, "even on four wheels."

"He's like," Lorrie agreed, "like a charge of electricity in the room." She lowered her voice. "And I never appreciated how big he is." The president's head and shoulders seemed immense.

"All of that force," the gent said, "trapped in that sorry chair. You know, I saw him in the last war, when he was in the Navy Department, and even standing at his full height back then – and he's a tall man – he made nothing like the impression he does now. He's learned how to do that." He shrugged. "Sometimes, though, the poor guy looks like absolute hell."

"Why wouldn't he? He's been leading us through the Depression all these years and now has a war against half the world. You'd look like hell, too."

He laughed amiably. "I do anyway, Miss Overstreet, and my burdens are nothing like his." He looked directly at Lorrie. "Well, shall we take up our courage in both hands?"

At the drinks cart, Lorrie reached out her hand to introduce herself at a moment when the president had an empty glass in one hand and rattled a steel shaker with the other. Taking in her uncertainty, he roared out a laugh that sounded manufactured, then handed her the glass. "There, my dear," he said, "never let it be said that your president never gave you anything." He poured the cocktail into Lorrie's glass and turned to the old gent. "Raymond, I'm counting on you to help us sustain morale in these trying times."

"You know me, Mr. President. Ever the patriot."

As Lorrie retreated, Roosevelt directed his noisy good humor at his next customer. After a sip, she decided that she would not be finishing the martini. Her father always insisted that his children drink the right way. For Jack Overstreet, that meant imbibing only scotch. On the rocks was acceptable; adding water was permitted, though disdained as the refuge of a rookie. You had to taste the liquor, he insisted, so you would always feel exactly how much you had drunk. And never, he had added, trust a martini.

* * * * *

Lorrie hunted for her name card on the table until she found it at the place to the president's left. After a quick scan to see if she could swap seats with someone – how could she talk with the great man for an entire meal? – she resigned herself to her fate. After a bellowed greeting from the president, Lorrie was relieved to discover that she was not expected to converse with him. He must be deaf on her side, she decided, which was slightly dispiriting. Despite her initial terror at having to chat with the president, she didn't like being classed as no more interesting than the floral centerpiece.

The president's conversational style alternated between close conversation with the Australian ambassador's wife on his other side, and questions shouted at other attendees down the table, which compelled them to reply at equal volume. When the man on her other side turned out to be Ray from the drinks cart, she decided she could survive the evening by exchanging banalities with him. That plan, however, went out the window when the waiters delivered an alarming first course.

Twelve shells circled her plate. In the middle of each shell, a moist membrane shimmered and jiggled in the candlelight. Having already ditched her martini, Lorrie wondered if she would find anything she could eat or drink all night. She lifted her fork and pondered how best to extract the membrane from the shell and deliver it to her mouth.

"Not an old hand with oysters?" Ray's question was posed quietly.

Lorrie smiled at him. "We don't see a lot of them in Chicago. Or not in my part of Chicago."

"No, we didn't have them much in Missouri." He nodded down the table. "Just remember, sweetheart, everybody here is faking it, too."

"Even him?" She cocked her head toward the president.

"Well, good luck with trying to figure him out. Let me know when you have." He picked up a shell from his plate. "We're allowed to lift this with one hand, then spear the meaty part with your fork. You can get away with eating only two, though three would be more polite. Don't worry. They don't have much taste."

Lorrie followed the instructions. The membrane proved to be slightly salty with overtones of rust, but could be a project to chew and then swallow. She finally swallowed and soldiered on to the second one.

Ray began to explain that he ran the government's Office of Facts and Figures.

"I've seen that name," she said. "It sounds slightly dry, and like it would be a lot of very detailed work."

"I suppose it isn't especially glamorous, but facts and figures are the heart of the war effort. The agency's name has an admirable simplicity and directness."

"But you're really a propaganda office, right?"

"Miss Overstreet, the Nazis have propaganda offices. We have only the humble Office of Facts and Figures." They shared knowing smiles. "Since I've been there," Ray went on, "nothing has gone out to the public that wasn't true. A few statements might have been incomplete, I suppose, but there is a war on."

After a waiter swept away the offending oysters, Lorrie reached into her purse for a cigarette. Instantly, the president held his lighter toward her with the flame ignited. After taking the first puff, she realized that he had conducted the operation without breaking eye contact with the ambassador's wife. Could he see out the back of his head? She turned to Ray and confided, "I'm thinking I should stub this one out and save it to show my grandchildren – the cigarette FDR lit for me."

"It's easier just to swipe an ash tray. That's what they're there for." Lorrie looked at the six-sided glass object in the middle of the table, which had "The White House" etched on it, along with an image of the building. "Everyone takes one," he added.

"How many times have you been here?"

"With Roosevelt? Maybe a dozen. Mostly back when I was writing for the St. Louis paper, which was when he cared more about what I thought. A couple of times when Hoover was president, but it wasn't easy to filch the ash trays then."

"My father says that Republicans are no fun."

"It varies. Coolidge was before my time, but he's supposed to have been as little fun as humanly possible."

Lorrie began to relax when the main course turned out to be pot roast, a dish that was just as dry in the White House as it had been in her childhood, beyond the power of gravy to rescue it. The peas seemed to have been cooked longer than the roast. She noted that the president ate almost nothing of his meal, though he had polished off the oysters with dispatch.

Ray proved an amiable companion, inquiring about her work at the civilian defense office, her time before that working for anti-fascist organizations that urged war preparedness, then about her family. She proudly explained that her father got her the job with Mrs. Roosevelt. He was the new Midwest region director of the War Production Board, a banker who volunteered for government service as a "dollar-a-year" man – on loan from his bank, taking no public money. Soon she was telling the family legend about how the young Jack Overstreet funded his six-month accounting course by catching stray cats and selling them to a nearby medical school where they would be dissected.

"You must be gratified," Ray said, "by our entering the war. After all your anti-fascist work."

"Not gratified, no. I could hardly embrace war. Both of my brothers are in the Army Air Forces Reserve, which is a worry. But I agree with Mrs. Roosevelt that this is a fight that we have to fight. No one else will do it for us. We can change the world."

"A few more families like the Overstreets and we'll have the war under control very soon." Ray offered her another cigarette. He, too, had given up on the food. After lighting them both up, he exhaled a plume of smoke toward the ceiling. "I agree that it must be fought. Hitler's a monster, and the Japanese are little better. But I was in the last war, you know, the one to make the world safe for democracy. It was a terrible business, and it seems we made things rather worse than better."

The president called out his desire for the attention of the diners, kicking off a round of toasts to the alliance of the United States and Australia and to victory in the Pacific. A few arch comments recalled their shared heritage as the detritus of the British Empire, now being called upon to rescue the country that had expelled their forebears.

When Lorrie reclaimed her coat, Ray offered her a ride home. They walked quickly through the brisk Washington evening to his car. She thought it felt like snow was coming, but she didn't trust her sense of the peculiar weather in Washington, which wasn't the South, wasn't the North, and usually was damp. Once inside Ray's Chevrolet, with its inadequate heater blowing cold air on them, Lorrie found his hand on her knee after he downshifted for a stoplight. Without missing a conversational beat, she lifted the hand and placed it on the gearshift. He must think she was pretty desperate to be interested in an old guy like him.

Streetlights shone on soldiers and sailors hurrying along the streets. "We'll be implementing blackouts soon," Lorrie said. "Especially on the West Coast."

"I was over in London a few months back," Ray said. "The darkness from the blackouts, right in the middle of the city, was hard to get used to."

She let the remark pass as he pulled up in front of the Kennedy-Warren apartments. She alighted quickly, calling her thanks back over her shoulder. She couldn't wait to write to her father about her dinner with the president.